PRAISE FOR

# *Did You Have the Life You Wanted?*

"Andrea Simon's new novel, *Did You Have the Life You Wanted?* explores the challenges and rewards of both youthful self-discovery and mature introspection through the eyes of Anita Rappaport, a woman whose early life allowed her to experience the revolutionary heyday of the 1960s. The narrative offers a first-hand account of the turbulent, volatile American political scene whose energy, possibility, and promise are later inflected by the musings of an elderly Anita taking stock of how her hopes and dreams played out over the decades. The resultant novel offers a rich account of one woman's coming to terms with her life story. *Did You Have the Life You Wanted?* takes its reader deep into the mind and heart of a woman whose life trajectory has proven both surprising and heartbreaking, inspiring, and tragic."

—**Mary Caputi, PhD,** feminist, professor, and author of *Feminism and Power: The Need for Critical Theory*

"A poignant and witty novel about a young woman from Brooklyn over some fifty years of her life with a group of stalwart friends who meet in the 1960s during the time of women's liberation, city race riots, a gritty Greenwich Village, and a rough, dirty subway. Some women change as time goes by, some leave the circle early, some last to the end. Through the book Anita, from stories and her camera, records the idiosyncrasies of her family, her jobs, and eventually her husband, her children, and her friends, asking herself, "Did you have the life you wanted?" Original and deftly written, the author brings an earlier New York to life. A moving and fascinating story."

—**Stephanie Cowell,** author of *The Boy in the Rain, Claude and Camille* and *The Man in the Stone Cottage*, recipient of an American Book Award


"When the title of a novel asks *Did You Have the Life You Wanted?*, I'm guessing most readers of a certain age will be curious enough to pick up the book and see what the story is about, while attempting to answer the title's question for themselves. At least this was my experience as I delved into this well-written fictional account of Anita Rappaport as she looks back on her younger days when she was a young social worker turned copywriter in New York City during the heydays of the late sixties and early seventies—an exciting time when danger lurked on city streets and sometimes on the subways. In this rich and thought-provoking story that explores friendship and the personal and professional lives of women, seasoned writer Andrea Simon, a lifelong New Yorker with numerous writing awards to her credit, takes the reader on an authentic and emotional journey where the past comes alive and depicts the joys and challenges, and sometimes sorrows, that come with lasting friendships and workplace and societal barriers. I highly recommend it."

—**Kathleen M. Rodgers,** 2024 MWSA Writer of the Year and author of *The Llano County Mermaid Club*


"Andrea Simon's latest book is a breath of fresh air: familiar and yet new. This excellent novel paints an engrossing story of a late twentieth-century examined life. Although psychologically sophisticated, it is written in a colloquial voice easy to access and to enjoy.... What begins as a young woman leaving Brooklyn after graduating from college and coming to live in Greenwich Village continues far beyond, reaching into middle and old age. The readable plot celebrates the power of female friendship through the vicissitudes of life: childhood traumas, a horrific attempted gang rape, career hurdles, and then fulfillment, a reluctant blind date that leads to a long loving marriage, the loss of friends and family to sickness and suicide, and the lucid description of her own cancer.... Family conflict is exposed with no sugarcoating, including the difficult relationship with her demanding critical mother, and her ever cruel brother .... From frenetic youth to contemplative maturity, Anita unites with old friends in person, by correspondence, or by memory. She concludes, 'Well, here we are, two old broads from Flatbush .... That's the beauty of old age ....We can do what we want.'"

—**Helen Schary Motro,** author of *The Right to Happiness: After All They Went Through* and *Maneuvering between the Headlines: An American Lives through the Intifada*


"Andrea Simon's vivid novel *Did You Have the Life You Wanted?* recounts the lives, the choices, and the inabilities to choose of narrator Anita Rappaport and her wide group of friends. Tracing the social and cultural upheavals of the '60s through the new millennium, this provocative novel will urge readers of any age to ponder their own pasts and the underlying forces that shaped their lives—patterns that are often indecipherable until they look back closely on the decades they have lived in."

—**Ruth Pennebaker,** author of *Women on the Verge of a Nervous Breakthrough* and co-author of *Pucker Up! The Subversive Woman's Guide to Aging*

"Andrea Simon's *Did You Have the Life You Wanted?* hooks you with startling events early on and keeps you reading with tightly written, kaleidoscopic, wise storytelling; and as a tribute to pre-2025 America, it promises to prove more important and relevant to post-2025 America than today's readers can imagine."

—**Mark Wisniewski**, Founding Editor of *Coolest American Stories*, author of *Necessary Deeds*

"*Did You Have the Life You Wanted?* is an insightful tour of over fifty years of American cultural history as seen through the eyes of a Jewish feminist in New York City. The novel takes us on a sweeping journey, beginning in 1968 and ending in 2019. At the beginning of the story, the protagonist, Anita Rappaport, age 22, moves from her parents' home in Brooklyn and works as a caseworker for the city's Department of Social Services until a violent incident sends her on a divergent path of self-exploration. Anita flees to Europe for a while, then returns to a more bohemian way of life among friends and lovers in Greenwich Village.... As the years unfold, Anita struggles to find a place for herself in a rapidly changing society marked by race riots ... growing feminist awareness, political activism, and the widespread challenging of social norms.... Her experiences mirror those of countless other women in the baby boom era, which is why the novel is so relevant and vital.... The characters are rendered with warmth and affection ... Novelist Andrea Simon has a brilliant way of poking fun at Anita and all the many wonderful minor characters in the book without disparaging them. Simon's dialogue is full of wit. She is a master at using humor to explore serious themes. *Did You Have the Life You Wanted?* is entertaining, far-reaching, and wise."

—**Katherine Kirkpatrick,** author of *To Chase the Glowing Hours*

OTHER BOOKS BY ANDREA SIMON

*Bashert: A Granddaughter's Holocaust Quest*

*Floating in the Neversink*

*Esfir Is Alive*

*Here's the Story ... Nine Women Write Their Lives* (editor and
contributor)

# *Did You Have the Life You Wanted?*

*A Novel*

ANDREA SIMON

Sibylline Press

Copyright © 2025 by Andrea Simon
All Rights Reserved.

Published in the United States by Sibylline Press,
an imprint of All Things Book LLC, California.

Sibylline Press is dedicated to publishing the
brilliant work of women authors ages 50 and older.
www.sibyllinepress.com

Sibylline Digital First Edition
eBook ISBN: 9798897409778
Print ISBN: 9798897409785
Library of Congress Control Number: 2025938361

Cover Design: Alicia Feltman
Book Production: Aaron Laughlin

This is a work of fiction. Names, characters, places, brands, media, and incidents are either the product of the author's imagination or are used fictitiously. Any resemblance to similarly named places or to persons living or deceased is unintentional.

**HUMAN AUTHORED: Any use of this publication to train artificial intelligence (AI) technologies to generate text is expressly prohibited.**

Sibylline
Press

*To Helene and Penny, who lived the life.*

"Nothing has a stronger influence psychologically on their environment and especially on their children than the unlived life of the parent."

—Carl Gustav Jung

# PROLOGUE: JUNE 2018

*My husband, Sergio, an oncologist, opened the front door of our apartment. Calling my name, he waited until I greeted him by the hall coat closet. Before taking off his sports jacket, he unbuckled his cracked brown-leather messenger bag and fished inside. He handed me a small greeting-card-size white envelope.*

*"This is from a patient," he said. "She saw your books on the table in the waiting area and leafed through* Blood Sprang from the Earth. *I told her it was a historical novel about the Holocaust written by my wife. Immediately intrigued, she unearthed the contents of her pocketbook and retrieved her notepad and pen. While I typed my examination notes into the computer, she wrote you this."*

*Addressed to me, Ms. Anita Rappaport, the black-ink handwriting was large. I recognized the style as similar to those of lefties—irregular, bold, multi-slanted—the penmanship of someone who is compensating for being different.*

*On the top left, the envelope displayed the patient's name, Betty Green, in cursive, filling half of the space across. But then underneath, there was her address, unmistakable: 165 Christopher Street, Apt. 3C. I was startled. Though I now lived on West 112 Street in Manhattan, my apartment was 3C. Still, this wasn't the coincidence, but maybe the pre-coincidence. Betty's building at 165 Christopher Street was that of my first apartment when I had moved from Brooklyn to the West Village, where I lived from 1967 to 1975.*

*I opened the envelope and there was a handwritten note on a white sheet of paper, 5 ½ x 7 inches. It said: "Dear Anita—I saw your book. Please come to our book club in my apartment. I will let you know when." She included her phone number. It was signed, "Elizabeth (Betty) Green."*

*"Wow," I said. "Who is this, Betty?"*

*"A patient with lymphoma. She also has Alzheimer's."*

*Sergio hung his jacket in the closet. As if anticipating my next question, he added, "She's lovely."*

*"How old is she?" I suddenly wondered if she could have lived at this building during the same time I had.*

*"In her eighties." Sergio's normally robust, Italian-accented voice lowered as if this were a state secret.*

*Too old for me, in my early seventies, to have had intersecting paths, I thought. "How is she dealing with her cancer?"*

*With the track lights on, I noticed the smudged and loose bags under my husband's football-shaped eyes. Had I not noticed this lately? I wondered.*

*Unaware of my scrutiny, Sergio said, "Betty, the patient, she's under control now, though she lost a lot of weight from the treatment."*

*"And the dementia? Does she have help?"*

*"I think her daughter visits often and she has friends, but she lives alone and still manages."*

*Sergio walked into the next room, the one I used as an office where he had a closet. He draped his messenger bag over the hook on the inside door and sifted through the hangers for the one that pressed his blue pants. He was fastidious about putting away his clothes and wouldn't allow me to help in fear that I wouldn't fold his clothes perfectly.*

*I sat on the red velour loveseat, crossing my long legs, trying to give Sergio the proper time to decompress. I couldn't control myself and asked, "Do you think Betty can read my book?"*

*"Can't you wait until I'm home for ten minutes before I get the third degree?" Sergio seemed to forget that he was the one who handed me Betty's note the second he came home.*

*"Sorry," I said. "I just wondered about her ability to respond to me."*

*"Yes, I think she will be able to read your book, though she may forget it afterwards."*

*"I'll call her," I said, thinking I'd better do it soon.*

*Sergio undressed and closed the door to the adjoining bathroom. I heard the rumbling of the shower and knew he would be scrubbing his tall, lean body, trying to rid it from the stench of his chemical-and-blood-stained scrubs that he had tossed in the hospital laundry basket.*

*I leaned back on the loveseat and closed my eyes. I had loved living in the West Village when it was more of a place for the bohemian: the folk singer, the out-of-work writer and artist, the semi-communist, the closeted suburbanite, the drag queens, and not the enclave of older, rich whites living in multi-million-dollar co-ops as it has become. I loved the acrid smell of pot and the vanilla-citrus taste of Orange Julius, of smoking Gauloises, and feeling the biting cold of walking westward toward the Hudson on Christopher Street in the wind tunnel of winter. Betty's note brought that past world to me in a sudden swirl.*

# PART I: REWRITING THE PAST

# CHAPTER 1: TRIP TO THE FIELD

Late June 1968

The dress had raised multicolored horizontal stripes. Rainbow ribs. It flared a bit on the bottom, brushing my knees, and the sleeves puffed out with elastic around my barely muscled upper arms. It was uncharacteristic of me to wear anything so fluffy and loud; I was a hippie who favored black, and jeans or *dungarees*, as we called them. But on this humid June day, a dress was the coolest thing to wear, and I wanted to look female and professional.

I expected to see an increased number of people on the streets because as a caseworker for the Department of Social Services (DSS), my designated "field" neighborhood of Ocean Hill-Brownsville was in turmoil due to racially explosive city-wide teachers' strikes emanating from the newly created Black/Latino school board's dismissal of nineteen predominantly white, and mostly Jewish, teachers and administrators from Junior High School 271. The action pitted the teachers' union against the community, and Blacks against whites, particularly Jews. The neighborhood swarmed with police officers, including those in plainclothes, parents, teachers, and protesters. Many local students who attended the still operational school loitered around the streets, avoiding the hotbed building. Nearly two-thirds of the parents stopped sending their children to school.

One of my Puerto Rican clients, who lived in a tiny apartment above a deli across from the controversial epicenter, had called me two weeks ago to report that she kept her twelve-year-old daughter, Amelia, home from J.H.S. 271 because her son had been hit in the back with a two-by-four.

When I had visited the family a few days later, Amelia said that at first she had enjoyed the teachers' new emphasis on the culture of Africa and the Caribbean, yet she was terrified of going into the building when the Black protesters came because her light skin made her a target. According to Amelia, when the troubles intensified, the teachers formed in conspiratorial clots and whispered to each other. Armed police patrolled the halls. To get inside the building, crowds squashed her, and she crawled under police barricades erected to separate the picketing teachers from community activists, some of them Black Panthers. Photographers and reporters jostled among the picketers. By the end of June, the governing board dismissed another 350 UFT strikers, adding to the tumult. When Amelia's brother came home unable to stand straight, school was no longer an option.

On this visit a week after my last, I navigated through the street throng to get to Amelia's apartment. Although I was usually uneasy once I got off the subway, super-conscious of my whiteness and role as an official "snooper," now my heartbeat sped up and my eyes blinked and crisscrossed as if they were honeybees escaped from their hives. It was like a war zone.

Dozens of helmeted police officers held nightsticks, trying to control barking German Shepherds. Police snipers with rifles poised on the rooftops. Helicopters buzzed overhead. A Black man held a sign, "Black People Control Your Schools," another's said, "Stop Teaching Race Hatred," and a woman's read, "Power to the People." A white teacher lifted his banner, "End Racism in Our Schools." Over a megaphone, a Black leader yelled, "We are going to take what belongs to us."

I avoided the school's block on Herkimer Street and walked toward another client's apartment past Ralph Avenue down Fulton Street. I was desperately trying to recapture the sense of uneasy calmness, if not desertion, that I had experienced in my "field" whose housing projects intersected with garbage-strewn, overgrown weedy lots and deserted, boarded-up tenements. In the beginning of May, before the strikes, I had rushed through the blocks of Brownsville, catching the chatter of teenage girls clutching their bookbags and passing around cigarettes, and boys standing atop the rusted rubble of landlord-burned buildings and car parts, and occasional groups of older women gossiping on a stoop.

The "field" was a strange word for this expanse of humanity amidst decay. But I was diligent; this was my first real, full-time job, and it required home visits. Though I had been a caseworker for six months, I had absorbed the utter uselessness of the system. When I had been on the job for only a month, a single mother and three small children came to my office after a horrendous fire destroyed their apartment. During the multiple roadblocks involved in obtaining emergency housing, my case supervisor detained the entire process for hours, insisting that the mother fill out three separate forms to locate the putative fathers.

Unbelievably, caseworkers were required to send absentee clients a form letter stating that since we couldn't locate them, they would no longer receive public assistance. I assumed this also applied to those who died. I never told my supervisor that I ripped up those forms, replacing them with handmade greeting cards with the words, "So Long," in bold letters. To continue my job, I adopted the mantra, "Do no harm."

And this was the way it was on that hot day. I was off to the "field," supposedly, to do as my supervisor wanted: locate "putative" fathers or record hidden televisions, in other words, to spy for the enemy. I memorized the list of minimum standards for special grants issued by the Department of Welfare. A family was entitled to one sofa and one drop-leaf table. An "adequate basic supply" of clothing for an adult woman included one hat, two cotton dresses, one "dressy dress," three pairs of panties, one girdle, and two pairs of stockings. Beyond these specified standards, it was up to caseworkers and our supervisors to issue more funds, for good reason, of course. I made sure that I didn't see extras, and when I could apply for more, I did. I had learned to lie to my superiors and visited the people I had grown to care about, hoping to help them circumvent city bureaucracy without reinvigorating liberal Jewish superiority. Although I never discussed religion with my clients, they must have guessed that I was Jewish from my last name, Rappaport. That day, aside from checking on Amelia, I had planned on helping one tubercular man get to a clinic, tutoring a teenager in math, and guiding the paperwork for an elderly woman whose oven had dangerous wiring.

*　*　*

Leafing through my casebook, I didn't see them coming, but heard the rumble of running feet, a stampede of herding noise and movement. I took a large intake of breath, forgetting to exhale until the air expelled in a gigantic whoosh. I felt a whip to my side and a sharp pain. *What was happening to me?* Terror arose in my throat like a fistful of vomit. I felt a tug on my shoulder, and my pocketbook disappeared. *No, no, not my pocketbook!* Arms and heads converged, yanking and dragging me. *I have to escape. I have to escape!* My heels scraped the sidewalk, and my dress rode up as my nylon panties swept the concrete pebbles. *My dress. Oh no!* It happened so quickly that I wasn't afraid for my life; instead, crazy thoughts overtook me: *My dress will be ruined. My money will be gone. How will I pay for the subway home?*

Arms dragged me further down a broken concrete pathway, my pounded body creating a smokescreen of dust, then bouncing up newsprint-strewn stairs inside a plywood-boarded, three-story tenement, and landing with a thud. The back of my head hit a sharp object, and I blacked out. What could have been seconds later, I opened my caked eyelids and saw the vestibule's silver mailboxes, some half-open, stuffed with supermarket circulars, others with doors hanging haphazardly on rusty hinges.

Hovering over me was a gang, maybe six or seven, Black teens, yelling and screaming, seemingly high. There were hands pawing over me, under my dress, snapping the elastic on my garter belt. An unrecognizable voice eked out from my parched lips, "Stop, please stop." *Who was that speaking?* That same voice told me to keep still, that soon it would be over.

"No, no," I screamed as prodding fingers inched under my panties. "Go away, please." I tried to move my arms to swat him away, but they were pinned down. It suddenly came to me like a shard of glass through my eyes that this was how my life was going to end.

There was tapping and knocking from behind the shattered glass door leading inside the building, and I maneuvered my back upward and twisted to view the source of the noise. The face of a gray-haired Black man with a scraggly beard appeared behind the glass.

"What are you doing?" he shouted through a large crack.

One boy said, "Why do you care? She's white."

The man said, "You better leave her be. There are cops around."

All I could think about were the photos of my six-year-old niece in my wallet. I said to the boys above me, "Take my money, but let me have my wallet."

The boys pressed tighter on top of me, pushing me again flat on the ground, when the man burst through the door. "Get the hell out of here," he yelled and plucked them off me as if they were leeches.

Then two middle-aged men and a woman appeared from the street side and chased away the boys, screaming at them to run away as fast as they could. The men lifted me up and led me out of the building. I crossed the sidewalk into the street. I felt safer amid traffic.

I ran down two blocks, looking over my shoulder, certain that the boys would catch up and pounce on me. Turning left, I spotted a police car and flailed my arms, uncertain if it was a mirage or the boys returning in a sedan, this time with their older, fiercer brothers. The car stopped in front of me and two officers got out.

"I was attacked," I groaned, pointing behind me. "Attacked."

"Where?" a lean officer said. He had a thick brown mustache and blue eyes and looked too young to be in a position of authority.

"There," I pointed again, "around the corner, further down, in a tenement, boys." My head pounded, and I ran my fingers over my hair to discover an egg-like lump. "Oh," I said, suddenly feeling faint.

"You'd better get in the car," the other officer said. "We'll drive there." This one was heavyset and balding, with gray temples.

I got in the backseat and directed the police to the street. Most of the storefronts and apartment buildings were boarded up except for two brownstones, where the helping neighbors now sat on the stoops. On the corner was an empty parking lot surrounded by a bent chain-link fence. It was easy to find the scene of the crime; it was the only building with an open door.

"There," I said, sniffing back the snot accumulating in my nostrils. It was then that I allowed myself to sit back and the terror of what just happened overflowed me like an umbrella of wet sticky air. I opened the window and stuck out my head.

"Close it and wait in the car," the younger officer ordered. I saw his name tag, and it said Brian O'Hara. "And lock the doors."

Both men took their guns from their holsters and raised them.

I reopened the window and screamed, "No, no, don't use your guns. Don't shoot them. They're only kids."

"Just roll up your window."

The officers disappeared into the building, and my heart thumped so rapidly I could barely catch my breath. I leaned into the front seat and examined my face in the rear-view mirror and gasped. My eyes were smeared black with mascara, and gray streaks ran down my cheeks. My hairband was missing, and my long hair bunched in clumps, wildly crisscrossing my forehead. Stretching my neck, I saw red welts and scratch lines traversing my skin like a monochromatic painting. I leaned further back and found darker and thicker patterns on my thighs, which were also wet with whitish-gray liquid. I lifted my ripped dress and noticed the elastic waist of my panties was torn and the crotch was wet and shredded. I smelled ammonia and the gassy vinyl of a new car. I must have blacked out again.

The car door opened, and both officers returned with guns tucked in their holsters.

Brian's partner was speaking into his walkie talkie.

Brian turned around.

"Did you catch them?" I asked, knowing the answer was no.

"They were long gone," Brian said. "I don't think they'll be back. They had been hanging out on the roof."

"How do you know?" I asked.

"We found used tubes of glue all over. They must have been high as kites. Who knows when the last time they was at school. You are one lucky girl."

How did Brian know I had been lucky? He never asked me what they did to me.

* * *

At the police station, I sat at Brian's desk while he asked me to describe the incident in detail. His right-hand fingers pecked on an upright typewriter.

"Can I ask you something?" Brian said.

I nodded.

"What's a nice girl like you doing in this hellhole?"

*"A nice girl?"* I swallowed my initial insult at this description and answered, "I'm a caseworker. This is my field."

"What a field! I don't see no flowers."

I pulled out a tissue from a box on Brian's desk and blew my nose. I could only imagine what he thought of my smudged and tear-stained face.

"How does your boyfriend feel about you coming here?"

*What the fuck is he asking about my boyfriend?* "I don't see the relevance of that question," I said, swallowing my anger.

"I guess I'm asking if you have a boyfriend."

"I've just been attacked, and that's what you want to know?"

"Sorry," Brian said. "I know it's been an ordeal for you. It's just that we don't often get girls like you in here."

"And I hope I am the last to come to the police station."

Another officer waved papers in our direction and Brian nodded. "Miss Rappaport, Anita," Brian said, sounding formal for the first time, "the sergeant will be here in a few minutes with money for your subway ride home. Do you need to use the phone?"

"No, thanks." There was no one I wanted to call. I didn't trust my voice.

Brian yanked out the form from the typewriter carriage and pushed it in front of me. It said, "New York State Incident Report."

"Can you sign?" Brian asked, pointing at the bottom where it said, "Complainant Signature." As I scrawled my name, I skimmed the narrative section and toward the top of the form under "Incident Type." In broken typewriter letters, it read, "Attempted gang rape."

I groaned at the words there in print before me. Up to then, I had been immersed in the car ride back to the tenement, watching the officers draw their guns. I worried that there would be violence, the losing of my pocketbook, and not having money to get home. Now, I wanted to say to Brian, "No, this is not true. I am fine, just an innocent bystander during a terrible time in the city when the students are undergoing stress." But I remembered the hands pulling at my underwear, the feral eyes of the boys, the searching fingers.

Yes, if the homeless man hadn't appeared by the glass door of the vestibule, it would have been "gang rape." Yes, that's what it must have been. But it was still a shock to see the words in writing.

Suddenly, the words in front of me blurred and dizziness crept down my face like an unfurling, gauzy window shade.

Possibly, I fainted, but I lost real time and was shocked into reality when I noticed a glass of water in my hand. I gulped it down even though it was lukewarm and tasted like rotten eggs.

* * *

Brian drove me to the subway and handed me five dollars from the sergeant and a business card as I got out of the car.

"Take this," he said. "It has my number in case you want to call."

"Well, I know the number of the station. I have a copy of the police report." I held up the manilla envelope as if to show him my proof.

"This is personal," he said, winking.

I took the card, opened the clasp on the envelope, and dropped it inside.

# CHAPTER 2: DRESS TOO SHORT

I had no memory of waiting at the subway platform, changing trains, squeezing among bulky riders, or arriving at the Christopher Street—Sheridan Square station. The mosaic lettering on the station's walls appeared when I looked up, and I dashed out the subway door before it closed. In that same fugue state, I must have walked those long four blocks home. Without my keys, which were stuffed in a zippered pouch in my stolen pocketbook, I took the elevator to the basement and searched for the super, José.

He was sitting on a backless stool at a makeshift wooden counter in his "shop," eating a sandwich.

"José, I'm sorry to bother you," I said. "Can I borrow the keys to my apartment? I lost mine."

"Sure," he said, swiveling his stool to the side where a large pegboard displayed keys hanging on hooks, each attached to a chain with the apartment number written in black marker on a white circle.

"I'll return it soon," I said. "I need to make copies at the locksmith."

"Take your time." José stared at my face in a double take. "What happened? Are you okay?"

"Sure," I said, too quickly, backing out of the room before he could question me further.

When I got to my apartment, I rushed to the bathroom to pee. Eager to leave the police station, I hadn't used the restroom there. Surely, I had to go then, but I had been afraid to leave Brian's side, despite his chauvinism.

In my bathroom, I looked in the mirror and again gasped at my face. The mascara and tears had smeared my dark-brown eyes into raccoon circles and my cheeks into inky blotches. My straight, waist-length hair hung haphazardly. A huge nest gathered atop my head. I imagined what José must have thought.

I was shaking uncontrollably but didn't allow myself to sit still. I had things to do. I made a list of items in my wallet: credit cards, driver's license (though I didn't drive), Social Security card, photo ID from the Department of Social Services, and the first-grade photo of my niece, Paula, grinning with missing front top teeth. Surely my brother, Ben, or sister-in-law, Aviva, would have an extra copy.

In the living room, I sat on the red-paisley Scotchgard-treated sofa and transferred the phone to my lap, calling as many numbers I could get from Information and the Yellow Pages.

When I hung up from Social Security after the operator insisted I didn't live on Christopher Street, according to her records, I leaned back. For a moment, that woman's assuredness almost made me question where I really lived. I made a mental note to report her arrogance to my roommate, Denise, who worked for Social Security.

The blare of the phone ringing in the well of my dress startled me, and I jumped. It was as if my lap proclaimed my distress.

"Hello," I said, expecting the Social Security woman's voice, verifying my phone number.

"Ani, hi, it's me," my friend Cindy said.

"Oh, Cindy, I wasn't expecting you."

"I called you at work and they said you were in the field. I figured you were probably home by now."

"Yes." I cleared my phlegmy throat a few times.

"You sound funny. Is everything okay?"

"Oh, just tired, that's all."

"How was the field? Any trouble from the strikers?"

"No, I bypassed the school."

I asked Cindy how her day went, knowing she was going for two interviews.

"They were horrid. I'll probably never work again."

"You will."

"Maybe I should try to get a job as a caseworker like you."

"You don't want to." I pictured my lanky, pale-faced friend and how vulnerable she would appear in the field. We had met two years ago at a summer job in the General Post Office on West 33rd Street. Having both scored 100 percent on the exam, we supposedly had the coveted position indoors. Ten minutes in the airless, un-air-conditioned basement bonded us as we envied our fellow test takers who scored below us, now temporary outdoor letter carriers.

"But all those available male caseworkers. You must admit that there are at least five men to every woman. You said as much when you got the job."

I recalled the male attention I received over the past six months. Three fellow caseworkers had asked me out, and I politely told them I didn't believe in dating someone from the same office, which wasn't completely true. Finally, the daily persistence of one, Rob Porter, wore me down. He was older than the others, in his thirties, and had been a record producer. He was short, stocky, with gray-streaked sandy hair and fine features—good-looking in an Aryan way, my mother would have said. My relationship with Rob turned sexual, reluctantly on my part. On two disastrous occasions, he couldn't get an erection and tried various positions and ointments until I was exhausted. He hinted that his impotence was due to my lack of enthusiasm, but his drug cabinet filled with unlabeled vials and strange mechanical devices told me otherwise. We agreed to break up, but now he was bordering on victim stalking. I didn't know how to disengage from him as he hovered by my desk each morning, bugged me to have lunch when we weren't in the field, and appeared outside the office building, waiting for me at the end of the day.

My supervisor, Kenny, in Rob's age bracket, also showed his interest with jealous-tinged negative comments about Rob. Though I found Kenny's Bobby Darin looks appealing, I kept to a business-only attitude, knowing his power over my job could be an issue. Besides, I had my heart set on Harold, a tall, long-haired man in his late twenties, who was also a photographer with a camera permanently slung over his shoulder. Everyone at the DSS had an alter ego, except for Kenny, who seemed to have no other ambition.

A few weeks ago, while I was searching for a case file in the floor-to-ceiling metal cabinets, I overheard Rob and Harold speaking behind the barrier.

"She's really great." Rob's scratchy, feminine voice was unmistakable.

"What's so great about her?" Harold asked. "She's pretty ordinary."

"Oh, she's like Earth Mother," Rob said. "Anita's hair is shimmering over her voluptuous breasts," he oozed.

And then, the nail that pierced my heart: Harold said, "I still don't see the big fuss."

I had slammed shut the file drawer and leaned against the cold metal. The steel handle dug into my back. All I could hear were Harold's words: "Pretty ordinary." That was me.

On the phone, Cindy interrupted my thoughts. I hadn't responded to her comments, and she made the sound of "ahem" a few times. "Are you still there, Ani?"

"Oh, sorry. I was just thinking about the men at work. Yes, the male ratio is great, but sometimes it feels like a horrible meat market, and I am hanging on a hook, my naked body on display."

"You're so graphic," Cindy said, laughing.

"I guess I am."

"Why do you sound so sad?"

"Now, don't get upset. I was attacked today."

"What! Now you're telling me? Oh my God, what happened?"

"I'm okay," I said without surety. "Really, it could have been worse."

After I quickly spurted the events, I said, "I know this is perverse, but the thing that bothers me the most is my missing pocketbook and the picture of Paula."

"Those kids have your keys. Shouldn't you get your locks changed?"

"I guess so." My voice was low, and I cleared my throat, realizing that I sounded too dismissive. I just wanted to lie down in my bed and sink under the covers.

"They could find your address and come for you. I mean it, Anita."

"I know you're serious when you use my entire name."

"This is no joke."

Cindy knew me too well. She realized that I was doing what I usually did when I was upset: using humor as a dodge.

She spoke louder and with more force: "I'm coming over now. I'll take the subway. Be there in an hour."

"Don't be silly, I'm fine. They were just kids high on glue. They didn't care about me."

"They have penises, don't they?"

"Talk about being graphic."

"You aren't going back to work, are you?"

"Well, I called Kenny, and he said I should take the afternoon off."

"That goes without saying."

All I could think about then was to hang up and escape to my bed. But Cindy was relentless. She wanted to know more about the reaction at work.

"After I spoke to Kenny, the unit supervisor, Regina, got on the phone. I had to go over the details with her. She had seen me that morning before I went to the field. And you'd never guess what she told me."

"What?"

"'I remember your dress. It was very colorful,' she said. 'By the way, Anita, I do think it was too short. We will have to review this for the other girls who go to the field. I will also recommend that women don't go alone.'"

"Oh, Ani," Cindy said. "It was not your fault. Regina should have known better." Cindy's voice began to break up. I was afraid she would start crying. That was the last thing I needed.

"Ha ha," I said, "Regina is a woman in a sexist system. Just like the policemen, she didn't even ask me how I feel. She was more interested in how this looks on her record. And you know the worst?"

"Don't tell me you were raped."

"No, but in the middle of all this, the policeman came on to me."

"That's no surprise."

After I hung up with Cindy, I went into the bathroom and turned on the water in the tub, making it the warmest I could tolerate. I opened the flap on the Mr. Bubble box and poured in the powdery soap flakes. As I watched the bubbles expand into iridescent cotton candy shapes overcoming my tub, I realized one thing: I was not going back to my job, ever.

# CHAPTER 3: THE AFTERMATH

As the afternoon progressed, I remained on the sofa, my mind a mishmash of random memories, crisscrossing each other like shuffled playing cards. My fingers smoothed the red sofa cushion, and I recalled going with Denise to Macy's and selecting this model even though it was too "red" and the thin material impractical, all the reasons Denise and I opted for the unexpected. It was our first real apartment purchase, and we wanted to make a statement of independence; it was the only major piece of furniture in our living room for a long time.

In November 1967, after seeing an ad in the *Village Voice,* Denise and I had walked the four long blocks from the subway on Seventh Avenue to 165 Christopher Street on the corner of Washington Street, and inspected the street-level, one-bedroom apartment with rust-colored window bars rendering vertical below-waist views of passersby. At the time, I knew little about this westernmost part of the West Village. After signing the three-year lease, we visited a few times before our official move-in date and observed from our barred windows young homosexual men on their way to the parked trucks by the abandoned piers along West Street. And once we moved in and positioned our red sofa for a lower-level view of the street, we'd see taxis and limos in the bus-stop lane under our window where well-dressed men emerged, undoubtedly leaving their suburban lives for clandestine pursuits along the waterfront.

Those thoughts of our first days in our apartment caused a well of grief in my chest, and I realized Denise would be hurt that I hadn't yet informed her of my attack. I dialed her number at work, and she answered in a rushed voice. Curious by nature, my dear friend would undoubtedly pepper me with questions. She would be compassionate and not press me too much. But she would want details, and she'd want me to do something, call someone. I had to lessen the fallout.

"Hi, Denise. It's me. I wanted to catch you before you leave."

"Oh, Ani. What's up? I'm on my way out."

"I was supposed to pick up groceries at the A&P, but I got home early, and I will have soup or a sandwich, so if you want something more, can you pick it up?"

"Why? Are you sick?"

There was no way I could fool Denise, so I gave in. "Now, please don't be upset, but I was attacked today in the field. I'm really okay, but I just want to chill."

"Oh, my God. I'm leaving this instant. Were you hurt? Did you contact the police?"

"No. Yes. Really, I'm fine. I'll tell you everything in person."

I hung up knowing I did nothing to stem the flood.

*　*　*

About forty-five minutes later, I heard the jangle of keys in the lock, and Denise opened the door, hanging the straps of her shoulder bag on the hall hook and plopping down a paper bag of groceries. A bunch of bananas spilled on the parquet floor. She sat on the hallway bench to take off her shoes, and she appeared as tall as the full-length mirror behind her. Although we were the same height of five feet five inches, Denise had a long torso and I had long legs, so when we sat, she seemed much taller. At parties, we had a routine called "Guess Who's Taller?" We'd each sit on a chair, side by side. Although our viewers normally figured there was some catch, they invariably chose Denise and appropriately oohed and aahed when we stood at the same height.

Denise saw me and rushed to the sofa, where I had remained for hours, not having the energy to make it to the bedroom. She inspected my face and smoothed my hair.

"You look intact," she said.

"Sit," I ordered, and patted the cushion next to me, as if she were a dog. Leaving out the line on the police report about "attempted gang rape," I related most of the story.

"How horrible," she said. "Do you think you should be examined by a doctor or nurse?"

"No! I just need some peace and quiet. I will lie down for a while in the bedroom and then have a little bite."

"I'll make you some tomato soup with rice, your favorite."

"By the way, I think Cindy is coming over, but please don't wake me."

"Cindy knows?"

"Yes, she called me when I just got home."

She was leaning into a hug, but I backed away and stood. As I walked to the bedroom, I could feel her posture become even more elongated and her slender piano fingers combing through her Jackie Kennedyish flipped bob, like she did when she was upset.

*　*　*

While I vowed never to sit again alongside the row of caseworkers, I returned to the DSS office in downtown Brooklyn. I showed up Monday morning following my attack, and went to my desk drawer where I removed personal items, such as a pink plastic tampon case, a pack of Marlboros, a Webster's pocket dictionary, a black-and-white marble composition book containing little-known and potentially explosive information

I compiled about the DSS's policy and treatment toward my clients, and a McIntosh apple browning around the core. I dumped these into an A&P shopping bag and left my single cactus plant in a coffee mug for the next Welfare worker to occupy my space.

Marching to my supervisor's desk, I deposited my bag on the top amidst a sea of forms and manila case folders stacked at cross purposes like angled Legos. Kenny's perpetual short-sleeved, wrinkled white shirt was sweat-stained under the arms, even though it was only 8:30 a.m. and cool for a June morning.

"What did you bring me?" Kenny asked. "Hopefully, a bag of donuts."

"No such luck, Kenny. These are my belongings."

"Oh? What does this mean?"

Kenny was a literalist and needed the obvious to be spelled out. "I am leaving," I said, drawing out the syllables.

"Leaving?" he repeated, as if shocked, which he couldn't have been. "I know what happened to you on Thursday. I even spoke to Regina about it."

"Oh, Regina," I said. "You mean the one who told me my dress was too short?"

"I am so sorry, Anita, that this happened to you. Regina said that there will be a new rule that women don't go to the field alone."

"And when will this rule be implemented?" My voice reeked with fatigue.

"She put in a request."

"Ah, the magic words." I was losing whatever little patience I had left. My neck felt hot and scratchy. I removed the elastic hairband I had wrapped around my wrist, gathered my long hair, and tied it into a loose ponytail. "Listen, Kenny," I said, lessening my sarcastic tone, "I am not staying here. I wanted you to hear this from me personally. I don't want to speak to Regina again. You can tell her."

"But you don't have to go back to the field, at least not until you feel safe."

"Oh, Kenny, Kenny." I wanted to tell him to use his balls for once, but I could see that he was trying to make me feel better in his own inept way. "It's not just about what happened to me," I said. "I don't want to help perpetuate this lousy system that spies on poor people and does everything it can to maintain stereotypes."

"I know you do what you can to help."

"Yes. Kenny, as a Jew, don't you realize that Black people associate the white oppressors with Jews—Jewish slumlords, Jewish politicians, Jewish bankers, Jewish teachers, and, yes, Jewish social workers?" I drew the nearest metal rimmed chair to the desk, sat, and rested my elbows on Kenny's stack of case folders.

"Jews have been and will always be on the side of social justice," he said in a professorial voice. "Look what has happened in the South—Jewish activists murdered in Mississippi in 1964."

"I know, Kenny, but you haven't been to the field in a long time. It's scary. I read that Black activists said ugly things against Jews."

"I don't deny that."

"One of my clients is on the board and I met some of the members. They knew I was Jewish and were very respectful," I said. My stomach gurgled, and I eyed the apple on his desk, debating with myself if I should reach out and grab it.

"And I have friends who are teachers at J.H.S. 271," Kenny said, breathlessly.

I knew he wanted to convince me to stay and was running out of arguments. I stood, getting ready to make my move out of the area, but Kenny ran his fingers through his hair and pounded the desk with his fist, dislodging folders into even more erratic positions.

He sniffed and bit his lips. "Two of my friends," he continued, "were among those ousted by the board. Like most of the city teachers, they are Jewish. They swear they had never experienced antisemitic comments on the picket lines or in the school."

"It's not necessarily based on real experience in the classroom."

"It all started," Kenny stressed, sitting straighter, "when the governing board ordered a bunch of teachers and supervisors to leave, and the UFT ordered them back. Some in the UFT leadership claimed that the community control board was made up of antisemitic Black nationalists."

I spotted Rob, who seemed to be rifling through the file cabinet. He was a lousy actor, sliding the drawers back and forth too quickly. I knew he was spying and waiting to get me alone when I left Kenny's desk area. This only made me resume my discussion with Kenny.

"I think a lot of racial strife is inflamed by politicians or people with outside interests, rather than actual community residents."

"I agree, Anita. But let me ask you this. You were attacked by a gang of Black kids. Can you ignore their race?"

Now Kenny got my full attention. "No, I can't," I said, feeling the rumblings of stomach distress. "This morning, there was a group of Black teens on the subway standing near me. While they were wearing school jackets and carrying backpacks, I started sweating and hyperventilating, maneuvering away from them."

"That's perfectly understandable."

"Maybe I'm a racist, but I never felt like that before. I don't hate the boys who attacked me. I actually feel bad for them, for their lives, for the fact that they had nothing to do and got stoned on the roof." I felt the tears forming and swatted my eyes with a dirty napkin on Kenny's desk. I was not going to cry here, not when Regina and Ron were lurking, readying to snatch me.

"Yes, but you are leaving Welfare."

"I am. I am not proud of myself. You can call me a hypocrite."

"No," Kenny said. "You are a brave woman."

I lifted my eyes and stared into Kenny's sky blues. He fingered his gelled tawny hair. A beautiful *goyisher punim*, or gentile face, as my grandmother would have said. But unlike Rob Porter's, Kenny's features were a bit too large and a bit too crooked. This was the first time I had heard Kenny show awareness of political or social events, or anything outside the realm of the incessant bureaucratic demands of this department. He sounded passionate and informed. Sadly, I had underestimated him. My former disdain for him faded, and I felt sorry for him, knowing he would have to face Regina and more.

"I know it's probably too soon, but what are you thinking of doing now?"

"I can't even go there now." I didn't have any idea what I would do next. I couldn't even think of what to buy for lunch on the way home.

"Nobody ever wants this job. You must have other ambitions."

"Oh Kenny, I don't know. My college counselor once advised me to be a teacher or when I showed little interest, a social worker, the only two options for college-educated women. So, I followed this advice, even though I am always drawn to creative pursuits. Right now, nothing makes sense."

"I hate to lose you, Anita."

"I am lost already, Kenny."

I clutched the shopping bag and walked down the long corridor toward the elevator. From my peripheral vision, I noticed my fellow caseworkers and ancillary staff gathered in gossipy clots, watching me. On the chance that Regina would be one of the onlookers, I was glad of my morning choice of attire: a black skirt that covered my knees.

# CHAPTER 4: ODD JOBS

Denise's parents, the Golds, still lived in the Madison neighborhood of Brooklyn on a tree-lined block with towering old oak trees and crowded two-story, semi-brick homes, a short bike ride from my brown-beamed Tudor corner-lot house, fancy from the outside but whose interior sorely needed a facelift with worn green wall-to-wall carpets and faded, peeling chartreuse wallpaper. One Sunday morning, Denise and I rode the IRT subway to Flatbush Avenue, Brooklyn College, opting for a train line a little further away so we could walk past our favorite spots along Bedford Avenue, including the verdant college campus, crossing into side streets, noting exterior changes in the Spanish-style stucco homes, until we reached her parent's modest attached house for brunch. Denise's parents were educated and, to me, sophisticated. Her mother taught French at James Madison, our high school, and had a genuine Parisian accent (she reminded me frequently), not like the other language teachers who gave away their Brooklyn heritage with each foreign syllable. Denise thought her mother was a snob. This was enhanced when Mrs. Gold admitted years after we graduated that she looked up the SAT scores of Denise's high-school boyfriends and expressed her disapproval without giving away her sneaky tactics. Denise's father, on the other hand, was modest and friendly. He was short and portly, and you'd never guess he was a full professor of history at Hunter College and wrote books on the two world wars.

Denise's twin brother was away in grad school in Massachusetts and her older sister was married and lived in Maryland, so Denise and I were the only younger company. While sitting in their dining room, bordering a mahogany piano, we passed around the wire basket filled with a variety of bagels.

"So, Nita, Pita, Denise here tells me of your troubles with the Welfare Department. So sorry to hear about it."

"Thank you, Mr. Gold."

"Yes, Anita, we were shocked. Can I say that?" her mother asked.

"Well, you already did," Denise answered in her "ready-to-kill" voice.

We smeared cream cheese on our bagels and took turns spearing pieces of Nova lox from a large platter.

"I may be able to help you with a job," Mr. Gold said, wiping cream cheese from his over-the-lip mustache.

"Oh, Daddy, that would be wonderful," Denise said.

In his research, Mr. Gold explained, he met many fascinating émigrés, one of whom was looking for an assistant, "part-time," he added, as if this would make a difference.

I still had savings from my college and Welfare jobs, plus I was collecting Unemployment, which I attained with the help of my father's uncle, who owned a shoe manufacturing business. This great-uncle supposedly hired me as an inventory clerk, pretending to fire me from this job after a month. The claims analysts at Unemployment never questioned why I'd leave a steady job as a caseworker to take one as a clerk.

Of course, I was interested, especially since Mr. Gold said that the job would take place inside the man's apartment, and I wouldn't have to travel to a dangerous neighborhood. The man, an elderly Romanian named Andrei, had been a young journalist and Communist dissident.

He was arrested in Bucharest in 1948 and imprisoned at a Soviet Gulag, where he endured unspeakable torture until his release in 1956. After a harrowing escape, he immigrated to Canada and eventually to America. Now at ninety-two, he was writing his memoirs. Through the years, he had accumulated many handwritten journals with observations and important historical details he had described on the telephone in a raspy, heavy accent that I couldn't quite identify.

I visited Andrei at his apartment in a prewar building a few blocks from Columbia University, near the Hudson River. With a hunched posture, skeletal face, and white goatee, wearing a moth-eaten cardigan, he greeted me by his door and led me to an enormous living room with an oak rolltop desk overlooking the river. The centerpiece was a huge, old black Remington typewriter, which clunked and whistled as I practiced pulling the carriage return lever.

I began work that first day and the routine remained in place for the two months of my employment. For three hours, usually after lunch, Andrei handed me written notes to organize and type. Sometimes, he presented one of his journals, underlined with marginal comments. One day's assignment rarely followed the previous one's. Dates were sketchy and often nonexistent. I found it difficult to put the work into a cohesive order.

On that first day, I questioned him several times about which event followed which and if he had any special reminiscences or personal anecdotes relating to a section in an early journal.

"I think this one occurred first," he said, pointing to an underlined passage.

Half an hour later, he reappeared at my side and insisted I look at a different document he had found that may be more important. By the end of that first day, I realized that my job was to edit and type the material, not make sense of it.

But I continued to ask questions. As the weeks passed, he opened up a little. I discovered that his wife and son were killed in the Gulag and that he had been ninety pounds at the time of his release, after suffering from the effects of frigid temperatures, hard labor, and endless torture. He told me all of this in a detached way, in bits and snatches, never revealing emotion and rapidly changing the subject.

Oddly, I understood his delivery, only vaguely realizing it was how I processed my attack in Brownsville. The more he revealed, however, the more I persisted in questioning him. His wife was called Maria, and she had hair the "color of ravens." She endured sexual humiliation, including being forced to run naked in the snow. Their son, Victor, who "laughed like a mouthful of bubbles," was snatched from his mother at eight months old and placed in an orphanage, where he died.

I thought about them at night as I tossed in bed, unable to sleep. I became obsessed with Andrei's story, because he was a rare living witness to an important and unique historical experience, and I realized that the past was slipping through my fingers. I thought of my great uncle and his family, who were murdered in a Polish village massacre during the Holocaust, and how my mother's family years before escaped pogroms and lost many relatives in their years-long flight from the Cossacks. Both sets of my grandparents immigrated to Ellis Island from Eastern Europe, my father's from Latvia, and my mother and her family from Eastern Poland (now Belarus). My grandfathers died before I was born, but my grandmothers lived until fairly recently. I was close to both, though each tried to bribe me to their side, hoping to sway my allegiance. They loved to tell me stories of their lives in the "Old Country," and I was always entranced by their abilities to escape hardship and relocate to a new land.

My obsession with Andrei must have had roots in my family stories. Soon, I narrowed my focus to the subject of survival, not just longevity but the persistence to prevail after undergoing inhuman treatment.

Sometimes these thoughts gripped me in a type of frozen stupor, and I felt waves of dark suicidal thoughts. Yet, I found relief in the mere recording of facts. In some sense, this was the perfect job for me. I didn't have to decide on a full-time position; I didn't have to answer questions; I didn't have to speak to strangers; and no one expected much from me. Andrei paid me in cash, so I didn't report my income and continued to collect Unemployment.

For a change, I wasn't the goody-goody girl. I had lied about my income and lied to Unemployment. Maybe all the subterfuge I learned as a Welfare worker taught me that the truth often interfered with justice. But, for once, I didn't feel guilty; I deserved a break, and I found it in researching Death. Here at Andrei's desk, I felt inexplicably at peace, typing, reading notes, and trying to make sense of the senseless.

* * *

One evening at my apartment, I saw an ad in the *Village Voice* with a bold headline: "Wanted, Copywriter with Teeth." It intrigued me. I asked friends in publishing what a copywriter was; I had thought that it was like an old-fashioned scribe who copied someone's manuscript. When I learned it had a broad application, I opted for creativity. I designed a brochure and drew a cover picture of a woman with a large open mouth displaying big white teeth. The title banner blared: "WANTED: COPYWRITER WITH TEETH." Inside the brochure, I wrote: "Last seen: Corner of Root and Canal." The rest of the "copy" overflowed with dental puns. I mailed the brochure to the address in the ad.

A few days later, I received a telegram, my first (and only) one. It said, "Please report for interview for Copywriter with Teeth." It was from a famous ad agency. I called and made an appointment for their earliest available time.

An "assistant" showed me the wall of client advertisements, including cigarette and pharmaceutical companies, and gave me a quick tour of the agency with "creatives" arranged in maze-like, glass-enclosed cubicles. For my interview, I entered the office of the advertising director, who said that mine was the most imaginative response they had received. Unfortunately, I had no portfolio of artwork or advertising, so I left pleased at the lesson I learned: To get attention, get attention. To keep attention, lie about experience.

This rejection didn't disappoint me, as I didn't want to work in the cutthroat pressure-cooker atmosphere of an ad agency, and I couldn't lie to the public about advertised products. But it armed me for my next interview weeks later as a junior copywriter at a scientific publishing company, specializing in Russian-translated journals, Theoretical Press in Chelsea. By then, I had a portfolio of writing samples, including college term papers on academic subjects, and introspective poems. I also presented my black-and-white photos of New Yorkers and their neighborhoods that I had been taking since my brother gave me his old rangefinder camera a year earlier. My samples were irrelevant, but serious.

At my interview, I filled out the customary paperwork and handed it to the receptionist.

The vice president, Michael Bernstein, a slight, white-blond, blue-eyed man from tony Scarsdale, only a few years my senior but wearing the thin-lapel suit of an executive, considered me for a personal talk. I was surprised. With only six months of full-time work experience, and as a caseworker, I was totally unqualified for the position, but was attracted by the *New York Times* classified ad that called for "college writing experience."

"What kind of writing have you done?" Bernstein asked, as he picked up my application from a stack of others, undoubtedly most with vague liberal arts degrees like mine, willing to trade a meagre salary for writing credentials. We all worked for our "résumé," an unexpressed way of putting off our lives.

"I write poetry," I replied, sure that my depressive, non-rhyming poems had nothing to do with Russian physics.

"Ah, poetry. I like poetry. Well, that is very good."

I got the job at Theoretical, to start in a month, at a whopping hundred dollars a week.

# CHAPTER 5: EUROPE ON A LOW IQ

I received an airmail envelope from my brother, Ben. Inside was a check for four hundred dollars. The note said: "I know you are out of work, so I thought this will help. We'd love for you to use it for a plane ticket to Germany in time for the baby's birth."

When I read this to Denise, she said, "That is so nice of him."

"Yes, but don't forget he needs someone trustworthy to help."

"In any case, the timing is perfect. I have two weeks of vacation due. Why don't we go to Europe, and you can visit your brother afterward in time for the birth?"

"I don't know," I said. Wrapping up details with Andrei, contacting the airlines, making hotel reservations, and packing seemed too much for me to handle. I had little money left in my savings account. Plus, I couldn't admit to Denise, or to myself, that I had a nagging foreboding of disaster, from dying in a plane crash to being rounded up in a pogrom.

As if reading my mind, Denise said, "Don't worry about a thing. I'll make all arrangements, including organizing an itinerary that focuses on Italy. Isn't Italian food your favorite?"

I had never seen Denise so sure of anything. She would be the perfect traveling companion. She was spontaneous, funny, and adventurous; we were entirely compatible. I could taste the pizza and veal marsala. Despite myself, I was excited.

* * *

Less than a week later, we left on Icelandic Airlines, the cheapest way to Europe, and headed for Luxembourg. During the flight, I opened my journal. It was empty except for the back page, which contained a poem that I had written a few weeks ago when I was going through my papers and discovered that dreaded police report. It was untitled:

do you really care

that I am bleeding,

or do you mind that my blood

drips on your white shirt?

does it bother you that

instead of getting polluted

you must tighten my bandages

and dirty your hands?

do you really care about

my blood

or, are you glad to be

the attendant,

while watching you have

something to talk about?

Although I didn't rip out the poem, I turned to the first page and wrote, "European Adventures." I was determined to turn the page, literally.

At the airport, we bumped into a familiar figure, Stewy Morgenstein, a popular boy from our high school. Denise and I both had a crush on him, but he never glanced at us. We exchanged a few words of surprise and politely went our way. I had a sinking feeling that our trip would not be as exotic as I had dreamed.

Armed with our only book of reference, *Europe on 5 Dollars a Day* by Arthur Frommer, we set out by train to our first destination: Florence. On the train, we opened our map of Italy and couldn't locate Florence. After finding Firenze in the appropriate spot, we learned our first European lesson: English language speakers did not know the correct place names.

When we arrived in Florence, we followed Arthur (Frommer), whom by now I was calling Artie, and headed for one of his recommended *pensiones*. Our proprietress was out of a Fellini movie. About five feet tall and rotund, she had wildly dyed hair in an unnatural brownish red color, clownish rouged cheeks, a double chin, and bright red lipstick that over-layered her lips onto her black mustache.

We weren't in our tiny room for more than a night when our hostess introduced us to a guest, Youssef, a thin, bearded young man from Tunisia, who bowed to us and murmured pleasantries in French. Denise, whose mother spoke to her in French since she was a baby, answered with a perfect accent, and this cemented their connection. He didn't know that I was the one who understood more French and told Denise in private Brooklynese what Youssef was saying.

We approached the city like researchers. We went to every tourist spot from the Duomo to the Ponte Vecchio, and adopted the mantra, where one said, "It's a Pitti" and the other answered, "No, it's a Uffizi." During that time, I wrote "Ode to Florence (or Firenze)," a much more cheerful addition to my journal, and took my watercolors to the Arno's riverbank and copied my version of Botticelli's *The Birth of Venus.*

On our fifth day in Firenze, Youssef introduced us to his friend, Habib, a short, clean-cut man in his early twenties who would act as my "date" on a trip to a swimming hole near Fiesole, ten kilometers outside Florence. The next morning, the "boys" appeared in front of our *pensione* on their Vespas. In my paisley Arnel dress, I sat sidesaddle and eventually plastered my now parted legs against the scooter's sides, my arms clutching Habib's waist. My terror quickly turned to exhilaration, and my long hair snaked around my face in a blinding frenzy as we dipped in and out of the serpentine road to Fiesole.

We stopped at a waterhole. Youssef posed for a photo, wearing Denise's purple flowered dress and a towel wrapped around his head, poking his face between the streams of a raging waterfall. Habib sprawled on a blanket, sipping from a bottle of Chianti.

Youssef invited us for a weekend with a local friend, Fabrizio, who had a camper. We spent the night at a beachfront in Cecina Mare, Tuscany, in the camper while Fabrizio, who was balding and weighed around 300 pounds, farted continuously in his sleep. The next day, on an inflatable raft, I hand-rowed away from Fabrizio, but he upset my balance as he climbed aboard. Eating greasy three-day-old lasagna leftovers reheated over a tiny campfire, washed down with cheap wine, I nursed violent cramps. Crowding into a tiny bathroom, more like a hole in the wall, I had watery diarrhea. That night, as I washed plastic plates at an outside spigot, Denise joined me.

"I am sorry about Fabrizio," she said.

I answered, "You owe me."

★ ★ ★

Our next stop was Rome, where we engorged on artichokes and rigatoni carbonara. On a bench outside the Villa Borghese, we conversed with a neighboring couple, charming Germans in their forties, the Schwankes, who spoke excellent English. We exchanged pleasantries about our backgrounds and itineraries. They lived in Frankfurt and had two young daughters, now staying at their grandparents. Insisting we visit them when we came to Germany, Mrs. Schwanke slipped a paper into my hand with her address.

In Rome, without the protection of Youssef and his friends, we attracted men of all types; most encounters were limited to a snapshot. There were a few more serious "dates," including one with a handsome entrepreneur who took me to an outdoor café where we sipped espresso and ate tartufo, made from chocolate gelato coated in cocoa and topped with whipped cream.

And then there were the scary times. One evening, on our way to our *pensione* on an unlit street, four young men pinned us against a wall, their hands plunging into our chests. We kicked and screamed, and they ran away, but the experience resurrected my fears. From then on, whenever a male approached us, I hid behind Denise, who was only too happy to flirt like crazy.

★ ★ ★

We often chose our next destination based on desire, rather than geographic proximity. This resulted in a convoluted back-and-forth travel, wasting a lot of time on trains, though I enjoyed daydreaming and looking out the windows. Wanting to honor our promise to visit our new friends, the Schwankes, we took a fourteen-hour overnight northern train from Rome to Frankfurt, knowing we would then return south to Munich for Denise's return to America and my travel to Ben's army base in Ludwigsburg, near Stuttgart.

In the train compartment, we turned down our reclining seats into sleeping position and turned off the lights when the window views became too dark to decipher in the middle of the night. Suddenly, we awoke to the humping of Slavic-speaking men laying on top of us, laughing, and reeking of alcohol. I felt thick hands pummeling my breasts. We pushed them off, turned on the light, and screamed at them as we pointed to the door. They left quickly, and I was again terrified by the sheer shock of the male sex and its infinite ways of accosting me.

Once in Frankfurt, we headed for the Schwankes. We contemplated hitchhiking but heard from the conductor that a violent rapist was picking up female hitchhikers on the autobahn. So we splurged on a taxi.

From Firenze we had sent the Schwankes a postcard with our intentions, signed with our full names. When we showed up at their lovely split-level house in the suburbs, with flowers in hand, Herr Schwanke answered the door, flanked by his fair-haired daughters. Frau Schwanke appeared in an apron, her face wearing a dour expression.

After an early bedtime, the next morning at breakfast, Frau Schwanke served us hard-boiled eggs, each perched in a hand-painted, flowered porcelain egg cup. Following the lead of our hosts, I tapped on my egg and missed; the delicate cup cracked. I apologized profusely. Frau Schwanke shrugged and repeated how they were going to church that morning.

As Denise and I said our *auf Wiedersehns,* we wondered why they had invited us. Did they think we would never accept their invitation? Did they change their minds when they saw our full names on the postcard? Did they cringe as Jewish girls used their bed linens and broke their chinaware?

★ ★ ★

A four-hour train ride from Frankfurt to Munich brought us to the final stop in our journey before we parted company. After checking into a hostel, the next morning, we took the twenty-five-minute train and then a short bus to the Dachau Concentration Camp Memorial Site. It contained the first regular German concentration camp (out of 44,000 camps and incarceration sites), where between 1933 and 1945, around 41,500 people died of hunger, exhaustion, disease, and some were executed. Over its time, it had over 200,000 prisoners.

We toured the enormous complex, which also housed SS facilities and a museum. The Crematorium Area was the most harrowing. With shaky legs, we walked through the "path of death": the clothing disinfectant chamber, waiting room, shower, gas chamber, and death chamber where the bodies were held until cremation. I saw the original crematoria with two huge steel furnaces encased within red-brick foundations, and smaller ovens, and then the newer and larger facility. Although these ovens didn't kill most prisoners, they helped dispose of the dead bodies.

I had never seen ovens that large and imagined Nazis sliding an emaciated Jew's body into the flames as nonchalantly as if it were a pizza pie. I recalled the framed prewar photo my grandmother hung in the hallway of her Brooklyn apartment. Her brother and his family stood in front of their wooden home in their native Polish village, looking more prosperous and fashionable than I had expected. Could Nazis have shoved my already-dead great-aunt Olga, her husband, Moishe, and their teenage children into these flames? Had they been transported to worse death camps where they were gassed or burned alive? Or, as we had suspected, had they been massacred, like so many in their area, in pits dug by locals? These thoughts were so overwhelming that I rushed out of the room, determined to learn more about their final days.

After hours reading the plaques and seeing the photos in the museum, Denise and I returned to Munich and fell into our beds at the hostel without eating dinner. From our windows, I heard the incessant blaring police sirens and could almost feel the thumping of boots up the stairs and fist-pounding on our door. If I hadn't promised Ben that I was coming, I would have taken the plane with Denise out of Germany.

I could have rewritten the title of my journal to *Europe on a Low IQ*. But were we really stupid? We made a list of goals and priorities. Yes, we went miles, hours out of our way; and we followed our instincts, ill-informed as they may have been. Yet, we were open to newness and made the most of the unexpected. Our motto was, "Wherever we go, we weren't there before." With all the headiness of travel, I was still emotionally fragile and inexplicably prone to violent thoughts. I felt like a victim, though I didn't seek sympathy or attention. Perhaps I had an innocent look that allowed males to pounce without fear of reprisal. My examination of the issue did little for me other than help blame the victim, which, in this case, was "me." I sensed, however, an important shift in my consciousness that perhaps began when I was researching for Andrei. Here, in Germany, even in the bowels of Brooklyn, I was linked to the history of persecution. I longed to express myself in a meaningful creative pursuit, and, most of all, I craved the peacefulness of inner acceptance.

# CHAPTER 6: A BABY BOY

At the Stuttgart airport, I hugged Denise extra hard as she boarded a plane back to New York, and I headed toward my brother's army base in Ludwigsburg. I hailed a taxi, but I didn't have Ben's exact address. He had joined the army as a captain because of his law degree, guaranteed to escape placement in Vietnam. My sister-in-law, Aviva, was about to give birth and needed moral support and help with her six-year-old-daughter, Paula.

The last time I received a note from him, he had been at his office and didn't know the street name or number of his apartment (different from the barrack numerals) and said he would forward it to me, which he hadn't. I had a phone number, and the connection was always busy.

Still operating on my spontaneous travel philosophy with Denise, I took a chance. How large could the base be? I'd find him somehow. I asked the taxi driver to head for the residential barracks, and I scanned the playground for Paula. It was around 10:00 a.m. and there were no visible children despite the sunny September weather; they must have been inside the school. Next, I stopped at the commissary and asked a clerk if she knew my brother. She shrugged but pointed toward the officers' barracks, and I asked the taxi driver (speaking in broken Yiddish) to troll the streets. Finally, I got out in a few places and screamed, "Aviva." At the third stop, a window opened on the third floor of a redbrick building and Aviva's mid-back-length, blue-black hair whipped across her porcelain face like a horse's tail.

"Aviva, Aviva," I yelled, waving frantically. "It's me, Anita."

"Oh my God," she yelled, and within minutes she lumbered down the stairs and appeared very pregnant as I was paying the taxi driver. We embraced loosely, as I kept from squeezing her belly. She was a vision of maternal health; tears flowed down my cheeks.

"Where in the world did you come from?" she asked. "I thought I heard my name but was sure it must be an aural hallucination. And there you were." She patted my face with her sweater sleeve and planted little kisses.

"I came from Stuttgart where Denise took a plane home. We had been in Munich. Didn't Ben tell you I was coming?"

"Yes, and no. He mentioned that you would probably come, but nothing specific."

"Well, here I am." Without speaking, Aviva took my arm and motioned to the front door, and I followed her up three flights to her apartment.

"It's perfect timing. Ben is away on some secret assignment for a few days. So it's just us girls." She bounced around the kitchen, opening the refrigerator and drawers, poured me a cup of coffee, and laid out a plate of cookies and cake.

As we gossiped around her round table in the nook outside the galley kitchen, I regaled my sister-in-law with tales of our adventures. After a quick lunch of egg salad, we headed for Paula's school. Gathered outside the building, surrounded by other girls, my niece saw me and zeroed in for a hug.

"Oh, Aunt Anita, I thought you'd never come," she cried. "Wait, Gerdy and Suzie, come, come." She motioned to her friends, who crowded around me. "See, this is what an aunt looks like." Paula beamed, pulling on one of her many colored-ribbon-tied pigtails.

"Ooh," a pudgy girl crooned and touched my face as if I were a newborn. I then realized that these army kids had been away from extended families so long they forgot their relatives.

Aviva and I spent the following two days at local cafes, indulging in apple strudel and Black Forest cake. She was not happy living in such a remote and sterile place and was dreading having a baby so far from familiar territory. She missed having a piano. With a music degree from Julliard, she had had a brief performing career before she had children. It took her two years to recover from postpartum depression when Paula was born, and then they were living in Philadelphia far from family.

One evening, after Aviva and Paula had gone to sleep, I was tossing in the sofa's pull-out mattress in the living room when I heard the slamming of the front door. Turning on the nearby lamp, I saw my six-foot-tall brother in a long wool green army coat swinging a duffel bag.

"Anita! Wow, you came."

I rose and stood on my toes to hug him. He smelled of cigarettes and alcohol.

"Yes, obviously, I'm here, though I have to admit it was hard finding your place."

"Why didn't you call me, Dodo?" He hung his coat and hat on wall hooks, revealing his normally curly light-brown hair now plastered and greasy. His cheeks had a blond stubble, and his gray eyes were filmy and red.

The hairs on my arm rose with that name, Dodo, and I ignored it. The clock on the side table read 2:05; it was no time for our usual negative repartee. I would take the high road.

"Have you been traveling?" I asked, even though I knew he had been somewhere "secret."

"Pretty much, but no sightseeing, just routine."

I gritted my teeth, trying to ignore his vague answers. I no longer cared where he had been and suspected that his secret mission involved women and booze and not military maneuvers.

"Is Aviva okay?" he asked.

"Yes, getting bigger and better. She can't wait for the big day."

"I hope she handles this birth better than Paula's."

"Well, we all know so much more about postpartum depression now. She is prepared."

"Oh, is she? I hope you can stay for the birth."

After his sarcasm, Ben's voice softened, and I immediately fell for his changed tone.

"Of course I will. I am here for the duration, though I am somewhat time-limited."

"Well, I wouldn't want you to miss your busy social life in New York."

With that remark, I told Ben I was tired, and he quickly left the room. I lay awake for another hour, going over our conversation and castigating myself for falling into old behavioral patterns. Then, on my way back from the bathroom for yet another pee stop, I saw Ben's coat hanging by the front door. On a whim, I touched the rough wool and smoothed my hands along the back. With my fingers seeming to have their own direction, they delved into his pocket and retrieved a train stub from West Berlin and a torn matchbook with the words "Big Eden Nightclub."

The next morning, I awoke to clanging in the kitchen and the aroma of coffee. After closing my bed and going to the bathroom, I went to the kitchen, expecting Aviva to be making breakfast. Instead, Ben was standing in front of a frying pan on the stove, fluffing up eggs with a spatula, the same way my father used to do. Ben wore a full-length apron that was probably designed for a pregnant woman.

"Ah, Dad's eggs," I said.

"Yes, remember he used to say that the trick was to make them look like popcorn?"

In the next minute, Paula dashed in front of me and screamed, "Daddy, Daddy, you're home."

Ben dropped his spatula and grabbed his daughter, tossing her in the air. "How is my little muffin?" he asked, smothering his head into his daughter's uncombed curls.

"I'm good, Daddy. Aren't I, Mommy?" Aviva appeared in the doorway, coming our way.

"Yes, pumpkin, you are good as gold." She kissed Ben on his cheek.

We sat down to eat the ham and eggs, complete with biscuits and jam. It was the best meal I'd had in months, and I buried all thoughts of family discord and impending birth tension.

For now, my brother was the king of the kitchen, and I would not spoil his reign.

My nephew, Max, was born the next day. He was a healthy seven pounds and had incredible lung power, screaming in such a shrill tone that it reminded me of the German sirens I'd heard in Munich. Aviva had been in labor for six hours and seemed more emotionally adjusted than she had been when Paula was born. On Max's day home, I volunteered to change his diaper and was so enamored by his little pink cheeks that I had my mouth open wide in a large oval trying to make a funny face and instead got a mouthful of baby pee. I literally learned to keep my mouth shut and decided that my most helpful job was to take Paula to the playground as often as possible.

Ben stayed home for two days and sulked in the living room lounger, rarely relieving Aviva; the tension between the two was great. It affected me greatly, and I was up each night, rehashing my brother's barbs. Although I loved spending time with Aviva and Paula, and baby Max, every time Ben entered our space, my spine stiffened, and I stifled my good humor. Since I was starting my new job at Theoretical soon, I had to leave by the end of the week, making my entire visit ten days. Part of me was relieved and the other part of me felt I was deserting those I loved.

"Oh," Ben said when I announced my departure. "I thought you could stay longer."

"I have a new job, and I have to get back."

"Well, at least you could enjoy Italy on my four hundred dollars."

There was so much I could have said. I was fuming inside. On cue, baby Max wailed from the portable crib in the master bedroom. Aviva was in the bathroom and Paula was playing at her friend's house.

"I'll get him," I said. I preferred the baby's screams to the ones inside my chest, ready for my brother. My mother had said to me that she was so happy that Ben sent me the money. He was so generous, she bragged. But I knew better. In my family, there were always strings attached waiting to be tightened.

# CHAPTER 7: THE LETTERS

In my senior year at college, I met a young man at Café Figaro on Bleecker Street in Greenwich Village, the place that represented for us repressed Brooklyn girls the romantic epitome of bohemian life, where we regularly trolled clubs for folk music with the likes of Peter, Paul, and Mary and Bob Dylan at the Bitter End. It was a Sunday afternoon, and Denise and I had been sitting at a sidewalk table for an hour sipping our cappuccinos, watching the passersby (probably other students from the boroughs). The windy spring day got to us, and we headed to a table inside, distractedly studying the yellowed copies of *Le Monde* plastered on Figaro's walls.

I heard a low, sexy voice ask, "Is this chair free?"

Reflexively, I said yes, expecting a nerdy guy to drag away our extra cane-back chair. Instead, he pushed the chair closer and straddled it.

"Can I join you?" he asked.

Wearing a black turtleneck sweater and tight black jeans, he had full kissable lips, voluminous hair, side-parted with a wavy forehead dip à la Jean-Paul Belmondo, and a heavy unidentifiable accent, which turned out to be Egyptian. When he, Jabari (shortened to Jake for acting purposes), sat at our table and asked to join us, my eyelids fluttered in an embarrassing retrograde manner that I would have scoffed at in a novel. I was in love with the idea that he was an actor, wrote music, admittedly smoked pot, and caused the waitresses to flaunt and swoon.

Jabari seemed equally smitten with me, almost ignoring poor Denise, and accompanied me on the long subway ride home to Brooklyn even though he lived in Queens. It was close to midnight when we got to my house, and we headed for the finished basement daybed, barely unbuttoning our shirts before we reached intimacy. Afterwards, instead of hearing the earth move, I was shaken by the rumble of the toilet flushing above us, expecting that my father was driven by his overactive prostate.

After we graduated from college, Denise and I drove up the California coast and north to Canada. After three weeks, Denise went home, and I stayed behind to visit my cousins in Los Angeles to see if I would consider moving to the West Coast. After about two weeks, I craved the unexpected: crowded subways, Spanish curses from construction workers, and New York pizza. During that time, Denise and I wrote each other long, newsy letters, many of which didn't arrive before I was back in Brooklyn. We had become accustomed to sharing the most intimate bodily functions, and Denise described her bathroom habits and dating fiascos in detail. She was deft at drawing caricatures of boyfriends, including one with a "huge" erection.

I was not such a visual artist, yet my letters included sardonic comments about my "entitled" Californian cousins who squabbled over the latest cars, and I fashioned novelistic depictions of weather and mood.

But the big news that Denise and I dissected was that upon her return to New York, she accepted a job as a claims adjuster for Social Security, putting off graduate school, much to the dismay of her professional parents. Miraculously, she found an affordable apartment in our favorite neighborhood, Greenwich Village. I was thrilled for Denise, but I was also jealous. It was time for me to come home and claim my turf.

My parents met me at the airport arrival terminal. Instead of greeting them, I spotted Jabari among the sign bearers. He lifted and twirled me around and abruptly let me go when he spotted my parents, whom he met once when he picked me up for a date. My mother nodded at him, and said, "We should go. We left the car in an illegal parking spot."

Jabari nodded back and uttered, "Mr. and Mrs. Rappaport, how are you?"

My father said, "Fine" and asked Jabari if he needed a lift. I was in shock because it wasn't like him to go out of his way, much less be hospitable to my boyfriends. But my mother wasn't having any of it and practically pulled me away from Jabari by my hair. Jabari said, "No thanks," to my father and backed away like a humble servant. I was so humiliated but managed to wave to him as he disappeared from sight.

Our house in Brooklyn was jammed with cartons. Now that I graduated from college, my financially strapped parents had a plan: downsize to an apartment, figuring I could adjust to a small bedroom. While I was in California, they finalized the sale of their house and signed a lease on an apartment in Rockaway Park with a sliding door, terrace view of the Atlantic Ocean. Their move-in date was only a month away.

A week later, my mother came into my room as I was writing Denise a letter, even though we were now in the same city.

"Who are you writing to?" she asked.

"Denise."

"Didn't you just see her?" she asked, barely hiding her sarcasm.

"So?" I wasn't giving her an inch.

"So, so. Maybe you should take up sewing with all your free time."

"And keep you in stitches?"

"Very funny, young lady. Did Denise do something special?" My mother sensed a change and was an experienced investigator of her family's shenanigans.

"If you must know, Denise moved to the 'City.'"

"Oh, I bet her parents are not too happy."

"They seem to accept her independence."

"They were always too liberal."

My mother only met Denise's parents twice and each time it was a school event, so she didn't talk to them for long. Although she would never admit it, I thought she was embarrassed because my father had lost his pharmaceutical product business, and she got a low-level job as an office assistant after being out of the workforce for years. Before she married, her two younger brothers and sister were still at home and her older brother worked in the insurance business and recently married. With no financial help from her parents, my mother supported herself as a single girl in Manhattan on an office assistant's salary. Eventually, her younger siblings attended city colleges while they worked odd jobs. My mother, however, was always self-conscious about her social and educational status.

"Anyway," my mother said, opening my curtains to let in the afternoon sun, "I hope Denise doesn't give you any ideas."

"I can speak for myself." Then, without a beat, I added, "Denise did ask me to live with her. Her apartment has a large bedroom."

"Are you crazy?" my mother screamed in her high-pitched voice. "You have just come home. Besides, you don't have a job."

"Well, that is not exactly true." By now, my head was pounding and my eyes teared. As I had feared, this would not be easy. The best course was to get it over with.

"It just so happens I found a job. Before I left for California, I sent an application to the Department of Social Services, and there was an acceptance in my pile of mail."

"You mean Welfare?"

"Yes."

"Well, you are just full of surprises, aren't you? Were your parents merely place savers for your behind?"

"There is no need to speak to me like this."

"Okay, did you think this through? Where will you work? In one of the dangerous slums, no doubt."

"It's hard to visit people on Welfare at Sutton Place." I uttered a fake chuckle.

The phone rang and my father, who must have heard our loud voices, did what he never did before: he answered. "It's for you, Frances," he screamed. "It's your sister."

My mother backed out of my room and rumbled down the stairs to the hall phone. I had hoped it would be one of her sister's long conversations, though I knew my aunt Reebie would not want to indulge my mother in her resentments. But I was wrong. Before long, my mother was back in my doorway.

"I blame Denise for all of this. She convinced you to move out of your home."

"What do you mean?" I felt danger inflaming my shoulders.

"I mean, she told you that you had to get away from your parents, that we are in an unhealthy relationship and a bad influence on you. Who the hell is she? After all, isn't she the one who said she hated her own mother?"

"How do you know this?" I said, fury building in my eyes. I fell on my bed, pulling my pillow over my face. Go away, go away, I willed.

"If you must know, I read your letters."

"What? How could you?"

"I was straightening out your room, and they were laying in a pile on your desk. At first, I just skimmed one and then when I saw my name, I felt compelled to read more."

"I can't believe this." I knew my mother was a fragile person and sensitive to slights, but I never thought she would betray me like this. The fury was intensifying, and I didn't know what to do with it.

"Denise is the one who is a bad influence on you."

"I just spent three weeks traveling with her. Am I some dope who doesn't know people?"

"She wrote poisonous things. And those drawings ... they're perverted."

"You never saw what I wrote to her." My hands curled into a fist. I was ready to punch.

My mother didn't mention the positive remarks she read. Denise stressed in every one of her letters that she would save mine, that they were beautifully described and composed like a novelist. She urged me to take my writing seriously.

"I can write letters, too," my mother whined. With that, she disappeared and returned in a few minutes, handing me an envelope. On the cover she wrote, "To Denise."

"What's this?"

"This is my answer to Denise. I typed it last night. Give it to her."

"I will not. And I will not stay in this house as long as I have no privacy."

★ ★ ★

That was how I moved out of my parents' home in Brooklyn and into Denise's new apartment on Christopher Street. Although my mother eventually visited and pretended to be friendly toward Denise, she couldn't fool me. She never forgave me for moving out, and she never forgave Denise for "influencing" her dumb, susceptible daughter. I never showed my mother's letter to Denise. As far as she knew, my mother was just as crazy as always, and my father remained oblivious to all emotions. As usual, we tried to guess his feelings by piecing together obscure clues.

★ ★ ★

After I arrived in New York from my three and a half weeks in Europe, Jabari was at the airport to greet me again. This time, my parents stayed in their new oceanfront apartment in Rockaway Park, Queens, and I took Jabari home to Christopher Street. That night, Denise gave us the bedroom, and Jabari and I had sex on my Beautyrest mattress, the same one I took from my childhood home in Brooklyn. I called my mother the next morning, and she had the good sense not to ask me how I got home from the airport.

"When will I see you?" she asked before we hung up. I didn't want to see her and ruin my good mood. Guilt assaulted me immediately, like a vestigial organ.

"Well, I'm starting my new job tomorrow. I'll call you."

Sometimes, I fantasized that there was a female goddess at the Pearly Gates who had a graph with a column entitled "Mother," which listed the number of times she asked her daughter to visit, and a column called "Daughter," for when she actually appeared. They never were even. Despite the Mother's claim to the contrary, the Daughter column was always the highest.

# CHAPTER 8: SOVIET SUBTERFUGE

On my first day at Theoretical, Michael Bernstein led me to a small open area near the Editorial Department and to my desk, which was a typewriter stand, jammed in the center between two larger desks, each occupied by a different department. To my left was Lydia Blank of Personnel (later renamed Human Resources), who disappeared regularly behind the tall copy machine, I later learned, to have sex with Joseph, the head of the Mail Department. My right elbow rested on the desk of Accounting, where Faye Williams pounded the buttons of an adding machine, whose trail of white paper swept the floor in bouncing curls.

With only inches separating us, facing me was the loveliest of faces, Shirley Baumann, who sat erect, slightly tilting her brown face toward her typewriter, her large mahogany irises rising through her cat's-eyeglasses. She had side-swept bangs, straight black hair puffing over her ears in a modified flip. The pearls in her drop earrings swayed as she nodded to me, and she continued clacking her long, red-painted nails across the keyboard. The sleeves of her black-and-white striped blouse billowed from the overhead fan whirring away. She had the side glance and grace of someone who saw everything but said little, but it was the slight smirk when our eyes met that gave me a sign that she was the one who knew it all. I was captivated at once.

Shirley was the head of the Marketing Department, and she was the only one of my desk mates who had employees under her ken, two women whose desks were at the other end of the congested square space. Our foursome was closest to Michael's office, which was one in a line of five similar small offices for the male executives.

Among the other college-educated females like me, there were two secretaries named Carol, both of whom were having affairs with their married bosses, one a shipping manager and the other a client liaison. I learned this after working for only an hour from the gossipy Lydia Blank on my left. Both Carols had desks outside their respective lovers. The younger and shorter Carol, I was informed again by Lydia, constantly talked about her boss, Ronald, who would visit her apartment after work at least twice a week. One night, I dropped off an envelope at her apartment and I glimpsed a full-length poster of Ronald plastered on the inside of the front door greeting me. Carol was horrified that I had seen his replica and laughed, muttering, "Oh, Ronald hates that thing."

The other woman in the office was Marilyn, a beautiful and tall Rita Hayworth look-alike, with long, curly reddish-brown hair, whose liaison function seemed vague, but who appeared way too radical in her politics to consider affairs with the oversexed, button-upped males of Theoretical Press. I discovered this not from Lydia, but rather when I met Marilyn in the ladies' room after lunch on the first day. She introduced herself and asked me how I liked the place so far.

"Well, it's a bit crowded but everyone is very friendly."

"Yes, you could say that." She smiled, her top lip at a slight slant. I wondered if she had Bell's palsy, but then she took a sip of water from a cup and swished it, gently spitting it in the sink. She had initially appeared so sophisticated that the gesture surprised me; by now, I expected her to brush her teeth.

"Sorry, I had a piece of tuna sandwich stuck in my teeth."

"No need to apologize. But you implied something about being very friendly. How long have you been here?"

"Only a few months. Oh, don't get me wrong. Despite the erudite subject of our work, everyone here is very informal, but I don't like to get too friendly with coworkers. You're lucky though, sitting next to Shirley. She's a real lady."

"And the others aren't?"

"Well, let's just put it this way. The men here have it good."

Theoretical catered to Soviet and Eastern European scientists. No one in the Editorial Department was fluent in Russian, or even had a basic knowledge, but we worked within the parameters of translated introductory material, supplemented by meaningless catchphrases, such as "invaluable as a reference for," "brings together the latest thinking on," and then we substituted the relevant category.

I learned this on my second day at Theoretical. The former copywriter had left me a publisher's style sheet, two pages of proofreading symbols, and a pamphlet listing the types of scientists and what topics they study. She wrote me a note: "Here are the basics. Good luck."

Michael Bernstein handed me my first big assignment. I was to write a book jacket and a brochure advertising their newest title, a Russian textbook on refractory metals. He explained the procedure: When I finished with the copy, he would give it to one of the executive editors who would correct it. Then I would work with the art department on the layout and design. He then gave me a ten-page English translation of the introduction and a chemistry textbook as references. I spent the entire day underlining and taking notes, sure that this job was beyond my capabilities. I didn't even know what refractory metals were and now I was going to advertise it to the world. I found a paragraph in the introduction and reworded it: "In recent times, refractory materials are becoming essential in the fields of national defense and the military industry." Then I looked at my list of scientists, and I wrote: "This breakthrough book will bridge the gap between research and practical applications. As an academic reference and as an industrial reference, this book will be invaluable to material scientists, engineers, physicists, chemists, and aerospace scientists." I added a few biographical lines about the author and put it on Michael's desk before I left the office.

The next day, Michael returned my copy and said the editor already reviewed it this morning and added a few words here and there but was very happy with it. "Make the few changes and discuss it with the Art Department."

I was in shock; sure they would discover my ineptitude and call me back with a dismissal notice. But Michael showed nothing but a smile whenever I passed him in the hallway.

My next assignment had to do with a journal on noise pollution. This time, I wasn't so intimidated and did a little research in Theoretical's "library," which was really a clothes closet. I could understand this subject and added a few lines of opinion and conjecture. These were immediately deleted by the editorial director, who simply wrote, "Stick to the facts."

Denise couldn't understand how I could write copy based on information from a foreign language about an obscure topic. My former job with Andrei prepared me to notice language quirks and summarize inexplicable material.

I realized, as I explained to Denise, the less I knew about a subject, the easier it was to write about it. Having gotten three Ds in college science courses, I was not fit to write about organic chemistry or electromagnetic radiation on the professorial level. But I could compete on the bullshit level with the best of them.

# CHAPTER 9: THE SUBWAY RIDE

November 1968

Even if I stayed at my Welfare job, I wouldn't have gone back to the "field" for months. On the opening day of school on September 9, nearly 54,000 of the city's 57,000 teachers stayed out of schools, not including a full staff that showed up in Ocean Hill-Brownsville, though student attendance was low. On Tuesday, October 1, there was a riot outside J.H.S. 271 with many police officers and locals injured. October 14 marked a third citywide strike. It wasn't until November 17, at the end of the fifth week for the third teachers' strike, that a settlement was ready for release. In all, from May-November 1968, schools shut down for thirty-six days, affecting over a million students.

Obviously, "my" field was not a safe place for anyone, especially another middle-class Jewish "do-gooder." My field was ablaze; budding crops burned to ashes haphazardly blown by conflicting wind currents, sticking to sidewalks and clogging nasal passages with allergic profusion.

The tumult in the city matched the turmoil in my insides and revived the details of my attack. I had masked some of the fear while I was away, despite threatening incidents I attributed to a foreign landscape. But since I returned to work in October, fears cropped up again as I saw hooded Black teens on the subway, a disheveled man jerking off on a bench in Washington Square Park, and heard late-night street screams coming in through my Christopher Street windows. Terror was everywhere.

I avoided unnecessary travel, restricting myself to neighborhood vendors. Even those excursions provoked anxiety. I was vigilant. As I walked, I scrutinized oncoming passersby, side-stepping teenagers in groups; Black or brown men; males with crewcuts, Afros, or ducktails; women who resembled men; or anyone who looked in my direction. Intellectually, I hated myself for acting on racial or social stereotypes; but emotionally, I had no choice. Panic gripped me, lodging in a rectangle around my eyes like outer-space plastic glasses, fogging my vision, pressing my eyelids in a band of sapping heat. I understood the expression: blinded by fear.

Thanksgiving would be my first real excursion alone. Denise had invited me to Brooklyn to celebrate with the Golds. I would have enjoyed that as I always felt comfortable with Denise's parents who represented "normality," based on their going out every Saturday night to a restaurant followed by a movie or a show. If I ever wanted to have a semblance of a relationship with my parents, I could never accept Denise's invitation. My mother had her issues with Denise's letters and the Golds' so-called pretensions, and even my normally taciturn father put them down as social climbers. He based this opinion on flimsy evidence, primarily that Denise's twin brother went to an out-of-town college, her father played chess, and her mother paid for expensive seats at the synagogue for the Jewish High Holy Days.

★ ★ ★

On Thanksgiving morning, I swallowed a tranquilizer, headed for the subway at West 4th Street, and boarded the A train to Euclid Avenue. There, I changed to the shuttle for

Rockaway Park. I was the only person waiting. Sitting on an unoccupied bench, I dozed off and when the train came, I ran to catch it and got in the last car. It was empty except for one man who sat near the door leading to the next car. To be on the safe side, I moved to the other end of the car and faced the glass door that overlooked the light-splashed halo of the gray tunnel. I opened my book, a novel called *The Chosen* by Chaim Potok, which took place in Brooklyn, and felt strangely comforted by its Williamsburg setting, though by now I was out of the borough and into the thin precarious connection to Queens's jutting peninsula.

In the flickering subway light, I glimpsed the man at the other end; he could have been a light-skinned Black or dark Mediterranean or maybe a Puerto Rican. He had close-cropped black hair and a scruffy mustache and beard. He wore black slacks and a brown leather jacket. His long legs spread wide, his elbows rested on his thighs, and his head pitched down as if he was nodding off. He raised his head and glanced in my direction. I turned a page in my book, hoping it was right-side up, which was ridiculous since the man was too far away to read the type.

I shouldn't have worried. By now, I was a tough cookie. Many men around the city had exposed themselves as I sat on park benches and in subway corridors. But all that happened before when I was a relative innocent. Now, I was becoming a soldier, ever on the lookout for danger. I should never have come. I should have called my mother and told her I was sick. It was too late. My heartbeat thrummed and sweat accumulated between my ample breasts. I couldn't help but glance in his direction. My old supervisor Regina at DSS would surely have said I was asking for trouble.

As if I willed it, the man unzipped his pants and whipped out his penis. From my vantage point across the empty subway car, his "member" looked enormous. It could have been a salami or a stick of dynamite as far as I could tell. What could I do? If I walked to the next car, I would have to pass him, and that was not an option. I could get off at Broad Channel, but the train was already deserted, and who knew what could happen to me on an empty platform? At least on the train, there had to be a conductor or maybe someone else would enter at Broad Channel.

When the train finally stopped, I couldn't move. Trembling, I sat there and turned a few pages of *The Chosen,* hoping that the title had nothing to do with my predicament. I remembered reading somewhere, probably in the *New York Times,* that men who exposed themselves were basically nonthreatening or harmless; they performed for the thrill of shocking someone. Usually, they selected victims who looked nonthreatening. And here I was, again, thinking of Regina, blaming myself for looking like I wouldn't bite off this man's balls.

During the next ten minutes, the Exposer and I played a game of chicken, or I should say chicken's chicken as neither of us moved from our seat. In our case, we lifted our heads, barely slanting and eying each other and then lowering toward the offending object. Although I couldn't see clearly, the Exposer seemed to have a dreamy smile and drooping eyes, certainly no match for the ferocity of his stroking hands. I tried not to focus THERE, but I couldn't help myself; it was as if I were willing him to come so that he wouldn't approach me with an erection.

Luckily, the doors opened at Beach 90th Street and two teenage boys tumbled in near me, not looking in the Exposer's direction. Then they got off at 98th Street and I was alone again with Him, and his member was still out and about. Finally, my stop came, and I ran out the door. As I hurried to the staircase, my eyes following the departing train, I spied the Exposer inside the car wiping his penis with something. At least he had the decency to clean up.

I jumped down the station's stairs, flew across the street and down the block to my parents' apartment building, which faced the Atlantic. On a summer day, assorted groups dragged portable chairs and coolers, preceded by skipping children, eager to plunk themselves in the debris-spotted sand or run along the boardwalk searching for a hotdog stand. On this chilly and cloudy Thanksgiving, there were a few families walking down the block but heading to the parking lots or building entrances, readying for their family feasts. By the time I got to the front entrance, the wind was strong, and I had to pull the massive glass doors with both hands, yanking my shoulder, sure that I tore my rotator cuff.

I stood in front of the elevator for a few minutes, ignoring the open door. I stilled my racing heartbeat. I wiped the perspiration from my forehead and breathed in and out as if directed by a cardiologist during an exam. With no one in sight, I slipped into the elevator, emerging at my parents' floor and making sure no one had climbed up the staircase to meet me.

My mother opened her apartment door and said, "You're late. We've been waiting for an hour."

The grandfather clock in the hallway indicated 2:15. "You told me to come at two, so here I am."

My mother's mouth opened as if she was about to object, but my aunt Reebie sauntered toward the door and wrapped her swollen arms and billowing red African-print dashiki around me in a fabric sweep. Instinctively, I pulled back and said, "You can't believe what I just saw."

"Richard Nixon on the subway?" Reebie offered.

"Another latecomer?" my mother said, this time with a bit of a giggle.

I related my saga of the Exposer, and the women trailed me to the living room where my father sat on his captain's chair against the glass sliding doors overlooking the beach. Without acknowledging me, he picked up his *New York Post* and flipped through the pages.

"His penis was huge," I said.

My father pushed his black-framed glasses against the bridge of his nose.

"Oh, God," my mother said, finally relinquishing the subject of timeliness.

"You should have told him, 'Put that thing right back where it belongs,'" Reebie suggested.

"What a great line," I said, immediately thinking I could use it for some essay title. "I hope to remember it for the next time. I won't go home on the subway. I should have realized it would be deserted on a holiday like this."

"I wish I could drive you home," Reebie said. She lived in New Jersey and passed through the Verrazano Bridge, too far from the West Village. "Maybe your father can drive you."

"You just got here. Let's not talk about going home yet," my mother said.

My aunt and I looked at each other and shut up. This subject would not be discussed again for the day, though it would be in our minds.

With that, we three women stared at my father. I was certain that he heard his sister-in- law, though he rarely spoke to her directly, but he seemed engrossed in his puzzle, erasing away with his pencil. I never understood their relationship. My aunt, a workers' compensation attorney, long divorced, and a single mother to grown twin girls, was always the voice of reason in an unreasonable family. She would point out the options in a dilemma, but never held back her opinion, even if it hurt the recipient. Her outspokenness often got her into trouble and that's why she was in a small law firm representing workers seeking redress for injuries or illnesses suffered on the job. She once worked for the government but hated the bureaucratic paperwork and preferred to work against corporate greed.

My father, who often saw himself as the family outlier because he was essentially unemployed—his rationalization for staying out of everything—thought my aunt was a hypocrite. "True, she'd represent the working man," he said recently, "but she'd also have greasy hands after the case is resolved." My mother usually defended her younger sister, but she also excused her husband.

As I could tell, both parties were hiding in their self-inflicted bubbles. My father would have respected my aunt more if she weren't overweight and slovenly; my aunt would have paid more attention to my father if he weren't overweight and slovenly. With their large horn-rimmed glasses and oily, gray-streaked hair, they could have been brother and sister, separated only by what they had in common: my mother, Frances, who was thin, shapely, and beautiful, but didn't know it. Her overdeveloped management tactics could have gotten her a partnership in my aunt's law firm.

The oldest of Aunt Reebie's twins, Abby (by five minutes) lived in Seattle and had a two-month-old son; the youngest, Ziggy (Reebie wanted names from A to Z), was in the Peace Corps stationed in Ghana. And since my older brother, Ben, was in Germany with his family, the only child around town available for Thanksgiving was me, the one with the strongest wanderlust (though currently severely challenged). Aunt Reebie and my parents depended on me to fill the space designated for offspring.

Sure, there were other cousins close to my age, sons and daughters of my mother's three brothers, but they were busy with their own lives, and we only saw them at Uncle Lenny's annual Chanukah party when he drank too much Manischewitz and pinched my behind more than once. Reebie's twins swore that Lenny felt them up when dancing, but Reebie insisted that her daughters were being overly sensitive. I had been surprised at Reebie's attitude as she was usually the first one to accuse a man of inappropriate behavior as she did in her advice for my Exposer. But Reebie had a soft spot for Lenny because he always called her Reebie the Rose, a delicate flower, and loved to tell Yiddish jokes. She figured if Lenny's fingers strayed, he couldn't have been serious, not to her girls.

So, I had a lot to put up with this Thanksgiving: keeping the peace between my father and Reebie, between my mother and her sister, between my parents, and saying a good word about all the good-for-nothing children who couldn't even make it home for Thanksgiving, though it wasn't really a holiday for the Jews, not like Chanukah or Rosh Hashana. My father thought the *mischugas* from my mother's family was so bizarre that he didn't have to participate, which was his normal mode of behavior anyhow. His family, the Rappaports, consisted of two first cousins who lived in upstate New York and ran a Kosher meat market; his sister and her children who lived in Los Angeles and had something to do with show business. There was enough dysfunction there, too.

My mother brought out a platter with cheese and crackers, and we crowded around the coffee table abutting the brown-leather sofa. I was waiting for the interrogation to begin.

Paramount in my mother's mind was my "situation," a new job with a questionable description. Unaware of why I left Welfare, she had been glad I wouldn't return to a dangerous neighborhood and wanted me to apply for a teacher's license, which implied "security."

Popping a cracker in her mouth, Reebie whispered to me, "How's the new job?"

I nodded.

That was enough of an opening and my mother asked, "What is it that you do in that place anyhow?" Her voice had such a tone of disgust, as if I had been working in a waste treatment plant.

"I write book jackets, catalog descriptions, and informational brochures."

"That sounds very impressive," Reebie said. "You were always so creative."

"Being creative never pays the bills," my mother said.

"Oh, Frances, go easy on the kid. She's only twenty-two. Her whole life is ahead of her."

My father, who had remained silent in his captain's chair, piped in: "She likes writing for the Commies."

"Must you be so crude, Richard?" Reebie said.

"Took the words out of my mouth," my mother said.

At least they agreed on something.

As if she sensed a cue, my mother got up and disappeared into the kitchen. Grasping the edges of a chipped, flowered, oblong platter, she delivered the turkey to the table, placing it down gently as if it were a newborn at a bris. It was a small bird, its legs trussed in white-cotton thread. Brown-bread and raisin-chestnut stuffing oozed from poorly sewn openings, the white thread crisscrossed cavernous holes like a handicapped spider. The bird was smothered in orange juice and white wine, my mother's latest basting discovery. From years of observation, I knew her turkey methodology: plunge the plastic basting syringe into the sauce, inject it every hour, and turn over the bird at least once. She would give that last task to my father, who, armed with oven mitts, was known to have dropped the poor bird more than once.

We hovered around the table, each walking around and filling our plates. The sweet potatoes were really yams, and they were the size of missiles. My father couldn't wait to describe the latest kitchen disaster.

"Your mother forgot to poke them with a fork, and when she opened the oven, they exploded all over. We had yams in the mashed potatoes and yams in the Brussels sprouts. I yelled to Frances, 'The Russians are coming, the Russians are coming. Hurry, close the oven.'"

"Very funny, Richard, it wouldn't hurt if you could have been a little more helpful."

"Okay," he said, "I'll have some vodka, and we can salute the Ruskies."

"Thanksgiving is hardly their holiday," Aunt Reebie said.

"Well, we can be thankful that they didn't send us to the Gulag," he said.

"They did enough to us with pogroms, why we came to this country in the first place."

"Here we go again," my father said.

"Can the two of you please stop with the sarcasms?" my mother's tone was also sarcastic.

We ate quickly and my mother disappeared before I finished the turkey. In my family, holidays focused on preparations—and all its attendant trouble—not on eating.

Bringing the coffeepot to the table, she said, "Let's have dessert in peace."

Reebie heard her cue and went into the kitchen, returning with two cake platters sporting her contributions: a gorgeously threaded apple pie and a lip-smacking tart cranberry pie.

"Did I tell you I stopped at the bakery in Brighton Beach?" Reebie said.

"Not a Russian one?" my father said, laughing.

"*Da da*. That's yes in Russian," she said, looking at me.

"*Spasiba,*" I said. I could play the game, too. There had been so many Russian references in my life lately, from Andrei to my job at Theoretical.

Our humorous remarks always had a hint of ridicule. One tried to outwit the other or get the last word. I was mentally exhausted.

As I bit into my slice of cranberry pie, my aunt leaped from her chair and said, "I must pee before I go."

"You're leaving already?" my mother asked.

"Traffic will be brutal."

"You could sleep over."

For the first time since dinner, my father seemed attentive, glaring at my mother.

"Where would we put her?" he asked.

"The daybed in the dining room is perfect."

"How about for a night bed?" he asked, slipping in a word joke, Groucho-style. I almost expected the duck to drop down and announce that "daybed" was the secret word.

As my aunt collected her Tupperware with leftovers and walked to the front door, my mother whispered to me, "Maybe *you* would like to sleep over."

"No, thanks," I said. I felt the rumblings of the Thanksgiving meal fighting in my gut and ran to the bathroom in time for the explosion. These bouts were becoming more and more frequent, and I worried about holding it together on the way home.

"Richard, do you think you can drive Anita home?" my mother asked. "It's too late for her to travel on the subway at this hour."

Since my mother failed her driving test five times, she was at my father's mercy. I recognized the tone when she'd ask him to drive her or one of her children somewhere. It was between groveling and nonchalance. She wanted him to offer graciously, though she knew this was impossible; she acted as if it were a spur-of-the-moment request, but she had undoubtedly rehearsed her plea and saved it for the last possible moment.

Per usual, my father tortured her with silence, the worst possible non-answer.

At the hall closet, my mother cornered me.

"Here," she murmured, looking over her shoulder. She shoved her fist in my face and opened her hand. There was a pack of neatly folded bills, a twenty showing at the top.

"What's this for?" I asked.

"I know you need the money. Just take it. But don't tell your father."

"I don't need it," I said. This wasn't true since I still had unpaid bills and my cash was low. Having spent more in Europe than I had expected, I didn't want to feel beholden to her in some weird mother-daughter way. I could imagine her normal weekly conversations when she would ask me when I was coming to visit, and I would feel guilty about owing her something.

"Will you tell me if you need it or when?"

I nodded and slipped my coat from the hanger. I resolved to leave but was equally resolute to avoid the subway. Taking a taxi would have cost too much, though I expected my mother would probably slip me a twenty by the elevator. Then there was the problem of finding a taxi. It was next to impossible to get the car service on the phone during a holiday. Then it occurred to me that I could hang out at the doorman's station, hoping that someone would be leaving and driving somewhere populated where I could then get decent transportation. Yes, that was my plan.

I heard my mother ask my father again, this time in a louder, angrier voice. Without responding, he walked to the hallway and lifted his jacket from the wooden wall peg, and secured his

Brooklyn Dodgers cap. He swerved his head, and I recognized his signal for me to follow him. I was getting a ride; I knew there would be a price.

Once in the car, I fiddled with the radio dial, hoping to find a news report that would encompass the dead air.

"Leave that," my father said when he heard a sportscaster discussing a football game between the Dallas Cowboys and Washington Redskins. I knew nothing about football, so I asked rudimentary questions.

"Who's the better team?" I asked.

"Dallas."

"Do you have a favorite player?"

"Nope."

Entering the Belt Parkway, a blue Oldsmobile stalled at the ramp.

"Go, you schmuck," my father yelled out his window.

It was quiet in the car for a few minutes until a taxi inched behind us.

"Stupid jerk," my father yelled.

Sweat was accumulating on my upper lip even though the windows were open, and the nighttime temperatures were hovering near freezing.

I tried to remember something about football, but all I could summon was the baseball statistics I had memorized over the years to stimulate conversation with my father.

"What about Ed Kranepool?" I asked. I was partial to the tall first baseman of the Mets.

"Now we're talking about baseball."

"How did you think he did this season?"

"Not so good, batting .231."

"Isn't that his lowest average in a while?"

My father's voice rose, and he glanced at me for the first time. "Yes, it was higher and so was his RBI."

"Do you think they will fire him?"

"Hope not. He's very dependable."

"Yes, dependable." Silence followed. I had exhausted my Ed Kranepool knowledge.

The sportscaster said something about a game between the Eagles and Lions. I was embarrassed to ask my father if they were football teams.

"What an asshole!" my father said.

"Who?"

"That mope on the radio. He doesn't know what he's talking about."

According to my father, there were so many dumb people on the roads cutting us off and on the radio misdirecting the conversation, it's a wonder we got anywhere.

The word "dumb" swam in my brain and I recalled a screaming, drag-out fight my father had with Ben when he was twelve and I was about six. I remembered his age because my father insisted he prepare for his bar mitzvah. This shocked my family because my father had never uttered a religious sentiment. Perhaps he wanted to prove something to his sister in California, who was married to a conservative rabbi and bragged about her wealthy congregation.

One day, when Ben was supposed to be studying with the rabbi at our synagogue, he came home and raided my father's liquor cabinet. By the time my father arrived, Ben was raging drunk in his room and blasting his music on his record player. I didn't see what happened, but I heard screaming and crashing sounds from my room next door. During the long fight, my father kept screaming, "dumb," "stupid," "idiot," "jerk." Finally, Ben emerged with an eye so swollen, my mother had to take him to an ophthalmologist. Ben didn't have a bar mitzvah, and afterward, the two males in my family never had a kind word for each other, though they seemed to have one thing in common: alcohol.

After thirty mute minutes, my father rounded the car onto Christopher Street and pulled in front of my building. He had several beers during dinner and probably had to use the bathroom. In the year since I had lived away from his home, he never stepped foot in my apartment. If he came to drop off or pick up my mother, he waited in the car. Once I asked my mother why he never came in with her. She said, "I don't think he wants to admit that you have your own life."

What she didn't add was the word "sex."

I opened the car door. "Thanks for driving me," I said, expecting my father to offer his chubby cheek for a peck. Instead, he leaned forward and pushed the lighter in, waiting to ignite his cigar. Probably he had been dying to puff away but knew that the smell made me nauseated. Not that he had been considerate; it had more to do with worrying about me vomiting on his buff leather upholstery.

"Let me know about Kranepool," I said.

"What about him? The season is over, dummy."

"If they renew his contract."

"Oh, that. Don't worry."

"I know he's dependable."

With that, my father honked in a "shave and a haircut" rhythm, and I opened the building's front door with my forced smile locked on my lips.

# CHAPTER 10:
# CHRISTOPHER STREET

## June 1969

As a Brooklynite, the closest I had come to Christopher Street, the oldest street in Greenwich Village, was when, as a college student, I climbed up the subway steps of the Christopher Street-Sheridan Square station and located a copy of the *Village Voice* in a newspaper kiosk in front of the Village Cigars on Seventh Avenue, which I folded and read at the nearby Christopher Street Park or Washington Square Park to circle the want ads and apartment listings way before I was ready for either. Occasionally, I'd meet friends for lunch at the Riviera Café on the corner of Seventh Avenue and the convergence of West 4th and West 10th Streets.

Now that I was a resident, I drooled over mounds of white-chocolate maple pralines, and handmade candies adorning the shop windows of the Li-Lac Chocolates, just west of Bleecker, and stopped for coffee at the Silver Dollar Diner opposite the Post Office. Sometimes, I'd go into a gay bar with Jabari, who liked the male attention, and I enjoyed being a curiosity—the only female (that I knew of).

Once, after a late-night movie, Jabari and I were sitting in the Silver Dollar eating hamburgers. It was after 1:00 a.m. on June 28, 1969. A local drag queen Lola, dressed in a grass hula skirt and long black-leather gloves, rushed in and screamed to no one in particular, "They're rioting. It's bedlam, there."

"Where?" a customer asked.

"At the Stonewall Inn. It's crazy, man." With her palm, she massaged her lopsided pompadour henna wig and stood at the counter as if it were a podium. "The pigs tried to arrest a butch and throw her into a police wagon. She resisted and was hit over the head with a club. She called out for someone to help. Finally, the crowd went crazy. Drags and fags and hippies are fighting the pigs. It's wild." She pursed her smeared red lips.

"Let's go see," I said, thinking that this could be history in the making. The visuals alone intrigued me.

"There are pigs all over. You don't wanna go there." Lola slumped on a stool.

"You'd better spend the night," I told Jabari. "We can sleep on the sofa. Denise will be in the bedroom. She won't care."

"No, I need to go home. I'm working tomorrow." After over two years of seeing Jabari, in our intermittent custom, I only recently learned that his uncle's falafel restaurant in Queens subsumed his artistic dreams.

"If you walk to the subway, you'll be in the middle of the melee. They can arrest you."

Jabari agreed to stay over and left by 6:00 a.m. As a break between vigorous sex, we slept for about two hours.

★ ★ ★

The riots seemed a long time ago, not weeks. I felt as if I lived on Christopher Street my entire life, because in the year and a half since I co-signed the lease, I was finally feeling the distance from my childhood home in Brooklyn and my parents in Rockaway. Christopher Street was my home; I walked the streets and explored the perpendicular detours with abandon.

For someone with such a terrible sense of direction, I never got lost in these quaint few blocks.

Yet, no matter how secure my path, I couldn't escape my fears. Since my attack as a caseworker a year ago, despite my sojourn in Europe where I experienced other sexual assaults, every noise that passed under my window still startled me. One night, two men sat on the ledge outside our apartment and argued so loudly that we heard every word, even with our radio tuned to rock and roll. One of them accused the other of being a "slut." There were more shouts and then a police siren. Denise tiptoed to the window and looked through the slats on the venetian blinds.

"They're putting handcuffs on them, and have their guns drawn."

"Oh no," I said, feeling an intense horizontal pain dividing the folds in my stomach. Immediately, I was back in the patrol car with the cops, searching for the boys after my attack. I saw them grab onto their guns, readying for action, entering the building as I waited for the sound of bullets piercing my young attackers. I thought I had submerged those images, but no, they lingered, ready to taunt me. There seemed to be no safe place, even outside my walls.

Knowing my anxiety and perhaps to lessen her need to ameliorate mine, Denise planned a party. It was the last thing I needed, but I wanted to satisfy her desire for normalcy.

Sometimes, we behaved more for the false appearance to others than for our true selves.

On July 4th, a Friday night, we hosted an Independence Day party, inviting my coworkers at Theoretical, including Shirley, Cindy and her boyfriend Jack, Denise's friend Arthur, and even some of my friends from Welfare. Everyone was told to bring a friend, so there would be new people as well. I didn't invite Jabari, as I kept our relationship private. Denise asked me the reason, since some of our friends hinted I invented him to avoid socialization.

"I don't know why, but I guess I don't want to worry about him fitting in," I admitted.

"Are you ashamed of him?"

"Not really. It's just we have a very weird relationship. There are no strings, no interference from others, nobody from the outside to offer criticism. I know he is not the person he pretends to be. He wants to be an actor and musician, but his accent and lack of experience, not to mention talent, are great impediments. I don't try to change him, and he accepts me without questioning my motivations. I suspect his family tries to orchestrate romances for him with nice Egyptian girls, but we never talk about this."

"Whew, that is some speech," Denise said. "He is certainly gorgeous and exotic. I can see the attraction."

That reassured me and I helped Denise with the hors d'oeuvres and drinks, concentrating on my disc jockey abilities and my 45-record collection. By 9:00 p.m. just before the fireworks, we opened the door to a barrage of people who seemed to take our invited time to heart. I positioned my old record player on the table in our dining nook, facing the living room, and lowered the needle to the first selection, "Dance to the Music." Cindy was the first to enter, grabbing her boyfriend Jack. They shook into the main living room, waving miniature American flags. Others joined instantly and before long, we had a conga line, swaying and gyrating to the music.

Next, I selected "Brown Eyed Girl," and I felt a tug on my arm. It was Kenny, my old boss. I forgot I had invited him; I had sent a postcard to the general department, and there he was wearing a red, white, and blue short-sleeved vest and oversized top hat. We did a jazzed-up slow dance, and he shouted "brown-eyed girl" in my ears, over and over.

Shirley brought her boyfriend Charlie, and they sat on my sofa, smoking cigarettes and munching on potato chip dips. Finally, I played "At the Hop," and Shirley dragged Charlie to the dance floor, where they squeezed among others. Lifting her flare skirt, Shirley showed off her legs and performed some amazing slop-dance moves, just like the ones I used to do as a teenager with my Black friends at the neighborhood Canteen Dance every Friday Night in Flatbush.

By midnight, everyone had left, and Denise and I slumped on our sofa to rehash the evening.

"What a night," she said.

"Yes, I had a great time. Just what the doctor ordered."

And for one glorious evening, with a mix of all kinds of people jammed into my living room, I felt at home.

# CHAPTER 11: THE PINK SLIP

## November 1969

Two weeks before Thanksgiving, Theoretical moved to a larger space a few blocks south, on West 19th Street, and for some strange reason Shirley and I were the only two women who got separate offices. I had missed my close contact with the "girls," but Shirley and I soon realized that if we kept our doors open, we could see each other's desks as the offices were in a direct line, with a huge open area of desks in between. To communicate our daily frustrations, we held up signs with colored folders, our system of semaphores. Marilyn, whose desk was close to my office, often sought solace in my cracking leather beanbag chair.

Through my interceding with Michael Bernstein, he promoted Marilyn to copywriter and named me as chief copywriter. I didn't mention to Michael that Marilyn also wrote poetry and painted in oils; her sultry looks were enough to get his attention. Unlike the other men at Theoretical Press, Michael didn't make a pass at the women, keeping especially respectful to Marilyn and me. Marilyn had decided he must be gay, but in the closet.

On a Friday morning in November, Michael stepped into the large rectangular-shaped editorial area and roared off a list of names—in no particular order.

"All of these people please report to Personnel," he said. "Everyone else, continue working as you were." I heard him repeat this message near the elevators.

Ten minutes later, Shirley walked into my office, which was located off the southwest corner of Editorial. "Did you hear about the firings?" she asked breathlessly.

"What firings? Are we at war?"

"Maybe we are. It sure feels like an attack."

"What the hell is going on?"

"All the people whose names were called were fired ... given pink slips."

"You're kidding?" I said, words I automatically uttered when I knew something shocking was true.

"I wouldn't kid about something like this. Can you believe it? Grace, Yolanda, Miguel, Walter, Franco, Johnny. They were given absolutely no notice. They were told to leave today, effective immediately. And so close to the holidays."

"But they all have families to support. How will they live on Unemployment?"

"I don't know."

Too startled to speak any longer, Shirley and I sat immobilized for a few minutes.

"Are you sure our names aren't on the list?" I asked. "He read them so quickly, and we didn't hear all his announcements."

"I don't think so. You never know in this place. If we come back from lunch and our desks are missing, it's a good sign that we also joined the unemployed." Shirley palmed the top of her black, flat-ironed hair, and added: "Oh, I forgot to tell you Cindy was on the list."

"But I didn't hear her name."

"She was told earlier."

"Oh my God, no! She just moved to her first apartment and was so excited." I shut my eyes as if it would block out Shirley's

Newport cigarette-clogged, husky voice. I was the one who recommended Cindy as an editorial assistant, our second job together since our summer working at the General Post Office before our senior year in college.

Shirley wrinkled her snub nose. Her long neck vibrated in a series of mini shakes. "I hope this doesn't mean she'll have to move back home. From what she told me, living with alcoholic parents was no picnic. I know what she means."

"So do I," I said. "Shirley, this is so incredible. I knew the company was in bad shape, but I never expected this. I feel so guilty."

"Why? It's not your fault?"

"I know, but we weren't fired. It's like we're dirty—like we escaped the gas chambers and survived for some bizarre reason, like we ..." Before I finished my sentence, Cindy stood in my doorway. Shirley and I looked at each other, the blood of complicity filling our cheeks.

"Oh, Cindy, I just found out. I'm so sorry," I said.

"Me, too," Shirley added.

"It sucks," Cindy sputtered. "They really gave us pink slips. I'm surprised they had enough foresight to order them."

"They're utterly heartless," I said.

"I know when I'm not wanted. I'm packing up and leaving ASAP. I came to say goodbye."

Cindy inched to my desk. She was a tall woman, nearly six feet, and her bendable limbs and penchant for green reminded me of the clay animation figure, Gumby, stretching even longer from my seat. I stood five feet five and peered up at her round hazel eyes. She maneuvered around the jutting of books and manuscripts cluttering my desktop and flung herself in my arms.

"Ani, I know others are worse off. But this is just too much for me now. I'm not prepared," she sobbed.

"I know," I said, patting her shoulders. "Why don't you stay with me this weekend? You shouldn't be alone. Stop here when you've finished packing and I'll go with you."

As soon as Cindy and Shirley left, I closed my office door, something I rarely did. I sat on my chair and swiveled away from the wall of glass, which overlooked Editorial, barely glimpsing outlined reflections of my long copper-brown hair flying from the oscillating desk fan, operating on cold days to compensate for the airless space. I faced an empty wall, the one surface in the office without a calendar, bulletin board, or poster. I stared into blankness, but before long, the blue-green wall became a movie background superimposed with action scenes. I could hear the flapping of home-movie film clogged in the projector; I could see my father opening his front door, slumped with bankruptcy in his captain's chair, penciling newspaper puzzles when he should have been circling want ads, watching the ocean waves from his Rockaway Park picture window though he never set foot on the beach.

About an hour later, Cindy returned, her bony face blotchy with smudged mascara. "I'm ready. I just said goodbye to Eddie and Roland—that hurt the most. The three of us were hired the same day …" She stopped abruptly.

I dialed Michael's extension and whispered into the mouthpiece: "I'm leaving for the day. I can't take it here any longer." I expected a tirade; instead, he said simply, "Okay. I understand."

We meandered down the hall toward the elevator and passed several coworkers carrying plants, cartons, shopping bags. They scurried about distractedly, like senile squirrels, frantically searching for the forgotten whereabouts of buried acorns.

Cindy and I bumped into Shirley on her way to the bank and lunch. "Want to join us?" I asked, suddenly feeling the need for Shirley's compassionate nature.

"So soon?"

"Yes, we're going to my place. We'll unwind and make some food. Maybe we'll do the town tonight. Who knows?"

"Sure," she said. "I need to call Charlie to pick up Elgin from basketball practice."

"Will Charlie be able to leave his job so early?"

"What job? You mean, will he be able to leave his bottle of whiskey?" It wasn't like Shirley to say something so negative about Charlie and then trust him with Elgin.

"Call him from my apartment," I said, electing to postpone comments on Shirley's revelation. Bad news seemed to pile on a revolving stepladder, each level requiring immediate attention, swiftly replaced by an approaching tier.

With a firm nod, Shirley wound her arm through each of ours, sweeping us into the elevator as if we were off to a great adventure.

# CHAPTER 12: FEELIN' GROOVY

I left Shirley and Cindy in my living room while I robotically opened cans of tuna, toasted white bread, and sliced onions in my narrow galley kitchen. Holding a tray filled with tuna-salad sandwiches, wine glasses, and a bottle of chardonnay, I headed for my sofa, where we rehashed the morning's events.

"I don't know about you, Shirley," I said. "But I for one never want to set foot in that place again. I can't believe that Michael would let someone like Walter go—Walter who has been with the company twenty-two years—without a moment's warning, without any severance pay, nada, zippo. He was so close to retirement."

"I know," Shirley said.

"And," I continued, my anger hastening the words, "the company is so cheap, it doesn't even have a decent pension fund. Walter will get a pittance for all his years. If we stay, it'll be like we're part of the Gestapo. Sometimes, you have to take a stand."

"For me, it's not that easy. I have a son to support."

"I'm sorry, Shirl. That was insensitive of me." I needed the job, too, but I rarely considered my family's recent history of poverty. I had a weird and inexplicable sense of personal financial assurance, although it could have been unadulterated denial.

"Let's not talk about it anymore," Cindy said. "I'm getting a vicious migraine. The thought of telling my mother. She warned me not to move out without a nest egg. God, let's change the subject. I need time to digest it all."

"Fine with me," Shirley said.

"I've got a headache, too," I said. "Think it's catching?" I sipped from my wine glass.

"I have just what the doctor ordered," Cindy said. She took out her cigarette case and pulled out a well-packed oblong joint.

"This is great stuff," Cindy promised, as she passed it around. Shirley raised her eyebrows and declined. Being thirty, seven years older than Cindy and me, and an Afro-American from rural Mississippi, Shirley had not tried pot before. Her brother frequented jazz joints in the South and was "hip" to the drug, but Shirley stuck to her Newports and alcohol.

I took two deep drags and handed it back to Cindy.

I sat all the way back on the sofa. The top of my head felt unbearably heavy, like a cast-iron frying pan cover. A sudden surge snapped my neck back. My eyes closed involuntarily, and patches of dizzy unconsciousness overtook my brain. I entered that dreamy, drifting state like those last mingling images of pre-sleep. Only I couldn't submit to sleep's peaceful abandon, and I couldn't lift my head and waken.

A force pulled me down, and I stretched out across the sofa. My arms locked straight by my sides; my legs extended like rigid sticks. I felt glued to the sofa cushion seats.

Lights and sounds merged. Tiny bells rang, and needle tips of luminescence flickered before me in a whirl of seasickness. My head grew larger than my body. My breath escalated; my lungs pumped like a heaving and wheezing accordion. Hot lava swept through my breasts; dotted lines of pain darted from my erect nipples like antiaircraft fire.

Yet, inside myself, I couldn't stop laughing—silent, strangulated cackles. My lips spread to clownish proportions. Feral animals howled in the kitchen. Shriveled cats crouched, buried in ketchup bottles inside my refrigerator door. I had to warn someone. But my outside body was both weightless and too heavy to move.

"An-I, ANI-ta, ANITA! Are you okay?" Shirley asked. I heard her voice through a long tunnel, an inverted echo, soft at first, getting louder as the sounds entered my ears.

I couldn't answer. My mouth froze in place. Someone must have removed my tongue; it was gone.

"I think she fainted," Cindy said.

"No. Her eyelids are fluttering."

"Maybe she's just sleeping and dreaming."

"No, she looks like she's having trouble breathing."

"Anita! Can you hear me?" Cindy yelled.

Through a bifocal slit, I saw Shirley and Cindy slink across the room and whisper to each other in the corner. Shirley, a speck in a distant field, glided toward me, each foot posed in midair like a ballet dancer. It seemed like hours before she completed the fifteen-foot distance to the sofa.

"Anita, are you okay? What's wrong?"

I opened my eyes wider and again tried to speak. A thick metal chain wrapped around my voice box. I was like a stroke victim, summoning Herculean energy to get my paralyzed limbs moving.

"Aniiiiita? Are you theeeeere?" Shirley's voice reverberated. As she came closer to my face, her words bounced off my skin, floated in the air, and rose to the ceiling beyond my hearing.

Shirley patted my arm. It felt sharp, hot and cold—a long blade of ice with a smoldering, searing tip. I had to warn her. "Please don't touch me, Shirley," I screamed soundlessly.

Shirley's expanded and distorted features spread out in a giant fisheye lens. Such sparkling brown irises, such a flattened nose! Her bulging eyes engorged mine, focusing in and out, sucking in my pupils. Her lips grimaced, disgusted and menacing.

I heaved my body away from Shirley's face. I was so tired. Awake and entombed in my own skin.

"She's sick. She can't seem to talk, and she's making strange grunting sounds," Shirley cried. "When I touched her, her face winced as if she was being stabbed. She's scaring me."

"We should call someone," Cindy said.

"You think the pot could be laced?" Shirley asked? "She must be having a bad reaction."

"She only had two drags. I smoked much more and I'm okay. Besides, it's from a well-used supply. I don't think it's the pot."

"Maybe we should take her to the emergency room," Shirley said. "I'm getting real worried. It could be a stroke or something serious like that." Shirley once worked as a receptionist in a doctor's office and took public health and nutrition undergrad courses, hoping to qualify for medical professional training. Then she became pregnant and everything changed.

I heard the conversation in delayed time. *No, they can't take me to the hospital. They can't. They can't. They just can't. I won't go. I'll show them that I'll be okay.* But I was still lying motionless on the sofa. *If I can just sit up a bit, the blood will fill my brain, and I'll be able to talk.* I strained and finally shook my shoulders.

Dread encased my body, causing this inexplicable havoc. Strangely, I didn't feel afraid. This was happening to someone else, someone who looked like me. I was an objective observer in a twisted horror film.

Again, I called upon all my strength. I needed to tell them I'd be okay. This certainty, despite the evidence, came from some primordial force. In my head, I latched onto an image from my journal, alongside a poem I wrote recently called "Suicide." I had illustrated a profile of a woman, incomprehensible consonants screaming from her open mouth. The top of her head lifted at an angle, the side supported by a large hinge. Inside her head, more consonants floated out, streaming toward the top of the page like dialogue bubbles. Despite this craziness inside her fortress, aching to be released, this girl knew that she would survive, or at least make a good show of it. I recalled the first stanza:

> I am no longer I
>
> And me has ceased
>
> To be objective I
>
> The world is You
>
> And they have conquered us.

"She's moving! I think she's trying to tell us something," Cindy said excitedly.

"Do you want to go to the hospital?" Shirley asked me.

I shook again as hard as I could.

"Do you want us to call someone?"

I squeezed my bones together and heaved out a push and sunk back down, barely showing a sign of movement, but utterly spent.

"She seems agitated. Let's leave her be for a while."

My friends spoke softly in the kitchen. The teakettle whistled. The radio played Simon and Garfunkel's "Feelin' Groovy." How ironic, I thought. Groovy, moovy, loovy. I am going loovy, loony. Little flecks of cubed iridescence swam behind my closed lids, teasing me like shooting stars in the blackened night sky. If only I could sit up a little. I tried again to move my waist, my chest. I was locked.

*Where is my life? Can I reach anyone, myself? Am I paralyzed forever?*

If only I could sleep. The instant my eyes shut, they flung open, and in that second, the world passed behind them, coming and going.

"Anita! Ani!"

*They call me Ani, Piri, Weary. Sit up you, Dreary. Get up, get going. Come back from hell.*

Hours dragged like days yet felt like seconds. Imperceptibly, I felt my arms stiffen. The Novocain was wearing out, and the ache felt great.

Little by little, like a silent massage, the air flicked a tiny section of my body, and each cell opened and strained, squeaked, and moaned awake. Finally, my shoulders became whole, and I could raise them a bit.

"She's moving!" Shirley shouted. "This time, she's really moving!"

Cindy rushed to me, rubbing her exhausted phlegmy eyes, coming closer to the sofa. She and Shirley became one, their faces weaving in and out of my sight, their voices wavering and modulating to a slow monotone.

"Ani, have you come back to us?"

I nodded but still couldn't speak.

A loud bong went off in my head.

"That must be Arthur. I called him." That was Denise's voice.

"Why?" Shirley asked.

"He's a social worker, and he's experienced with things like this. We need help."

Arthur, freckle-faced and paunchy, came in the door, looped over to my sofa, and sat on the edge.

*Get off Arthur,* I shouted inside myself. *Go away! Don't you dare touch me.*

"Anita, you're safe with us," he said gently. "Perhaps you had a hysterical reaction over some deeply rooted traumatic episode. Denise told me that you all had a very upsetting day. Maybe that triggered something in your past."

*I'll kill the bastard. Who the hell is he to espouse this psychobabble over me? I'm not a case in a textbook.*

The clock on the wall melted like the Dalí painting, *The Persistence of Memory.* Two more hours lost. Slowly, I came to myself enough to speak. "Ugh," I mumbled.

"You should go to a doctor," Arthur said in his sane, masculine voice. "First to a neurologist to make sure nothing is happening with your brain."

"And then where should she go?" Shirley asked Arthur as they spoke around me, louder and slower, as if I were not there at all—the way people talk to the disabled and the hard of hearing.

"If there's nothing physically wrong with her, she should see a psychotherapist. She needs help."

I squirmed in my space and mumbled, "Toilet." Cindy and Shirley each grabbed me under an arm and dragged me to the bathroom. After I peed, my head flopping back and forth as I sat on the toilet, the women led me back to the living room.

The game of Risk was lying near the couch, on top of a pile of old newspapers and magazines. Arthur opened the box and spread out the game board on the parquet floor.

"Let's play," he said.

"Now?" Shirley asked.

I knew I could count on her to see Arthur's inappropriateness.

"Yeah, it'll be good for her, for all of us, to get our minds off this, to refocus."

"I agree with Arthur," Denise said.

*Turncoat. When did she become so compliant?*

I could barely stand. With Shirley's help, I dropped to the floor. She placed several pillows between my back and a side of the sofa.

They started to play. Cindy said to Shirley, "Here, take China, you need it."

Shirley said, "Thanks, here's Venezuela."

"That's a good move," Denise said.

I propelled my hand back and forth from country to country.

Arthur shouted, "You girls are too much! Can't you see? This is a game of intense competition. You're supposed to take over each other's territories, not give them away. You must be aggressive."

"Well, I don't feel like being aggressive," Cindy said.

I slumped on my pillows and closed my eyes.

"I think she wants to sleep," Shirley said.

Territories, countries, and continents floated around my brain. Argentina, Egypt, Northwest Territory, Eastern Australia, South America. *If only I can sleep, I'll be okay. As long as nobody touches me. Iceland. Siberia.*

* * *

The girls helped me to the bedroom, and I collapsed on the bed, my behind finding a familiar indentation on my Beautyrest mattress, my nose inured to the rank odor of years of urine-soaked underwear, period flows, and more recent seeping of sperm all commingling in Rorschach blob stains under the violet tulip twin fitted sheet, delivered by my mother on her first official visit to my first apartment away from her.

"I'll never forget what you said to me when you left home after college," my mother recently repeated for the hundredth time since I moved out almost two years ago.

"What?" I had asked, bracing myself.

"That if you didn't leave then, you'd lose Denise."

"Well, that's true," I said. "Denise had the apartment and would have gotten another roommate."

"And that apartment," my mother said, "a real hovel with bars on the windows."

"I've seen worse."

"I couldn't get over the fact that you left our house for such a small place. After all, we had all those empty rooms."

I said, "Did you ever hear of any child leaving home for a bigger space?"

Why my mother's words haunted me at this moment, I couldn't say. If she had seen me now, a babbling weakling stuck to my childhood bed, she would scream at me to get dressed and pack a bag. She'd hail a taxi to her apartment in Rockaway, a sheen of self-satisfaction dripping from her lips, and deposit me in the dining room she converted to a guest nook for me—or, God forbid, my brother—for exactly this reason. The only person worse at that moment was Arthur, pacing around the room, his chubby cheeks blown up under his swollen Jewfro, morphing into one giant circular balloon.

I squinted at the night table and noticed that it was 3:00 a.m. The last time I remembered was noon when we got home from the office.

Somehow in the night, Shirley went home.

"I still think we should call someone," Arthur said, standing in the bedroom doorway. "We shouldn't wait. At work, an elderly woman swooned in group therapy, and she insisted on resting on the couch while the group continued. She had a stroke."

"Arthur, you're making it worse," Denise cried. Finally, she replaced Shirley as the voice of reason. She also knew Arthur the longest since their mothers had been high-school friends.

Cindy announced she was walking to the Seventh Avenue subway and wanted Arthur to go with her, as she was afraid to go by herself in the dark.

"Should we be leaving Ani?" Arthur asked. "Besides, why leave at this ungodly hour?"

"Things seem to be under control," Cindy said. "Denise promised to call me. I'll come back if Ani is worse. I think she needs to be alone."

I wanted to sit up and wrap my arms around Cindy. She was just fired, didn't know if she could afford to live in her new West 17th Street apartment for the next month, and realized that what I needed most at that moment was for Arthur to go away. I heard the door slam and left my body. Only this time, I fell asleep.

# CHAPTER 13: NAME ME
# A VEGETABLE

On Saturday, I slept until almost noon. Denise made me a bowl of tomato and rice soup. I swallowed two spoonfuls and only that because she stood over my bed and watched me, squinting her wide-set emerald eyes to kaleidoscopic slivers, her soft sandy curly hair resting in curlicues on her forehead, still damp from a shower. At that moment, she resembled an adult, yet a still petite Shirley Temple; I almost expected her to tap dance when I put the spoon to my lips.

"So, how do you feel this morning?" she asked.

"Like I'm underneath an elephant."

"I'm happy to hear your voice, at least. When I came home last night, you didn't seem to recognize me and grunted. I've been very worried."

"I'll be okay." The words came out the way you say you're fine when you meet someone you know in the street after you had a tooth pulled.

"You sound so sure. Cindy told me that you reacted negatively at Arthur's suggestion about seeing a professional."

"Oh, don't mention Arthur."

"Well, he knows a lot."

I didn't want to spend my energy badmouthing Arthur, especially to Denise who always defended him. "I don't know what happened to me, but I will survive. You can reassure Arthur for me." I could feel the heat of anger invade my nostrils and activate the cilia. I had enough of people wanting to get into my head. Enough!

"Why are you so sure you will survive?"

"I don't know why." I immediately felt terrible for my dear friend, who I knew was only thinking of me. "Okay, I was terrified. I should say I am still terrified. To think that your body can take over your will is unimaginable."

"You sound entirely too rational. Do you think it was from smoking the pot?"

"Maybe, but I only had two drags. It was as if everything in my head needed to burst out and the slightest puff of pot and poof. So many p's—I'm alliterating."

"Don't make a joke out of this. It's serious." Denise's voice thickened and sounded like she was going to cry. She placed the bowl of uneaten soup on a tray and left for the kitchen. I could hear pots clanging and cabinets slamming. The phone rang and Denise mumbled from afar, sounding congested. She returned to my side and reported that Cindy had called and was also worried about me.

"I'm okay, really," I said. "I've been keeping a lot of stuff buried."

"What things?"

"My crazy childhood, my crazy parents, my crazy brother." I really didn't want to analyze myself anymore. I was now spouting obvious causes, basically to stem Denise's questions.

"Do you think getting attacked has anything to do with this?"

"I'm sure it didn't help. But don't forget, I was attacked almost a year and a half ago. I thought I was getting my life back, and now this." Finally, that elephant on top of me seemed to press harder and harder and I found it difficult to breathe. I wheezed.

"Are you okay?"

"My entire body is in some kind of delayed shock. Like it's operating on its own."

"Well, I for one can say that I am scared."

"Me, too," I said, adding under my breath, "I guess."

Eventually, I got out of bed and made it to the dining room table, where Denise brought me a tall glass of water and ordered me to drink. She leafed through the *New York Times* while I pretended to sort my mail. We didn't speak for a while.

Finally, I said, "Let's talk about ordinary things."

"Okay," she said. "I forgot to tell you that Jabari called."

"When?" I wanted to see his gorgeous face, to have his long fingers massage my back. Knowing him, he wouldn't ask me tons of questions. He'd only want to make me feel better.

"About an hour ago."

"Really? I didn't hear the phone."

"You were in a deep sleep."

"I guess. What did he say?"

"He just asked for you. I told him that you were fighting the flu and still sleeping. He said not to wake you, at least I think he said that. I can't always understand his accent."

"I know. I guess he's back in town. He was going to Puerto Rico for a week and then, I don't know, he did his usual disappearing act. Sometimes I think he has a wife and two kids somewhere and only calls me when they go away."

"Like Puerto Rico?"

"Maybe."

"You don't sound very perturbed."

"I'm not. I've known Jabari for over three years, and this is our relationship, if you can call it that."

Denise sat straighter. She was certainly aware of my comings and goings with Jabari, though I rarely analyzed it. "You know by now that every few weeks or even months, he phones. We see each other every night for a week. We have hot and heavy sex. I am utterly satiated, physically. Then we don't see each other for a long time. I almost forget him when he suddenly reappears."

"And you're both okay with this arrangement?"

"He likes that I put no demands on him. He knows I go out with other men, and I assume he is seeing women, or one woman. We never talk about it."

"Maybe this is healthy."

"It's enough for me, now. Only sometimes I worry that his mysteriousness is really something unsavory."

"You think he's a member of some crime syndicate?"

"Maybe. I don't know enough about the Egyptians. Maybe it's a pyramid scheme."

"I see you have your sense of humor back. Drink your water."

"Is it from an oasis?"

I obediently gulped, suddenly so dry, my lips chapped from fake grimaces in my stupor.

Then Denise said in a low voice, "I can always make you some Jewish food, guaranteed to stick to your stomach, but good for what ails you."

"You mean brisket?" I asked.

"Brisket or Stanley," Denise said.

Sure enough, I felt a wave of laughter gathering in my throat. "Ah, brisket," I crooned, and my chest heaved in hysterical spasms. Denise burped, leading to a series of suppressed giggles until we were both holding our sides.

"Don't get me started," she said. "Remember that part-time job I had in college, as a rehabilitation assistant at the Jewish Home and Hospital, and they gave me that board game for patients to try out?"

"Oh, no," I said. "How could I forget?"

"The Director of Recreational Therapy had asked me to test it to see if it was appropriate for the patients."

"Yes, Cindy and I were your test subjects."

I remembered we were at my house in Brooklyn, lounging on the drab green living-room carpet. Denise read the instructions in a serious tone. It went on for pages. Cindy took a pad and jotted down notes. Then it became so complicated, she made a graph of the various strategies.

"All three of us burst out in hysterics. Nobody could understand the rules, and it seemed to be the worst game for anyone, especially patients with dementia," Denise said.

"I don't think I ever laughed that much." I could still recall the severe pain in my side and the snot dripping down my face. "To get back to the brisket," I said, "do you still associate brisket with Stanley?"

Stanley was Denise's brother-in-law, and he looked nothing like a brisket. But Denise had this strange ability to associate people with a specific food. It had nothing to do with physical resemblance or even word similarities.

"Stanley will always be brisket. And my sister, Rebecca, is noodle pudding."

"That's so random," I said.

Denise went through the list of people and their food monikers: "Your niece, Paula, is broccoli, my aunt Alice is canned Dole pineapple, especially the ones with the hole, and my nephew Aaron is asparagus."

"But how does the food come to you? Do you think about the person first?"

"No, it's automatic. Either it comes or it doesn't. Sometimes, more than one person has the same food. For example, my mother's friend Allison is also pineapple."

"Maybe it's the similar spelling of the name."

"No, it's usually not the case."

"I know you have said that you can't think of a food associated with me. Have you changed your mind?"

"Sorry, nothing comes to me. That won't change."

"Not even a fruit or a vegetable?"

"No."

"I guess it's better than being a brisket," I said.

"That's a good title for something."

I borrowed the pencil on the table, reserved for the crossword puzzle, and ripped a page from a notepad. I wrote, "It's better than being a brisket." I planned to place it into the empty carton I kept for story or essay ideas.

"But, Denise, close your eyes, think. Could I also be a pineapple?"

"Nothing there. At least I got you into thinking about something else."

I suddenly felt dejected. I knew that this ability of Denise's was weird and unpredictable. But why was I the only close person in her life who had no associated food? Couldn't I be even a lousy Brussels sprout? I longed to be a vegetable.

My eyelids flickered, and the heaviness returned.

Two hours later, I awoke with a full bladder and peed for a long time. I was clear-headed enough to walk outside and sit against the redbrick ledge outside our apartment, resting back on the wrought-iron spikes. I had promised Denise that I would return home within the hour, but it was uncomfortable, and I decided to buy milk and a loaf of bread.

Walking aimlessly, I found a deli/grocery, its windows plastered with cheap newspaper discounts, posters for Coca Cola, and a large sign announcing Green Stamps. I pushed open the door, jingling with bells, and was awash with the stale, dusty closeness of crammed merchandise: ripped-open cartons of soda and candy bars, aisles blockaded by potato chip bags, racks of magazines and newspapers, a table of assorted packaged pastas and baked goods, and a cloudy glass meat counter with ugly slabs of pink cold cuts.

I looked for the refrigerated section and veered toward the man behind the cash register. He was bald, with graying sideburns, and had a thick, black mustache. All I had to do was utter the word "milk," and he would point me in the right direction. I sidled up to the man as if I had stuffed bags of M&Ms into my pockets. He nodded at me, and I stumbled down an aisle, sweat gathering under my armpits, unable to form the word.

I passed a display of fruits and vegetables. The lettuce was brown, the cucumbers had mushy brown spots. There was a bowl of cut broccoli, its stalks were uneven and flaccid. I thought of Denise, wondering if the state of the vegetable's freshness influenced her hallucinogenic imaging.

In a section with paper goods, I noticed a reach extender leaning against the aisle. Ah-ha, toilet paper. I could always use a roll, and besides, I wouldn't have to ask anyone for help. I pressed the lever and aimed for a roll on a tall shelf, grabbed the paper covering, and depressed the roll into my willing hands. Delighted with my prowess, I sank another roll with the swift grace of a fly fisherman. Balancing the rolls, I headed for the register, and when the counterman asked me if that was "all," I nodded and plunked down my coins in the exact change.

Outside the store, I walked another block and found a stoop outside a brownstone. I sat and waited for my heartbeat to calm. I still didn't have milk and bread. I was ruled by muteness. I headed back to Christopher Street and went into the A&P on the corner of Seventh Avenue, across from the Christopher Street Park at Sheridan Square. The A&P. Surely, I could find a carton of milk and a loaf of bread there without having to utter a word.

# CHAPTER 14: RAISING THE FLAGS

On the first Monday after the mass firings, all eight of the desks in Theoretical's open Editorial/Sales Section were empty except for the one in my direct view, belonging to Marilyn. I had passed the Art/Production Room on the way to my office, and there were only two employees rather than the usual six. Shirley no longer had her two assistants, so Michael now enlisted Marilyn to facilitate Shirley's mailing lists.

Before I sat at my desk, the phone rang.

"Hi, it's me," Shirley said. "Is your desk still there?"

"Yes," I said, suppressing a laugh. Last night, we had spoken on the phone and Shirley reminded me what she had said on the day of the firings, "Don't forget to check your desk tomorrow morning. If it's missing, it's a good sign that you no longer have a job."

"It's deadly quiet in this place."

"I know. How do you feel? I spoke to Denise several times, and she assured me that you are a survivor and doing as well as expected."

"I feel woozy but getting better." I didn't admit that I struggled with holding my head up for a long time and rested it on my desk every few minutes, that as I sifted through Theoretical's untranslated Russian journal articles, my brain felt similarly to the Cyrillic alphabet in front of me, indecipherable and unpronounceable.

"Are you coming home with me tonight?" A few weeks ago, Shirley invited me to attend her son's basketball game and sleep over at her apartment in Bedford-Stuyvesant.

"Do you still want me?"

"Of course I want you. Why wouldn't I?"

I didn't remind Shirley about the pot incident. I was embarrassed that she saw me that way, weak and out of control. She had asked me how I was feeling last night on the telephone, and I told her "much better." Mainly, though, I was reluctant to go anyplace, especially if it meant sustained activity. My body could betray me again. However, I didn't want to disappoint Shirley, and her motherly warmth often soothed me. I would go.

From my long view, I noticed Shirley holding up one of her makeshift flags, which signaled that I was getting male company. Before long, Henry, a graphic artist, snuck into my office. He had a Canon 35 mm camera strapped around his neck, digging into his long Mick Jagger-style hair. He plunked down on the floor opposite my desk, and aimed the camera up at me, first at my face, and then he weaseled under the desk and positioned himself between my legs.

"What are you doing?" I yelled good-naturedly.

"I'm zooming up your skirt."

"You are a definite pervert."

"You mean pre-vert."

"You're both pre and per. If you snap a picture, I'll kill you."

"You know I would never do that," he said, abruptly standing, wiping his red flannel shirtsleeve across his eyes in a fake show of tears. "I just came to see how you're faring. This place is like a morgue."

"It is. Cindy called me this morning. She asked me to get her sweater from her locker. She was crying."

"She's a real sweetheart. I hope she's okay."

"I hope so, too. How's your department?"

"We are only two now. Walter is gone, and we're waiting for a higher up to tell us what to do. We have at least four jobs in the works. I feel like quitting in solidarity with our comrades."

"I feel the same."

By the end of the day, I had a steady stream of visitors, despite the low number of employees. Marilyn came into my office and plopped in her favorite spot: my beanbag chair.

"This place is like a morgue," she said.

"Henry said the same thing."

"We should do something."

"Like what?"

"Organize the staff. Picket outside."

"I agree, but there are so few of us left, and many really need their jobs."

"I'll think of something." Marilyn's voice was low, almost a whisper.

During the day, whenever someone passed our view, Shirley raised the "flags," holding up several colored folders simultaneously. We phoned each other and complained, perfecting the art of looking busy, even though there were hardly any people who noticed us.

No one did much work. Either we were too depressed or too confused.

★ ★ ★

On the subway to Bedford-Stuyvesant, riders squashed Shirley and me against a pole, but we gossiped all the way from 14th Street. That morning, at a coffee break with Shirley and me, Marilyn mentioned that she was going out with a Black man, Clinton. I was surprised because Marilyn had never mentioned his race before, and I had watched Shirley's face to see if she had a reaction, perhaps a resentment. Shirley hadn't lifted an eyebrow.

"That was the first time I heard Marilyn talk about a man," Shirley said now, her tan leather pocketbook thrust into my side.

"I know, she keeps personal stuff personal. Not like us."

"Anyhow, Marilyn is such a beautiful girl," Shirley said. "Her posture is straight even in those horrid chairs we have."

I wondered if Shirley was deflecting the racial question, but I let it go. "Yes," I said, "she has an elegance and otherworldliness to her, like she doesn't belong anywhere."

"Before Walter was fired, Marilyn used to help him with some of the brochure designs. I remember one drawing she did of a man sitting at his desk. His face resembled Michael's, who was delighted."

"Yes," I said. "Cindy went to the High School of Music & Art when Marilyn was there. She said Marilyn was one of those untouched girls, but someone very respected."

"What do you mean 'untouched'? Like a virgin?"

"No, I think she had boyfriends, but she didn't mingle with the other girls. She was a loner, but not because of anything. Most of the kids looked up to her. Apparently, she was a great painter. Her talent and her exotic looks set her apart."

"I can believe that," Shirley said.

"She even had a show at the school's art gallery. Cindy said she had a review in a local paper."

"What kind of painting style did she have?"

"I saw three of her paintings that she stored at some relative's loft basement on the Lower East Side. She paints in an abstract expressionist manner, large canvases with bold colors and distorted figures, like her idol, Willem de Kooning. I don't know if you know him."

"No. I'd love to see her work."

That day in the basement, Marilyn had shown me two very large canvases with saturated colors and odd amebic shapes. And the third was a smaller one, a self-portrait, in color sections but definitely recognizable. The woman in the painting's head was down, her face hidden.

"What is she doing at Theoretical Press?" Shirley wondered.

"You can say that for almost anyone there, especially the women."

I was still thinking of the racial question and plunged in. "You know, Shirl, back to Marilyn's boyfriend."

"What about him?"

"Does it bother you that he is Black?"

Shirley and I rarely talked about race even though the issues were constantly in the news and on people's minds.

"Why should it bother me?" she asked.

"I don't know. I guess because I thought Black women resented white women taking their men."

"Well, it doesn't make me feel good. We Black women don't need the competition. But I don't hold it against Marilyn. She's not the type to be with a Black man just to show off. Besides, if this was in the South, it would be a much bigger deal. I've seen more mixed couples in New York, even in Brooklyn."

"True," I said, thinking of my maternal grandmother and her sisters who constantly gossiped about anyone who went out with or, God forbid, married a non-Jew.

"Here's our stop," Shirley said. She slipped her arm through mine, and we made our way through the crowd and up the stairs to the street. Before we cleared the block, three Black male teens approached us from the opposite direction. I slid my arm from hers, grabbed her wrist, and squeezed it tightly.

"Ouch," she yelled.

Shirley knew of my attack. Though I never mentioned the race of the young men, I was certain she knew they were Black from the neighborhood itself. Now, the oncoming guys nodded at Shirley, and I felt her slowing pace.

"You're with me," she said, simply. "Boys from my street."

With that, Shirley took her arm and placed it around my shoulders, declaring that I was hers, and we swept past them, while Shirley slightly tipped her head.

"Two more blocks and we're almost at Elgin's practice game."

# CHAPTER 15: MAGIC WORDS

Though I had visited many Black people's apartments in Brownsville when I was a caseworker for the city, I had never been inside a Black person's home for a social reason. After we picked up Elgin at the YMCA, where we watched the last half-hour of his game, we turned onto Hancock Street, and I thought we had gone instead to London's plushest neighborhood. Magnificent brownstones, most in pristine condition, walled in by black wrought-iron fences, lined the block. We stopped in front of the most elegant, with glass-paned wooden double doors. A mini-Juliet balcony molded with pedestal reliefs rose above. A black lacquered staircase, each balustrade topped with a tiered cake-like design, bolstered the brownstone stoop. At the basement level, we bypassed the row of garbage cans. Through an arched front door, we entered a dark hallway of the two-bedroom apartment that Shirley shared with her eight-year-old son.

Shirley never spoke of Elgin's father except to say that they had been married in Mississippi. At some point, he left, and she migrated to New York to find a job, leaving Elgin in the care of her mother for six months when he was a toddler. Now there was another man in her life, Charlie, who came to Theoretical Press on three occasions to pick up Shirley after work.

Past the stair landing, we stopped to hang our coats on wall hooks and walked into an eat-in kitchen with a knotty-pine, rectangular table and three cane-backed, padded-seat chairs. Elgin threw his bookbag on the table and opened the refrigerator.

"Would you like a drink, Anita?" he asked. His smile activated deep, vertical cheek dimples, and his large, upturned eyes shone like flashing marbles. The parallel immediately stuck me, but these were not Greek sculptures. This Elgin's marbles were green. I had never seen a Black person with green—or blue—eyes.

"I'll take what you're drinking," I said.

"Are you sure?"

I could have agreed to Kool Aid or a beer, but I was fairly certain that Shirley was a strict Southern, health-conscious mother and wouldn't allow her son, either. Soon, we were tapping our glasses filled with Pepsi Cola and Elgin said, "To health." He grabbed two chocolate-chip cookies from a platter and excused himself to do his homework while Shirley prepared dinner.

"Is he always so charming?" I asked.

"Can't you tell?" Shirley asked, slicing a head of lettuce in the sink.

"Tell what?"

"That he's putting on a show for you."

"Well, I am already his captive audience. And those eyes."

"My ex-husband's. I think he had some Irish ancestry. Probably a slaveholder."

"Really?" I said, my heartbeat quickening the way it did when I visited my great-uncle Leonard, who talked about his first wife and three sons who were killed in the Holocaust because they were stuck in Poland. Leonard had been visiting his brother in New York for the World's Fair in 1939 and remained to make money to bring his family to America. By the time he had enough for passage, he couldn't locate his family.

My eyelids felt heavy, and I wanted to lie down and rest my head. It was almost like I felt last weekend after smoking pot. I couldn't freak out here, not in front of Shirley and Elgin.

"Can I get some ice?" I asked Shirley.

"Sure. Help yourself."

I opened the freezer and stuck my head close to the inside. I lifted the tray's metal lever and held two cubes to my forehead, running them across until water dripped down my cheeks. The cold alerted my senses and dulled the fatigue that was gripping my upper head.

"Are you okay?" Shirley asked. "You turned white."

"I can't say the same."

We both laughed, and my chest heaved. I inhaled a few long breaths to stave off the impending hysteria and drank the rest of the Pepsi in nonstop gulps.

While we were eating Shirley's homemade lasagna, which she had removed from the freezer and heated up, and a salad, there was a knock at the door. Charlie came in, his arms laden with orange chrysanthemums, and a white cake box tied with a red-striped string. Before he finished his meal, Elgin grabbed the box and sliced open the string with his knife and squealed in delight. "My favorite," he said. "Strawberry shortcake."

Charlie had a booming voice with a New York accent and not a Southern drawl like Shirley. He was about five feet nine inches, with tightly cropped, graying hair and a white mustache. He must have been about fifty, at least twenty years older than Shirley.

"Let's all have dessert," Charlie called, opening the cabinets and taking out small plates.

Shirley looked at my half-eaten lasagna and back at her son, picking off a strawberry from the cake, and then at Charlie, who pulled up a chair from the hallway and straddled it.

"Let's wait until we all finish our supper," Shirley said.

"Don't let me interrupt," Charlie said, slicing a piece of cake for himself.

"I am happy to eat cake," I said, recognizing Shirley's discomfort. I got the impression that Charlie normally got his way, which was surprising to me. Shirley was the most competent and secure decision-maker I'd ever met, especially for a woman in business. She often told me how she had worked her way from a file clerk to a supervisor to a department head by being pleasant but assured, a winning combination in a white man's world.

As we sat at the table drinking coffee and licking the crumbs from our cake, I directed the conversation to a personal level, ever curious about Charlie and Shirley's relationship.

"How did you two meet?" I asked.

"Charlie was the first person I talked to when I came to New York."

"Yeah, she was a greenhorn, coming to Brooklyn from Mississippi. The rooming house owner was my cousin, who happened to also be from Mississippi. So, I hung around a lot."

Charlie poured himself a whiskey without offering us a drink.

"And he brought strawberry shortcake every Friday night," Shirley said.

"I knew how to win a lady's heart."

Charlie refilled his drink and excused himself; although I sensed that he normally slept over as his coat and jacket were hanging on the hall hooks, and I had noticed shaving cream on a bathroom shelf, though it could have been Shirley's.

Shirley walked Charlie to the front door to say goodnight, and I poured myself a shot of whiskey into Charlie's glass and sipped. Why, I couldn't say. I hated the taste and smell. I didn't know why I did things anymore; I was a mystery to myself.

When Shirley checked on Elgin, he was sitting at a small desk in his room. I came with her to say goodnight.

"I told you to go to bed."

"I have to write an idea for a story and can't come up with anything good."

"What did the teacher ask you to write about?" I asked.

"Our favorite animal. I couldn't think of one. I like dogs, but everyone writes about them."

"Have you been to the zoo?"

"Yes?" With a question in his voice, he turned to his mom for verification.

"Remember last summer, we went to the Prospect Park Zoo?"

"Yeah, that's the one," Elgin said.

"And what was your favorite animal there?"

"I liked them all. Monkeys, oh and the tigers."

"Oh, how about the elephants?"

"Yes, I saw them there, and I saw a movie about Dumbo." Elgin's voice broke as if he were going through puberty. I was so gratified by Elgin's enthusiasm, my mind raced with animal images, realizing I should stick to what he suggested.

"Well then, how about using an elephant for your story? A boy like you with an elephant?"

"But how could the boy fit the elephant in his apartment?"

I laughed at the visual, at his literalness. "Maybe his mother owned the zoo, and the boy took care of the elephant. They were special friends."

"Yeah," Elgin said, "and the boy could be Nigle."

"Why Nigle?"

"Elgin backwards."

"I love it," I said, truly touched by Elgin's ideas. I almost welled up.

With that, Elgin scribbled a few words on this homework page and hopped on the top bunk bed. Shirley leaned in and kissed him on the cheek.

"Can I get one?" I asked. I thrust in my face without waiting for an answer.

As we walked back to the kitchen, Shirley said to me, "You were great with him."

"He's easy to love."

Shirley beamed and said, "Let's have another piece of cake."

★ ★ ★

I went to sleep in the bottom bunk bed under Elgin's. Shirley checked at least three times to make sure I was comfortable, insisting I take her bed instead. The last time she came in, I pretended to be asleep, but felt her warm hand patting my head and tucking in the covers under my feet. When I heard her leave, I untucked my feet and eventually went to sleep with my journal on the floor in case I woke up and needed to write.

I awoke at dawn before anyone stirred. As I put my foot down to make my way to the bathroom, I noticed my journal was open, with letters scrawled in a downward slant, some overlapping and others clustered into words. I couldn't make out meaningful phrases, and it felt like a passage from Lorem ipsum or Greeking, the dummy text the Art Department used to estimate layout. I interpreted some words when letters were missing or merged into long chains:

*It was something that Charlie would visit a woman with a sleepover, an inappropriate plan. Everyone had a level of intake necessitated and found themselves a scarf, letters, nothing all or thought that bringing their babies are here, they are coming and coming. You substituted landing orange lights swing in bulb and they illuminate us but catching only. We just don't reach each other anymore. We try to type but the letters are in the range coming if typing ... short bursts got waylaid to fluggy shorts. We meet others we know who are sleeping or mesmerized by the swish swash of mounting ... All you needed to do was get out early on the street to play ball ... We are all like disconnected tiles rising and collapsing … And I did this after Shirley went to bed and snuck out and left me with Elgin and I got to thinking … he would curl his lashes and offer up his eyes to the boy. His mother was lost in a puzzle of dead words.*

I was dumbfounded. *When did I write this? Did I get up in a drugged stupor and write? Who wrote this?* Certain phrases stuck out: "We just don't reach each other anymore," "We are like disconnected tiles," "lost in a puzzle of dead words."

*What was happening to me? What did it mean?* I began to tremble uncontrollably and crashed on the bed.

When I was in college and couldn't memorize my textbooks or even organize the facts into notes, I put a book under my pillow and hoped that osmosis would penetrate the feathers into my brain and imprint information as if an invisible carbon paper was the intermediary between the pillow and my scalp. In those days, I believed anything.

Now, I couldn't imagine how these mysterious words appeared in my journal. Had I slept with it pinned under my side, perhaps I could have summoned the idea of an unknown mystical force. But the notebook was still in the same place I left it before I went to bed, its pages splayed next to my shoes under the bed frame.

With mounting terror, I believed what I had denied before. It wasn't only my body that was failing me. I was losing control of my mind.

Just to make sure that I wouldn't fall asleep and wake again to write another indecipherable piece, I placed my journal on Elgin's desk next to his homework page. He had written the title of his story, "Nigle and the Elephant."

# CHAPTER 16: SENTENCE COMPLETION

Arthur was in our apartment at least three times a week. He lived about a thirty-minute walk away, near the Bowery, and found all kinds of excuses to ring our bell or knock on our windowpane, normally involving extra food that he had in a plastic bag, carefully squished in a Tupperware container, sent by his mother via her mid-Manhattan office messenger to her poor son starving in the bowels of what she called "Manhattan's worst neighborhood with bums sleeping on the steps" to his fifth-floor walkup. It took me a while to realize that he was romantically interested in Denise, confirmed one evening when I came home from a dinner date.

On that night, I had made myself a cup of tea, thinking that Denise was asleep as the bedroom door was closed. Denise wandered into the galley kitchen and opened a package of sugar wafers and placed them on a dish.

"Would you like tea?" I asked, noticing that Denise's face was pinker than her usual pink and her green eyes focused downward.

"That would be nice. And another for Arthur, if you don't mind."

"Arthur is here?" I was confused, as he often came and went before dinnertime.

"Yes, he's in the bedroom." Denise wore a smirk of complicity.

"No?" I said, giggling.

"Don't say anything," Denise said. "Just make us some tea."

When we sat on our red-paisley sofa, Arthur emerged from the bathroom, his denim work shirt opened to reveal curly brown hair on his chest. I thought of gulping my tea and making an excuse to go out again, aiming for Sheridan Square's Christopher Park to sit on a bench.

"Hi, Anita, just the person I wanted to speak to," Arthur said, sitting on a large red silk throw pillow on the floor near the couch.

*Oh, no, I hope he doesn't bug me again about seeing a psychotherapist.*

"Please don't hate Arthur," Denise said, always trying to minimize interpersonal tension.

"Why? Is he going to commit me to an institution?"

"Don't be silly, Ani. He just wants to help you."

"Did I ask for help?" There was just something about Arthur's insistence that felt intrusive. It was possible, I realized, I just resented his importance in Denise's life. "Sorry," I mumbled without conviction.

"Okay," Arthur said in a loud voice. "Please, Anita, I don't want to upset you."

I hated when people said that. "It seems like both of you don't want me upset yet continue to say upsetting things."

"Just listen for a few minutes," Arthur said, his voice mellowing. "If you don't agree, I will never bring it up again, I promise."

Arthur reached into his jeans and pulled out his wallet. He flipped through the business cards and put one on the coffee table. It said, "Manhattan Psychotherapy Clinic (MPC)."

"I spoke to a psychiatrist there. He said they would interview you and then refer you to a suitable therapist. Payment is on a sliding scale."

"I don't want to see a psychiatrist," I said, sounding like a ten-year-old. I imagined being whisked away in a straitjacket, huge attendants injecting me with brain-numbing substances on the way to electroshock therapy.

"I think most of their therapists are psychologists. It's just talk therapy on a comfortable chair. If you don't like the therapist, you don't have to continue."

Speaking of "talk" therapy, Arthur spoke at length about the procedure, anticipating my objections. Looking at his ardent, business-like delivery, it was difficult to remember that he and Denise had just been on my Beautyrest mattress having intercourse.

Instead of going back into the bedroom, Denise and Arthur stayed on the sofa as I took the used cups of tea into the kitchen. I rinsed them out, wiping my hands on my jeans, feeling the hard edges of the business card through my pocket. I assumed Arthur would leave soon, and I was about to disappear into the bedroom when I heard guitar music. Arthur was vigorously strumming his expensive 1964 Gibson Cherry Sunburst, while Denise kept her used Yamaha on her lap, unplayed. Her lovely soprano sang "Love is Just a Four-Letter Word," almost as good as Joan Baez, and Arthur had the good sense to hum along in the background.

I remembered the crazy words I wrote in my journal at Shirley's house. I reread the paragraph many times. It made no sense. It was one thing for my body to betray me by freaking out on pot or even exploding my bowels at inopportune times. But on each of these occasions, I was there, conscious of what was going on, even if I had little control. Now, there was a part of me that came out when I wasn't there. Maybe I would get up in the middle of the night and walk naked through the streets like my grandmother did when she was in the throes of Alzheimer's. *Oh, God, what was happening to me?*

* * *

One day at lunchtime, I took the train to the Upper East Side and walked into the MPC. There was no recent major event propelling me there, other than that morning when my lips froze as I asked for coffee at the local luncheonette, and I walked out empty-handed. I didn't trust myself anymore; I couldn't control my bodily parts or my mental state.

For weeks after Arthur left the clinic's card, I fingered it in my wallet but didn't take it out. Arthur appeared a few times a week, staying later and later until Denise asked if he (and they) could sleep on the living-room sofa. Although this arrangement presented me with logistics issues, like having to wait until I heard noises before I could open my bedroom door, at least Arthur never mentioned MPC again. But the initials remained in my head.

After exiting the elevator, I registered with the receptionist, who instructed me to fill out a questionnaire, then wait for an intake interview. The interviewer would then evaluate my answers, and the information would go to the referral committee, who would recommend a therapist. So, I wouldn't meet the therapist today. This was a great relief.

I sat on a stiff wingback chair in the waiting room with a clipboard and paperwork. Two paintings on the walls above the black-leather couch caught my attention, and I couldn't focus on the questions. Thick black paint strokes dominated each painting in unrelated zigzag patterns, overlaying dark brown blobs and gray backgrounds. I stood and moved back a little, trying to get a better perspective and realized that these were faces, one a male, noticeable by a brown lumpy beard, and the other a female with twisted breasts crossed like a scarf. Surely, these must have been a Rorschach type test, designed to evoke negative emotions from repressed patients. They scared me and I almost got up to leave, but I would have to report to Arthur one way or the other, and it was better to get this over with.

The first form, "MPC Personality Index," directed the respondent to check "true or false" on the space next to each question. Forms were to be mailed back to MPC within five days.

Skimming the questions, I noticed they included the words "almost" or "sometimes" and focused on dark thoughts and feelings. I hastily went through it, checking off "false" for questions like "I feel almost all people are extremely selfish" and "I believe that few people can be trusted." I checked "true" to more self-evident ones like "I have sometimes felt depressed" and "I am handicapped a great deal by feelings of inferiority."

There was a second form, entitled "MPC Sentence Completion," filled with underlined words like "tense," "fear," and "unhappy." Well, what did I expect, sunshine and bunnies?

By the time I got to this one, I felt less resistant. I went from Number one: "I hope and work for peace" to "I feel depressed when I think too much" to "My greatest fear is having no one that cares" to the more revealing "My father is a pitiful person." I finished with: "My childhood seems nostalgic but in retrospect must have been traumatic."

On the back of the form, I scribbled:

*It is very difficult for me to answer these questions honestly. Many asked for an absolute "yes" or "no" answer. Each one requires qualification. I'm somewhat against these questions as I feel they tend to put people in categories. Also, some of them reminded me of certain "abnormal" conditions, and I am too conscious of their apparent or real intentions for me to answer freely. For the sentence completion, it was also hard to be direct since part of my problem is a difficulty in expressing what I feel. I found myself analyzing the questions as to what the answers would mean and thinking too much before I answered. I did try my best to be honest.*

In less than ten minutes, I finished and handed the papers to the receptionist.

"But you're supposed to take these home and think about them," she said, her long pink fake nails sifting through the papers.

"I spent enough time thinking about them."

"Okay. Go back to the waiting area. Someone will call you for an intake interview."

With any luck, I thought, I'll be out of here and still have time to grab a sandwich for lunch. But, as I sat on the couch, with the terrifying faces above me, I felt that in my denial of the test's motives and my need to outsmart them, I already gave away too much.

I didn't have to wait long. Leslie, a young Japanese woman with white lipstick, called me into a small office. She opened a manilla folder and asked me questions from a list, including, "Are you sexually active?" to which I answered "yes." Further prodding focused on my current sex life, which was, I thought, not so "active." I mentioned that I had a long-time liaison with Jabari from Queens, whom I saw sporadically, and a new relationship with an Armenian teacher named Sirak. I had met him in Washington Square Park while we stood nearby listening to two folksingers. We only had two dates and during our last one, I had noticed he was snorting coke before we had sex.

"How old is he?"

"Why is this relevant?" I could see that Leslie wasn't looking up at me. "Okay, I don't know, in his forties."

"Where did you meet him?"

I explained in detail, even including the singers' song choices. I had no idea what she would find relevant.

"How long did it take for you to have a sexual relationship?"

I debated whether this information had anything to do with my problems and stuck to the facts. "That evening."

These clinic people hear all kinds of kinky things and must be trained to show no emotion. However, Leslie's curvy eyebrows lifted. Certainly, in this day and age, sex on the same day couldn't be so unusual.

"Can you be more specific?" Leslie asked.

Glancing at her notes, I was sure this question was not on her roster.

"I went to his apartment, and we smoked pot. I think he also sniffed coke as he offered it to me, but I said no."

"Why did you refuse?"

"I don't see the relevancy of this."

The image of Sirak's lean body and his skin-tight dungarees gripped me. Only last Sunday, we stopped at Inspiration Point, the Grecian Temple on the Henry Hudson Parkway. We huddled inside under the crisscross trellis interwoven like a grape arbor, held up by Doric columns. Amidst views of the George Washington Bridge and the Hudson River, Sirak pressed his body to mine, and we made out for so long that the next time I looked up, the sky had darkened over the Hudson.

Leslie tongued her lip as if she were wearing candy lipstick. She scrolled her pen down the page and read a few obligatory lines from the clinic, announcing their privacy and legal obligations.

"Well," Leslie said as she closed her folder and looked at me directly for the first time.

"One more quick interview for you."

"The shrink boss?"

"Yes, and then we will refer you to an available therapist."

"Only one who is available? After all this preliminary discussion and forms?"

"Of course, we will match you with a professional who is right for you."

★ ★ ★

As if drawn from central casting for a Sigmund Freud doppelgänger, the chief psychiatrist, Dr. Friedrich Meyers, entered the intake room. Complete with a trimmed white beard, middle-parted gray hair, and bushy eyebrows, he wore a double-breasted trench coat even though it was May and the weather was warm. He unleashed his sash, slipped off the coat, draped it behind his chair, picked up the folder left by Leslie, cursorily leafed through it, and finally lifted his head to face me. "So, Anita, can I call you by your first name?" He had a pronounced German accent.

"Yes," I said, suppressing my answer. "Can I call *you* by *your* first name?" I remembered my friend Audrey, who had addressed her eye doctor "William" as she read from his name tag, and he replied, "My name is Doctor Klein if you don't mind, Audrey."

Without reply, he began, "I see from your file that you are having sexual relations with an older foreign man who abuses drugs."

"This is one relationship, and I have only been going out with him for less than a month." I felt my back go rigid against the metal frame of the chair.

"Ahh, but do you like having sex with older men?"

"Age has nothing to do with anything."

"Sometimes it helps a patient to have a successful sexual relationship with someone who is considerate."

"I didn't come here to talk about my sex life." Nausea gripped me, and I took a gulp of air. I couldn't throw up in front of this man.

"Why did you come here?"

"My roommate's boyfriend is a social worker, and he thinks I need some professional counseling."

"Do you think you need counseling?"

"I guess so." My voice lowered.

"Is this upsetting you?" Dr. Meyers stood and arched over the desk, laying his hand on my arm. "I don't want to upset you." He patted my arm.

"I am not upset," I said, careful to clear my throat and speak clearer.

"I see. And what do you want from therapy?"

"I want to be more in control of myself."

"Are you often out of control, as you say?"

"I had an experience after smoking pot."

"Did it increase your appetites?" He turned his head and seemed to smirk.

Fury was building in my chest, and my eyes stung. *What was I doing with this creep?* I wanted to get out of there in the worst way. "What is the purpose of this interview? Will you be my therapist?" I dreaded the answer.

"Oh, no. I am too busy. But I can see you periodically to review your therapy."

"I would like a female therapist."

"Why is that?"

"I would just feel more comfortable."

Dr. Meyers wrote something on my chart. I wasn't sure if he noted my preference or if this added to his composite of me as someone with "male trouble." The phone rang, and Dr. Meyers said into the mouthpiece, "Okay, I will be right there."

"So, Madeline, we are finished here."

"My name is Anita."

"Oh, very sorry. We will call you with the name and address of a qualified therapist who will try to help you find out why you are attracted to unsuitable older men."

I wanted to deny this ridiculous characterization and tell him to go to hell. In record time, he lifted his trench coat, buttoned it, and tied the sash as he walked out the door. One memory came to mind: During a lunch break at Theoretical, I was walking along Broadway with Marilyn and Shirley. I was in the middle. We passed a handsome, middle-aged man walking opposite us. As he approached, he opened his trench coat, looking squarely at me. He was completely naked. In my commutes to work, I had seen so many men exposing themselves in the subways, it became a joke in the office with someone regularly asking me, "See any penises this morning?" And then there was the Exposer on the train to Rockaway.

What did it matter, anyhow? I had asked for a female therapist. I wouldn't have to deal with men in trench coats, at least in a therapist's office.

# CHAPTER 17: MIND READER?

I didn't get my requested female therapist. The name Leslie gave me over the phone was Gregory Katz, and his office was on 89th Street and West End Avenue. I made an appointment for Monday night.

It was a fourteen-floor, prewar building, and Dr. Katz's office was on the twelfth floor. There was no thirteenth. The doorman asked who I was, consulted a sheet of paper with names, and pointed to the elevator. There were four apartments on the floor, and the hall was painted a dark gray with black trim. Swallowing several times and wetting my lips, I dug into my brown-leather Coach pocketbook and pulled out a roll of multicolored lifesavers, biting off the first circle, red being my favorite. Dr. Katz stood in front of the open door. The doorman must have called him on the intercom; or he was expecting me and wanted to welcome me in the best way. I had decided in the elevator that I would give him the benefit of the doubt and not be my usual skeptical self. But, by then, I had little faith that MPC would come through for me.

Although he was probably about forty, Dr. Katz was stooped at about five feet seven. With curly but thinning nut-brown hair, he wore black slacks and a gray sweater. He looked pleasant and unintimidating. After my experience with the sleazy Dr. Meyers, I was relieved.

"Hello, Dr. Katz." I nodded.

He was gripping a pipe, and I could smell the cherry aroma. Though my father smoked cigars, which made me ill from the thick, woody smell, I was more favorable to pipes. Dr. Katz didn't light up and used his pipe to point down the hallway and said, "Follow me to my office, and please call me Gregory. I am not a doctor. And if I were, we are on equal footing here."

*So far, so good.*

We walked down a long hallway with the wall on one side. The other side faced glass-paneled French doors, behind which I could vaguely see bookcases. At the end of the hall, we stepped into Gregory's office, which had two facing black-leather reclining chairs, a brown corduroy couch, and a floor-to-ceiling bookcase. A small desk held a phone, pad, and ashtray. Gregory tapped out the tobacco from his pipe in the ashtray and left it sitting in the well. He motioned me to sit in the recliner opposite him, and I curved forward, afraid that if I leaned back the chair would thrust into a recumbent position. "Is this your apartment or an office?"

"Both," he said.

"I notice that you smoke."

"A nasty habit."

"I smoked, too. Cigarettes. I started when I was thirteen, stopped a year later, and took it up again in college."

"Was it the stress of studying?"

"I don't know. The Surgeon General's Report on Smoking and Health came out in 1964, and the notoriety made me want to smoke."

"Even though there was proof of its lethal powers?"

"Maybe because of that."

I surprised myself at my forthcomingness. I had also vowed in the elevator that I would only reveal what was necessary. Now all I could think about was having a cigarette, though I had stopped smoking (for good) in Europe. I popped in another lifesaver. This time it was green, my least favorite, but it was good at masking the nicotine desire.

"Do you want to smoke now?"

I studied Gregory's face, and his soft woody eyes crinkled with sincerity. I almost fell back in the chair. "Are you a mind reader?"

"In my profession, that is the goal."

"Touché."

"You can smoke if that makes you feel better."

"I have actually stopped smoking but weaken occasionally." Everything I said seemed to have a double entendre.

"Well, Anita, can you tell me why you are here today? Why do you think you need therapy?"

"Did you read the questionnaires I filled out?"

"Yes, but your answers were vague. Anyway, I'm not a fan of those forms. They are too restrictive and obvious. I have a feeling that you already figured that out."

"Yes, I hate those types of questions. I never did well on multiple-choice or short-answer tests. They cause me to panic. Sometimes I can't understand the questions, think of too many possible answers, or try to parse out the preferred answer by the wording of the question."

"Maybe you're too creative a person."

*Is he trying to butter me up?* "Maybe I am just stupid and can't understand the question."

"I don't think you're stupid."

"Then I successfully fooled you."

"Why do you think you're stupid?"

"My father always calls me 'jerk,' 'mope' or actually 'stupid.'"

"And what do you answer him?"

"I usually don't say much." I glanced at the bookcase and noticed that the hardcovers with colorful jackets were on the lowest shelf, and the bound-leather textbooks jammed the top.

I had a sudden urge to get up and inspect the paperbacks in the middle, to see if I had read any.

"And your mother?" Gregory said, redirecting my attention. "Does she think you're stupid?"

"She says my older brother is like my father, good in math, and I am like her, good in English. But I think she means we females are both stupid."

"How did you do in school?"

"I got As in subjects with essay questions and Ds in those with multiple choices. And on the morning of the SATs, I overslept for the first time in my life. Then when I did take it months later, I freaked out. I couldn't understand the questions so I tried to imagine there was an answer pattern, like maybe the last answer was 'a,' so the next answer may also be 'a' to fool us."

"And how did this system work?"

"Not well. But funnily enough, I did better in math than English."

"What did your mother say?"

"She never asked about my scores."

We spent the rest of the session like this, talking about studying, tests, and college, and I never answered his question about why I needed therapy. I suspected that even with all my evasions, I'd said enough to give him clues.

★ ★ ★

On the third week of therapy, Gregory met me by the door as usual. This time, he didn't rush down the hall with me trailing. He stopped midway and pointed to a painting on the wall. It was a landscape in oil, with a simple house tucked away in a forest of green trees underneath huge puffs of clouds. It wasn't remarkable by any standards, but the softness of the brown roof and the ochre sides of the house shone in the sunlight, and it gave me an inexplicable sense of peace. Past the front lawn, a triangular pond with rocks the size of potatoes seemed to float downward, leading my eyes off the canvas. I wanted to live there.

"Nice," I said.

"Thanks. I hoped you would like it. I painted it a few years ago during a brief stint as a would-be artist."

"Oh, I'm impressed," I said. I wanted to ask him more but realized that this was not proper protocol.

Back in his office, I sat back and thought again about our relationship while Gregory filled his water glass from the cooler.

*Why had Gregory revealed such a personal detail? Was it a technique to get me to do the same?*

There was still so much I didn't admit to Gregory: my pot freakout, my phobias of talking to strangers or dealing with the public, and the inexplicable essay I wrote at Shirley's. Cindy begged me to tell Gregory about being attacked as a caseworker and that I never cried or got emotional about it. She said it wasn't normal to keep everything inside, as if I didn't know.

Cindy was right, of course, but I just couldn't open up to him, not yet.

Gregory had further plans for me, though.

"Anita, I have a group therapy session here every Thursday night at seven. There is an opening, and I want you to come."

"Group therapy?" *Shit, more wrist-slitting.*

"Yes, I find that it is very helpful to have others share their problems."

"You are getting rid of me?" I felt my cheeks redden. I knew this wouldn't work out.

"No, you will continue seeing me in individual sessions. The group would be additional. Try it. What can you lose?"

"I can lose money, and I can lose my Thursday evenings."
"I thought you were a risk-taker."
"Okay, you know how to get me."
"Only superficially."

# CHAPTER 18: BLOOD
# ON THE COUCH

After a month of me saying almost nothing, I was adamant about stopping group therapy. Then at our last meeting, Gregory announced that Awilda, a middle-aged Spanish teacher, would be leaving the group. She was the only one I liked, and that cemented my desire to drop out until Gregory asked if we knew anyone who could substitute for Awilda and someone who wasn't necessarily his patient in individual counseling.

I immediately thought of Cindy. She had been so depressed about losing her job at Theoretical and then having to move back with her parents, who were in the middle of a war over Cindy's sister, who had just gotten pregnant. I mentioned Cindy to Gregory, and he wanted to know if it would be a problem for me to have a friend in the group.

"Absolutely not, I mean not Cindy. She is the best, and her presence will make me feel better. But there is one obstacle. She lost her job and money is tight."

"Remember, there is a sliding scale. The clinic may make a deal with her."

That's how my darling Cindy came to group therapy.

The group included Norman, a single, white Jewish man in his thirties, who wore a black-and-white-striped polo shirt and black slacks at every session, and I suspected was a hoarder; Barbara, a Catholic, divorced mother and empty nester in her late-forties, masked her loneliness by solitary drinking and guilt-ridden casual sex; Julian, a gay college student, flunking out and practically homeless; and Michelle, a seemingly happy housewife with two teenagers, an accountant husband, and an Upper Eastside apartment, with the pulled-together face of too much plastic surgery and the over-thin body of a concentration camp victim.

I sat on the couch between Cindy and Michelle. Barbara occupied the "patient's chair."

Norman and Julian leaned against large pillows propped against the wall.

"Why are you here?" Norman asked Cindy.

"There was an opening, and I wanted to support my dear friend Ani."

"You mean you don't have your own issues?" Barbara asked in a know-it-all voice.

"Of course, I do. I am on Unemployment, living with my soon-to-be-divorced parents, and in a dysfunctional relationship."

"Now, you're talking," Barbara said. "Who is your co-conspirator?"

"My boyfriend Jack is a hippie who wants to be rich. He also wants me to cater to his every need and resents my current problems."

Unlike me, Cindy had no trouble speaking about herself and fit in with the others as if she had known them for years. In a convoluted motion that only Cindy's flexible body could make appear natural, she slipped off her sweater and swept it over her knees.

"What, may I ask, is your attraction to Jack?" Michelle asked in a whisper.

"Yes, I'd like to know this, too," Julian said. Normally shy, Julian often spoke after someone else paved the way.

"Okay, you both can ask," Cindy said. "Sorry if this is superficial, but Jack is really cute. He's tall with flowing rock-star hair and a soft beard. He has a toned and fit body with hard muscles, and sex is great with him."

"And the problem is?" Barbara asked with a dismissive tone.

"He smokes too much pot but can perform well when he's stoned. He's very creative and musical. He plays the guitar, but not like everyone else. He doesn't just strum three chords to folk songs. He knows how to play 'Malagueña.' And with a pick."

That's why I loved Cindy. She had a gift for words and could summarize a person in one line. She fell for his Spanish guitar playing, and that was it. Unconsciously, she fingered pretend strings as she described his music. I could almost hear the rattle of the maracas.

Gregory piped in. "Cindy, what does Jack do for you as a woman? Is he supportive of you in your current struggles?"

Right on, Gregory, I thought, saying what I wanted to say but couldn't because I didn't want to confront Cindy, knowing that she was vulnerable, and that Jack was a phony piece of shit.

I was quiet too long and my silence, as usual, was becoming the elephant in the room. Since I joined the group, I couldn't speak except for a few lame observations about other members of the group. When they asked me questions, I answered in monosyllables. I spent a great deal of time rehearsing imagined responses. It was as if this was a big multiple-choice test, and I was anticipating the best answer.

★ ★ ★

After two months of Group, my fear of speaking encased my vocal cords like a Mafia cement block. This immobilization didn't happen in my consciousness-raising group, where I was talkative, funny, and in control. My friends in the CR group never challenged me in that way. There, I felt accepted and respected, that I had an intellectual platform. In group therapy, it was different. In individual therapy, Gregory asked me about this dichotomy, and I couldn't explain my growing terror in the group, how the more I clammed up, the harder it was to speak.

Sometimes in group therapy, I was unable to concentrate on the speaker, internally rehearsing an opening for me to jump in. When others questioned me, I responded with a terse statement, never revealing much. I couldn't understand this fear. It reminded me of when I was a child in elementary school and Roddy Spivak, who was often my seatmate and endured my frequent nosebleeds, made fun of me incessantly, causing me to retreat from others. My reluctance to speak in public lasted through college, where a mandatory speech test landed me in the clinic for two years of oral exercises. I had thought that Cindy's presence would make me feel more comfortable; instead, I was growing tired of her obsession with Jack.

One night, Barbara began the group. "Something has been bothering me."

"Well, that's why you're here," Norman said.

"I know, Norman, but this is not about me." She accidentally pressed the bar on the recliner, and the chair snapped back. She let out a surprise "ooh" and righted herself. "This is about Anita."

At the mention of my name, my palms moistened; I felt like a child castigated by Roddy Spivak.

"Ooo, Anita, precious Anita," Norman whined.

"There is no need for sarcasm," Gregory said.

"There you go, defending Anita, like you always do." Norman sounded like a jealous nine-year-old.

Barbara interrupted, "I want to address Anita." She looked directly at me. "You just sit here like an observer." She turned to Gregory, "And you never challenge this. It's as if you are her defender. With Anita, we are walking on eggshells, and it makes me uncomfortable."

"Barbara, I'm glad you can say how you feel," Gregory said.

"Anita can take her time," Julian said. "So, Anita, what do you say?"

I wanted to hug him.

"I'm curious, Anita, about your response to Barbara's anger," Gregory said.

"I didn't say I was angry."

"Okay, maybe you are uncomfortable."

I glanced at Cindy, squeezed next to me in our usual position on the couch. She took my hand and kneaded it, murmuring, "It's okay, we won't bite." At that moment, I hated her.

I began, "It's not that I sit back and think I am better than you all. It's just hard for me to open up here, and I can't tell you why. The longer I don't talk, the worse it becomes. I am almost unable to speak."

"We are here to support you," Cindy said.

How did she become one of "them"? I wondered.

"Wait," Barbara said, "okay, we are here to support you and all that fuckin' crap."

I had never heard Barbara use a curse word, plus be so aggressive. *Did I not judge her properly?*

She continued, "I want to know why you're here, Anita. Why are you wasting our time?"

"I'm sorry," I said. "I have issues, too. Things have happened to me that I can't control."

"Like what?" Barbara unfurled her crossed legs.

"No need to be so direct," Cindy said.

"I am who I am, Cindy." Then again turning toward me, Barbara said, lowering her tone, "We are basically here to help you change bad behavior, not to enable you. This is true for all of us."

Sweat trickled down my spine and I squirmed in my seat. I hated this kind of attention.

"Bravo, Barbara. And that's why I love group therapy," Gregory said. "All I have to do is sit back and watch you all come to grips with the reality of your lives."

"That sounds so smug," Barbara said.

"He didn't mean anything," Michelle said, sitting forward, pinned to my other side.

"He talks about us as if we are predictable rodents, behaving in a set pattern. And you, Michelle," Barbara said in her most audacious tone, "automatically defend him like you defend your husband."

Michelle's eyes watered. Relieved to escape the group's scrutiny, I felt sorry for her and handed her the nearby box of tissues. She blew her nose several times and dabbed her eyes.

"Barbara, you don't have to be such a bitch," Cindy said, her back straightening.

"Who are you to talk? You can't keep a steady job. Thank God for Anita, who seems to find temporary work for you. And don't get me started on your choice of boyfriends."

My heartbeat slowed, and I regained a steady pulse. "Cindy is a wonderful, loyal, and giving person. She doesn't deserve your remarks. You don't even know her," I said.

By now, Cindy was actively crying, the first time I had ever seen her with wracking tears.

"Anita, I'm sorry that I am a burden to you."

"You are not. Barbara, shut your goddamn mouth."

Barbara twisted her lips in a tight hole and sneered at me.

The talk went on and on, and Gregory let the criticism flow more than usual. I sat and listened to them emote, relieved that the focus was off me. I planned to tell Gregory that I was quitting the group. *What do I need this shit for?*

★ ★ ★

Predictably, in my next individual session, Gregory challenged my need to quit the group while trying to make me feel that this was a pattern of destructibility. "I won't tell you not to quit, Anita. But I think we should examine why."

"Why do you have to speak like nurses, using the 'we' instead of 'you' or 'I'?"

"Okay, I will ask you directly. Why do you want to quit, and what is it about the group that makes you clam up?"

"I really don't want to spend all my time here analyzing my feelings about the group. This is a waste of my time and money. So, I have a problem speaking to the group. Maybe I feel a lack of control. It's not a one-on-one relationship. But I normally don't have problems with a group, so why do I have to borrow new problems? I have enough with my old ones."

"Lack of control is an interesting observation. Do you feel a lack of control here?"

"Why do you have to turn everything around to us, to you? Sometimes I feel that shrinks only perk up when there's a chance that their patients may have feelings about them."

"We are in a relationship, whether you think so or not."

★ ★ ★

At the following group meeting, before everyone sat, I spoke. "I want you all to know that this will be my last group meeting.

I apologize for not being a good member, for not speaking about myself. Obviously, I have an issue about control, but I will continue to deal with this in individual therapy."

"Finally, she speaks," Barbara said. "What are you afraid of? We won't bite you."

"I know. It isn't you or the others. It's me. I am a group failure."

"Oh, Ani, you are not a failure," Cindy said. "Besides, you enjoy our CR group."

"Come on, don't feel sorry for her," Barbara said. "That's how she manipulates everyone."

After a few minutes of the two women going back and forth, Cindy mentioned Jack's name, and the conversation changed to male domination, and I sloped back on the couch cushion. My intestines were rumbling, and I felt bubbling vaginal movement and pressure on my ovaries. I had my period and was wearing a Tampax and a sanitary napkin, as it was my second day and the flow was heavy. A wetness seeped into my underwear, and I ignored it, figuring I would go to the bathroom on the way out of therapy, a fitting end to my last session. But I couldn't wait as the gurgling and wetness increased. I stood to make my way to the door and Cindy yelled, "Ani, Ani, you left a pool of blood." She pointed to the couch.

"Oh my God," Barbara said.

"I am so sorry," I uttered, and pushed open the door, holding my hands under my crotch as if to protect the hallway from my bleeding insides.

★ ★ ★

The bleeding lessened, and Cindy and I took a cab to my apartment. She slept over and insisted I call my gynecologist in the morning. Before office hours, my bell rang. I couldn't imagine who would come over so early in the morning on a weekday.

I opened the door and gulped. It was my mother.

"Mom, what in the world are you doing here at this hour? Is everything okay?"

"Oh, your dad dropped me off on his way to Larry's shoe store. He's helping him with his books. You know your father is good with numbers."

"And why are you here?"

My mother explained that there was a fire on West Broadway nextdoor to her silk-screen place. Her boss said it wasn't safe to go inside and to take the day off, and she took a chance to come over, hoping to convince me to take a few hours off and go for breakfast.

"Why didn't you call first?"

"I tried but your phone was busy."

From the doorway, I looked at the wall phone and saw the receiver dangling onto the floor.

"Shit, Denise must have knocked it off this morning on her way to work. She does that when she grabs her coat from the nearby hook."

By then, Cindy came to the hallway, rubbing her eyes. "Oh, Mrs. Rappaport," she said, "is everything okay?"

"Well, it seems like I'm not your only guest." My mother reeked of sarcasm.

"You may as well come in and sit. I'll make coffee."

As I walked away, my mother yelled, "Oh my God, is that blood?"

I felt wetness between my legs. The bleeding seeped through my pajama bottoms.

In the taxi to St. Vincent's Hospital, my mother scrunched in the backseat between me and Cindy. I sat on a folded bath towel and put my head down to prevent the dizziness from overtaking me.

My mother kept staring at me. "Thank God, I came on time," she said, questioning me about when this started. Cindy tried to answer for me, but my mother ignored her. Finally, she said, "Could you be miscarrying?"

"Absolutely not," I said. "This is the normal time for my period." I remembered all the times I sat in my family's TV room in Brooklyn wrapped in a thick blanket, freezing when everyone else was in their shirtsleeves. Always, my mother would look at me and say, "What's wrong with you? You're not normal."

I pressed my forehead against the back of the driver's seat, trying to block out those images.

As we entered the ramp to St. Vincent's emergency room, I felt globs of blood flow down my legs. After filling out paperwork, a nurse and an attendant helped me onto a gurney in the hallway next to a man who had been shot in the head. Luckily, the wound was covered with a bloody towel, and I didn't have to stare at his brains.

Finally, they moved me to a curtained cubicle and wiped the blood from my legs, giving me several pads and a stretchy gauze panty. The resident's brilliant diagnosis was that I suffered from a heavy period and that I should double up on birth control pills. I asked if my frequent bouts of diarrhea could have exacerbated my vaginal bleeding. He shrugged and said he didn't think so, but I should follow up with a gastroenterologist. We left and returned to Christopher Street. My mother and Cindy propped me up on the sofa, which was becoming my place for recuperation.

Hours later, my mother left. Her parting words were: "This never happened when you lived at home."

★ ★ ★

That night, tossing in my bed, I thought of my last night at group therapy. Ironically, my bloody mess was none other than an accumulation of all the unsaid things I left in there, nothing more and nothing less. I spilled my guts in the only way I could.

I turned on the nightlight and reached for my journal. Flipping the book to the last entries, mostly jottings on daily activities, I smoothed a fresh page. I had the title before I knew the first line. It was called, "The Elephant on My Shoulder," and I continued the analogy of this beast that began with the story idea I had presented to Elgin. Only my elephant was not Elgin's towering figure of protection. It ended with the stanza:

And then, my elephant,

My beast of depression,

Takes over.

It slows my heartbeat,

Blocks my tear ducts,

Smothers my voice,

Winning the battle of my head

And the war of my soul.

# CHAPTER 19: CR GROUP

Although Shirley declined my invitation to the consciousness-raising group because our monthly Sunday meeting times interfered with her church and Elgin's activities, she longed to hear all the news the morning after. Before I finished my first sip of coffee, Shirley held up her flag, this time two triangles, one white, one black, pasted on a typing page.

"What's up?" I said into the phone.

"So, how was the meeting? Details. I want details."

"It was at our place. Of course, Denise was the co-host. Marilyn and Cindy came. Also, Denise's friend Sonia from the hospital she used to work at; she's a psychologist. And Bonnie, she's the one I worked with at Welfare. She was also a caseworker but is an elementary-school teacher now."

"I can see the connection." Shirley giggled.

"You take what you can get."

"Don't I know it."

"Well, it was very interesting, as usual. We talked about birth control, abortion, and masturbation. Shirley, you have to see for yourself."

What came over me, to be so bold, after my experience in group therapy? Perhaps I had a multiple personality disorder: there was the meek, fearful Anita, and the confident social orator. It also surprised Cindy, to see my two apparent contrasting sides, though she seemed less confused as she said last night, "I always knew you had it in you to be a leader."

"I could never talk about such things."

I could feel Shirley blush from across the room.

"You don't have to if you don't want to. But Shirl, you won't believe what happened after the meeting."

"What?"

"Well, Denise, Cindy, and I went to the drugstore on Eighth Street. Cindy bought a vibrator. It was long and looked like a banana. And get this, it was brown. We opened it on the street."

Again, I surprised myself at my *chutzpah*. I thought I was "liberated," especially with Jabari, who seemed to have no limits to foreplay and sexual positions. But to use battery-operated devices that looked like penises was outright brazen. Shirley wanted to know if we had tried it on the street, also worrying about the appropriateness of it all.

"No, but Denise said, 'I want one, too.' And I said, 'Me, too.' So, Cindy said, 'Let's go back and get the damn things.'"

"Denise and I were too embarrassed to go inside the drugstore. Cindy called us 'a bunch of scaredy-cats' so she went inside herself." I only prayed I wouldn't run into anyone I knew. God forbid my mother decided on another surprise "visit" to my neighborhood.

"Oh, no. Then what happened?" Shirley asked.

"Within ten minutes, Cindy returned with a bag. Inside were two vibrators, one white and the other brown. I got the brown one."

"So?"

"So, nothing. I didn't try it yet."

"What are you waiting for?"

"I guess to penetrate the racial divide."

"Very funny."

She changed the subject, claiming that Michael Bernstein entered her area and was heading toward her. But I suspected that she was horrified by our behavior—and a little titillated, because later in the afternoon, she said that maybe she would come to the next CR meeting, as long as we promised not to talk about vibrators or masturbation. There were so many jokes I could have used, but refrained, totally delighted that she would join our group when she could rearrange her schedule.

"I can't wait," I said, holding onto the phone.

I heard Shirley speaking to Michael Bernstein. "Of course, Michael. Our mail machines seem to be having a problem with vibrations."

That Shirley. She always knew how to crack me up.

★ ★ ★

Denise's friend, Sonia, lived in a huge brick complex on West 96th Street. Past the steel gray security desk and to the right in a bank of elevators, Denise pressed fifteen, and the door opened to a mammoth gray carpeted hallway. Thankfully, signs pointed us toward 15F, and Sonia was waiting for us in the hall- way, a floppy-eared, rust dachshund wrapped in her arms. The animal yapped in that small-dog-annoying way that crawled up my back, and Sonia nuzzled the pup, whispering, "These are my friends, Vivian. No need to bark."

Vivian looked up at her mistress, turned to us, and blared even louder.

"Welcome to my home," Sonia said as if we had never met there many times, sweeping her free arm across the open living/dining room. It was as if this were a model apartment; everything was neat, without a personal effect. No pictures on the white walls; a beige velour couch crowded with large geometric throw pillows in various hairy styles: white shag, thin pink loops, crewcut fringes, plus a brown scooped-out rectangle with bolsters that served as Vivian's bed and took up three quar- ters of the couch.

Just as I was arranging the pillows to make room for seating, the doorbell rang and Vivian jumped out of Sonia's arms, running in a frenzy and yelping at the door.

"Sorry," Sonia said as she welcomed Cindy inside. By then, I had stacked the pillows on the floor with Vivian's bed on top, as she no doubt desired. We maneuvered into the small kitchen, each arranging what food we had brought. The joke among us was that, except for Cindy who liked to cook, especially chilis, none of us prepared anything special for our meetings. Instead, we were "responsible" for whatever we brought. Without discussing beforehand, each miraculously provided something different. I usually brought a barbecue chicken; Denise stopped at the A&P and picked up potato salad and coleslaw; Cindy made some kind of guacamole; and Sonia, to appear sophisticated, had tabouli salad and hummus, prepackaged from the neighborhood deli. Bonnie was usually the only one to be brave enough to buy dessert; she brought Entenmann's crumb coffee cake.

We loaded our paper plates and sat on the couch and in two director chairs, waiting for the last one to arrive: Marilyn. Living in her parents' converted garage apartment in the Bronx, she normally borrowed her father's car and drove. The rest of us lived in Manhattan except for Cindy, who now came from her parents' house in Flushing, Queens, where we never went.

Finally, there was a knock on the door; Vivian seemed more interested in a plush toy bone that Cindy brought than in the newcomer. Marilyn burst into the open front door, her broad face damp, her coppery-red hair a frizz. I was expecting a story about traffic and parking. Instead, she darted toward the bathroom and when she came out, said, "Hey, I'm sorry I didn't have a chance to get anything. I could go out and pick up some dessert from the deli."

"No need," Sonia and I said simultaneously, as we had done at all our consciousness-raising group meetings so far. This was our second year, and the group dynamics were set; we knew the score, at least as far as the food.

Since this meeting was held at Sonia's, it was her turn to organize the conversation, another procedure we had never discussed but seemed to work.

"Well," Sonia said, scanning a sheet of paper. "Here is the list of our proposed topics. I vote for, 'How I Am Like (or Unlike) My Mother.' Everyone in favor, say 'aye.'"

The "ayes" were almost unanimous, except for Marilyn, who said, "Didn't we discuss our mothers before?"

"Yes," I said, "but it never gets old."

"Maybe we are the ones getting old," Cindy said. "What do you have in mind, Marilyn?"

"Nothing in particular, but maybe we can delve more into that topic by focusing on our body images."

"Now that's a subject we have never discussed," I said, and we all laughed.

"My mother never cared what I looked like as long as I was presentable," Denise said. "All she cared about were the neighbors' view of her family, a reflection of her own abilities."

"I guess, we're back to talking about our mothers," I said.

"How about your mom?" Cindy asked. I sensed her experience with my mother when I was bleeding sparked more of an interest.

"My mother is very contradictory. Obviously, as Cindy and, of course, Denise knows, she has trouble with boundaries and undermines my independence. On the other hand, she has an unusual background and considers herself 'modern.' She even lived with my father before they got married."

"Really?" Marilyn said. "That *is modern!*"

"Really. I think they wanted to make sure they'd be miserable. And, get this, my mother once admitted that she had a back-alley abortion."

"Wow," Marilyn said, sitting up and staring at me.

Something like pride got to me. My mother was beautiful and articulate, there was no question. But she also was locked in a bickering marriage with almost no physical tenderness. I didn't want the group to think that I was bragging.

"Once I mentioned to my mother," I said, "that I would never get married. She seemed aghast at the prospect. So, like a lawyer, she methodically made a case for marriage. She said, 'It's for security.' I answered, 'I don't want security.' Then she said, 'It's to have children.' I said, 'You don't need to be married to have children.' Then I pointed out that I didn't know any happily married people. She said, 'Happy schnappy. Marriage is not to be happy.'"

"Oh my God," Marilyn said. "That's unbelievable." Marilyn walked to the kitchen and returned with a plate of carrot sticks and pita bread. She bit into a carrot and then spit it into a napkin.

Bonnie sipped her wine and clinked her glass with Sonia. Both sat on the carpet, each with an elbow on the shag pillow. "I was wondering, Anita, about your mother," she said. "Do you think that her remarks about marriage reflected dissatisfaction with her life?"

"Of course," I said, immediately sorry as I realized that my response was an insult.

"But do you think her life choice depended on the times she lived in? I mean, how much choice did she, and all our mothers, actually have?"

"A great question, Bonnie," I said. "Our mothers were, on the whole of course, products of their times. With the Depression and the War, our mothers were more interested in security. I don't think it occurred to them to fulfill themselves."

"I agree," Marilyn said. "Females of that time had little options. Not that we have that many, either."

"My mother was extremely intelligent and intellectual," I said. "She grew up poor and had to take a commercial diploma, not an academic one. To her, the next step after high school was to go to 'business.' Happiness was not a concept."

"I guess this was not really a choice," Sonia said.

"My mother really wanted to go to college," I continued. "She inquired about enrolling at Brooklyn College, and they told her she needed to take high-school academic courses like algebra. She said, 'I'm too old to take algebra.' We didn't question her."

"How old was she?"

"Forty."

"Wow."

"Didn't she go back to work, though, about then?" Denise asked.

"Yes, she had to for financial reasons, when I was a teenager. She was so nervous on her first day back, she got off the subway on the way to work and threw up on the tracks."

"I think if my mother had a choice, she wouldn't have had children," Bonnie said. "She always seemed so burdened."

"My mother lived for her kids," Cindy said.

As I thought about our mothers and their historical restraints, I compared my life choices. While I was more financially secure than my mother and had more educational options, as a woman, I was still limited. At this point in my life, I still had no sure career path, no field to pursue, no mentor to encourage me. While I didn't know what I wanted, I was learning what I didn't want. How was I better off than my mom?

I felt like a goldfish smacking my puckered lips against the glass walls of a murky fish tank.

"How about you, Marilyn?" Sonia asked. "You never talk about your mother."

We all looked at Marilyn expectantly. She put her paper plate on the floor and gathered her hair together as if she was going to pin it up. Then she let it fall into place.

"My mother," she whispered, "died when I was four. She had breast cancer." Thick tears dropped down Marilyn's cheeks like tiny silver balls, and she flicked her tongue from side to side as if to catch the drops.

"Oh, so sorry. We have been so insensitive," Sonia said.

"No, no. How could you know? When I hear you all compare yourselves to your mothers, I take it all in. Sometimes I can't get enough." Marilyn licked the rim of her water glass. "I want to hear what mothers and daughters do, how they relate to each other. It's a vicarious thing."

"That's understandable," I said.

"And then a part of me wants to scream at all of you. I want to yell, 'You had a mother, just be grateful.'"

"Oh, I'm so sorry," Sonia said again.

"Sometimes we are too full of ourselves," Denise said.

There followed a distinct quiet. Even the dog stopped snoring, picked up her head, and swiveled around, as if wondering what was going on.

Suddenly, all our petty grievances seemed just that, petty.

This was one of the first times Marilyn had talked about herself in personal terms. Cindy had told me that in high school, the students were afraid of Marilyn's aloofness. In her yearbook, it said, "The girl we admire and want to know better." They had wanted to dub her the Ice Queen but recognized the meanness of making this her permanent moniker.

"I didn't mean to sound so bummed out," Marilyn said to me as we broke for coffee and huddled in the hallway, waiting for the bathroom.

"You were only expressing how you feel," I said. "I'm sure the other women were glad to hear about your feelings and would welcome more about how your mother's death impacted you growing up."

"Do you mean the other women or you?" Before I could respond, she said, "Sorry, I am just not used to all this sharing and caring stuff. I was a failure in group therapy."

I thought of my group therapy and how the others resented me for withholding emotions. "I didn't take to group therapy, either."

"Really? That's hard to believe. Here, you are the linchpin of the group. You keep the discussion flowing. Your insights are inspiring."

"Thanks so much. I need to hear this. But Marilyn, if I can say from my own reluctance to share, here in this supportive female environment, this is not therapy. We don't need to delve into forbidden territory. It's about understanding ourselves and our places in our society, what holds us back from being the best we can be."

Marilyn nodded. "I'll try harder," she said.

I felt like the biggest hypocrite in the world. All my so-called insights were more like opportunities for sounding rational rather than true efforts at behavioral changes. Who was I to judge Marilyn, a person who suffered real tragedy? When we went on and on about our mothers, she was wishing she had one to complain about.

We returned to the couch with our coffee cups and broken pieces of cake; God forbid one woman would eat a whole slice. Another subject I thought to explore, maybe with the title, "I'll Just Have a Sliver."

★ ★ ★

"I would like to get back to our conversation," Marilyn said, now to the group. We all sat more erect, including Vivian the dog. "Having my mother die was, of course, the most pivotal event I experienced in my life," she said, inhaling deeply. "My father tried hard to fill in for her absences, coming to our sporting events and piano recitals for me and my sister. But of course, he couldn't know what it felt like for a girl, especially for my sister, who was thirteen when my mother died."

"Every girl needs a female role model," Denise said.

Marilyn continued, as if she were the only one in the room. "My aunt Esther would come over a lot and comb my hair; it was always a tangled mess. She'd take me shopping to buy skirts and dresses, but frankly I was pretty much a tomboy and had no idea what it meant to be female."

"I think women of that era thought they could solve every problem by going shopping," I said.

Marilyn's body pivoted on the director's chair. She spread her legs, dug her elbows into her knees, and faced down as if she were talking to her feet. "I used to take my mother's photos to the bathroom and study them. Once, I found her old makeup box in the closet and smeared powder on my cheeks with blots of rouge, applied lipstick, and taped her photo to the mirror to see if we looked alike, but I looked more like a clown than a daughter."

"Did you realize how pretty you were … and are?" I asked, lowering my voice as if I would be waking Marilyn's dead mother.

"No, I never felt pretty, though people have told me I was. I feel like I have been fooling others because I am an artist and can make my appearance appealing. Now, I'm good with hair and makeup."

"That's sad," I said. "You are an extremely beautiful woman, inside and out." I surprised myself with a few tears slipping down my cheeks.

"Once," I said, moving my head around the group, "when we got our official class photos from the sixth grade, I showed them to my mother. Most of the girls wore white blouses and blue quilted skirts. My best friend at the time, Jane, wore her hair like mine: long in a ponytail, with the top combed straight back. I said to my mother, 'Look at Jane and me. Don't we look like twins?' 'Absolutely not,' my mother said with an indignant voice. 'Jane is plain looking.'"

"Why is this bad?" asked Marilyn.

"I was so shocked that I was speechless. Jane was plain looking. I had never considered such a thing. Did this mean that my mother thought I wasn't? This had been my only memory of my mother saying anything positive about my looks."

"Another sad story," Denise said. The rest of the women either nodded or said "yes."

Finally, Bonnie, who had squirmed on the floor pillow, seemingly unable to find a comfortable spot, spoke. "My mother was obsessed with her appearance, and consequently mine and my two sisters."

Bonnie was the one woman who epitomized fashion, with her beige kid gloves and matching clutch bag, to her perfectly curled flip, and her prominent circle pin on her white starched collar. Yet, for someone so clothes conscious, she was stooped and awkward in her movements.

She said, "My mother often repeated that girls are nothing without their looks. I always knew that I had to work harder than most with what I've got."

"So sad," Denise said. "And how about you, Sonia? I know you're close to your mother."

"Yes, my parents were Holocaust survivors and had no living relatives, except for my mother's distant cousin in Israel. My parents are very protective of me."

"That's natural, considering," Denise said.

"It is, but it can be very suffocating. Maybe that's why I became a psychologist, to figure out why my parents have merged with my personality. But I have to say that for me, in terms of looks, I always felt beautiful. I never questioned it."

I looked at Sonia. With her short, dullish ash-brown straight hair, bangs covering a broad forehead, a pug nose, and full lips, her features could have been pretty on another girl, but on Sonia they were too small for a wide face. Her blue eyes were noticeable, but they bulged under heavy lids, and she gave the impression of a frog. It wasn't that she was funny looking; on the contrary, she was certainly acceptable, and she dated frequently. Of all the very attractive women in our group, she was definitely like my old sixth-grade friend Jane, the plainest. So, the question really was, did it matter what you really looked like for your mother—or for you—to think you were acceptable?

This was the question we all left with but did not speak out loud. Nobody wanted to offend Sonia. I suspected that the others felt as I did: jealous that Sonia had a mother who made her feel beautiful. And for Marilyn, it was another story.

# CHAPTER 20: POWER
# TO THE PEOPLE

September 23, 1971

I knew Marilyn was active in Black politics—her boyfriend Clinton was a lawyer for the Prisoners Solidarity Committee—so it was no surprise that she called me to announce that the bus was leaving for Albany on Thursday morning, in two days, to protest the Attica massacre, and Clinton would have a seat reserved for me. Although my latest fears bordered on agoraphobia, somehow, I wasn't afraid of protest crowds. I had ridden to Washington for the Poor People's March in June 1968 and beforehand to the Vietnam Peace protest rally in 1965.

But they were before my traumas. The 1968 March was only days before my attack in Brownsville. Now, going to the bodega in the Village was inexplicably more fearful. When it came to fighting for other people, especially if I didn't know them personally, I was still fearless. When it came to fighting for myself, I was a basket case. I was beginning to understand this distinction.

I didn't need Marilyn to convince me to go to Albany; all I had been thinking about in those awful days since the September 13 riot were the newspaper and TV images of head-shaven Black men, their arms raised on their heads, sprawled on the Attica yard, strewn in bloodied and torn clothing, surrounded by gas-masked troopers with drawn rifles; barred prison windows, each pane shattered by bullet holes, spreading the glass with spider web patterns. It was a massacre by bullets, and someone could have superimposed the bodies on the images of Jews shot in mass graves, only this time the faces were Black.

It all began on September 9 at the state prison in Albany called Attica, when inmates held thirty-nine hostages (prison guards and employees) for four days. In response on Monday, September 13, state police and correction officers launched what was termed "the worst riot in US history." Forty-three people were murdered in a barrage of gunfire. Of the dead, thirty-three were inmates.

On the next day, a Tuesday morning, I spotted Marilyn at work. At her desk, she was typing furiously, sipping coffee, and murmuring to herself. I wasn't used to seeing her so busy the first thing in the morning. Usually, she was scanning the newspaper before she began her work.

"What's up?" I asked.

"Oh," she answered, startled. "I am writing an op-ed for the newspaper. I promised Clinton to have it ready by ten. He's stopping by to pick it up."

"About what?"

"About what happened at Attica. We want to get something in print before it gets worse."

"That's great," I said. "Can I help?"

"Be on the lookout for Clinton and let me know as soon as you see him. I don't want Michael to catch my boyfriend interrupting me at work."

"Will do," I said. I returned to my office and sat at my desk. As I looked up, I noticed Shirley waving her "magic flags" at me.

I dialed her extension. "Anything wrong?" I asked.

"I was wondering what Marilyn is working on. She passed me on the way to her desk without saying good morning. It's not like her."

"She's writing something about Attica for Clinton."

"Oh," she said. "For Clinton."

"It's important," I said.

Shirley switched topics to what she brought for lunch, and we hung up. I peered at the long view to see what she was doing. Her head was bent as if she were writing something. I felt dumb. Shirley didn't need me to remind her that Marilyn was doing something important. And she certainly didn't need me to emphasize that what Marilyn was doing, she was doing for a man, a Black man.

★ ★ ★

On the bus, nine days later, Clinton's deep voice reverberated through a bullhorn. "Thank you so much for coming," he boomed. "Our brothers," Clinton said, although mostly everyone on the bus was young and white, "our brothers, all they wanted was clean water and privacy to pee."

"Right on!" a protester in the back yelled.

"We heard that they slashed the throats of hostages," another shouted.

"Lies, lies," Clinton cried. "Lies, lies," he repeated as he swayed down the aisle. "Everyone was mowed down in the yard, like chickens to the slaughter, their necks and heads twisted, even though the men had their hands up the whole time."

Clinton went on and on, but I was no longer listening. Instead, I watched Marilyn gather leaflets from a satchel, handing a bunch to a selected number in aisle seats. Her long hair was crimpy, and

I had the idea that she curled it tightly to look more like a Black sister. I instantly dismissed the thought, ashamed that I doubted the sincerity of my friend, who had always been the most idealistic and honest person I knew, beyond reproach in my book.

In my pocketbook, I found a paper folded in fourths. I opened it and read it to myself. It was a typewritten letter to the *New York Times* that I sent, but, of course, it was never published.

Inspired by Marilyn's "faux" op-ed, I wrote:

*I have been watching television news and talk shows nonstop. I listened to the emotional testimony of a correction-officer-hostage and a lawyer-negotiator, both of whom spent almost five grueling, torturous days at Attica. The guard says he would have personally paid for airline tickets for the prisoners. The negotiator pleaded for time, reason, and human concern. Meanwhile, the "other side" opined that those "hardened criminals" should not have been allowed to intimidate anyone, and that when the prisoners didn't release the hostages at first, the National Guard should have moved in at once. The prisoners would have gotten reforms in time.*

*Not only is it unbelievable that the governor didn't make a personal visit, that Nixon applauded the "decisive action" of the governor, that the National Guard had to use guns instead of an alternative (thus killing the hostages, ironically), but former "white liberals" continued to view the situation from their plush Manhattan apartments unaware that people who have been persecuted, dehumanized, punished for countless years don't think the way they do. And thank goodness they don't.*

Once we got to Albany, we walked orderly in the streets past row houses, deserted stores, and boarded-up windows. Black passersby idled on the sidewalks, giving our crowd, which swelled to at least a thousand, little notice, as if we were the white interlopers we were.

"Fee-fi-fo-fum—Rockefeller is a crumb," Clinton shouted. Others followed the refrain.

"Attica means fight back," another man screamed.

"Rockefeller and Nixon are murderers," Clinton yelled.

I could feel those around me pick up steam, walking a little faster, pushing ahead.

About three miles farther, we reached the Capitol steps. Thomas Solo, a member of the negotiating team to end the Attica rebellion, stood at the lectern. He said that the decision to storm the prisoners was not only up to Rockefeller, but to Nixon and the "whole white ruling class."

Clinton chanted again, "Murderers." Cheers went up.

Solo continued, "Jail the rich, free the poor—power to the people."

Without thought, I joined the next chant, "Run, Rocky, run … People of the world are picking up the gun."

Red and orange banners floated above me, "End slave labor, free Attica."

A woman held up a photo of Rockefeller that said, "Wanted for murder, the butcher of Attica."

A group of construction workers booed us as they jumped into a truck. Then they blared their horns.

On the way home, while Clinton moved up and down the aisle, complimenting the group for their courage, Marilyn slumped in her seat as if she were collapsing. Soon, she stood by my aisle seat, two rows behind her, and we complained about our exhaustion.

"Hey, Marilyn baby, can you bring us some water?" Clinton called from the back of the bus.

She looked at me and shrugged. "Sure," she yelled back. But before leaving my side, she said, "Remind me to talk about this at our next consciousness-raising meeting."

"What?" I asked. "You mean, Attica?"

"No," she said, "I mean that prisoners' rights are our rights, as long as you're a man."

And then, she moved to the front of the bus where she rummaged in a cooler for Coke bottles and thermoses for the protesters, mostly men whose thirst needed quenching.

I thought of one of our CR discussions about how we women often were attracted to powerful men and considered those who were tamer and conciliatory as being weak. I remembered one time Marilyn said that in her experience, men assumed she would like rough sex. "They have a rape fantasy, that women really want that."

One of us—I couldn't recall who—challenged Marilyn: "Did you ever confront a man who said that?"

Marilyn had said, "Yes, I did. But I don't think I was forceful enough. He kept trying despite my asking him to slow down. Eventually, though, I gave in."

She later explained that her motivation was a combination of fear and the confusion about what was expected of her, her role as a woman.

"It's the old blue balls syndrome," I had said, relating how an old boyfriend once said that I was a cocktease. My refusing to have intercourse caused him to have blue balls. I had imagined a terrible condition where the testicles glowed like sapphires.

The internal bus lights dimmed as night darkened. The bus driver slammed on his brakes at a gas station near Middletown, and I awoke with a jolt, my mind still immersed in a dream where I was walking with an unknown woman toward her house, nestled high on a cliff overlooking a valley. On the way, there was a gate that was like a wall, cemented and sturdy. It was higher than my height, but I couldn't get close. Since it was partly ajar, I was afraid that if I went through it, I would fall overboard into the chasm of the valley. I got dizzy and backed away, sure that I couldn't control myself from falling.

As I tried to digest the dream, I recalled a psychological test that we had learned in college. It involved several "givens," and the respondent had to fill in the particulars. One of them was that you found yourself in a forest and there was a fence. The questions were, "What kind of fence? How high is it? Do you climb over?" The obvious interpretations were that the fence represented your obstacles in life and how you chose to over-come them. I remembered my friends' answers, ranging from "a short fence that I jumped over" to an "insurmountable steel tower." Following this example, my dream represented an unap-proachable challenge, one with dire consequences. I had no idea who my mysterious woman was, but since I had just spent the day with Marilyn, she was a good guess.

Several bus riders got out to use the restroom. I felt a tap on my shoulder. "Don't you need to get out?" Marilyn asked. "I didn't want you to miss the chance."

"Oh, thanks," I said, still groggy from my dreamworld. I stood and moved down the aisle toward the front door.

"Watch your step," Marilyn whispered, her arm on mine.

The line to the bathroom was long and straight. I shivered in the cool September night.

"There's no toilet paper," a man said as he exited the bathroom.

"Anyone have any tissues?" Marilyn yelled. The men mostly shrugged. The four women on the line fished in their bags and pulled out wads of used and fresh tissues, passing them down the line to the men who needed them.

# CHAPTER 21: NAKED TRUTH

A few weeks later, at another protest, Marilyn met a woman who verbalized her frustrations: Angela Davis. In calling America's prison system "totalitarianism," Davis focused on the dehumanization of prison life, a system of nonexistence, that could metaphorically relate to the growing sense of female invisibility in the protest movement that is essentially male. According to Marilyn, Davis recognized the collective consciousness of political prisoners, necessitating a confrontation with totalitarianism. Marilyn felt that Davis used psychological and sociological intellectualism to explain repressive behavior. Not that she necessarily agreed or disagreed with these observations. Marilyn was more focused on Davis's ability to publish her views and be recognized as a female political voice.

"It's not what she says," Marilyn explained to me one day in the ladies' room of Theoretical Press. "It's that she says anything and seems to have a platform for her voice."

"I see your point." I spoke from the toilet seat inside the stall. I heard the faucet's force in the sink and took the noise as a diversion to cover my groaning cramps as I violently rid myself of that morning's scrambled eggs, bagel, and coffee, followed and preceded by a Kent light.

"Are you okay, Ani?"

I sat for another minute, hoping to catch the last of the spasms, embarrassed that Marilyn must have heard my bowels erupting. "Sure," I said, rotely.

"I don't know how you do it," she said. "I know you are sick every morning."

"How do you know?"

"I know, I just do. You're not as good at hiding as you think you are."

"I guess running to the bathroom is a dead giveaway." I didn't tell anyone except Denise that I recently went to the gastroenterologist who ran all kinds of inhumane tests, including a barium enema. He prescribed pills to help control the situation, but they brought me only mild relief.

"I bet it doesn't help you that I am spouting politics in the toilet."

"Where it belongs," I said.

"Touché."

"You mean, 'tushy'?"

"Wipe that away," she responded.

"It's all behind me."

"I can see that if I don't stop you now, there will be no end to this."

"You said, 'end,' not me." I flushed the toilet and opened the stall door.

"Ani, can I ask you something?" Marilyn's normally throaty voice lowered, barely audible.

I checked under the stalls for any legs. We were alone. "What is it?" I was sure that Marilyn would suddenly scream some intimate political gossip.

"I know you have intestinal issues."

"Sorry if it smells in here."

"No, I mean I know you have a condition of some kind."

"Yes, ileitis. It runs in my family. My uncle and cousin have it. We have screwed up intestines and crampy diarrhea."

"All the time?"

"Pretty much. But I must admit that I am not as careful as I should be about what I eat. I should cut down on coffee. And cigarettes don't help, although I keep quitting. I confess that I recently bought a pack. I find it difficult to put a piece of paper in the typewriter without craving a cigarette. For my intestines, I take medication."

"And that helps?"

"Somewhat. Luckily, I haven't needed surgery. My uncle has had about half of his small intestines removed and my cousin has had surgery twice."

"That's terrible."

"As far as inheritance, I think all those matzoh balls and latkes adhered to our insides. Having major guilt producers for relatives increases the acid indigestion."

"Does acid cause it?"

"Nobody seems to know what causes it for sure. Why are you asking?"

"Well, look at my ankles." Marilyn lifted her pants legs and rolled down her socks.

"They look swollen."

"They are swollen. I went to my internist, and he sent me to a rheumatologist, thinking I had gout or arthritis."

"Aren't you too young?"

"I had X-rays, blood and urine tests, ultrasound, but they don't know what it is. I have to see a GI doctor now. My father found someone in the Bronx at Montefiore near him, and I have an appointment next week. In the meantime, I can hardly touch my ankles. They are so painful."

"Could it have anything to do with the protests? We were cooped up in the bus for hours and then we walked and stood still for a long time, plus we had no sleep. Who knows what you could get from that experience?"

"I would agree with you, but I've been having this problem for months before Attica."

"I'll go with you to the doctor if you want."

"Thanks, Ani. My dad will go with me."

As we left the bathroom, Michael appeared at the door as if he were waiting for us. "There you both are," he said in a conspiratorial tone. "Just the two I am looking for."

"Did you come in person armed with pink slips?" Marilyn asked.

As usual, I was amazed at her nerve.

"No, but I have this." He waved an envelope. The return address was from a textbook bookseller in North Carolina. "Read it," he said.

Marilyn opened the envelope flap and took out a letter. Attached with a paper clip was one of our brochures; I recognized Theoretical's open-book logo on the back. In a thespian voice, Marilyn articulated each word: "We are very disturbed by the attached advertising brochure." Marilyn stopped reading and looked at me, knowing I had written the copy.

"Go on," Michael said.

Marilyn continued, "This is not the moral message we wish to portray to our esteemed academic community. There is no place for nudity in our literature."

"I don't understand," I said, thinking that maybe somehow the printer had mixed up our artwork with a pornographic client. I thought of the time last year when I sent a poem to a literary contest and the rejection was addressed to Miss Gladings. I always wondered if Miss Gladings got my acceptance by mistake.

Marilyn turned over the brochure. There on the cover was Leonardo da Vinci's *Vitruvian Man*, his perfectly proportioned body inhabiting the vertical space, reaching out for the circle within the square, attempting to explore all conceivable dimensions.

"They object to this!" I said, my voice rising in incredulity.

"No way, José," Marilyn said. "Unbelievable."

"Wait," I said, and ran to my office. I leafed through the file on da Vinci and found the quotation I wanted and returned to Michael and Marilyn, who hadn't moved.

"Here," I said. "Let me read what da Vinci wrote in one of his notebooks: 'By the ancients man has been called the world in miniature; and certainly this name is well bestowed, because, as man is composed of earth, water, air and fire, his body resembles that of the earth.'"

"That's amazing," Marilyn said. "We should include it in our response."

"There is more to the letter," Michael said.

Marilyn read on: "Theoretical showed a total disregard of our nation's code of ethics and moral rectitude. We expect a new and revised brochure posthaste."

"They've got to be kidding. This must be a sick joke," I said. "Michael, just inform them this is da Vinci, not scrawled graffiti on the subway."

Marilyn said, "This is probably the same person who prays to the statue of Robert E. Lee in New Orleans and who thinks that *Inherit the Wind* is a book about farting."

"Sometimes," I said, "I think that we New Yorkers are the true hicks. We have no real idea about the narrow ignorance of most Americans, which makes us just as ignorant."

"Listen," Michael said, with increasing authority, "we have to respond. Apparently, this man, excuse the pun, is up in arms. He wants us to design a new brochure. Can you handle this, Marilyn? I know you don't usually do the art, but Ani has bragged about your talent. I remember the wonderful sketches you did for the book cover on physical chemistry. So, work with the designers here and come up with an alternative. And you, Ani, will be in charge of the copy. See if you can have something for me to send to the client by five o'clock."

"But we can't capitulate to him," I said.

"I can't take a moral stance here, Ani. This is now about our jobs. Ronald said this is our number-one client, and he has a lot of influence."

We didn't say anything, but Marilyn and I exchanged angry looks. I was waiting for her to quit or blurt out something outrageous, maybe mentioning Angela Davis and what she would do. Just this morning, she had reminded me that Angela had come close to being fired for her views. She had been hired to teach at UCLA, but the UC Regents tried to dismiss her for associating with communism. The chancellor defended her right to academic freedom, and she kept her position.

"Well, girls, what do you say?"

"First, please don't call us girls," Marilyn said.

"What's wrong with that? My mother calls her mahjong group 'the girls.'"

"It's different coming from a man."

"And I call my friends 'the boys.'"

Sometimes it amazed me that Michael, despite his tightly fit three-button suit and skinny tie, enjoyed sparring with Marilyn. And maybe if he had another life, he would have joined her on the picket lines.

"*Nu?* Marilyn."

"Okay, okay. We'll have something on your desk by five."

"Make that something, really something."

"Don't worry, boss," Marilyn said, slapping his shoulder. "I'm an expert at making something out of nothing."

I couldn't help myself. I stuck out my arms to the sides and spread my legs. "Just call me Vitruvian Man," I said.

"You mean, 'Woman,'" Michael corrected.

"Right on! Just don't call me 'Vitruvian Girl.'"

# CHAPTER 22: DECEMBER ROMANCE

One night when Arthur was sleeping over, he opened the living-room sofa and tucked in the top sheet. Denise was not home yet; she was taking a film course at the New School with our friend Sonia. Instinctively, I helped Arthur fluff the pillows in place and smooth out the cotton comforter.

"Sit," Arthur said, patting the blanket, which had been the one I pilfered from my childhood room in Brooklyn.

"I wanted to ask you something." He sounded serious, like he was going to pop the question.

At that moment, I felt like a guest in his house, not my own.

"What?" I asked, breathing in, trying to calm my racing heart. I was full of internal questions: Was he going to quiz me about the status of my mental health? Did he want me to move out so he could have Denise to himself?

"Don't look so stricken. This isn't bad. I was just wondering if you would be interested in meeting a man I work with at Elmhurst, a doctor from a small town in Italy. He doesn't know too many people and I think he would love to meet an American woman to go out with."

Relief flooded me like a cool breeze, though I wasn't sure about going out with someone who probably barely spoke English. "You make it sound like I would be doing a *mitzvah*."

"It would be a good deed for sure, but I really think he's a great guy. He's extremely intelligent, like you."

*Arthur thinks I'm intelligent?* I almost fainted on the sofa bed. From his soliciting manner and his overprotection of me when I had my pot incident, I had assumed he was considering having me committed to a mental institution rather than hiring me as a matchmaking candidate.

"What's his name, anyway?"

"Sergio. I think you will like him. My secretary, Ellen, thinks he's hot."

"Why doesn't she go out with him?"

"She's forty-five, married, with three kids."

"Picky, picky."

"What does he look like? Is he a real greenhorn? The therapy clinic thinks I have a serious thing for foreign types."

"It's hard to avoid that in New York."

"So?"

"He's tall, at least taller than me, maybe six feet, has dark hair, almost black, large gray eyes, and wears glasses."

"I'm not in the market for a boyfriend."

"I know you go out with different guys. Look, Ani, I'm not asking you to marry this guy. One date only and who knows, you may even like him."

"Okay," I said. As usual, I gave in to Arthur. There was something about his manner and assurance that melted my resolve. "He can call me. But I'm not promising anything."

* * *

Sergio called me the next evening, although I almost hung up on him.

"Is this Anneeta Rape-port?"

"Who is this?" I asked, ready to slam down the phone.

"I am Sergio, friend of Arturo, I mean Arthur. We work in hospital together."

"Oh, Sergio, hello."

"Hello, good night," he said.

"What? Are you hanging up?"

"Hanging? I don't know what that means."

I then realized that he must have read in some English language book that you said "good evening" to someone and instead he confused it with "good night."

"Would you like a date?" he asked.

"Sure," I felt like saying, "but not with you." Instead, I opted for kindness, assuming he must have been sweating on the other end.

"When?" I figured he would know that word.

"Saturday at six, okay?"

"Yes, that would be fine."

I gave Sergio my address and didn't have the heart to belabor the conversation, so I had no idea if we were going to dinner or for a walk around the park.

In getting ready on Saturday night, I had changed outfits twice. First, I wore my bell-bottom jeans with my tooled-leather belt and a blue-and-white striped cardigan. Then I thought maybe it was too sexy and cultish, and I opted for something more conservative: brown wool trousers and a short matching jacket. If I had been trying to hide my hippie demeanor, I couldn't disguise my straight, overlong hair. I couldn't resist a multicolored red-carnation hairband and moccasin fringe boots.

When I opened the door, he said, "Anneeta?"

I said, "Sergio?"

We both laughed at the ridiculousness of our introductions, and I showed him inside, directing him to sit on the sofa and take off his coat. He was wearing a pink silk dress shirt, gray slacks, a super-large fleece-lined suede jacket with leather buttons and fleece-topped pockets, and pointy black, patent-leather shoes. When I laid his jacket on the sofa, he said it was his father's. Coming from Italy, he didn't own a winter coat. His looks surprised me. He had gorgeous gray/gold-flecked eyes, long lashes, shiny dark-brown hair, a little lighter than mine, and ash brown stubble on his mustache and beard. I was used to being with good-looking men, as Jabari could have passed for bad boy Belmondo in *Breathless*, and my former Armenian boyfriend, Sirak, was another sexy man complete with dimples and blue eyes, but Sergio was definitely hot in a more understated manner.

After sipping from a glass of water, Sergio homed in on my two red-wooden bookcases, one against the wall and the other at right angles, acting as a semi-divider between the living space from the dining table. He squatted and fingered some of the book's spines.

"Did you read all these books?"

"Most of them are mine. My roommate Denise's books are on shelves in the bedroom."

"I see you have books of Oriana Fallaci." He held up *Nothing and Amen*.

"Yes, I like her very much. She is controversial, but very brave. Especially her views on Vietnam."

"She is Florentine. I went to medical school there."

"Where were you born?"

"On the Amalfi Coast, in a small mountain village. My father took tourists on donkey rides over the twisting coastal paths."

After ten minutes of chitchat, Sergio suggested we go to Arturo's Italian restaurant on West Houston Street. Apparently, Arthur had suggested it, laughing at the name similarity.

As we walked down Christopher Street, Sergio asked, "Can I hold your hand?"

I wasn't sure if I understood him properly or if he was putting me on, but I said yes, and he slipped his leather glove into my wool one and squeezed his fingers around mine.

In the middle of the street, he halted, looking concerned. "What is this?"

"What?"

"These big circles and all the smoke. On my way here, one of them exploded in the air. It almost hit me in the head."

"Oh, no. You mean the manhole covers?" I was confused.

"Manhole? What is that?"

"If you take the lid off, a man can fit inside and goes underneath to fix the steam pipes."

He continued to question me about the underground network, of which I knew no answers other than Ed Norton's experience on the *Honeymooners*.

"We have such holes in Italy."

I wouldn't touch those lines for anything and kept a mental note of all the double entendres passed between us in the ten minutes that we walked to the restaurant. If this would have been a conversation with an American guy, I simply would have thought he was trying to act coy and innocent. But Sergio appeared truly interested in asking me permission to hold my hand and the history of manhole covers. Despite my normal skepticism, I found his naïveté endearing.

The restaurant was small and crowded, and I had trouble understanding Sergio's English. He kept asking me to repeat myself. While we were waiting for our food, he opened his wallet and took out a small, folded paper. Opening it, he pushed it over the table to me.

"See," he said, "it's you."

"There was a pen-and-ink drawing of a woman in hip-hugger bell-bottoms and long hair standing in front of two red bookcases. On top it said, "Anita." I recognized my roommate's hand.

"Denise?" I asked.

"*Si,*" he said. "Arturo, I mean Arthur, gave it to me so I could see you first. It is beautiful, no?"

"As a drawing, yes," I said.

We ate pizza and smiled a lot. I learned that his mother was a shepherdess with a fourth-grade education and that his brother and sister worked in a dairy factory. How he got to become an intern in New York seemed as mysterious to me as the various markings on the sewer covers that led to the subterranean maze and formed the marked trail back to Christopher Street.

# CHAPTER 23: POPULAR TOPIC

June 1972

Since Cindy was now living in a rooming house with her boyfriend Jack in Staten Island, and it was her turn to host the consciousness-raising group, Denise and I volunteered our apartment to save transportation hassles. At our last meeting, we didn't have time to select a topic, so we spent the first few minutes of this meeting choosing one. As usual, Marilyn was late or could be a no-show. About six months ago, she quit her job at Theoretical Press and then disappeared for two months. When she called me, she mentioned she had moved in with Clinton, who lived in the Bronx, and was waiting tables at a Mexican restaurant in East Harlem. Best of all, she was painting again.

When Cindy had arrived an hour before, she complained about commuting from Staten Island, which took almost two hours.

"Why don't you sleep over tonight?" I asked.

She agreed that this would help relax her because she hated walking the Staten Island streets, especially at night.

"Last week, I was on the bus with Jack. You haven't seen him in a while. Now his hair is even longer and shaggier. He hasn't cut it in ages. He has a full mustache and beard and looks like Jesus Christ. I was wearing my blue serape, you know, the one I knitted for my mother, but it was too big for her. Remember that diet she was on, eating grapefruit?"

"So?" I was annoyed at Cindy's inability to stick to a story.

"Oh yeah. Well, we were getting all these looks from the squares on the bus. There were three greaseballs, complete with tight t-shirts and bulging cigarette packs popping out of the sleeves."

"And?"

"And they were making snide remarks, like, 'Are you slumming in Staten Island, you hippie freaks?' Finally, we got off before we wanted to, and they screamed from the window, 'Commies, niggers, go home where you belong.' I'm telling you; they gave me the creeps. There was violence in their voices."

"That's horrible," I said. "Maybe you should move."

"We can barely afford to pay for one room."

The bell rang as Sonia, then Bonnie, and finally Shirley came. She was now a regular member, though she always seemed preoccupied and came late and left early. We gathered in the living room. Denise set up the red enamel fondue pot, a Christmas present from Shirley, who had discovered cheese fondue at a publishing party and was dying to try chocolate. Denise followed the recipe, and we all stood around the coffee table, dipping our long steel forks into the bubbling brown mix and plucking out a piece of fruit or a marshmallow.

"Delish," Bonnie said, biting into a chocolate-covered banana chunk.

"Let me taste yours," Sonia said.

"Take your own."

"But I don't know if I will like it," she whined.

Although Sonia was originally Denise's friend and Bonnie was mine, I suspected they had bonded and were more than just friends. If so, they would be the first lesbians in our group.

Right now, we had a Black Baptist woman (Shirley), two Ashkenazi Jews (Denise and me), an Italian Catholic (Cindy), an atheist of undetermined ancestry (Marilyn who rarely revealed anything that personal), and now two possible lesbians (Bonnie, Jewish, and Sonia, Puerto Rican Catholic). We were becoming representational of what I wasn't sure.

"Let's not wait for Marilyn," Denise said. "It's already eight o'clock. And she may not even come."

"Okay," I said. I opened the drawer in the coffee table and found a lined yellow pad and flipped through it. "Here," I said, "is an old list we made of topics. We could do, 'How we act dumb with men.'"

"Yeah, that's always a good one," Denise said.

I began the conversation: "It reminds me of an old boy-friend, Gary, who took me bowling. I say took me, because in those days, boys invited you out and paid for everything. When I got home, my brother asked me who won. I told him that I did, and he asked our scores. Mine was about seventy-five more than Gary's. My brother was horrified. 'You mean you beat his pants off?' he shouted. I didn't know what he was talking about. Finally, he explained that I should have faked my game and let him win, maybe get some gutter balls."

"I know," Cindy said. "I was always better than my brothers in baseball, and yet the boys never asked me to play in their game."

"We had to be nice and pretend they were smarter and better athletes. What was wrong with us?" Bonnie asked.

"Maybe this is a little off subject, but what kills me is the premium women, even liberated ones, put on spending time with guys," Sonia said. "Like if she gets a date with a man, she thinks nothing of rescheduling one with a woman."

"You're talking about straight women," Bonnie said, smirking. Lately she had admitted going out with women but said nothing about being involved with Sonia. I suspected Sonia wasn't ready to come out of the closet.

The intercom rang, and I buzzed back without questioning, expecting Marilyn. I waited by the door and then poked my head out. Nobody was there. I returned to the group. "Well, maybe it's me, but this subject isn't going anywhere," I said. "Let's look at some others: 'The Myth of the Vaginal Orgasm,' 'Miss America and the Swimsuit Competition,' 'Should I thank my husband for doing the dishes?'"

"I don't know," Denise said. "Nothing thrills me."

"Oh, here's one: 'How we perceive ourselves and how others see us.'"

"We did that before." Sonia said.

"Yeah, so what?" I said. "I think it's the root of every other topic."

And so it was decided.

We heard tapping and someone calling my name at our street window, and Denise investigated. Marilyn yelled through the open window that the intercom wasn't working. I rushed to the outside door and let her in. In the lobby's light, I looked at Marilyn and almost fainted. I took a double take. I hadn't seen her for about three months since she hadn't shown up at the last meetings, though I had spoken with her several times on the phone. Her face was gaunt, with dark hollows on her cheeks. Her bloodshot eyes were smudged underneath with bagging skin. I gaped at her once-glowing mane pulled back in a rubber band with dull wisps framing her face. She was out of breath, and her forehead was beaded with perspiration. I wanted to cry.

"Sorry, I practically ran here from the subway." She kissed me on the cheek, and I squeezed her shoulders that felt like long bones.

We entered my apartment. "Sit down," I said, bringing her a glass of white wine at the sofa.

"What did I miss?" she asked.

"We were just beginning. The topic is 'How we perceive ourselves and how others see us.'"

"Oh, that one again?"

Everyone laughed in a forced way. I could tell from their raised eyebrows and stares that they were as shocked as I was at Marilyn's appearance.

"What's so funny?" Marilyn asked.

"Oh, some of us really like this subject. I'll start." I knew that if I had to wait for the others to speak, I would clam up like I did in group therapy. Plus, I sensed that Marilyn didn't realize how bad she looked and wouldn't tell us much until she felt comfortable. So I plunged in: "I see myself stuck as a depressed adolescent, but others think I am basically funny and even-keeled. Arthur even once called me intelligent. I was surprised."

"You are definitely funny, but I don't know about even-keeled," Cindy said. "You are extremely intelligent. I know you've been phobic after being attacked and after that pot incident. And you have certain phobias. Sorry, am I giving away too much?"

"No," I said. "But I was hoping this wouldn't be group therapy. More like women helping women."

"I am there for you," Cindy said. "I'll keep my mouth shut."

"No, I want to hear what you have to say."

"Okay," Cindy said. "I wear all these hair coverings: a baseball cap when I'm talking to my father, a wide hairband when I play the guitar, a straw hat when I go to the beach with you girls, and a crushed felt fedora when I'm on a date with a guy. But when I am with myself, I don't wear a hat."

"Very, very poetic," Shirley said, with an air of annoyance. "What I want to know is why you can't wear what you want to wear." Even though Shirley had gotten used to our middle-class angst, sometimes her patience wore thin. She got up from the armchair and stood near Marilyn and smoothed her hair. "How're you doing, babe?"

"I'm okay I guess," Marilyn said.

Cindy continued, focusing on Shirley. "I don't feel like you have this problem. You seem so self-assured that you wouldn't take bullshit from anyone."

"As a Black woman in America, I have to keep my mouth shut many times, so I will be seen as a Black woman who knows her place. But this is not who I really am. At Theoretical Press, I am the only Black woman in a position of power, limited that it is, including the low pay. I worked very hard to get there. Two women I supervise are also Black, but they keep to themselves and don't socialize with the others, all white, in similar jobs, though they are friendly enough."

"This sounds exhausting," Denise said.

"And I'm a Southern woman and not a college gal like you all. I'm supposed to keep political and social opinions to myself, not cause waves." Shirley excused herself to call home and check on her son.

"Stupidly, I never questioned my parents," Denise said. "When it came time to go to college, they only had enough money to pay for one of us, me or my twin brother. We both did very well academically. He went to Yale, and I went to Hunter College. I accepted their opinions that he was the smart one and, of course, he was a boy."

"And what you left out, Denise," I said. "You graduated *summa cum laude*, and he didn't."

"But I always had to study."

Intrigued by Shirley's answers, I asked her, as she came back into the room, "How do you want to be seen?"

"I don't think about that," Shirley said. "I am a mom first and I go to work. I'm tired most of the time. Coming here for this group is something extravagant. My aunt watches my son, and my boyfriend gets angry that I am spending too much time with radical white girls."

Denise stood and took the fondue pot back into the kitchen, returning with a bowl of sour cream-onion soup dip and a bag of potato chips. She ripped open the plastic and poured the chips into an empty bowl, then passed them around.

"Do you think that men ever talk like this?" Marilyn asked, playing with a potato chip. As usual, Marilyn zeroed in on the theme or point, deleting the personal detritus. She probably would be the one in composition class who could formulate a hypothesis and thesis statement.

"I doubt it," Denise said.

Marilyn got up and rushed to the bathroom. Cindy gave me a look that said, "What's up with her?"

I shrugged. Everyone turned to the hallway, their eyes following Marilyn's path to the bathroom. "I'm very worried about her," I whispered to Cindy.

"Me, too."

All were quiet for a moment. I didn't want everyone to stare at Marilyn when she returned so I continued: "For me, I always remember this quote by poet John Greenleaf Whittier, a kind of guiding principle: 'For all sad words of tongue and pen, / The saddest are these: "It might have been!"'"

"I just don't want to reach my deathbed and wonder why I didn't do what I should have done or been what I wanted to be."

"Why is that so important?" Cindy asked.

"I look at someone like my father, who was unlike most of my relatives who came to this country with nothing. He was born in New York. His immigrant parents became successful. He had money, and a chance for education. He dropped out of one college, and they got him into another. His parents helped him start a business. He gambled away all his money, couldn't manage his employees, and went bankrupt. He was smart and funny and now he sits in his chair and sleeps most of the day."

"Talk about a sad story," Sonia said. "How do you see yourself then, Anita?"

"It is my yardstick, from which I measure everything. To not be like my father."

"You never told me this," Cindy said, rubbing her thick eyebrows and flicking off phantom dandruff. She sounded hurt, as if I kept something to myself that I should have shared.

"It's not a secret."

We used the break to make coffee and arrange a platter of chocolate-chip cookies. With all the chocolate fondue, cookies did not seem like a treat. By the time Marilyn returned, we were all unenthusiastically nibbling on them.

"Are you okay?" I asked Marilyn. All eyes turned to her.

"As good as I am."

"So much chocolate," Bonnie said. "Not good for pimples."

"Now you're talking about how we see ourselves," I said. "Shirley is divorced with a boyfriend, Cindy and Marilyn have boyfriends, and oh, I forgot Denise has Arthur. I'm kinda in a relationship, Sonia and Bonnie are unattached."

Bonnie said, "We are only unattached by men." Sonia blushed.

"Yes," I said. "We are defined by our relationships or lack thereof. And look at our so-called careers? Shirley rose from a file clerk to a bona fide department head; Denise is a claims adjuster for Social Security; I'm a copywriter and former caseworker. Although I've been at Theoretical for almost four years, I am starting a new job soon, also as a copywriter."

"Oh, really?" Shirley said, her eyes widening. "When did you expect to tell me?"

Her tone was laced with anger. I had never seen her like this. "So sorry. I only decided last night."

What had I been thinking, blurting this out before I told Shirley? We had both been going on interviews, but still. If she accepted a new job without consulting me, I know how I'd feel.

"Where?" Shirley asked.

"For Happy Frogs Magazines. I will be writing ads, book jackets, and catalog copy for their children's book division. At least it's something I can understand, and it's more money. Unlike Theoretical, it's a large organization and may offer other opportunities."

"You don't sound very enthusiastic," Bonnie said.

"Well, I am not thrilled about this kind of writing, though it may be challenging. Besides, I will be bereft without Shirley."

"You interrupted your train of thought," Bonnie said.

"Yeah, I was listing our jobs. Marilyn is a painter and works as a waitress; Cindy has had lots of temporary jobs and is a great guitarist; Sonia is a therapist; and Bonnie is a teacher. We don't have a secretary here."

"Being a secretary was the goal for women in our mothers' generation."

"I know, Bonnie. And, in college, women were expected to be teachers or in the social service professions. That's why I studied sociology and became a caseworker. Not that social work and sociology have any relation. Now I feel aimless. My job is temporary. It has nothing to do with personal expression. My relationships with men and to my job don't define me."

"The way I see it," Marilyn said, "some of us have jobs, not careers. Sonia's as a psychotherapist and Bonnie's as a teacher are careers. Denise fell into Social Security; it wasn't a planned destination. Shirley was promoted into better jobs not pursued by males. Our work lives, and even our creative aspirations, are traditionally female. We are all products of our times."

"You said it," Cindy said.

"And to get back to our topic ..." Denise said.

"You mean the thesis statement?" I said. "We see ourselves as reflections of our situations."

"Well put," Cindy said.

"Maybe you should be a writer, not a copywriter," Sonia said, slapping me on the back.

"Well, my mother once pleaded with me to take a typing course. I said, 'If I ever have a job where I have to type, I'll kill myself.' And what do I do all day?"

Everyone yelled, "TYPE."

"And maybe we see ourselves as reflections of our expectations?" Marilyn said.

"Our generation is the first where we can choose," I said.

"Theoretically, yes," Marilyn said. "Pardon the word. But opportunities do not match. Freedom can have its drawbacks."

"Yes," Shirley said. "Freedom is not for the faint-hearted."

"I think we are all speaking in intellectualisms," Cindy said. "Nobody has mentioned feelings."

"I feel sad," I said. "I feel like we missed the boat, and I am drowning." This was more than I ever admitted in therapy, group or individual. I could feel my eyes water.

"Me, too," Cindy said.

"I'll drink to that," Sonia said.

Marilyn ran back to the bathroom, and we remained in our seats, silently waiting for the toilet to flush.

"It must be something she ate," Sonia finally said, to break the silence. "Could it have been the fondue?"

Marilyn snuck back into the kitchen and returned with a glass of water. "It seems I am always missing something."

"Nothing much," I said. "We're just taking it in."

"Well, I was just letting it out."

"Speaking of which," Shirley said, "as a polite Southern girl, I will break the stereotype and ask you what everyone is too chicken to ask."

"And what is that?"

"We are concerned about your health."

Sometimes I felt that Shirley was the only adult in the room.

"Do I look so bad?"

Nobody answered.

Marilyn broke the silence: "I know I look like shit, pardon the expression. I have some crazy intestinal disease. The doctors can't pinpoint it. I'll be okay, please don't worry."

We all smiled and said some empty pleasantries. Denise turned to a fresh page on the pad. "What should we talk about next time?"

"How about something happy for a change?" Sonia said.

After the women left, when Denise and I were washing the dishes, I asked, "Tell me the truth, did I talk too much? I feel like I monopolized the conversation."

"Coming from you, that is rich."

"Why?"

"Didn't you tell me that you spent months in group therapy and never uttered a word?"

"So?"

"So, it's time to get some of it out. Besides, I think you helped stimulate a good conversation and gave us a lot to think about."

"Are you sure?"

"Sure. And you kept us all from dwelling on the awkward situation with Marilyn.

"Oh, Denise, one more thing."

"What?"

"I think that you would have graduated *summa cum laude* from Yale."

# CHAPTER 24: KNOCK THREE TIMES

Once I exited the elevator at Happy Frogs, I faced a glass-topped wraparound reception desk, above which were displayed the HF logo and a mural of children and animals tumbling down a playground slide. I had noticed this cheerful scene during my interview but hardly gave it more than a glance.

Happy Frogs was as different from Theoretical as a publishing company could be. First, it represented American children's picture books and magazines as compared to Russian academic research textbooks and journals. Second, the walls of Happy Frogs were plastered with their book jackets and magazines, spotlighting dancing amphibians, cherubic boys and girls, whereas Theoretical's covers were basically monochromatic and featured geometric shapes and zigzag patterns.

The chief copywriter Ingrid, whose tall, blonde looks fit her Scandinavian name, met me at the reception lounge and led me to my office, which was the size of my Christopher Street living room. There were no windows, but one wall abutted the Art Department and Ingrid's office was on my other side.

Minutes later, my next-door artist neighbor Bernice popped her head in the door and announced that the best way to communicate with me was to bang on our adjoining walls. "As the song says, knock three times if you want me." She was a bubbly, cherubic sort, and I instantly warmed up to her and answered, "Twice on the pipe."

As a direct contrast to Bernice, our boss Edward arrived and ordered Bernice back to her office and addressed me as Ms. Rappaport. In his early sixties, Edward or Mr. Sterling, wore a tweed jacket with suede elbow patches and a white button-down shirt. He seemed like the quintessential academic, but I soon learned that he lived in the suburbs and was addicted to golf with a miniature putting green in his office. Unlike Theoretical, the people I met didn't gather in sociable clusters, chitchat in the halls, or have sex in the elevators. No, Happy Frogs was a proper place. I missed everyone at Theoretical and even longed to see the calming face of Michael Bernstein.

My first jobs were to proofread copy for their book catalog and write a dust jacket blurb for a heavily illustrated children's hardcover and an author's biography. At the end of the day, I left my copy on Ingrid's desk and collected the pages the next morning. She had only minor copy edits. I made the changes and then Ingrid delivered them to Edward. By the end of the second day, my boss returned my work, this time with several red circles around words and marginal notes. An intensive rewrite was in order, and I stayed an extra hour in the office and came in early the next day. I handed my revisions to Edward and said, "Here's the copy. I hope you like it this time."

In a nasal, feminine singsong, he said, "Here's the copy. I hope you like it this time."

"What?" I asked, confused.

"Just repeating your accent. So Brooklyn."

My cheeks flushed, and I didn't trust my voice not to stutter. I backed out of his office. For the following week, Edward found every opportunity to make fun of my voice. I tried to avoid him by using Ingrid as a go-between. She was always sweet, and I was certain this had not been the first time she had interceded with our very haughty boss.

That Friday, as I was leaving work and pressing the elevator button, Edward appeared gripping his brown-leather briefcase undoubtedly filled with my inadequate copy.

"Have a nice weekend," I managed to squeeze out.

"Have a nice weekend," he said in that horrible imitative voice.

By the time the elevator reached the ground floor, I got my courage up and yelled at him for making fun of me. As I walked to the subway, I felt proud of myself for speaking up. At our apartment, I related the entire episode of Edward's remarks to Denise, complete with my courageous retort.

"Oh, no," she said.

"What?"

"Please repeat what you said to him."

"I said, Mr. Sterling, you should not make fun of other people's infirmaries."

"Infirmaries?"

"Oh, no," I said, immediately recognizing the malapropism. "I was so nervous; I said 'infirmaries' instead of 'infirmities.' I'm sure he told his wife, and they had a good laugh."

★ ★ ★

I returned to Happy Frogs that Monday. Unconsciously, I found myself over-elucidating and harboring a faux British accent. After another week, my "wallmate" Bernice knocked three times and I appeared in her doorway.

"Anita," she said. "If you want to survive here, you have to rise above Edward's insults." I nodded, thanked her for her advice, and returned to my desk, but not before I took magic markers and construction paper from her bookcase. At my desk, I drew a Black woman sitting at a desk, holding up colored folders that looked like flags. She smiled broadly and her arms crisscrossed in an expansive wave. I didn't think I ever missed anyone that much.

I taped Shirley's picture to my right wall and cut brown strips and glued them around the drawing, resembling a window frame. In the background, there were two other heads behind the woman at the desk. One had long reddish-brown hair and the other's head was taller and had soft curls. Though Marilyn and Cindy no longer worked at Theoretical, they were together behind Shirley, cheering me on in my new space. I lifted my water glass in a salute to them and whispered, "To you girls, my dear friends." I waited a second to hear my words repeated in a nasty imitation. There was silence.

# CHAPTER 25: KNOTS

"**I**'m dropping out of therapy," I said to Gregory before I sat. Normally, I blurted important information as I was ready to leave, which Gregory explained was common for analysands. We neurotics, he said, including himself, need to eke out what we fear the most, but don't want to face the consequences. That was why we were in therapy. In my case, if I didn't say it in the first minutes of the session, I would have chickened out. I had been thinking of quitting for a long time, and it was now or never.

"Let's talk about it," Gregory said, inching forward in his black La-Z-Boy. He picked up his pipe from the ashtray and lit it, the first time he had done so in my presence.

"There's nothing to say."

"Okay, nothing is par for the course."

"Are you criticizing me?"

"No, it's just that as Barbara from the group had observed, sometimes getting information out of you is like pulling teeth."

"Maybe you should have been a dentist." I immediately thought of the "Wanted" brochure I created with dental puns. About to say, "We can bridge the gap," I resisted, knowing Gregory would think I was using a defense mechanism like intellectualism, or maybe a term more appropriate to the oral stage.

"You successfully dropped out of group therapy by not showing up."

"Maybe that wasn't so successful then? I lacked courage. And that was two years ago. This is now. I am confronting you in person. doesn't that mean I am much healthier?" I tilted back in my chair and stretched to reach the headrest, always too high for my short-waisted posture.

"Yes, you are." Gregory then discussed the various reasons people quit therapy, and I was lost in the maze of his words. It was as if I were taking the SAT test again and could define each word but make no sense of the conglomerate meaning.

"Where are you?" Gregory asked.

"Oh, you don't want to know."

"Don't I?"

"There you go, turning everything into a question."

"Maybe this is more like what R.D. Laing talks about in *Knots*. You told me the book impressed you a lot."

"It did," I said. "I remember the words at the beginning of the book, something about playing a game or playing at not playing a game. All these confusions of meanings or should I say intentions of meanings?"

"Wow, that's good. You have a great memory."

"I remember another one that used to drive me crazy. It was about equating not feeling good with being bad and therefore unloved. And it ends with the kicker: if you are loved by someone then that person is bad."

"This is why we therapists make a living," Gregory said.

"There were so many examples, and I can identify with all of them. My mind is one giant knot." My throat felt sore, and I reached into my pocketbook for a pack of trusty Lifesavers, peeling back the top. "Care for one?" I asked.

Gregory shook his head. "This kind of convoluted thinking is a good defense mechanism," he said. "You successfully managed to use up the first ten minutes of our session. Can we go out and come in again?"

"Do you mean you won't charge me for the beginning?" I was feeling kind of cocky at this point, like I had the upper hand, at least when it came to delaying tactics.

"Why do you want to drop out of therapy?"

"I have told you everything there is to know. I am as good as I will ever be and have gone as far as I am capable of going. We spend a lot of time in word games."

"Would it be better for you if we got straight to basics?"

"Maybe, but I am just tired, tired from trying to analyze myself."

"How did you feel when you dropped out of group therapy?"

The mere mention of the word "group" put me in a more defensive mode. Why does everything come down to group? I wondered. When would that failure ever be put to rest? "Oh, that dreaded group," I said. "I did the right thing, but I was weak. I worried that Barbara would accuse you of enabling me or something like that or maybe treating me with kid gloves."

"Did you really care what she thought?"

"I want everyone to love me, even those who I hate."

"This sounds like something out of *Knots*."

"Yes."

"Let's get back to us. I'm glad you and I can talk about this. If we could work differently, how would you envision it?"

*Here it came, I couldn't avoid it.* "You should be more aggressive with me." *There I said it.* "I need someone who challenges my knottiness."

"Can do." Gregory reached for a tissue from the box near his ashtray. He blew his nose. I could swear I saw his eyes redden.

"So, am I hopeless?"

"Actually, I feel very hopeful for you. You want to get better and are taking care of yourself."

"Not very successfully, though."

"Don't try to get in the last word. Let's begin with your feelings. How is your anxiety level lately?"

"High." My voice rose as if I were singing opera.

"How so? Be specific."

I inhaled deeply twice and lowered my head toward my knees, feeling the blood rush to my temples. The waves of tension floated around my head, meandering, undulating in curlicue patterns with me inside, steam emitting from their heated coils.

"Do you want a glass of water?"

I shook my head. "I'm okay," I said, more out of habit than actuality.

"You know, Anita, you've had a life filled with trauma."

"I have?" I felt as if I were back in the Police Department and reading the charges for the first time: Attempted gang rape.

"Yes, you have. Your childhood was rough. Your father is a depressive, probably an alcoholic; your mother had a Dickensian childhood and is definitely disturbed. When it comes to your relationship with her, she has poor boundary control. Your brother was into his local gang growing up and now bullies your sister-in-law."

"He's not that bad."

"Okay, didn't he fight with you growing up? I mean, give you a bloody nose on more than one occasion?"

"Aren't all older brothers like that?" The words came out without me thinking and I realized I sounded just like my mother, making excuses for Ben's bad behavior.

"Let me continue with your family history. Your grandfathers died within two years when you were a child; extended relatives were killed in the Holocaust. You were sexually assaulted by someone, I suspect your grandfather, as a child, and again, more recently, by a gang. You suffer from several diseases. You were the designated "sane" one in the family and given a lot of household responsibilities. You were left alone a lot. I think this qualifies as trauma, no?"

"Not so different from many people."

"Not many that I know, and not many who come to me."

"Do you think this is why I freaked out smoking pot and why I'm practically agoraphobic?"

"Yes, I do."

"Can I be fixed?"

"Of course." Gregory stood, patted me on the head, and squeezed my hands clenched in a fist on my knee. "What you need is some quiet and uneventful time."

I closed my eyes and leaned back again. Gregory turned off the lights. I thought of the last conversation I had with Marilyn recently. I had barely recognized her voice on the phone.

"Ani?" she had breathed, sucking in air as if she were smoking a cigarette.

"Marilyn? Is that you?"

"Yes, me. I wanted to tell you something."

"Of course, sweetie. What is it?"

"I'm not doing well."

"Oh, no. What happened?"

"I don't want to get into the state of my health or lack of it. I just wanted to say thank you."

"For what?"

"For sticking with me, no matter what." She wheezed in a long whiff of air and coughed.

Finally, someone else got on the phone.

"Hello?" a woman said.

"Yes, who is this? Is Marilyn okay?" I was horrified that Marilyn was on her deathbed. *How could this be?*

"I am her visiting nurse, Violet. She is resting now. I know she wanted to talk to you."

"Can I see her?"

"Not now. She will tell you when."

"Give her a kiss for me." It was such a dumb thing to say, then.

"Where are you now?" Gregory asked again.

"I'm with my friend Marilyn. I can't stop thinking about her. As far as me having an uneventful time, I don't think that will happen for a while."

"I'm sorry for that." He turned on the lights and moved toward his bookcase, running his hand down the spine of books on the shelf adjacent to his height. "Oh, look, I just happened to find *Knots*. Maybe Laing is trying to tell us something."

"And if he is, we probably won't understand it."

"Before we go, I want to address something you said. You wanted me to be more aggressive. So, I'm going to ask you directly. Are you game?"

"I guess so. What do you want to know?" My heartbeat raced. I was hoping Gregory would look at his watch and realize we were probably running out of time. But Gregory was not Gregory today.

"A few subjects. First, let's start with your father's father. You have hinted that you were very young when he died, but you had several dreams linking him to sexual inappropriateness."

"Yes, I feel like something happened, but I can't be sure. I was maybe three or four and he used to come into my room in the country when I took a nap. I had a stuffed teddy bear that he gave me, and I think he did something with it, but I can't be sure. I just can't remember, and truthfully, I don't want to besmirch his memory based on some vague flashes. Everyone tells me he was a wonderful person."

"Okay, we won't pursue this now. But if you continue with our sessions, we will work on this, I promise. I would like to do some memory work with you, like hypnosis."

I hated the idea of being totally out of control. *That does it, I am definitely quitting.*

"But before our session ends, I want to ask you about your brother. I feel your memory here is clearer. Every time we talk about him, you tense up. You defend him, but I don't feel like you believe what you are saying, more like you're retreading old excuses."

A sudden swoosh of heat enveloped my breasts, and my head felt heavy and wobbly, like a marionette. *Oh, no, was I going to freak out like I did on pot?*

"What is it Anita? Are you unwell?"

"I don't know."

"Can you close your eyes and sit back? Try to free your mind from your anxieties."

"Easier said than done."

"Count to ten."

"Are you going to hypnotize me?"

"I can do it, if you want."

"No, I don't want to swallow a whole onion like I've seen on TV."

I knew what I should confess to Gregory. Only, I had never told anyone, and it was stuck in my throat like a giant lump of congealed fat. "My brother ..." I mumbled.

"What about him?"

"In the Catskills, where we stayed at a bungalow colony every summer, there were a lot of kids. Ben was the leader of a group of six boys, two of them, Micky and Louis, were our twin cousins, sons of my mother's oldest brother. There was a wooded area on the property with an artificial lake, more like a pond. When I was about five, Ben, who was eleven, invited me to go swimming with the boys; likely, my mother ordered him to take me. We wore bathing suits under our shorts and T-shirts. It was late in the afternoon and cloudy, so we had the place to ourselves. The boys tore off their outer clothes and jumped into the water."

I stopped abruptly, as if I were underwater with them.

"Go on," Gregory said. "Should I get you a glass of water?"

I shook my head. "The boys got out of the water, and I was still standing there with my clothes on. I was scared to go deeper without a tube. I usually swam in the bungalow pool as the bottom sloped so that there was a shallow side to hold onto.

"'Take off your clothes,' Ben urged, and I stripped to my suit. 'Come on, you can take my hand.' I followed him in, and we tiptoed around the rocks, and I lost my balance. Ben tried to hold me up and then the other boys joined us, and we formed a line, and they tugged me out farther. Somehow, I dropped under water and Ben reached down and pulled my arms and undid my bathing suit top, waving it around for all to see."

I instinctively crossed my arms over my chest. "Isn't time up yet?" I asked Gregory.

"Don't worry about it. I want you to go on. Did you remain in the water?"

"I trod water back to the shoreline and frantically looked for a towel. Before I knew it, the boys surrounded me. Louis pointed to my chest and taunted, 'Look at those little titties.' His brother continued, 'I wonder if everything about her is little. Take off your bottoms.' I shook my head, breathing heavily as the tears came." I stopped abruptly. My chest hurt. Surely, I was having a heart attack.

"Take your time," Gregory said softly.

"'Anita is a chicken!' the twins screamed in unison. My brother joined in. 'Anita is a chicken.' I don't know what possessed me, but I needed to let them know I wasn't a chicken. I slid down my wet bathing suit bottom and stood there shaking."

"Oh, no, Anita," Gregory said. "Can you continue?"

"I may as well get the whole sordid thing out. So, like I said, I stood there shaking and crying. Then Louis took his finger and traced a line of freckles on my stomach that formed a triangular pattern pointing downward. 'Look, look,' he said, 'this leads to her twat.'

"I don't remember much after that except that the boys gathered closer to watch, and they repeated the word *twat*. Then Louis took a stick and lowered the direction toward my vagina.

"Finally, Ben yelled, 'Okay, enough. Put your clothes on, you,' and then he stopped, and said, 'you twat.' The boys broke out in hysterics. I gathered my shorts and tripped as I placed my leg in the hole. I held my shirt to my chest and ran to our bungalow, not sure of the way."

"That's terrible," Gregory said. "Boys, bullying, sexual assault, all that is far too common, and I'm so sorry this happened to you."

"At least my brother stopped them."

"Here you go again, defending him. It should never have gotten that far. He didn't really protect you. Sometimes watching and not saying anything is worse than committing the crime. Your grandparents' family was in the Holocaust. You know all about the crimes of omission."

"Yes, it's true. But I was to blame, too. I was such a chicken; I shouldn't have taken off my bottoms. I egged them on."

"You were an innocent little girl."

"Maybe."

"No maybe. Did you tell your parents, your mother?"

"No, I would never tell my father. And, my mother, I was too ashamed. I was afraid she would yell at Ben and then he would punish me. I didn't tell anyone."

"That's very sad," Gregory said. This time, he blew his nose into another tissue and his voice was clogged. He got up and moved toward me and loosened his arms. I suspected he was going to hug me but thought better of it. I sat immobile.

Gregory returned to his chair, and I continued, "As he got older, my brother's crazy behavior with his 'boys' was much worse, drinking and drugs, staying out late. My parents were already beside themselves. Plus, my mother always urged me to be nice to him, and in a way cover up for the things he did, like when he didn't do his chores. She didn't want to anger my father. And then, a terrible thing happened when he was a teenager."

"What?"

"Ben was supposed to join his neighborhood friend on a drive to Coney Island. He couldn't go at the last minute because my father needed him to pick up a prescription from the pharmacy. His friend, eighteen-year-old Barry, was behind the wheel. Sixteen-year-old Tommy was in the passenger seat and his younger brother, Eddie, lay across the backseat. Police reports stated they were involved in a three-car collision. Three people died, five injured. Tommy and Eddie died at the scene. The driver, Barry, was taken to the hospital and charged with DWI. He died a week later."

"Whew, how horrible. Your brother must have been wracked with guilt, survivor's guilt."

"Yes, in his case, he just became more sadistic."

"So, you kept all this to yourself."

"Yes."

"A lot to handle for a little kid."

"The worst part was that every summer after the lake incident, one of the boys would say to me, 'Do you still have those freckles?' or call me 'twat girl'; and if the others were around, they would all laugh hysterically. I dreaded seeing them and ran away as fast as possible."

"I am so glad you are telling me about this. One thing I want to say, though, do you see a similarity between this gang of boys from your childhood and the gang who tried to rape you when you were a caseworker?"

"Wow. I didn't make the connection."

"Just think about it."

"I will."

"How do you feel now?"

"Strangely lighter."

"Good. I'm proud of you. Now, I'm afraid our time is up."

# CHAPTER 26: ARCHIE'S GIRLS

The phone rang on a Saturday morning at six. I sat up instantly. No one called me this early. Groggily, I answered, expecting that one of my parents had died.

"Ani? It's me, Marilyn." Her voice was more like a groggy whisper.

"Oh, Marilyn," I said. "Where are you? Are you okay? Your voice sounds weird."

"I'm in the hospital, have been for three weeks."

"My God, Marilyn." I stopped breathing and didn't move. I was shocked but not really surprised and resisted the urge to say, "Why didn't you tell me?"

"Yes, it was an emergency. Burst intestines. Peritonitis. It was awful."

"That sounds awful. How do you feel now?"

"Weak. But the doctors are trying a new medicine. They finally realized that I had been misdiagnosed again. My father found me new specialists at Columbia. Montefiore sent them all my records."

"Well, we know that it wasn't gout as they first suspected," I said, as if summarizing Marilyn's health could lessen her symptoms. "And we know it wasn't leukemia, thank God. But I thought they had agreed it was colitis."

"Yes, but granulomatous colitis apparently is different from the now-diagnosed ulcerative colitis, and I am now taking a new medication. Cross your fingers."

"Of course." I resisted the temptation to badmouth the medical profession, who totally screwed up my friend, even though her well-connected father found the very best people in the field. I also thought of my own intestinal problems and my upcoming schedule for another barium enema, yet another of the medical profession's tortures.

"Anyhow, Ani, what's happening with you? I feel like I have been out of touch with the ordinary world. Sorry, I didn't mean you were ordinary."

"Can I come visit you?"

"I don't know, Ani. I look terrible."

"That's hard to imagine. You are truly the most beautiful woman I know."

"Thanks, darling, but if you come, promise me you won't gaze at my looks. I lost a lot of weight since I saw you last."

"I wish I could say the same," I said, immediately sorry I opened my big mouth. Why is it, I wondered, that so many of us are awkward with sick people or those who lost a loved one?

★ ★ ★

When I entered Marilyn's room the next day at the Columbia-Presbyterian Medical Center in upper Manhattan's Morningside Heights, I first thought I had mistakenly entered the children's ward. Marilyn's body seemed dwarfed under the bedcovers. At second glance, I noticed that her formerly luscious red-brown hair was shorter, darker, and matted in sticky clumps. Her once-sparkling, sunlit-brown eyes were dulled-muddy sockets, and her shrunken face was that of an ancient skeleton. When I remembered that she had warned me not to react, I held my breath and let it out in tiny wisps.

"Marilyn," I said, leaning down to kiss her cheek.

"Ani, you came. I didn't want you to see me like this, but I'm so happy to see your beautiful face."

"*You* are the beautiful one," I hated the words spewing from my uncensored mouth. I sat on a chair next to her bed. "Are you in pain?" I asked.

She didn't answer but stared at me. I felt her eyes bore into my innermost soul, and, at that moment, she conveyed her certain knowledge that there was no hope left. I blinked as if to erase her look, and handed her an Archie comic book, featuring Betty and Veronica in the title underneath the banner "Archie's Girls." I found it in a vintage store in the Village. I remembered how she dressed as Veronica for the Gay Pride March a few years ago and walked down Seventh Avenue holding hands with Cindy, who appeared in a blonde wig as Betty.

"Oh, Ani, it looks like an original Archie."

"It's from the 1950s. I'm afraid that it has a chauvinistic tone."

"Doesn't everything?"

"True."

We leafed through the comic, and I read the bubbles on the cover as Betty says, "Boys think they're the greatest things; but it's us girls who pull the strings!" To this, Veronica replies, "They're the ones who wear the pants; but we're the ones who make them dance!"

"You said it," Marilyn laughed. As if the antics of the girls exhausted her, she closed her eyes for a few minutes, and I thought she was asleep. I was about to leave when she opened them and stared again at me, directing her gaze at my eyes.

"Thanks so much for coming," she whispered. A lone tear inched down her right cheek, settling in a hollow. She rested her hand on the comic's cover.

Afraid to get closer, I blew her a kiss with my hands and said I'd visit her again soon.

As I walked to the elevator, I hated myself for not saying, "I love you." It would have been inappropriate, I reasoned. We didn't normally say that to each other. If I had said it to her now, she would have known that I understood her penetrating gazes. But to not have said it was cowardly. In a trance, I got in the elevator and remembered the photos I saw on a recent TV special featuring the liberation of Auschwitz. Marilyn could have been there huddled in her wooden bunk wearing an oversized blue-and-white striped uniform and a torn, dirty kerchief around her head.

Two days later, I got a call from Marilyn's sister.

"Is it over?" I asked, not surprised, but still shocked.

"Yes," she choked out, informing me of the funeral arrangements.

Marilyn died from the consequences of misdiagnosed ulcerative colitis, the consequences of wasting away like a concentration-camp victim, and the consequences of an exploding intestine. Yes, it was a consequential death. She was twenty-seven years old.

★ ★ ★

Cindy and Shirley planned to meet Denise and me on the subway platform near the middle car at the Times Square station. Denise wore black silk pants and a matching jacket, her "interview" suit, as she called it. Between the lapels, she sported a white silk blouse with a ruffled front edged in black and matching buttons. This outfit was so unlike Denise's normal attire, which veered from simple, monochromatic shifts to apron-like jumper skirts for her new job as an old-age-home recreational therapist; but her fashion-conscious mother bought her the black suit to inspire more acceptable choices—and possibly influence her daughter to reapply for her former, more "stable" job at Social Security.

This was the first time Denise wore the clothes, which she reiterated on the train as she fidgeted with the annoying neck tag, and this would be the last time she would wear it. My choice was an old dress I bought for a college dance: a short-sleeved, black, Swiss-dot sailor number with white organdy trim and a long necktie. In its day, its full double-lined skirt guaranteed a graceful twirly lindy, my all-time favorite dance, but I worried that it was inappropriately festive on this hot Sunday afternoon in August.

Since Denise and I had to remain on the train, we expected to stand by the open door, stick our heads out, and look for Shirley and Cindy at the platform stop. If they weren't there, we'd get off and wait. We were concerned that we wouldn't see them in the crowds; but as the door to the Bronx-bound car opened, I immediately spotted a mixed-racial duo wearing black peering into the doorways. Shirley looked sophisticated in a tailored speckled-gray suit with diagonal black stripes, and Cindy was her elongated usual hippie self in a handmade wrinkled black peasant dress with gathered puff sleeves and a square neckline. Her nod to decorum was a plain white ribbon woven through the bangs framing her blondish bob, plus she had embroidered a red ribbon stripe with a line of tiny yellow chickens about four inches from the dress's bottom.

We waved them inside the subway car and stood, arms hanging from the triangular metal grab handles, sporting our best black-and-white inspired outfits, heads down, peering into our fleeting images in the graffiti-smeared window glass, appearing like penguins frozen on an Antarctic floe. But we weren't dressed for a Halloween parade or a frigid research-station-themed fashion show.

On the way from the subway to the funeral parlor, we four friends of Marilyn walked arm in arm, breaking apart for passersby and re-arming as if we were interlocking puzzle pieces snapping into our gouged holes. When we were a block away, I withdrew my arms and stopped.

"What?" Shirley asked. "There's nobody coming."

"I know," I said, my voice cracking. "I don't want to go inside. How am I going to read my eulogy with Marilyn's father, her sister, her brother, her aunt, and her boyfriend, Clinton, staring at me in the front row? I just can't do it."

"You can."

"Do you want me to read it?" Denise asked, knowing I was terrified of public speaking, as well as too upset to be coherent.

"Didn't Marilyn's sister call you and ask you to compose a eulogy?" Cindy asked.

"Yes," I said. "She will be giving one and asked me to write something. But she didn't say I had to read it. If she can do it, who am to refuse? I just don't want to freak out, especially with Marilyn's loved ones there. They've had enough sorrow to last a lifetime."

"You can do it," Shirley said again, putting her arm around me. "Marilyn thought the world of you. You were her true friend. You know she didn't make friends easily."

"I know. I just can't believe she's dead. I mean, who dies at twenty-seven? She will never have the life she was supposed to have."

"Who says that she was supposed to live more than twenty-seven years? Maybe that's what she was supposed to have. Maybe that's what God intended for her."

I knew Shirley was a Baptist and maybe believing that God had a plan comforted her, but I was a devout atheist, a living oxymoron. At this moment, I wished that something could console me; all I could feel was the utter devastation of Marilyn's death. All I could see was her gaunt, ashen face, her racoon-mask eyes fixating on me, daring me to live her life for her.

# CHAPTER 27:
# KILLING ME SOFTLY

### August 25, 1974

My shoes felt like antique hand-forged irons, and I heaved each foot to make the next step. My heartbeat quickened, and I felt dizzy. *Please, God*, I begged, forgetting I was a heathen.

*Don't let me faint here across the street from the chapel.*

Somehow, I made it up the steps and through the door. There was a sign with Marilyn's name, directing us into a waiting room.

"I won't go to the viewing room," Cindy said. "I want to remember Marilyn as the gorgeous woman I knew."

"She was cremated," I said. I could understand why people believed in burning the dead, but after seeing the Dachau crematorium, and suspecting that those relatives who hadn't been murdered in village massacres were probably gassed in Treblinka and thrown into large cremation pits, I cringed at the idea of the normal practice. I imagined Marilyn lying on a conveyor belt, shoved into the furnaces and incinerated. I could almost smell her exploding flesh disintegrating into ash and see her bones reduced to slivers. I ran to find a ladies' room where I threw up in the toilet bowl.

We floated into the waiting area, propelled by several people pushing behind us. Marilyn's father and his sister, Esther, were sitting on a couch; I had only met them once when they came to Theoretical Press to take Marilyn out to lunch. At the time, I was struck by their bigger-than-life appearance. Marilyn's dad was about six feet four and had white hair and a white goatee; her aunt was also tall, reaching six feet in high heels. She had dyed super-black hair, though she wore no makeup I could discern. They seemed to be sophisticated actors, yet I knew her dad was a lawyer, and her aunt worked in the Kitchen Department of Sears. Now sitting, they seemed old and shrunken; her father's beard was straggly, and her aunt's hair was laced with gray roots. They both hunched as they spoke and sucked in their slackened cheeks as if they had been on a starvation diet to match Marilyn's deterioration.

Marilyn's older sister, Meg, was visibly pregnant, and stood with her brother, George, whom I recognized from a photo, and another man who must have been Meg's husband. They were hugging two elderly women. Clinton, Marilyn's boyfriend, rushed to us and embraced me. His unshaved face was scratchy as he brushed my cheeks.

"Oh Ani, I am so glad to see a familiar face." His voice was clogged with tears. He mopped his eyes with a handkerchief. "Sorry, I've been holding it together up to now."

"Let it out," I whispered, though I wished he would calm down, as I couldn't summon a comforting word.

"Ani, thanks so much for coming," Meg said, and we hugged. "This is my husband, David. David, this is Marilyn's good friend, Ani, and her other friends. Sorry, I don't know your names."

I introduced Shirley, Denise, and Cindy, and we all mumbled our "sorrys." I nodded to David and said, "Nice to meet you," as if we were at a party. If that wasn't the dumbest thing to say.

"You have your piece?" Meg asked me.

I nodded again.

"We'll call you in the middle if that's okay with you."

"Whatever is good for everyone."

In a "receiving" line, we swept by Marilyn's father, brother, and aunt and gently patted their hands, again murmuring our sorrows. They nodded. It seemed to be all anyone could muster.

Once inside the chapel, we stopped by the door.

"Let's sit in the back," Cindy said.

"But you should sit closer to the front," Shirley said, turning to me. "After all, you're giving a eulogy."

"You all have to sit with me," I said, my body bordering on catatonia at the thought of separating from the three of them.

"Okay, let's aim for the center," Denise said, always the mediator.

Marilyn's father was the first to speak. At the lectern, he recalled how he shared his love of painting with Marilyn and how his daughter's well exceeded his own talent, and how when Marilyn was about six, they built a dollhouse and painted each room a different color with handmade furnishings representing exotic countries. He stopped abruptly, as if he had lost the oxygen in his lungs. Then, replacing a few words, he recited the Dylan Thomas poem, "Do Not Go Gentle into That Good Night," written for Dylan's father.

At the last stanza, he replaced the words "my father" with "my darling daughter":

And you, my darling daughter, there on the sad height,

Curse, bless, me now with your fierce tears, I pray.

Do not go gentle into that good night.

Rage, rage against the dying of the light.

And he repeated, "Rage, rage against the dying of the light."

The sobbing in the audience was audible, and I felt like a knife sliced across my throat, cutting off the air. Meg and

George related childhood stories and recited passages from *The Little Prince* and *Winnie the Pooh*. With both staring directly into the audience, and I thought searching for me, I lowered my pocketbook to the floor and gathered my typewritten pages, readying for my rise. Instead, they swiveled to the other side of the audience, and a tall man, a younger version of Marilyn's father, walked down the aisle, climbed the stairs to the stage, and sat on the piano bench. I had not noticed the black Steinway before, instead focusing on the lectern at the base of the stage. Meg introduced the man as her uncle Robby. In the meantime, George suddenly appeared next to the piano with a Martin acoustic guitar strapped around his shoulders. Robby did what everyone seemed to do on this sad day: he nodded. Meg moved to the piano and parked on a stool. Clinton joined the group and looped his arm around Meg. Robby played the introductory notes to "Killing Me Softly with His Song," while Meg, in a Roberta Flack soundalike, paused on the words "dark despair." She continued the lyrics and Clinton bent to the mic and they harmonized during the last stanza.

As they sang, I closed my eyes and imagined Marilyn wearing a hippie headband across her forehead, her hair flowing in a fiery mop-like crown like Janis Joplin, playing her electric guitar as she had so often accompanied Denise and Cindy in our Christopher Street singalongs. She would plug in her Gibson, unafraid to electrify the air as my parquet floor reverberated with the rhythm, and I would be grateful that we lived on the ground floor with nothing but the Hudson River rats beneath our boards. Even then, Marilyn defied the convention of our small female group, unafraid to yell her guts out, but so withdrawn without her instrument. And now, with her family onstage, her father, aunt, and uncle in the front row nodding profusely, I realized that her multiple talents were so inborn that she took them for granted, not taking credit for how uniquely she soared.

"What an act to follow," Cindy whispered to me.

"I know."

This time, Meg stepped back to the lectern, held the microphone, and called my name. I had to go on. How my legs carried me down the aisle, I had no idea, but I placed my speech on the shelf, adjusted down the microphone, and scanned the audience for Shirley, not the only Black woman but nearly so. I saw her beatific smile and read "A Poem to Marilyn," which I directed to her as if she were alive.

I read on and mechanically turned the pages. I looked up and focused on Marilyn's father in the front row. He was weeping and resting his head on his sister's shoulder. I could not continue. *Who was I to bare my soul? What was my pain compared to his?* But if I left the stage then and there, I would forever be sorry. I continued to read, honoring the characters she loved to recite: Winnie the Pooh, the Mikado, Babar the Elephant; recalling the causes she took to her heart, from Vietnam to Attica; appreciating her talents in writing and art. I labeled her "A free spirit/Way before it was fashionable," and called her both Alice in Wonderland and Angela Davis, and mostly herself, "at all times."

I read another page, and when I uttered the last words, "I love you," the words I should have said to her on our last day together, my voice was barely a croak. Cindy and Shirley each ran down the aisle and grabbed an arm and led me back to the padded wood pew. Denise whispered that my poem was "amazing and would have made Marilyn proud." Shirley said I brought Marilyn back to life. I craned my head into my lap and wept, knowing that what Shirley had just said was impossible.

Clinton returned to the stage, moved the microphone and adjusted it, and sat on a stool. He pressed into the mouthpiece and said, "This was recorded by Judy Collins and written by Leonard Cohen. It's called, 'Hey, That's No Way to Say Goodbye.'"

And then he sang how he loved Marilyn in the morning and added his own description of her wild red hair upon the pillow. Clinton interrupted the song, reached behind him, and lifted a large posterboard facedown from the floor. It was a black-and-white blowup of Marilyn, her lips closed but forming a slight smile as if she knew something important about us and was keeping it to herself. Clinton resumed singing, this time staring at the photo and ending, "Your amber eyes cloud with tears," and then he repeated the song title.

★ ★ ★

We stumbled out of the chapel while several people yanked my arm and murmured how much they loved my poem. Once on the street, we strolled a few blocks toward the subway. On the corner, there was a darkened window with a yellow neon-light sign called Patty's Pub.

"Let's go inside," Cindy said.

"I can use a drink," Denise said.

"I'm game," Shirley said.

They dragged me inside the dimly lit bar. My friends ordered beers, and I asked for a daiquiri, the only cocktail besides Brandy Alexander that I had enjoyed. The bartender, a double of Hoss Cartwright from *Bonanza*, said, "A what?"

"A daiquiri," I repeated with a question: "You know, the drink with rum and lime juice?"

"I know, girlie. You don't have to tell me what's in the drink. I just have little call for it here in the Bronx. Maybe you gals came from somewhere else."

"Yeah, we're from the moon," Cindy said.

Hoss placed my drink, complete with a slice of lime slit into the cocktail glass, on a tray with the beers and brought it to our small round table. Without hesitation, I drank the entire glass and motioned to "Hoss" with two fingers. I got up to examine the Rowe Ami jukebox, the song titles arranged in rows above the screen that displayed a psychedelic slideshow of whirling designs. I selected my three songs for a quarter and slung over the machine while Janis belted out "Me and Bobby McGee," and I sipped my second daiquiri.

I gyrated to the music and soon a mustachioed man in black leather pants tapped me on the shoulder. He pulled my arm onto the tiny stage, which was more of a linoleum square, and we did a tight slow dance. He smelled of sweat and whiskey, and I could feel the bulge in his pants as he ground into me.

"Hoss, hit me again," I yelled, and he placed the drink into my raised hand, which rained down my hair like iridescent dewdrops. I realized that my bladder was bursting and excused myself, but my partner held onto my hand and followed me down the hallway to the ladies' room. Before the door, he took my drink and slid it onto a nearby side table. With his slobbering mouth over mine, his hands lifted my dress, and he found my panty lines and slipped his finger into my vagina, pinning me to the wall with his leathery body. I wanted to get away from this strange man, but I longed for his finger to continue circling my clitoris. I felt a sharpness and assumed his nail was long and jagged. I unsnapped his fly. "Fuck me," I whispered. "Fuck me."

"I want to fuck your insides out," he responded.

"Ani, what are you doing?" Cindy cried. "Get away from her." She slammed between us and pulled me away.

"No, I want this," I slurred.

"No, you don't," Cindy said. She yanked me into the ladies' room and pushed me into a stall. "Get yourself together, Ani. Do you really want to fuck a complete stranger on the day of Marilyn's funeral?"

"Yes," I said.

"No, you don't."

I rolled down my panties and let go of my bladder. Once outside the stall, Cindy swabbed my face with a wet paper towel.

I didn't recall much of what followed except that before we returned to our table, I said, to Cindy, "Please don't say anything to Denise and Shirley, especially to Shirley, about that man in the black leather."

"Don't worry," she said, "my lips are sealed."

Somehow, we found a yellow checkered taxi willing to go to Manhattan and tumbled in, three of us squashed on the backseat with me in the middle and Denise on the jump seat, keeping an eagle eye on my slurring speech and lolling neck. I must have passed out because I remembered nothing of the ride, and the next conscious moment I had was lying on my Beautyrest mattress in my bedroom on Christopher Street. Denise told me the next day that we had to stop near the ramp to the Major Deegan Expressway so I could vomit. I was mortified, sure that Shirley, who had once confided to me that her first husband had been an alcoholic and that her boyfriend, Charlie, was also showing signs, and she had no more patience with lushes. Denise assured me that Shirley understood and knew that drinking was not my habit or had not been my habit.

Mostly, I was ashamed of how I behaved on a day that I was honoring my friend, Marilyn. What would she have thought of me? I knew that she smoked pot and had an occasional drink, but I also thought of her agreement with Shirley at one of our consciousness-raising meetings about addictive behavior and how it was not only self-destructive but dooming to a relationship. Drugs, she said, were okay to enhance an encounter but not to overwhelm it.

What I was realizing was that when someone young died, every word she had uttered became engraved in metal or wood, inked over, and printed on a scroll to be unfurled like a torah, portions read, re-read, argued about, but always revered. Marilyn knew this, I was sure.

# CHAPTER 28: MOVING SOUTH



It was time for change. Though Denise and I had been room-mates since 1967, we continually faced threats by interlopers, namely boyfriends. This was for me, the worst thought, that Denise and I, who never had a fight, could fester serious resentments. No. Not us.

The major issue was sleeping arrangements in a one-bedroom apartment. First, Arthur stayed over at least five nights a week. Often, I gave Denise and Arthur the bedroom and slept on the living-room convertible sofa, uncomfortable that it was. It was easier to have access to the rest of the apartment. Then, when I got sexually involved with Sergio, we had very little privacy if we slept on the couch, as Arthur usually left early in the morning and Denise was a light sleeper and heated milk in the middle of the night.

Sergio's best friend from Italy, Giovanni, was also an intern at Elmhurst Hospital in Queens. They shared a one-bedroom apartment near the hospital. Sometimes, I slept at Sergio's place when Giovanni was on night duty; and sometimes Sergio slept in my apartment when Arthur wasn't there.

Giovanni was expecting his Italian fiancée to arrive, which would further complicate everyone's lives.

Denise and I had talked about one of us moving out but seemed unable to advance this conversation into action. Then one night after work as we were preparing dinner, thankfully without our boyfriends, Denise said, "Ani, we have to discuss our apartment situation."

"I know," I said, feeling a sharp pain shoot through my stomach.

Post-college, I soon moved to Christopher Street with Denise. I had never lived alone. I dreaded making decisions about apartment purchases or repairs without consulting Denise, and I depended on her rational common-sense advice about my daily work problems. She was the one person who understood my deep need for creative expression and my inability to find satisfaction as a copywriter catering to clients' needs. She often said to me, "Ani, if you're so frustrated, why not write your own stories? Your poems, essays, and even your creative pieces from college are so wonderful." My answers to her were usually preceded by "I don't have enough time," or "Nobody but you would be interested in reading my work."

"What do you want to say?" I asked Denise, regaining my outward composure.

"I am ready to look for my own apartment. I think one of us should move out. The sooner the better."

I knew she was right. This time, I had to face it. But I couldn't explain why her words felt like the biggest rejection, worse than the ones I imagined getting if I ever wrote fictional stories and sent them to magazines.

"I guess you're right," I said, suppressing what I wanted to say, which was, "Do you no longer love me?"

"Unless *you* want to look and move out," she said.

To show that I was not the chicken shit I was, I said, "Okay, I'll look through the *Village Voice* for apartments." The voice inside of me said, "How can you leave Christopher Street?"

★ ★ ★

Within weeks, I found a tiny apartment on Thompson Street, between Spring and Prince, south of Houston Street, a few blocks beyond the border of Greenwich Village. The area was called SoHo, south of Houston. I knew the neighborhood because my mother worked at a commercial ink-supply company in an industrial loft on West Broadway, and her famous client was Andy Warhol, who bought supplies for his silk-screening work. SoHo also overlapped Little Italy, and the inhabitants included older Italians, as well as artists enticed by the lower rents of industrial lofts. Since the district was designated a landmark in 1973, it was rapidly becoming gentrified, as former West Villagers were attracted to the cobblestone streets and large commercial buildings and the growing art scene.

I was lucky to find an apartment on the third floor of an old, white brick four-story building sandwiched between similar nondescript low-rise dwellings. The apartment itself was the same size as the building's studios, except someone sliced into the living room to create a miniscule bedroom, only large enough for a double bed. When I bought a new bed, I stood under the mattress and pivoted it into the room. I was stuck underneath until I pushed with all my might and turned the mattress to fit snugly into the rectangular space, with literally no room to spare.

Otherwise, the apartment had an open galley kitchen and a living room not much larger than the bedroom. I packed the room with my parents' old brown upholstered chairs, stuffing exposed, and my former twin mattress from Christopher Street served as the living-room couch.

The worst part was that the ceiling between the bathroom and living room had a storage compartment, and when I opened it, roaches literally ran down my head. The wallpaper was white with black-flocked designs that looked like spiders. With all this, the rent was twenty-five dollars cheaper than Christopher Street at $140, and I grabbed it. Bugs and all, this was mine, and I got over my feelings of rejection from Denise. It turned out that I enjoyed my solitary home life.

★ ★ ★

Now that my mother worked two blocks away, and unlike her surprise visit to me when I lived on Christopher Street, she called me at least once a week, usually on a Wednesday, to meet after work for a quick dinner at the English bar and grill near my place before she took the long subway ride back to Rockaway. Occasionally, if my father was helping at his friend's shoe business on Duane Street, he would pick her up at the restaurant, always after we finished eating. He still never came up to my apartment, although he often ran into the restaurant to use the bathroom.

One Wednesday, I heard a knock on my door shortly after I arrived home from work. It was my mother who was hyperventilating, sweat beads collecting on her forehead.

"Mom, what are you doing here?" I asked after leading her to my old bed that acted as my couch in the living room. Then she excused herself and went to the bathroom. I was sure when she turned on the light there, the roaches scattered. When she returned to the "couch," I brought her a glass of water. A roach crawled on the kitchen counter.

She inspected the glass and wiped the rim with her sweater sleeve.

"It's clean," I said.

"Sorry, I tried to call, but I was already on the street when I decided to come, and the phone in the booth was busted. I thought maybe you'd like to grab a bite. Your father is picking me up at the restaurant at seven."

Fortunately, I had made my bed and took out the garbage. I was expecting Sergio that night after his hospital shift. I was only too happy to leave with my mother as I could see her eyeing my place with disappointed lip-smacking tsk-tsking. On the way to the restaurant, she offered to buy me a real sofa so that "nobody has to sit on that old lumpy bed." She had never offered to buy anything for my Christopher Street apartment, I think because she never forgave me for living with the letter-writing traitor, Denise. I declined her offer even though most of my hand-me-down furniture was way too big for my tiny boxlike apartment. But they were now mine, and I was basically content.

That is until Sergio had announced a new wrinkle in our relationship. This happened after I was on my own for only three months.

"Giovanni's fiancée, Lucia, is coming to America in two weeks."

"Oh, that's nice," I said, not thinking.

"Nice, yes. But the apartment is too small for three. I was thinking. Can I move in with you?"

"What?" I said, even though I had heard his words.

"Move in with you. It will be temporary until I find a place."

"Oh, temporary, okay. But you know I haven't been on my own for long."

"I know," he said in a sad voice. Clearly, he had expected a better reaction from me.

★ ★ ★

That weekend, Cindy moved in for three days. I had gotten her a freelance proofreading job at Happy Frogs for our new catalog, and she didn't want to commute from her apartment in Staten Island, where she still lived with Jack. I think she really needed an escape from Jack, and I welcomed her, even though it would leave me only a week after she left to enjoy my apartment without another person.

To celebrate our time without men, we invited Denise to join us. When she entered the apartment, she cradled a package covered with striped wrapping paper.

"This is for you, Ani. It was the best housewarming present I could think of."

I tore open the paper and held in my breath. "Oh, my God. I just leafed through this last week at the 8th Street Bookshop. I was going to go back this weekend and buy it."

I held up the large softcover book, *Our Bodies, Ourselves,* and pressed it to my chest.

"This is the best present ever."

Denise grabbed it from me. "I have spent hours reading my copy and took it upon myself to underline certain passages in yours, though I haven't read it all yet. Just to skim it is enough to realize how groundbreaking it is."

"Wow," Cindy said. "I remember the amazing review in the *New York Times*. I can't wait to read it."

We settled on the floor of the living room, gathering the bed/couch bolsters for support. Denise opened the book at the beginning. "Okay, just to whet your appetites, listen to this, in the first chapter called 'Our Changing Sense of Self.'"

"I love it already," Cindy said.

Denise read a few paragraphs explaining how unlike the promises we were fed as girls, most women were not totally fulfilled by marriage, motherhood, and/or a typically feminine job. To remedy this, women needed space to discover who they were apart from primary relationships in order to become fully functioning adults.

"Wow," I said. "This is straight out of our CR discussions."

Denise continued: "The chapter puts out the purpose of the contributor thinking: 'to figure out how we wanted to change the ways we thought and felt about ourselves … what it means to be female.'"

Denise flipped through the pages and showed us the photos of women with children, with power tools, playing a violin, discussing issues, taking self-defense classes, at abortion clinics; gay women; older women. There were in-depth drawings of birth control and stages of pregnancy.

"Get this, Ani, women said they found it took a long while to feel comfortable and trusting in a group."

"Finally, someone recognizes this," I yelled. I felt as elated as if I had just published my own book.

"There's so much about our repressed adolescences, using words like 'suppressing,' and 'constricted,' and 'anger.' And listen, one woman said that her parents saved money for her brother to go to college and not for her."

"Denise, this is exactly what happened to you." I shook my head in disbelief.

"Unfuckinbelievable," Cindy said.

"Maybe someone had a tape recorder at our meetings," Denise said.

Cindy lifted the book from Denise's lap and scanned the table of contents and fingered the pages. "This is amazing. All the subjects we talked about in our CR group: menstruation, birth control, abortion, contraception. And wow, actual photos and drawings of the female reproductive organs. I have to study these."

"Cindy, you'll have plenty of time to read this while you're here. I grabbed the book from her and clasped it to my chest. I was thinking of putting it under my pillow like I used to do with my college textbooks.

"I'm going to call Sonia and Bonnie to buy a copy, and xerox some pages at work and give them to Shirley when I see her at our weekly lunch. We must consult them for our future meetings."

"What I liked the most," Denise said, peeling it from my chest and caressing the cover, "this book gives us the tools to take control of our physical and mental health."

* * *

By now, I had established a routine and Cindy accompanied me on my neighborhood errands after work. We stopped at the local bodega at the end of my street for fruit and vegetables and cold cuts. We bought freshly ground chopped meat at the butcher's around the corner and entered the lime-green storefront of Vesuvio's Bakery on Prince Street where we purchased sliced Italian bread. Finally, I felt comfortable greeting the local vendors, and calming down the phobias I had developed for such a long time following my attack in Brooklyn. It felt good to plan my own meals, buy my own ingredients, and even prepare for company, this time for Cindy.

We gathered around the card table I jammed in the few feet of empty space fronting the kitchen area, and ate what was before us: bread, cheese, Greek olives, sliced tomatoes, and washed down with cheap wine. A Joan Baez album was playing on the hi-fi.

"This is nice, Ani," Cindy said.

"Yes."

"And what's nice is that it's just us girls."

"You mean us women."

"Sorry, it's been a while since our CR meeting to remind me of the proper lingo. After studying *Our Bodies*, I should know better."

"By the way, are you still going to group therapy?" I asked.

"Yes, Gregory is keeping me there, gratis. We aren't telling the clinic. The others don't know."

"You mean he's encouraging you to lie? What a shrink!"

"You know he's a sweetheart. He cares about us, I mean, as people."

"I know. I threatened to leave him several times. But I will soon. Especially now that I have this place on my own. I have to be more careful with money."

"At least you have your own place, and it's in a great location."

"I'm lucky. Tell me, how is the group doing?"

"Oh, the same old, same old. Barbara challenged me again for speaking about Jack. She wanted to know why I stay with someone who has no job and has substance issues."

"Why do you?"

"Oh, not *you*, too."

"Okay, I'll let up. I am glad not to hear from Barbara anymore."

"She got on your case a lot about not speaking. Can I ask you why you never really opened up when you seem to have no trouble in our CR group?"

"I've tried to analyze this with Gregory. You may or may not have noticed that in the CR group I can talk about a topic and I'm happy to bring up any personal details. No one challenges me if I don't answer. I feel supported by non-critical people. I am interested in exploring feminist issues. For group therapy, it was different."

"How so?"

"Well, I keep a lot of personal stuff to myself, as you know. I don't want to dredge it up with people whom I consider strangers. I haven't even told Gregory all of it by now, though he pretty much has guessed most of it."

"Would you tell me? Or Denise?"

"Of course, I trust you both. It's me, I can't explain it. I've always felt that I have secrets that I would never tell anyone, that I am an expert at fooling people into thinking I am normal."

"Do you think that you have fooled your best friends, too?"

"No, not consciously. My mother always complained that I have too many friends. She says that when I was living at my parents', Denise called me so many times a day, even when she took a crap."

"I don't think of Denise that way. She is very sane and controlled. Besides, she always complains of being constipated."

We laughed and drank some more wine.

"I have a joint. Do you want?" Cindy asked.

"Oh, no. Not since my pot freakout. I won't touch it."

"Okay, I won't push it. Do you mind if I smoke?"

"No, of course not." Again, I lied to one of my friends. I minded. I minded. I minded. I didn't trust myself around secondhand smoke. In my new life, as a single woman in my own apartment, I had to stay in control. I just had to.

# CHAPTER 29:
## ONE VALISE TO STAY

Winter 1976

One night after the new year, the bell rang from the down-stairs vestibule intercom, and I had the immediate thought that it was my mother again with one of her "surprise" visits. But it was after ten and I knew she had probably been snuggling in her own attached twin bed in Rockaway by then. I couldn't understand the voice from the intercom, but buzzed back any-way, even though a woman on the first floor had recently been followed home by a pervert, and she managed to call the police, who arrived before the man got past the mailboxes. I heard enough of the voice to assume it was Sergio, though he had said that he would be on call at the hospital.

I was right.

Sergio appeared at my doorstep with an old brown tweed valise with leather corner reinforcements. "I haven't found an apartment yet," he announced as if I didn't know. He spent all his free time at my place. "And, besides, Giovanni is getting married next month."

What that had to do with his living situation, I didn't know. Unless Giovanni was planning to give up his apartment, Sergio was still technically homeless.

Sergio's belongings already took up two drawers in my dresser. He had been living with me two months after he promised to look for another place. Now, I realized that he never planned to go anywhere else.

"What does this mean?" I asked, even though I knew his answer.

"I want to stay with you, roaches and all."

Maybe it was the last words that got me. Sergio looked like a lost boy, wearing his father's oversized jacket, lugging the same valise he brought from Italy. He wanted to be with me. Did he mean permanently? He was adorable and funny and smart. *What more could I want?*

I was twenty-nine, and, as far as my family was concerned, bordering on spinsterhood. When many of my mother's siblings and children joined us to celebrate my great aunt Anna's ninetieth birthday at her retirement home, I brought Sergio. Aunt Anna repeatedly asked me why I wasn't married, and I answered, "Nobody's asked me." That didn't shut her up, and the next time she asked during the party, I said I was a lesbian. Overhearing, my mother yelled, "She's only kidding." Either my announcement embarrassed my mother, or she hoped that Sergio and I would get married and put an end to the speculation.

Throughout the day, Aunt Anna never remembered Sergio's name and called him "doctor." To her, that was even better than being Jewish. As we hugged goodbye, she took me aside and said, "Anitaleh, I'm just living to see you married." I answered, "Then, why would I want to kill you?"

Without saying much, I lifted Sergio's valise and placed it on the bedroom mattress. Unsnapping the clasp, I opened the cover and reached inside, lifting a stack of his shirts lying on the top. I unfolded each one, slipped in a hanger, and hung it in a newly created space in the far right of my already bulging closet. Before I finished unpacking, Sergio grabbed my waist from behind and dragged me on the mattress, which was strewn with crisscrossed wire hangers. He pressed me down, and I felt the cold wires dig into my back. He began little kisses on a downward path toward my pubic bone. "Ouch," I complained at first, and then hummed as his lips continued. "Wait a second. I'm getting my diaphragm," I said and hopped off the bed.

Afterwards, back in the bathroom, I removed the diaphragm that was dripping with jelly and sperm. As I washed it under the faucet, I noticed a tiny hole in the center of the crater. I had stopped taking birth control pills a few months before because my gynecologist was concerned about the high estrogen content of the extra doses I took to control my bleedings. So, I didn't have much experience with the diaphragm. But I knew that a hole of any size was not good.

I kept this to myself. I didn't want to ruin Sergio's first night of "official" homecoming, and I hoped the rest of the diaphragm did its job. Besides, I was not at the most fertile time of my cycle. On this night, I also didn't ask Sergio to leave and avoided discussion of our future. Instead, I made another decision. The next day, I handed my resignation to Edward, who simply said, "not surprised." Maybe that was similar to people who move to another house when they are on the verge of divorce. One definite change would be enough.

★ ★ ★

It wasn't easy finding another job. I had been at Happy Frogs over four years and about the same time at Theoretical; I certainly had enough experience as a copywriter in the publishing business. At both places, writing became rote and formulaic. I longed for something more expressive and personal, so I accepted freelance assignments, hoping to enhance my skills and opportunities. I edited manuscripts for a publisher of craft books, created an employee newsletter for an insurance company, and researched travel brochures for physicians attending conventions in exotic locales. Again, Denise marveled at my ability to work on unfamiliar material. I reminded her what Truman Capote once said about Jack Kerouac: "That's not writing, that's typing." In my case, "This wasn't writing, it was fooling."

During one job interview, filling in for a reporter on sick leave at a community newspaper, the publisher handed me a legal pad and ordered, "Pretend that you're writing an article about me. I want you to interview me now."

"What?" I said. "Now?"

"Yes," he replied. "I'll give you fifteen minutes and then write it up, type it, and hand me the finished product."

I had little time to freeze and focused on his unconventional yet direct style, asking him what he enjoyed about being a boss and what he looked for in an employee. This seemed to loosen him up, and I wrote a lively feature. I got the job, which lasted for a few weeks. I admired this man and felt it was one of the best learning experiences I had, not necessarily as a writer but as an interviewer who had to think quickly on her feet.

Even though Sergio now contributed to the apartment's upkeep, my savings were running low, and I needed a full-time job. While commuters were traveling from the boroughs to Manhattan, I reversed course and went against traffic. I had two potential interviews, one in Long Island City and the other in Jamaica. Stupidly, I thought Long Island City was on Long Island, far from Manhattan, and went for the interview in Jamaica, which turned out to be a longer commute. The job title was the Assistant Director of Public Relations for the Queens Borough Public Library, located at the main branch.

Despite the long subway ride to Jamaica, I took the job. My duties included writing press releases, brochures, and newsletters advertising the borough's events and branch openings, as well as new book reviews for the entire system. I was also supervising several employees, including clerks and artists. It seemed like a responsible position, with the potential of working with other city agencies.

On the second day at the job, my boss handed me a Minolta 35 mm camera and assigned me to take photos of a branch opening attended by the very short Mayor Abe Beame and some very tall library officials. With the true meaning of learning on the job, I inched backward and framed a perfectly acceptable wide-angle shot. So inspired, I used a local school's darkroom to develop the black-and-white film and prints. There was nothing like the thrill of seeing an image emerge from the developing solution and manipulating time and light exposure to get the picture just right. This was a new avenue of creativity for me.

I longed for this type of freedom in my personal writing. As an adolescent, I would creep around my house in the middle of the night and grab a snack, usually cold leftover pizza, return to my room, and scribble my innermost feelings into a journal entry or depressing poem. As I aged, I wrote short stories and essays, most of which featured words I summoned from the dictionary and emotions copied from my daily soap operas. I collected these pieces in an old carton and never looked at them again.

In my jobs, I manipulated words; I responded to clients' needs, but *I* was missing. When people asked me what I did for a living, I never said I was a writer/editor, though this profession appeared on my income tax forms.

# CHAPTER 30: OVER THE MOON

Motivated by the desire to avoid literary fraudulence, I registered for a fiction writing course at the New School, taught by Broderick Sudberry, a famous children's author and novelist. He was in his fifties, portly, and handsome, with side-parted, long silver-fringed hair. I walked into the classroom and sat in the back. Broderick had a warm and expressive voice with strong opinions about stylistic icons such as Hemingway and Faulkner. He wrote magazine pieces about the publishing world and his friendships with literary luminaries. I was excited to be in such distinguished hands.

Broderick had a predictable routine. He would select an assigned sketch or exercise, ask the student to read, and dissect it, normally with a supercilious tone as the poor victim turned red and faked giggles. Early in the semester, Broderick called for our next assignment: a fully realized short story with believable characters.

That night, I returned to my tiny, roach-infested apartment and settled into my parents' former brown easy chair. Sergio was on call at the hospital. I balanced a yellow legal pad over my knee and jotted down notes for my short story. I wanted my characters to a have real-life conflict, to write what "I know." Before long, I described my imagined breakup with Sergio.

Avoiding the violation of his privacy, I changed Sergio's name and hair color.

Within a few hours, I wrote the first pages and sketched out the plot. The fictitious Randy and Annie became as real to me as the black-and-white photo of Sergio and me framed on the bookcase shelf. Before the next class, a familiar terror from college courses and group therapy gripped me: public speaking. I wrote on a yellow note and stapled it to the cover of my story. It said, "Please don't ask me to read this aloud."

The following week, Broderick rifled through the stack of stories on his desk and pulled out one. I recognized the attached yellow note; my heartbeat increased, and my mouth soured with bile. Sure enough, he said, "I will read this student's story. She doesn't want to read it herself." I was certain he was staring at me. I slumped into my chair and lowered my face.

As Broderick read, his voice soared on polysyllabic words and on flowery similes. He delivered his finest comic impressions of the dialogue, showing fake anger whenever Randy spoke and whiny tones for the female protagonist, namely me. He was like my old boss at Happy Frogs, who got pleasure at making fun of my nasal Brooklyn accent.

After finishing the story, he wrote the characters' names on the blackboard. Under each name, he asked "volunteers" to name personality traits, offering the first one for Randy as "weak." The rest of the lesson used my story as an example of overwriting, among other excesses. At the end of the class, Broderick called the students to pick up their stories on the way out. I was the last on line.

"Mr. Sudberry," I said. "Why did you select my story to critique if it was so terrible?"

"Because it was the best in the class."

That was little comfort as I went home and inspected his circled and underlined words. His handwritten comments were profuse. Not one of them was complimentary. That was it, I thought, shoving the story in the bottom of the cardboard box that contained old poems and journals.

* ★ *

The next morning, the phone rang when I was about to leave for work. It was later than usual as I had been throwing up in the toilet. It was my gynecologist, who said what I'd expected. I was six weeks pregnant. Surprising myself, I was happy. A baby, growing inside of me. A baby with Sergio's large gray/gold eyes and shiny dark-brown hair, and my button nose and sense of humor.

This time, I called Sergio immediately and reached his pager. By the time he answered, I was in my office. "What's up?" he asked with concern. I normally didn't call him at this hour.

"I want to have a special dinner tonight, at Arturo's."

"Oh, what's the occasion?"

"I'll tell you in person."

"Are you pregnant?" he asked, almost yelling.

'What? Did the gynecologist call you?"

"Of course not."

"How did you know?"

"I heard you retching the other night. I put two and two together and got three!"

"Brilliant," I said.

"They don't call me doctor for nothing."

"Really? Are you happy?"

"Over the moon," he said. "We'll talk soon. I love you."

"Ditto," I said, feeling like I did when Sergio was driving too fast and taking a turn without signaling. What was I doing?

When I got to Arturo's, Sergio was already sitting at a booth in the adjoining room. There were a dozen red roses in a tall white vase in the middle of the table.

"How did you have time to get these?" I asked.

"You forget that I work in a hospital, and people visit the flower shop."

He leaned in and kissed me, tasting of alcohol. He quizzed me about every word the doctor had said.

"As I was leaving his office, Dr. Caravaggio said, 'I know your son will be a happy little fellow.'"

"I was barely six weeks pregnant; I wondered how he could know already. 'How do you know it's a boy?' I asked, remembering all the old wives' tales about the shape of a uterus or the direction of the baby's bump that determined sex."

"What did he say?" Sergio asked.

"He said, 'Doesn't everyone want a boy?' I was shocked. But then he's from Sicily and is ready to retire. He's too old or too obtuse to be politic. At that moment, I decided to change doctors, hoping to find a female gynecologist."

"I'll ask around for one," Sergio said.

"He told me to make six months of appointments before I left his office."

"What did you do?"

"I made my way into the receptionist area and turned around, and said, 'Oh, Dr. Caravaggio, my husband and I want a girl.'"

I anticipated that Sergio would be upset that I disrespected his colleague, a fellow Italian immigrant who helped him settle into this country. Instead, he surprised me. "While I would be happy at any sex, I'd be extra happy if it's a girl."

# CHAPTER 31: THE NEWS IS OUT

I remained in Sudberry's fiction class. I refused to give up entirely, but I lost belief in my ability. Midway through the course, I met my sister-in-law, Aviva, for dinner before my class, as was becoming our routine on Tuesday nights. Aviva was waiting for me in front of the Taste of Tokyo on West 13th Street. I spotted Aviva, six years older, with her tight jeans and ponytail, looking like the undergraduate females who flocked to the New School's film programs.

"Look at you," I said. "You don't look a day over eighteen."

"And my mouth is watering just like a child."

Trying to revive her career as a pianist, Aviva studied with a tutor who lived on 11th Street near the New School. On those days and nights, she enlisted her daughter, Paula, then fourteen, to watch eight-year-old Max, until my brother, Ben, returned from his job at a criminal defense law firm in Manhattan to their brownstone in Park Slope, Brooklyn. However, this arrangement was fraught with uncertainty, as Paula was often engaged in after-school gymnastics or band practice. Ben specialized in DWI cases and was at the mercy of the emotional demands of the firm's partners and clients. He also had a penchant for forgetting his home responsibilities. All this created great emotional stress for Aviva; her youthful looks belied her problems.

The door opened, and a Geisha-dressed waitress led us to a front table in the narrow space where we watched slides of

Japan's gorgeous snow-capped Mount Fuji flickering high on the opposite wall.

"Remember last time, what we got? It was delicious," Aviva said.

"All I remember," I said, "is that John Lennon and Yoko were sitting at the end of the restaurant, and we couldn't stop turning around and staring."

"That's what I miss the most," Aviva said, "running into famous people in the city."

"What, you don't see stars in Brooklyn?"

"I'm sure if we hung around Brooklyn Heights more, we would."

"When I came to the Village with Denise as college students, we often went to Bleecker Street, to the Bitter End. One night, we were waiting for the show to start and drinking wine. A hulky, gorgeous man approached our table and asked in a deep, gravelly voice, 'Can I sit here?' He was pointing to an empty seat across from us, facing the stage. It was Kris Kristofferson, and he waited there until it was his turn to sing. We returned many times to see him perform and kept hoping he would sit with us."

"Yeah, he's pretty gorgeous."

The waitress brought us glasses of water and menus. I watched her white face paint and crimson bee-stung lips, waiting for a crack in her expression. She was stoic, faintly bowing and backing away.

"How is your piano playing going?" I asked Aviva.

"It's coming back. Even though I've been practicing at home, it's not the same without a rigorous professional at your back."

"I'm so glad you're doing this."

"You are the only one."

"Isn't Ben supportive?"

"Maybe theoretically. He would tell you he was. But he gets so mad at me for taking time away from his needs that sometimes I think he is going to sneak up behind me and smash the piano's fallboard on my hands."

"That's harsh."

The conversation slowed as the waitress approached our table with soup and salad on a tray. I had a flash of my brother when he tried to teach me the electronic keyboard that he bought with the money he earned washing cars when he was fourteen and I was eight. I couldn't remember the notes and he kept screaming, "Start in the key of C. Remember EEG, EEG, you know, lull-a-by and good-night."

I asked my brother then, "Where should I place my fingers?"

"I showed you a million times," he had answered. "Start with your right hand, place your thumb on E, next to middle C. Are you deaf?"

I had been petrified of his rising anger and felt as if he had been speaking a foreign language. At my mother's urging, he tried a few more times, with more recognizable tunes, but it was no use. Years later, when I was more interested in taking lessons, Ben insisted I couldn't use his keyboard, ever.

"Ben doesn't always have patience," I offered Aviva, after we slurped our miso soup. I didn't feel like relating the keyboard incident to her and ruining her mood.

But it didn't matter. Her face had already reddened from the heat, and I noticed tears inching down her cheeks.

"Aviva, what the hell?"

"So sorry, Anita. Sometimes your brother can be a downright asshole. He gets these really bleak moods and locks himself in his office and won't answer knocks on the door or calls for dinner. If the kids try to reach out to him when he's like this, he will lash out with the most insulting comments."

"Oh, no," I said.

"Yesterday, he called Max 'retarded' because he wasn't sure of the math homework, and then I held back his hand when he went to slap Paula for not taking out the dog on time. The dog had peed in the hallway and Ben stepped in it."

"Oh, shit," I said. I didn't belabor my brother's shortcomings with Aviva. She knew I had similar issues with his bad behavior, which only exacerbated since his friends' teenage accident.

As we waited for our sushi and tempura, Aviva excused herself to go to the bathroom. I watched the slides of Japan's cherry blossom trees and remembered that terrible year following the car accident. My father's sister in California had died of a heart attack at age forty-six. Their parents had both died of heart disease when they were also in their forties. It was also the year that my father lost his pharmaceutical business at the age of forty-two, the year my mother abandoned all dreams of going to college and took a full-time office job, the year we moved to a run-down house in Brooklyn, and the year my father gave up on life.

All my mother ever said about that time was, "Your father was in the wrong profession. He couldn't take the stress and worry about his employees and clients. His parents pushed him to make money. He really wanted to be a math teacher, but nobody encouraged him. He could deal with abstract problems and not those involving humans."

Suddenly, I felt sorry for my brother. Looking back, there was so much going on in my family during that time that he couldn't have gotten the emotional support he needed.

Aviva returned to the table, her cheeks cleaned from mascara smudges. After eating our dinner, sticking with our chopsticks, we waited for the red bean ice cream. Aviva asked me about my latest writing assignment.

"Just a short, short story that is supposed to have only two characters. Mine is about a man who struggles with guilt from his past."

"Very intriguing. Tell me more."

"In my story, a man graduates from law school and looks for a job. Still atoning for his teenage guilt over a car accident, he wrestles with his conscience, which stands in for the second required character. He ultimately devotes his life to helping young drivers convicted of DWI."

"Ooh, so close to home."

"It usually is. I think it was Jonathan Swift who said that *Gulliver's Travels* was his most autobiographical work."

"Don't ever show that story to Ben."

"I wouldn't dare."

"Sorry, that's great that you're writing. I want to read your story."

"I'm not sure I'm ready for anyone to read my work."

"No pressure."

"First, I have to get past my teacher's remarks. I don't even know if he will appreciate the story. He can be unbearably sarcastic and chauvinistic."

"I can relate to that," Aviva said.

Plunging my chopstick into the ice cream, I speared little holes into a face. It was time for me to stop procrastinating.

"What in the world are you doing?" Aviva asked.

"I guess I'm making a baby."

She smiled and then moved closer to my face. "What?" she yelled. "Are you?"

I nodded, my face getting the color of the red beans. "You're the first person I told."

"And you waited until dessert?"

"I was saving the best thing for last." I made a joke out of it, like I always did. The biggest news of my life was the hardest to tell.

Aviva was beside herself. Jumping up and down, bumping into the waitress as she left us the check. "I can't believe it," she said about ten times. We talked a little about what the doctor said, what I needed to buy, who to tell. As we left the restaurant, she whispered, "Don't tell Ben yet." I didn't ask her why because I knew. She didn't want to ruin the news for me.

# CHAPTER 32:
# WEDDING BELL BLUES

### Fall 1976

The explanation for our marriage proposal was like conflicting stories from two witnesses at a crime scene, only our contrasting versions rooted more in our philosophies than our remembered accuracy. In Sergio's account, I was pregnant (due to a faulty diaphragm) and practically begged him to marry.

Anyone who knew me would have suspected that the translation from his original Italian was faulty. I hated the idea of tying myself down to one person for the rest of my life. It took me years of suffering 1950s conservative indoctrination to become sexually free.

Every married couple I knew, my parents in particular, stayed together for the sake of their children, the sake of convention. Mix that with a dose of fear, security, and low self-esteem. My parents had never shown physical affection; I couldn't point to one instance of them kissing, except once when my mother landed a smack on my father's cheek as a joke, and he made the sound of a raspberry.

Anyone who knew me would recognize that I never would have begged anyone to marry me and that I would go to the altar kicking and screaming.

So, I couldn't explain how we came to the agreement. One day, we were discussing my pregnancy, a fact I welcomed wholeheartedly. Even if Sergio had denied saying so, he did mumble, "Maybe we should get married."

I answered, sitting across from him at our tiny dining table, "Having a baby nowadays doesn't necessarily mean marriage."

We shrugged.

"You know my family is provincial. Everyone has big families. They don't expect me to remain single."

"Even my family, no matter how cosmopolitan, touts the benefits of sharing an income and childrearing. Not that they require a license."

We were entirely too intellectual. I grabbed his hand and led him to the couch in the living room. We leaned against the bolsters. I hoped that a little intimacy would encourage our genuine feelings. We sat silently. Sergio played with a clump of my hair, forming a long braid.

If I had to dig further, it was enough that Sergio escaped the narrow constrictions of his native villagers' and family's religious practices. It was too much to ask him to accept single parenting. He wound the braid around my ear and kissed the top of my head. Though it was warm in the room, I shivered. If I had to succumb to norms, if there was any man I could do this with, it was Sergio.

I didn't say yes, and I didn't say no. The baby needed two unequivocal parents. For this, I was sure. I wanted a child. I loved Sergio; he was an honest, intelligent, down-to-earth person. I still doubted that any relationship could last. The future no longer had to be permanent.

And there was something else that preyed on my thoughts. The phrase we had heard throughout our younger years, "Don't Trust Anyone Over Thirty." I condensed all my major life decisions—having a baby, getting married, and probably leaving my exhausting library job—before that dreadful milestone, while I could still be trusted.

"Let's do it," I said.

"Maybe with a pinch of enthusiasm," he said, squeezing my thigh.

Somewhat reluctantly, I agreed to shop for a wedding dress at Lord & Taylor with my mother, Aviva, and Denise. I insisted we bypass the Bridal Department and head directly to what my mother described as "formal dresses," and I prayed these weren't the horrible organdy sleeveless numbers I bought as a bridesmaid to women I hardly remembered.

I sulked in the dressing room while the "women" brought me light-colored dresses, and, to my insistence, something not too fancy so I could wear it again (and not at another wedding). With the saleswoman's help, my mother produced three white gowns slung over her shoulder, including one she said was perfect for the "mother of the bride."

"You can wear whatever you want," I said in a voice befitting a preteen. Shuffling through the others without trying them on, I added, "These are not for me."

Denise knocked on the dressing-room door, apparently coming from a different direction.

"Here, look at these. I love the light coral one. It goes with your complexion."

For Denise's sake, I slipped on the scooped neck, peasant-type dress, which would have been perfect for Cindy's tall frame, but looked like a sack on me. There was silence in the tight mirrored space. Just when I said I would wear jeans, Aviva burst in without knocking, her arms loaded with a rainbow of dresses.

Although her selection was better, with one beige sheath passable, I excused myself and told the others to wait there.

After a few minutes of looking through racks, I saw a long black straight dress with a scooped neck, thin shoulder straps, and a sheer pink jacket with bell sleeves. Delicately threading it under my arms, I presented the dress to my "attendees."

"Black to a wedding!" my mother yelped. "This is not a funeral."

"It's nice," Denise said, trying to sound conciliatory.

"I love it," Aviva said. "Try it on."

I slipped the silk dress over my head, and it flowed, barely bypassing my small, three-month pregnancy belly, and landed appropriately by my ankles. Aviva held up the jacket and placed my arms into the sleeves. After she tied the top loop, she said, "Ta da, may I present to you, the bride."

Denise clapped. My mother remained quiet, her way of acceptance.

★ ★ ★

Aside from Sergio buying a two-button, pinstriped, dark-blue suit, we hardly prepared for the big day. In strict feminist fashion, I insisted on keeping my maiden name, which Sergio never contested. Being a foreigner, he acquiesced to many of my ideas, as I often hinted that these were American customs, which, of course, they weren't. I also insisted that the Justice of the Peace not read the customary marriage vows, especially including the word "obey."

To ensure this, I wrote our wedding vows. Sergio had little to add; he said he trusted me to write what was in his heart.

★ ★ ★

At City Hall in Brooklyn, we waited for the judge along with our small party: my parents; Ben, Aviva, Paula, and Max; Denise and Arthur; and for Sergio, his best man, Giovanni, his wife, Lucia, and Sergio's nephew, Matteo, who had come from

Italy to attend college in New York. The only one missing from my nearest and dearest was Cindy, who was somewhere on the West Coast, and Shirley, expected at the luncheon afterward.

In one of the judicial wood-paneled rooms, we gathered around a long conference-room table, and my father, with the prompting of my mother, presented the men with carnation boutonnieres for their suit lapels, though he pinned his to the collar of his striped sports shirt. Normally, my father didn't address Sergio directly; I assumed due to Sergio's inability to understand American sports. This time, my father explained the traffic pattern in downtown Brooklyn and Sergio nodded with his arms folded and his boutonniere slanted. Paula yawned and Max played with the tape-recorder buttons.

"Stop touching that," Ben yelled at his son. "I am going to record the ceremony."

Finally, a legal associate entered and told us to follow him to a huge room with murals of historical men.

The judge stood at the lectern, and I handed him our vows. "Please read these instead," I said.

He nodded and placed the paper under another. Then he spouted the traditional vows, directing Sergio to repeat. Sergio pressed toward me and whispered, "What does *thee* and *thou* and *troth* mean?"

I didn't answer. I turned to the judge, "We wrote our own vows. Please read them."

He said, "I will, afterward."

I said, "Please leave out the word 'obey.'"

The judge ordered me to repeat after him "and to obey, till death us do part, according to God's holy ordinance; and thereto I give thee my troth."

I was silent.

Without missing a beat, the judge picked up my written vows and read:

*We hope that marriage will not change our basic commitment to each other but instead reinforce that commitment. We hope that we will continue to care about each other, to listen, to sympathize, to help each other grow as individuals and to share in that growth. We wish to respect each other's feelings, to encourage each other's interests, and help each other in whatever difficulty or need arises. We will try our best to remain free people alone so that when we come together, we will be adding another dimension to ourselves by sharing and caring. This is what we hope will guide our lives, what we hope to give to each other and to all those we love.*

The rest was a blur. I was consumed with fury. *Why couldn't the judge listen to me? Why did he have to read the traditional vows first? What was it to him?*

After the ring exchange and kiss, we walked outside the building; and joining Denise and Arthur, were my aunt Reebie, Shirley, and Charlie showering us with rice. I threw my bouquet, and it skidded down Rebbie's fulsome chest until she caught it. It was fitting, as she was the only unattached one, though as far as I knew, she enjoyed her single status.

Before we went to our official dinner at Mary's Italian Restaurant in the Village, we stopped by Denise's apartment (and my former one) on Christopher Street. Denise and Arthur served champagne and hors d'oeuvres. I was happy to see our old red paisley sofa bed, Denise's and my first joint purchase, and a black-and-red woodblock that I made in a printing workshop, hanging over it. I had so many memories of lying there, from being rigid after my pot-smoking freakout to making out with Sergio on our first date. And I had so many memories of this my first apartment.

Christopher Street was the right place to be on this day, my official farewell to being a single woman in Greenwich Village.

"I would like to make a toast," Ben said, raising a plastic champagne glass.

"Yes, I would like to join," Shirley said.

Charlie clinked her glass.

Ben boomed, "To Anita and Sergio. May they have a long and happy life."

My Aunt Reebie added, "And may they keep their aggravation to a minimum."

We all sipped.

"Wait, wait," Paula yelled. "We forgot to play the tape recorder."

"Oh, I want to hear the ceremony," Shirley said.

Ben set up the tape recorder on the coffee table and pressed "play." When the judge asked me to repeat the phrase with "obey," there was a noticeable silence.

"Is there something wrong with the tape?" Charlie asked. "I don't hear anything."

Ben pressed the fast forward and rewind buttons until he got to the same phrase. There was silence for my part. Nothing. He advanced the tape a few minutes, and the judge read the vows I wrote.

"Well," Ben said. "You didn't have to worry that you said 'obey.' Obviously, there were no words."

"But I said, 'I do,' after *our* vows."

"Still," Ben said. "Officially, you're not really married."

# PART II: SKIPPING AHEAD

# CHAPTER 33: NOT AGAIN



I couldn't shake the dream. As I sat in front of my office computer, my fingers automatically spread at the ten-finger method position on my keyboard. I didn't click on the word processing program or activate my fax. I didn't even procrastinate with Solitaire. Not when all I could envision was the scenario in my dream. It was back in 1987, and my sister-in-law, Aviva, paced around her bedroom, clutching her side in pain, wheezing, not quite okay but alive when she shouldn't have been. In the dream, I perched on Aviva's bed, watching her in amazement, unable to be happy that I had my beloved sister-in-law to myself, unable to remind her that she died nine months before, unable to say what she needed to before she died. All I could do was think, no, this wasn't true. Aviva was suffering, still. Again, she must die. Again.

Back in the dream, I had finally spoken to my sister-in-law and once more we arranged the schedule for Aviva's children. Again, we discussed the nature of the pain, and again, we denied its significance. The worst part was the knowing looks in Aviva's pewter-colored eyes that said, "I'm tired. I'm dying." But mostly, they said, "I'm angry. I'm angry with you for taking Ben's side in the divorce, even if he's your brother. I'm angry with Sergio for letting me die. I'm angry with you for being healthy. I'm angry at you for living."

The dream was with me at lunchtime as I pressed against the coffee shop counter, trying to eat a turkey club sandwich.

The dream was with me at 8:30 that evening when Sergio came home from the hospital and mixed a batch of Bloody Marys.

"Did you go for your mammogram today?" he asked, pouring the red liquid into glasses.

"I had to reschedule. The printer screwed up our osteoporosis brochures. Shirley and I had to go downtown."

"Don't put it off too long. You know it's important."

"You don't have to remind me that my sister-in-law died of breast cancer. You don't have to remind me that my business partner just had breast cancer. You don't have to remind me that it's all over the fuckin' place."

"I know I don't. Remember what they say, 'Denial is a river in Egypt.'"

"Sergio, there are just some things I don't have a sense of humor about, and this is one of them. I'll go, just don't bug me. Not today."

"Why not today?"

"It's just, well, I don't know. I just don't feel like it, okay?" I couldn't talk about my dream, not when just yesterday I had congratulated myself for finally getting through a full week without obsessing about Aviva, without driving Sergio crazy with "what if" scenarios that threatened to destroy our marriage. After thirteen years since Aviva's death, it still haunted me. In my family, as in his practice, Sergio was always the doctor first, and the first to be praised—and blamed.

There was only one time in my nearly twenty-four-year marriage that Sergio forgot that he was a doctor: when I went into labor with Giorgia in 1977. After my water broke and labor began, we called my gynecologist, Julie Linden, who met us at the hospital. "You're still only a few centimeters contracted," she said. "Go home. The first baby takes long."

By the next day, I was crazy with unremitting pain. I had not eaten or drunk anything.

Sergio called Julie again and we met her at the hospital. Still no progress. This went on for a third day and Sergio was pacing and screaming like a crazy person. Finally, he said to me, "You're having the baby today if I have to pull it out myself."

At the hospital, everything spun around quickly. Apparently, it was now an emergency. The baby was too big; they prepped me for a C-section. Sergio was not allowed in the operating room. I found out later from Julie that he sat scrunched in the waiting room and didn't talk to anyone. When Giorgia finally appeared, she was gorgeous though jaundiced. Sergio was weeping when he told me she was in the isolette. By the time we took her home, she regained her rosy complexion and suckled me with abandon.

"Today, I feel like forgetting everything and just getting drunk. Any objections, doctor?"

"Not a one," he said, taking the glass from my hand before I finished. He put his thick, hairy arms around me and kissed my lips. I could taste the lime he always sucked before he drank a Bloody Mary and I winced.

The alcohol helped me fall asleep instantly, although I got up at three in the morning, my eyes refusing to rest. At least I could remember no dreams and remained in bed, allowing my mind to wander.

This used to be my biggest pleasure: free-associating. Four years before Aviva died, she and I escaped our families to take a long weekend in Mexico. We sat at the airport lounge for two hours waiting for our delayed flight. While Aviva was restless, getting up several times to go to the bathroom, to buy magazines, I was content to watch people around me, my imagination spinning tales about their relationships, their destinations, the lives they left.

Two rows behind me, there had been a family of four, including two small girls, one about six and one barely walking.

I could picture them for years. The mother, an overweight brunette in a hooded sweatshirt, lifted the giggling little girl up a few times while the father, a bearded, tall guy, sat near his older daughter and helped her draw in a pad. In the surrounding tumult, they seemed a contented, insulated bubble. It surprised me as I always thought of airports as places of rushing and tension, and I thought about my youngest, Beth, then nearly three, who in her second-born effort to gain her father's attention, repeatedly examined him with her little doctor's kit. And the giggling baby aroused an image of my firstborn, Giorgia, when she was less than two and squirming out of my arms at the Cloisters Museum in Manhattan's Washington Heights. Normally a well-behaved child, this time she escaped my clutches and ran into the outdoor garden and plucked the flowers. After I drew her away several times, with a severe guard watching us, I bit her in the arm. To this day, at the age of twenty-three, she still talked about this assault.

"How could you have bitten me?" she had asked.

I had no answers; I was just as mystified. If this happened today, they would haul me off to children's court and take away my child.

These thoughts had both nurtured and upset me. I thought of myself as a fun and loving mother, the first parental choice over Sergio if asked, yet I had a few blemishes. I turned to the window and focused on a plane taxiing on the runway. I missed my family, especially my girls, who would always be my heart.

When the plane was finally ready for boarding, Aviva looked as if she had been traveling for days, her tan safari jacket wrinkled and unbelted, its pockets stuffed with lipstick-smeared tissues. I had boarded the plane, my denim blazer fully buttoned, almost disappointed that I had to interrupt my daydreaming.

At this middle-of-the-night awakening, though, my thoughts were not soothing. They drifted back over Aviva's last year, lingering over familiar territory like a sniffing dog. I kept seeing Sergio walking through the front door, heading for the refrigerator before he said hello. I would follow him, waiting until he opened a beer, until he delivered his latest report. How my heart pounded with terror that he was going to tell me this was the day that took Aviva.

As an oncologist, Sergio had a difficult life, and I had learned not to ask about his patients unless he volunteered. Even though he wasn't in charge of Aviva's case, he worked in the same hospital; his patients were on the same floor, sometimes in the same room. Naturally, he knew everything.

During all those days, weeks, months that my sister-in-law was in and out, when she had a mastectomy, followed by chemotherapy, he knew what he didn't want to know. And during all those days, when Sergio mentioned Aviva, I bombarded him with uncontrollable questions until he'd slam the bedroom door and escape into a bath. Of course, the minute he was out of sight, I'd call my mother, and she'd ask what Sergio knew.

I got up to go to the bathroom, careful to close the bedroom door so that the light didn't disturb Sergio. In our years as a married couple, I learned he could sleep through a hurricane but would awake instantly from a flash of lightning. Being a chronic insomniac, I observed such things about people.

From the downstairs bathroom, I followed the vague illumination of the Manhattan skyline that projected through the window of our Roosevelt Island duplex, where we moved in 1979 when Giorgia was two. The nearby study was clogged with jutting bookcases and dusty exercise equipment, and I was covered with bruises from late-night encounters. To protect myself, I flailed my arms around as I entered. Closing the door, I sat at the desk, watching the city lights. The sky was a deep-gray wash, interrupted by darker inkblots. Even at this hour, there was no such thing as pure blackness.

My thoughts flipped backward. Sergio had related what happened weeks before Aviva died. Since Aviva's parents were dead, my mother, Frances, took charge. She had cornered Sergio in the hospital's solarium. "Why can't the doctors do something?" she had begged. "It's like they've already given up on her."

"They're doing what they can," Sergio had said, looking down on his petite mother-in-law, his hunched shoulders making his six-foot frame seem neckless.

"That's not good enough. This is not supposed to happen. She's only forty-eight. A mother or mother-in-law is not supposed to outlive a child."

When Sergio had reported this to me, I thought immediately of Marilyn and her parents.

She had been even younger, twenty-seven years old. At least Aviva had children: Paula and Max, then at the time of Aviva's death, in their twenties. Their parents had been divorced since she was seven and he was five. My daughter, Giorgia, had been ten and Beth was seven; I was grateful they had their childhoods intact with both their parents, though they were still too young to be declared "safe."

Finally, Sergio had convinced my mother to sit down. Taking her hand in his, he said mechanically, "This is not your decision to make. Aviva does not want heroic measures to be taken. Let her go in peace."

"You call this peace!" Frances screamed. "Every bone in her body cries from torment."

She withdrew her hand and held it over her eyes as she sobbed.

"That's why you have to let her go."

"Never," she said. "I will never forgive them."

And with those words, Sergio was condemned, along with the whole medical profession.

While I could appreciate the unfairness of my mother's vitriolic attack, I felt the same.

"I must forget all this," I muttered, pulling the chain on the green-glass hurricane lamp. The brochure on osteoporosis lay on the desk. On the back page, directly on top of the sponsoring pharmaceutical company's logo, was a smudge the size of a thumbprint. That morning, when I was supposed to go for a mammogram, Shirley, my business partner now for three years, and I sat on the floor of the printer's office removing the marks with pencil erasers. We completed only half the fifty-thousand-run and hired two teenagers to help the next day so that the job could be delivered in time for the doctors' conference.

This had been the biggest project since we had formed our editorial/design company, with Shirley in charge of the business side and me as the creative director. After our years in numerous publishing jobs, we both had been disgusted with our sexist and incompetent bosses, and during a wine-infused lunch, we became entrepreneurs. Not agreeing on a company name, I had opened the dictionary at random and pointed my finger to a listing. It was "factotum, a person having many diverse activities or responsibilities." We had been so struck by that seemingly other-worldly choice that we decided this would be our company name even if it betrayed the good sense of choosing a name that sounded good on the telephone and had a meaning that everyone understood. Fate was our guide.

I took a pencil from my desk drawer and erased the stain. Dark-pink eraser flecks dotted the brochure in a marbleized finish. I brushed away the evidence. Eraser bits would be greater proof of failure than the initial smudge. Sometimes clumsy cover-ups were worse than honest mistakes. Not bad, I decided. I would remember that line and use it somewhere. Who knew when it would be required to compare some product to Watergate?

# CHAPTER 34:
## THE LAST ERASURE

By 4:30 p.m. the next day, Shirley and I, along with our teenage helpers, finished the last erasure. We left the printer and returned to our midtown office, immediately checking the client's written delivery instructions.

"I'm going for a break," Shirley said, opening her desk drawer and reaching for her purse.

I didn't look up from my computer, on the other side of our rectangular, light-filled loft space, but I heard the office door creak shut. I was certain that Shirley was now standing in front of our office building on Second Avenue and 55th Street, smoking a cigarette. And my heart sank. I had vowed a week ago that I would no longer get upset about Shirley's smoking. I thought I had talked myself into that "denial" Sergio had mentioned. Denial may be more than a river in Egypt but an ocean with tidal-wave potential.

The phone rang and Shirley, just returning to the office, ran to her desk. "Hi, Louis," she said. Her voice was raspy but loud. "Yes, they'll be there tomorrow morning. I know we're a day late, but you'll have them in time for the conference."

While Shirley was still speaking to our client, I picked up the phone, pushed a button for the second line, and contacted the printer. "Kevin, are you sure the cartons are going out now?" I asked. "Have you checked them personally?" Kevin reported that the cartons were almost all loaded on the truck, which would move in thirty minutes. Yet, I couldn't dislodge the ball of anxiety from my stomach. I had too much experience in the publishing business to know that a printer's promise was about as reliable as a contractor's estimate.

"I called the printer," I said, as Shirley put her purse back into her desk drawer.

"Don't tell me the brochures fell out of the cartons and got rolled over by a tractor-trailer."

"Nothing is impossible. But if you can believe Kevin, they're almost on their way."

"After what we went through, I think I may have osteoporosis from bending over and making all those erasures. But, thankfully for me, thin blonde women are the highest risk group."

"Blacks are not immune," I said. "And you know, your age is another factor."

"So, I'm only sixty-one. I'm still too young."

"How about your smoking?"

"I was waiting for you to mention it. You smoked, too."

"I haven't had a cigarette since I gave birth to Giorgia." This was not the total truth. I didn't go to Smokenders until I was four months pregnant. When Giorgia saw a photo of our wedding dinner and noticed a cigarette in my hand, she accused me of being the reason she was only five feet, two inches, four inches shorter than her sister. And what I never confessed to her was that I had a short bout of postpartum depression with Beth and for a few weeks, I snuck a cigarette from a pack in my underwear drawer, though I never smoked around the children.

"I don't smoke that much, anyway," Shirley said. "A few cigarettes a day doesn't mean a thing."

"Shirley, I'm gonna say something, and I hope you don't take it the wrong way. But, you know, sometimes things happen, and you don't really care about the niceties anymore."

"What do you mean?"

"I mean. Fuck it. You had breast cancer, for God's sake. How can you smoke?"

"My cancer was cured."

"I know. Thank God you were lucky. But I can't, I refuse, I will not lose another person to it. It's bad enough that this disease has haunted my family and even my business partner. I can't escape that. If you do nothing to prevent it, I'll only feel like I let it happen." Tears fell down my cheeks like tiny weights. "Look," I stammered, "I'm ruining another brochure."

Shirley smiled. "Here." She threw her pack of Newports into the garbage. "I'll do my best. And Anita, you didn't let Aviva die. It was not your fault." When I didn't respond, Shirley continued, "And it was not your fault that Marilyn died, either."

★ ★ ★

That night, I had a dream about Shirley. We were walking through a wooded trail in the country somewhere. What began as a wide, meandering swath soon turned into a narrow, pebble-and-weed strewn, steep uphill path overlooking bottomless space. Shirley was ahead and slipped on a rocky cliff, slid down, and was about to topple over the ledge. I crouched and grabbed Shirley, dragging her back to the path. I tried to straighten. The ledge was so treacherous, I couldn't get a solid footing and knew my only option was to reach my leg over a precarious iron railing, which required more strength than I had. *Where was Shirley?* I panicked. *I had helped her and now she's gone. She deserted me.* Finally, I lifted my leg over the railing and got to safety. Shirley was standing there after all, not offering her hand but waiting in case of emergency.

The feeling of urgency was so severe that I woke, jerking my head and peeking at the clock. 3:00 a.m., the same time I had been waking up all week. I was amazed how blatant my dreams were becoming. There was no need for a shrink. At least I had survived the danger, the first heartening thing that had happened to me in a long time.

★ ★ ★

In the morning, while I was showering, Sergio came into the bathroom to say that my mother was on the phone.

"What's wrong?" I asked.

"Don't ask me," he yelled over the rushing noise of the water. "She no longer confides in me. It's like I'm a leper."

"Tell her I'll be right there." I wrapped a bath towel around me, and, without patting myself dry, went into the bedroom, leaving a trail of wet footprints.

"Ma?"

"Anita, is that you?"

"Who else would it be? What's wrong?"

"Why should something be wrong?"

"You usually don't call me at seven in the morning. Come on, Ma, I'm dripping for God's sake."

"It's your uncle Bernie."

"What? What happened to Bernie?"

"He had a heart attack."

"No! How bad?"

"He's in intensive care. Maybe you can ask that husband of yours if he can find something out. They won't tell me a thing."

"Ma. I'm so sorry. I don't want to drag Sergio into this, not again."

"I'm not asking him to interfere this time. I don't want him to kill another relative."

"God, Mom. You've got to stop doing this. Sergio was an absolute prince during the whole time of Aviva's illness, especially in her month in the ICU. You have no idea what he did. Not a day went by when he didn't spend as much time with her as he could, the first thing in the morning, the last thing at night. He was on the phone constantly with her doctors. Just lay off already."

"Are you going to ask him?"

"Okay, Ma. I'll call you back."

"Don't get me involved," Sergio said before I could open my mouth.

I was grateful he had overheard. Now I didn't have to manipulate the situation. "Just one phone call," I said. "Uncle Bernie is in intensive care. My mother just wants to know how he is. Please. I promise I won't ask you anything ever again."

Sergio sat on the bed looking at me. The towel spread on the bedsheets, exposing my smooth, beige skin, wet bubbles hanging above my breasts like a beaded necklace, my nipples hard from the chill. He picked up the phone and called the hospital.

"He's okay," Sergio said, hanging up. "Your mother was right. It was a heart attack. But he's stable now. He's gonna make it."

"Thanks," I said, kissing Sergio on the cheek.

He slid his hand down my chest and cupped my breast. "Umm," he said, "we still have time."

"Let me call my mom first." I led his hand down over my wet pubic hair and dialed my mother.

"I'm sure he's fine," I said for the third time. "Yes, Sergio spoke to the resident. I know he's only a resident. Please, Ma. Can't you just be happy that Uncle Bernie is going to live?"

I let my hand rest on the phone, almost expecting it to ring again, almost expecting my mother to call and say, "How can Bernie be alive? How could he make it when my own daughter-in-law didn't? Why did God take a young, talented musician, a mother, and not a bitter old man?" I sat for a moment before I realized that Sergio's hand was gone from my crotch. I heard his electric shaver in the bathroom.

★ ★ ★

"The brochures have arrived," Shirley screamed as I was hanging up my coat. "I just spoke to Louis. He thinks they're beautiful."

"Thank God," I said as I walked to my desk, gripping a paper cup of steaming black coffee. "Sometimes life is fair."

"Wow, that's heavy for 9:00 a.m." Shirley massaged little circles into her cheeks, a habit she had acquired ever since she cut down on smoking.

"Don't mind me. I'm heavy with dreams. Which reminds me, I had one about you."

"Really?" Shirley sat up straight. Raised in a small town in Mississippi, she retained a firm belief in supernatural portents.

"This is not so mysterious. In fact, I'm kinda embarrassed. I hope you won't be angry at me."

"Why?"

"I guess because in the dream, I helped you over a dangerous precipice. You were safe and sound but didn't do anything to help me."

"Is that what you really think I would do?"

"Of course not. I trust you would help me. I don't know what it means. At least we both survived. I found that very comforting."

"Maybe you don't really trust me," Shirley said, sounding confident rather than hurt.

"Maybe I don't trust you won't leave me like Aviva did."

We said nothing more until the messenger arrived an hour later. It was one of the rare times in our business that we weren't on the verge of some crisis with an artist, typesetter, client, or printer. We knew when to be quiet with each other, which is why we were such good partners.

But my words to Shirley stayed with me all day and into the night. "Maybe I don't trust you won't leave me like Aviva did," I repeated to myself, right before I fell asleep. I vowed that if I smelled smoke on Shirley's breath one more time, I would quit the partnership.

There it was again. That same dream from the other night. That same dream about Aviva in her bedroom, alive, but suffering. Only this time, Aviva stopped pacing and sat next to me on her bed, coming closer, closer. I woke drenched with sweat. And again, it was 3:00 a.m.

Why is this dream haunting me? I agonized, shivering as my body adjusted to the wind-chilled gusts coming in through the air-conditioner vents in my bedroom. A late-February snowstorm was brewing outside; the spotty light around my darkened bedroom window alerted me that the night was busy.

I tried to push the image of a sickly Aviva out of my mind; I didn't want to remember my sister-in-law this way. I recalled when she went back to performing. I summoned images of her last concert, her long legs wrapped in a knot under her piano bench, unfolding gently to depress the pedals. And there was Aviva so many years before, lying in her hospital bed, this time tracing the mouth of her newborn son who sucked the creamy colostrum from her breast. Life. Aviva was life. *How can such a vital presence be silent? How can my sister-in-law not be in this world? In my world?*

I rolled onto my back and glanced to my other side, able to notice the flattened covers. Sergio's low-toned snoring was absent. I felt my way toward the study and peeked through the semi-closed door. Sergio sat at the desk, his hands pressing into his eyes. I tiptoed toward him and patted his shoulder.

"Can't sleep?" I asked.

"A resident called. A patient of mine was admitted to the hospital."

"Oh, I didn't hear the phone," I said.

"I was in the kitchen getting a glass of water and got it on the first ring."

"Anything you want to talk about?"

"No, go to sleep. I'll join you soon."

Instead, I moved closer to the window and propped my forehead against the cold glass. I watched a dizzying shower of whiteness, the snow blotting out the city. At first light, the scene would be blessed with virginal emissions. By the time I'd get to work, the shoveled, rock-salted, and brown-splotched snow would be piled in mound-like obstacles, seeping through my cracked leather boots, soaking my socks, reddening my toes, chilling me for the entire day. By the time I'd get to work, the promise of purity would be marred with grime, just like the eraser residue that stubbornly clung to the back page of my brochure.

Tomorrow, I'll call the women's radiology center. Maybe they could give me an appointment for a mammography before the end of winter.

# CHAPTER 35:
# THE LAST GENERATION

## September 2001

In 1982, my father was admitted to the local Rockaway hospital for congestive heart failure. He had been there for about a week, and although he was in the cardiac ICU, his prognosis was good. On the following Saturday morning, we left our daughters, Giorgia, then five, and Beth, two, with a babysitter, and went to my mother's apartment, where she had breakfast waiting for us before we would all leave to visit my father. The phone rang and my mother answered.

"It's for you," she said, handing the receiver to Sergio. "He asked for my son-in-law, the doctor."

"Yes, this is Mrs. Rappaport's son-in-law. Who am I speaking to?" Sergio said into the phone. A minute passed, and then Sergio said, "Oh, no. How did this happen?" He remained still for a few seconds after hanging up the phone.

"Who was that?" I asked.

"Dr. Nelson from the hospital, the guy we met last weekend."

Sergio's voice was on the verge of a stutter. I immediately realized the news. "Is my father dead?" I asked.

"Yes," he said.

My mother screamed, more like an inhuman wail. "Nooo," she finally eked out. "Are you sure?"

"What happened?" I asked, a vise clenched around my own heart.

It seemed my father had died from a pulmonary embolism. Sergio suspected that the hospital didn't administer a blood thinner to my father, a customary procedure. At the time, we were too shocked to pursue this. As the weeks followed, I was convinced that we had a viable lawsuit, but my mother was adamant about avoiding a prolonged legal battle. She did what the bereavement experts say was the worst thing: she made a major life-altering change. Unable to withstand her isolation in her beachfront community during the off-season months and the long commute to work at her managerial job in Manhattan, she moved to a senior apartment building on Roosevelt Island to be close to us. Taking the tram and bus to her downtown office was a lot easier than the long subway ride from Rockaway.

Soon thereafter, she officially retired from the silk-screen company and went to the office occasionally to what she called, "straighten things out." Her prodigious energies did not go to waste. As my mother became involved in local politics and elected president of the Senior Center, I witnessed her often-public contentious behavior and intrusive presence. Feelings about my father's sudden death and my unresolved anger were superseded by my mother's constant needs. Several times a week, she appeared on my doorstep to complain that she heard I went for a walk with friends and didn't invite her; twice, she received an Express Mail envelope with a threatening anonymous message: "Ask for forgiveness NOW!" It was not unusual for a local vendor to report an altercation with my mother, though some expressed admiration. One time, waiting at the bus stop, which was across from the Senior building, I spied my mother naked in front of her window.

When we visited my father's grave on the anniversary of his death, I nodded to the graves of my Rappaport grandparents, two immigrants from Latvia, who had gone from sewing scraps in a Lower East Side factory to owning a profitable sweater business. Then I noticed something I hadn't seen before. The date of my father's birth was incorrect. I may have been the one to have written the date, but more likely it had been my brother who was in charge of the headstones. It was fitting, I thought then, that my father, who could have been anything he had wanted, ended up dying from a mistake in judgment and a typo cemented in stone.

* * *

In 1999, on a brisk late-summer Sunday, my mother insisted that my daughters and I accompany her to the cemetery. She wanted to be sure we were aware of her wishes. It was her birthday; she had reminded us. We couldn't refuse.

With Beth, a college junior, holding the leash of our Springer Spaniel Ruby, we walked to the garage and picked up my mother in front of her building. Weakened by weeks of painkilling cocktails to treat a severe case of facial shingles, my mother needed a cane or wheelchair to get around. On this day, deciding that her cane would be sufficient, she maneuvered into our Jeep and read us the instructions to the cemetery, hopefully a twenty-minute drive away in Queens.

We came to the cemetery entrance and followed the sign inside, parking in a treeless lot. Outside, the sun was beating down and the humid air felt thick. I chastised myself for not checking the weather report that morning; Frances didn't do well in the heat. After leading her, hyperventilating and perspiring, up and down the aisles, we realized we were hopelessly lost. We finally found the office, studied another map, went back into our Jeep, and drove a few blocks farther into the proper entrance and eventually found the correct row.

Beth let Ruby loose, while Giorgia followed her along the walkway. I was a step behind.

"Why did you let the dog go?" Giorgia asked her sister.

"You try controlling her," Beth said.

As I watched my daughters argue, I only hoped the dog wouldn't dig in the grass and unearth bones. When we finally reached the Rappaport plot, eight grave sites arranged in two rows, my poor depleted mother practically collapsed on the stone bench perpendicular to the graves.

"I'm very happy to see that the graves are well taken care of," she said. "I can thank your brother for paying the bill." I didn't have the heart to tell her I was the one who had signed the check.

Then she pointed to my father's grave and said, "See to his left. That's where I'll be—soon." After Giorgia, Beth, and I protested in unison, like a Greek chorus, my mother raised her finger toward the distance ahead and said, "I'll be facing that beautiful oak tree. It's peaceful here."

★ ★ ★

Nearly a year after my mother's death in 2000, my daughters and I planned a cemetery visit to wish my mother a happy birthday.

In the car, with Giorgia at the wheel, I remembered that stifling day, how my mother insisted we make sure the plots were taken care of, how my mother slumped on the stone bench panting near her final resting place. I remembered my feeling that in coming to Frances's future grave, we had almost killed her.

Why was I feeling guilty again, when my mother often told me how much that visit meant to her, how she hadn't been too tired afterward to enjoy a brief stop to eat sandwiches at a park near the cemetery?

All morning, I had felt the well of grief rising. As we made our way to the cemetery, I prepared myself. This time would be hard. Unlike my lifetime of emotional sabotage, this time I feared that I'd break free in front of my children. Maybe I'd beat my breast and fall on my mother's grave like a born-again supplicant. Until then, I had everything under control. The funeral was grand with standing-room only. We dispersed her belongings in record time. I hadn't arranged a formal unveiling for the following week, the actual one-year anniversary of my mother's death. This day, on Frances's birthday, alone with my two girls, would be enough.

On the drive, in between needless reminders to Giorgia about the turn on the second entrance, I chattered incessantly. "Are you upset?" I asked.

With one hand clutched around a paper cup of coffee and the other on the steering wheel, Giorgia seemed unable to manage a third task, such as speaking. Instead, she nodded.

"I am," Beth piped in from the backseat. Beth always had a special affinity with my mother.

"I'm upset, too," I said, "even if I don't show it. She was a much better grandmother than mother."

"Should we stop to buy lilacs?" Giorgia recalled her grandmother's favorite flower.

"Jews don't put flowers on graves," I said. "They place small stones on the monuments to show they were there, to show that the deceased is still loved and remembered. I guess stones last, and flowers don't. Besides, it's probably impossible to get lilacs in late August."

Returning to silence, we drove onto the street leading to the cemetery, bypassing the first entrance and making the correct turn into the parking area. We walked up the designated hill, and stopped at the turnoff point, passing an elderly man wearing a brown uniform and carrying a hoe.

I mentioned row *R* after our last name and asked if we were going in the correct direction.

"You're right on it," he said with a grin. Two of his front teeth were missing. "Yes, you're on the right track."

Turning right on row *R*, we followed the path and there it was: the family plot.

In slow motion, I approached the gravesites. I had approved my mother's engraving and saw a photocopy of her tombstone. But still, to be here …

"Grandma's grave is crooked," I said.

"I feel good about that toothless groundskeeper," Beth said, as if this was a natural response to my comment. "It's nice that Grandma will have a friendly person tending her."

"The grave slants to the side," I insisted. "Maybe there won't be enough room to put a coffin in one of the two empty plots." I had an instant image of the gap-toothed groundskeeper lowering my plain pine coffin into that space, only to find that it didn't fit and that there was no space for me, or for Sergio.

Beth, the more emotional of my daughters, began to sniffle, which increased in intensity. "I keep thinking of those Friday nights," she said, between sobs. "When Grandma gave me and my friends her bedroom and slept on the living-room couch. She just wanted us to have fun. I remember the time she sat on the toilet seat while us girls washed and set her hair and applied makeup on her face." Then Beth's crying became hysterical.

I remained on the bench, like a statue. Giorgia put her arm around her sister.

Our time must be up; we have to go this instant. I rose and somehow moved to my mother's grave. "I'm thinking of writing my own stories," I blurted to the mound. Feeling selfish, I added, "Giorgia filmed a day on a new television series. She had her own trailer parked in front of Brooklyn College, three blocks from our old home. Beth has begun law school this year. She's a great student. Otherwise, we're all well."

The girls and I stood for a few minutes, each in our own world of repression.

Giorgia moved to the stone bench and gazed at the bed of ivy forming the ground cover of the eldest relatives. Beth joined her, burying her head inside her sister's chest. I stood to the side of the bench and began my final rounds. I said hello to my uncle Hershel, who died too young, grinned recognition at my grandmother, nodded shyly at my grandfather and great-grandmother—those I never knew. I allowed myself to linger at my father's side, embarrassed for him in front of his family, knowing what I knew—that this man had squandered so much potential, that this man wallowed in lies of omission, that this man took from me my right to speak. Then I recognized his incorrect birthday, and for only a moment, my anger at my missing father melted into compassion.

At my final stop, I ran my fingers along my mother's engraved name. I mentally surveyed Frances's life, her immigrant and poverty-riven childhood, her being forced by a male school adviser into a commercial diploma, her subsequent jobs as a bookkeeper and office manager, her final forays into leadership at the Senior Center. Such a singular person, I thought, how would I ever live life without anticipating her opinion? How would I ever make peace with her frustrated ambitions? I thought of that famous Marlon Brando line, "I coulda been a contender."

"Yes, Frances," I pretended to say, "you coulda been a congresswoman, a senator, professor, or the head of a corporation. You coulda been a woman with power and influence. You coulda, shoulda."

"Girls," I said, motioning them to my side. "Don't let this happen to you."

"What?" Giorgia said. "Do you mean dying?"

"No, silly. Don't die with regrets."

As a clot of three, we backed up and continued toward the end of row *R*. Though I vowed to return next year on my mother's birthday, I turned around for another look.

"It's peaceful here," I said, recalling my mother's words when she sat on that same bench. An overwhelming feeling of belongingness encompassed me. I didn't want to leave this place, this place where I had dreaded coming. My family was here; I was home.

# CHAPTER 36:
## "THE LINGERING CHILL"

### Fall 2001

After four years of owning Factotum, Shirley and I closed our business for two weeks for some much-needed time off. Normally, we would rotate our vacations, though rarely did we handle every problem without interrupting the other. It was the nature of our business, we soon learned, to be stuck on a roller coaster of stress, each client a needy child with inexplicable demands. There was the bank who needed their newsletter to be constantly updated at the last moment; the pharmaceutical company who insisted on ugly stock art to replace our fine artist's expert renderings on their patient aids; the travel agency who wouldn't pay us to visit the city we were writing about; the major insurance company, who was always late paying its bills. Instead of suffering through crazy bosses, we now had crazy clients.

Not that we were ready to quit our business. Surprisingly, we had never been in the red, though our salaries were just adequate. Shirley had sacrificed the most, giving up a secure job at a major publisher. For myself, I was at a professional crossroads: dissatisfied, but terrified of an uncertain future.

Since Sergio couldn't take a vacation, I stayed in New York and basically chilled, visiting museums and parks, and having lunch with friends. After a week, I tackled the junk in my bedroom closet. I opened an old carton of ancient writings that I stored on a top shelf. Mostly, I found old poems and journals. On the bottom of the pile, there was a stapled story titled "The Lingering Chill." What a horrible title! I took the yellowed and stiffened typewritten onion-skin pages to my bed and rested against the headboard, feeling a familiar knot twisting my esophagus. The story was from Broderick Sudberry's fiction writing class, nearly twenty-five years ago.

On the cover page with my name, Broderick wrote, in pencil and underlined, "Do Not Ask Her to Read!" His comments were: "This is thin but has some possibility. The introspection contributes to the shallowness of the character. Let's read and discuss style? Irony? Clues of Motivation? Particularly Randy. You overwrite. Edit your work more carefully."

I turned the eleven pages, reading Broderick's notes in the margins. There were not that many of them and they were also in pencil, not in the red ink of my reimagined memory. On the first page, first paragraph, Broderick circled the words "subterranean" and "quickened," as well as the phrase "February air increased its boldness." He bracketed a section that featured "aberration of warmth" and wrote, "Ugh!" At the end of that paragraph, he wrote, "overwritten."

I scanned the rest of the story and noticed more circled phrases: "somnolent stupor," "unexpressed aching within the recesses of her heart," "pregnant silence," and "twinkling smile of tender reminiscence." Much to my surprise, there were only minimal negative comments, including "too much" and "what does this mean?" Four pages had no marks. Had the red-inked disparaging comments remained solely in my head?

Finally, I read the story. After I got past the long weather descriptions with excessive metaphors, I focused on twenty-eight-year-old Annie, who is home alone, prepared to read a book, and suddenly interrupted by the telephone. In the subsequent conversation between Annie and Randy, I learn that they are a couple who separated after two years of living together. They carry on a simple, information-packed conversation, each reporting on their recent adjustments to single life. The story continues with Annie's introspection, and her home life with her cat, Ella, until Randy calls again and suggests he come over "to pick up some things."

When Randy arrives, Annie quickly notices the changes in his appearance and behavior: a new haircut and a switch to another cigarette brand. Annie observes Randy's relationship to the cat, showing their different styles of affection. Further discussion leads them to the bedroom for a "final" act of sex. After a few pages, Randy leaves and Annie returns to the bedroom, wondering if Ella knocked over the ashtray on the mattress.

Broderick Sudberry had been right about this story. It was loaded with clichés, overwriting, bad metaphors, and navel-gazing. But something new struck me in this uninterrupted rereading. The pacing was good, the interiority cogent, the dialogue realistic, the tension maintained, and, importantly, the relationship was believable. I could see why Broderick said this was the best story in the class. Yes, it needed a good copy editing, but it had heart and a workable structure. Not such a bad first story. Why had I only remembered his sarcastic tone, his nasty comments, his ridicule? Why had I misremembered the number and color of his comments?

I often wondered what would have happened if Broderick had been a more encouraging teacher. Would I have applied to top-notch graduate programs that offered well-published professors with ties to agents and publishers? Would I have had several novels and essay collections visible on bookstore shelves and library stacks? Would interviewers have asked me to name the influential books on my bedside table?

Mostly, I tried to find something good that came of my literary choices. Could all the jobs I held after I left the Queens Borough Public Library in the 1970s have helped me hone my writing and editorial skills? Did my co-ownership of a company give me confidence to take risks? I kept thinking of my parents' failed careers and that haunting quote by the poet Whittier about what "might have been." I wanted to break the chain.

I took my first serious plunge when I enrolled in a short-story course at the New School, this time with a female teacher who used prompts from Natalie Goldberg's book *Writing Down the Bones*. During our second class, the teacher read a prompt about recreating an unforgettable childhood memory. As I wrote, my pen pressed so hard into the paper that it ripped jagged lines. I could hardly control the flow of images. My brother, Ben, and his gang were before me on the page, as they examined my naked, shaking five-year-old body. The scene was so vivid that I quickly turned it into a story of eleven pages, unconsciously matching the same number as "The Lingering Chill," though this one was called "Take Off Your Bottoms." And this time, there was no yellow note; I read the story aloud in class, though my voice broke on the verge of tears.

The woman who sat next to me in class loved the story and gave me the name of her uncle who was a famous literary agent. I called him the next day, and he invited me to mail him my story. A few weeks later, the agent called and said he loved the story. "You are a comer," he said. "I want to start you off with a few magazines and build you a reputation. Then we can talk about a novel."

I was so flabbergasted how this had so easily fallen into my lap that I didn't feel too disappointed when the agent told me that the editor at the *Atlantic* liked the story but declined to publish it as I had no credentials to speak of. I guessed that my

Factotum bestseller, *The Parkinson Disease Handbook*, didn't count as much. Not long afterward, I received a note in the mail from the agent saying that he was retiring and only keeping a few notable clients. Of course, I was disappointed, but by that time, I had already written half of my novel.

*  *  *

It was not an easy road to get a novel published. I soon learned that it was even harder to get an agent interested in my work. Younger agents wanted authors with a track record, with a story that gelled with a popular event or one written by a celebrity. They seemed less interested in literary quality than the sales potential. As for a publisher, it was a catch-22. Major publishers required an agent; an agent required an interested publisher. After countless rejections from agents, I sought small independent publishers who didn't require an agent.

Another two years of rejections and I was ready to put my manuscript in that cardboard box in my bedroom closet on top of "The Lingering Chill," when suddenly I received an offer from a small feminist press. By then, Shirley and I had closed Factotum permanently, and she joined a major trade publisher as its "first Black woman vice-president of marketing." I didn't know what to do, so I continued to work for my clients on a freelance basis.

On a warm, May afternoon in 2003, as I sat in my office working on a script for a video employee health newsletter, I heard the front door slam. It was four in the afternoon, and I was expecting my daughters for a rare mother/daughter lunch.

"Giorgia, Beth?" I called.

Before I got a response, twenty-six-year-old Giorgia stood in my office doorway wearing what I could only describe as a "smirk."

"What's up? I asked. I just spoke to your sister. She will meet us at the restaurant in a half hour." I noticed a bulge under Giorgia's hooded sweatshirt and a brown edge of a mailing package above her zipper, opened at breast level.

"What's under there?" I asked.

"Wouldn't *you* like to know?" She took a few gulps from a plastic water bottle in her hand.

"Did you get it from the doorman? Is it for me?"

"Not everything's for you."

"Okay, Miss Smart Aleck, give it over."

"You'll see." Giorgia rushed to my desk and grabbed scissors from a leather-bound pencil holder. Then she unzipped her vest and pulled out a slim corrugated envelope.

"Let me see. Where's it from?"

"Can't you wait for a second?" I felt like a child.

Giorgia turned the air conditioner to the highest setting. "It's like a tomb in here."

"I must admit, even *I'm* hot."

I sat back and let my daughter proceed at her own pace. After all, she just had her first documentary produced after leaving a short career in acting. She certainly had the right dramatic flourish.

With a few deft slashes through the glued flap, Giorgia opened the mailer and before I could register what my daughter had in her hands, she said, out of breath, "Ta da, here it is Mommy ... your book."

I didn't immediately see the book. I was transfixed by my daughter's face. She was crying.

"Oh my God," I said. "I can't believe it's really here." I caressed the cover—a black-and -white photo of a rural road, with the shadowy back of an adolescent girl walking into the forest. Above the title, *TAKE OFF YOUR BOTTOMS,* was my name, Anita Rappaport, in a 1950s flourishing, all-caps script.

"I'm so glad you were here when it came."

For a few minutes, I said nothing, cradling the book in my lap, smoothing the glossy cover. I closed my eyes.

"What? What is it?" Giorgia asked.

"I don't know. I'm feeling overwhelmed, I guess." My breathing was coming out in honks.

Giorgia stood by my side, and we took turns flipping through the book, looking over each other's shoulders.

"It looks good, really good," Giorgia said, her cheeks returning to her natural lightly freckled, pink tone.

"Hmm. It does. They did a good job. I'll admit I was a little worried, but the paper and color are first-rate. I expect a delivery of more author copies soon."

"Let's bring it to lunch to show Beth. She'll be so happy. You can be proud."

"I am." I said the words, but they came out too easily. I *was proud, I was.* But the whole experience was unreal. With the book resting in my hands, I waited. I waited for it to implode, to burn itself from within. I waited for the phone to ring and hear the awful truth: that Sergio had paid for the book to be published and that this was the only copy. I waited, expecting to see that it was not my name on the book cover, that there was a terrible spelling error in the title.

# CHAPTER 37: BOOK PARTY

## Fall 2003

Two weeks before my first book party, I reviewed the list of RSVPs. Though I was hosting the party in my Morningside Heights apartment, where we'd moved three years before, I had hired a caterer to provide the food and help serve. I needed to inform the caterer of the exact number of people attending. Out of the fifty-two invited guests, five hadn't called, including my dear friend Shirley.

I worried I had sent Shirley's invitation to the wrong address. Shirley now lived somewhere in New Jersey, but I couldn't remember the town's name. During the past twenty years, Shirley had moved several times within a fifteen-mile radius, though I had visited only one house: a split-level that Shirley shared with her grown-son, Elgin, daughter-in-law, and twin teenage grandson and granddaughter. Through the years, I had squeezed all of Shirley's addresses into a single, four-inch-long page of my little blue book, scribbling some phone numbers sideways to fit empty space, neglecting to cross out old entries.

The relationship between us had been unpredictable since Shirley and I dissolved our business over a year ago after nearly six years as partners, the last two practically on a part-time basis. Recently, when I met her for lunch at her new office, I had jokingly referred to our parting as a "divorce," and she jumped at me in a way I had never seen in all our years as friends.

"Don't ever say the word 'divorce.' It gives the impression that we are no longer together and parted with animosity."

"I am so sorry, Shirl." Though my apology was sincere, I possibly offended Shirley in a profound way and that explained her recent silence.

With my party coming up, I had also fretted that Shirley wouldn't know many people, that she would sit in a corner, shy and friendless. A Libra in truth and spirit, I wanted everyone I knew to love everyone I knew. Could it be that Shirley didn't want to socialize with my friends?

I lifted the receiver and dialed the clearest entry in my phone book. Shirley said hello on the second ring. Accustomed to hearing Shirley announce our company name, I almost didn't recognize my friend's raspy voice.

"Did you get it?" I said, without preamble, as if there had been no interruption in our past conversation.

"Anita? Is that you?"

"I thought you'd know my voice anywhere." I twisted my finger around a corkscrew ear lock.

"I can't believe you're calling. I was just thinking of you."

If anyone else had said that I would have rolled my eyes, but I knew Shirley was telling the truth because I often felt the same way. Although we hadn't seen each other more than half a dozen times since our business dissolution, we kept in touch by telephone. If each hadn't heard from the other by about a month and a half, one would phone just as the other said she was going to. Shirley often said we had telepathy. I never wanted to destroy this belief by telling my friend that the absence of contact over time was triggering associations, not some mystical bond.

"Did you or didn't you get my invitation?" I asked.

"I did."

"Good. I thought I sent it to your old address. I can never get used to these New Jersey towns. To me, they're just exits off shopping plazas." Knowing that Shirley's nerves had sabotaged her driving test numerous times, I couldn't imagine her being stuck in a place that depended on a bus or car to the city. "When are you moving back to civilization, anyhow?"

"The farther away I am from the Big Apple, the more civilized I feel."

"But the commute must be murder."

"It's not much more time than coming from Brooklyn."

"That's great. I admit I was a little concerned. Okay, I can't take the suspense. Are you coming to my party or not?"

"Anita, you must know I'd never miss your first book party."

I felt Shirley's warmth envelope me, and my neck and shoulder muscles relaxed. I could picture Shirley's wide, gleaming smile. How could I have imagined that Shirley would feel uncomfortable with strangers?

"I'm so glad you said that, Shirl. I was concerned when you didn't call."

"I'm sorry. The invitation is sitting on my desk. I meant to call. You should have known to count on me."

"I can't wait to see you." I hung up, relieved.

★ ★ ★

On the afternoon of my party, rain fell softly at first and gathered intensity. "Good that you didn't have it at an outdoor venue like you originally planned," Denise said, helping me lay out plates and silverware along the buffet table.

"I know, but I hope people won't have trouble getting here."

"It's only rain. Don't worry."

"I was thinking of Shirley. She has to come all the way from New Jersey by bus, then take the subway uptown and walk several blocks."

"Isn't your cousin Jeffrey coming from Boston and Sergio's sister from Virginia?"

"I guess so, but they're all coming with someone."

"Shirley's a big girl. She'll be okay," Denise said impatiently.

"Well, you know Shirley."

"Yeah, but she was your friend, more than our friend. After the years of our CR group, you worked and socialized with her separately."

"I guess so. It wasn't deliberate. More to suit her responsibilities than anything else.

"My God, Anita, will you relax about Shirley? You forget that I also saw her at your office Christmas party. What was it, about five years ago? I loved talking to her then, and she had a good conversation with Arthur about computers. She looked like she was having a good time."

"Arthur is your husband, he doesn't count."

"I'll forget to tell him you said that."

★ ★ ★

My daughters and two of their male friends, one a six-foot, long-haired Brit who charmed my friends with his accent and affectionately tousled Giorgia's hair, and the other a former college friend of Beth's, volunteered as my waitstaff, dressed in black T-shirts and pants. They circulated with platters of hors d'oeuvres and plastic flutes of champagne. I surveyed the guests, who formed unpredictable, mini-interlocking couplings along my two right-angled, pink-and-green flowered couches or stood around the edges of my oblong dining table lined with platters of plastic-wrapped sushi and stuffed grape leaves. It was remarkable. My physician cousin Mindy stood face-to-face in an animated conversation with a woman from my writing group; Denise was introducing a gay neighbor around the room; my childhood friend now living in Connecticut was whispering to a recent freelance colleague from Brazil. And Sergio and my "waiters" made sure that no one was sitting alone. I was delighted but realized that Shirley was nowhere in sight.

By a little "fake" prodding from Denise, who arranged one of my dining-room chairs in the center of the living room, I opened my book for a reading. From the days of my silence in group therapy, unlike my mother, I rarely felt comfortable as the center of attention. I cleared my throat and adjusted my eyeglasses. I focused on Beth, who sat on the floor in a basic yoga lotus pose.

She kept nodding.

"Here goes," I said, and read the first two pages, where I introduce the main character as her family pulls up to their ramshackle bungalow in the Catskill mountains. Then I looked up and took off my glasses. There was prolonged applause. Sergio, normally reticent in social settings, placed his two fingers in each side of his mouth, between his pursed lips, and produced a loud, melodious wolf whistle. While I heard such screeching sounds from boys growing up in Brooklyn, I was shocked that my foreign-born husband could have passed for a native New Yorker, at least sound-wise. Later on, I did cursory research to find that there were various theories on the derivation of the sound, but most agreed that it emanated from the mountainous regions of Southern Europe to warn shepherds and dogs of wolf sightings. So, perhaps Sergio brought more credibility to the sound.

A few of my guests, who hadn't yet bought my book, gathered around Giorgia, who was the official salesclerk. They joined others who brought their copies and formed a line while I signed my name. I kept thinking of my mother, who would have loved this event, probably finding a way to grab the spotlight. I recalled one of her famous lines, which she said even before I finished this book: "I just read the worst book, I don't know why yours isn't published."

★ ★ ★

After dinner, Denise asked about Shirley.

"I don't know where she is," I said, quelling my anxiety. I didn't tell Denise that I suspected the worst. Then again, if it were a bus or subway accident, I reasoned, there would have been word by now. My guests who had driven would have heard about any disasters on their car radios. But even if they had, would they have known the victim's name, and that she was my friend?

More likely, something important came up. Maybe Elgin got sick, or it could have been one of his twins. Elgin was an amateur football player; maybe he was injured. But why hadn't Shirley called?

"She did have a lot of trouble with her teeth," I said to Denise as the caterers scooped coffee into the percolator's trough.

By the end of the party, a sense of certain dread gripped me.

"Call her," Denise said for the fifth time that night.

"I will. I know it's nothing terrible. She lives with her son. He would have called me." I remembered when Shirley had been diagnosed with breast cancer early in our partnership. It was a simple case, no spread. They had gotten it all. Stage I. Though you never know. If it had metastasized by now, Shirley would have mentioned it when we spoke two weeks ago, but then perhaps she just found out something. Still.

I couldn't admit to Denise why I hadn't called Shirley immediately. It was this persistent fear that Shirley had forgotten about the party, or that she didn't want to come and was too embarrassed to call. For me, hurt feelings often overrode concern.

"I'd never miss your first book party," Shirley had said the last time we spoke. I repeated the conversation several times in my head and went to bed, reassured. It was probably some stupid mix-up on Shirley's part. There had been many over the years: Elgin's school accidents, Shirley's last-minute meetings. And last year, I waited in Shirley's office lobby for almost an hour only to discover that she hadn't gone to work. She had an emergency at the dentist and later said she had tried to call me. Some people were just not good at making and keeping dates.

Of course, there were all kinds of unpleasant explanations. But not between Shirley and me. Not between the dynamic duo, our old boss, Michael Bernstein, used to call us. I was almost twenty-three when we met. Shirley was nearing thirty. Even then Shirley seemed so sensible, beyond the need to indulge in feminine wiles. Her full-time responsibility was raising a son alone in Bedford-Stuyvesant. She was, always, the most mature person I knew.

The day after the party, I couldn't stand the worry and weakened. My heart was thumping as I dialed Shirley's number. A male answered.

"Hello, Elgin?"

"Yes."

"Hi, this is Anita, you know, your mom's friend."

"Sure, how are you?"

"Fine, and you?"

"Can't complain."

"You can, I'll let you. Really, I was kind of concerned about your mother. Is she around?"

"Actually, she went fishing. She wanted to take advantage of the warm weather."

A Southern girl at heart, Shirley preferred to spend the afternoon with her hair pinned back, her forehead wrapped in a scarf, and a fishing pole in her hand.

"Oh, then she's okay?"

"Yeah, fine."

"Tell your mother I called."

"I will. Nice talking to you."

Still, Shirley didn't call. Days passed and then two weeks. If Shirley were in trouble, surely Elgin would have told me. His mom had gone fishing, he had said.

"Maybe she's going through a life crisis," Denise offered during a phone conversation. "You know, she is living with her son and his family. You mentioned she was considering early retirement. It's sometimes hard for people who have been so goal-oriented and responsible to focus on their own needs. It can be traumatic."

"I know, but she had said she was having the time of her life. She would have told me otherwise," I said, but doubts remained. Maybe I didn't know Shirley as well as I thought.

Maybe Shirley wouldn't have told me.

I tried to put Shirley out of my thoughts and concentrated on my work.

After emailing two submissions to clients, the phone rang. It was Denise and, as usual, the subject of Shirley came up.

"It's possible that Shirley could have a dependency problem," Denise said.

"Ever since you got your MSW two years ago, you really sound like a social worker. It doesn't mean the whole world is in or needs recovery."

"It's just that avoidance is typical of the chemical abuser."

"She does not, I repeat, does not have a drug or alcohol problem." I hung up, but with a loud thud that reverberated for several minutes. I couldn't concentrate on my work. Finally, I called Shirley again.

"Yes?" Shirley said in a distracted tone.

"I'm glad you're alive."

"Anita?"

"You still remember my voice?" I couldn't control my teenage spite. I hated when others did that, but now I wasn't myself.

"Listen, I meant to call," Shirley whimpered. "I didn't tell you that I handed in my resignation last month. The commute was too much. I want to find something closer."

"Why didn't you tell me?"

"It all happened so fast. There's been a lot of construction work on the turnpike, and for months it took over an hour to get to work and almost two to get home. I couldn't take it anymore. I meant to call you."

As a fearful New York driver, who rarely took the wheel, I normally would understand traffic issues, but Shirley's excuse smacked of dishonesty. I felt the acrid taste of betrayal.

"That's a lot of wasted time."

"Now, I don't know what local business will hire me."

"You're still so young, not even sixty-five yet."

"That's old in the business world. Believe it or not, I just got this part-time nothing job, a few days a week, up the road from me. Temporary. Dull office work. I'm home on a lunch break now. I have to go back. I'm already late."

I couldn't believe Shirley was rushing me off the telephone. *Who was this woman?* I was a mixture of tears and fury, still holding onto the idea that she was keeping something important from me.

"But, Shirley, are you okay?"

"Yeah, why wouldn't I be?"

"You didn't call me, you know about the party."

"Oh, no! I forgot that it was on the seventh."

"It wasn't. It was on the fourteenth."

"I didn't look at the invitation."

"And Shirley, why didn't you return my call?"

"What call?"

"I spoke to Elgin. He didn't tell you?"

"No, he didn't."

I swallowed. "You know Shirley, I'm very hurt, hurt that you didn't even remember." This was the first time I criticized Shirley. I felt a torrent of humidity wash over me like I was stuck in the surrounding aftermath of a waterfall.

"Oh, Anita, you know how much I love you. You have to know that."

"I guess so, but Shirley, are you sure everything is okay?"

"Sure. I really must go. Listen, I'll call you tonight and we'll talk."

"Okay," I said, hanging up, certain that Shirley wouldn't honor her word.

★ ★ ★

Sure enough, Shirley didn't call that night. My line wasn't even busy. There was no excuse. This time, I had spoken to Shirley directly. There was no invitation to misplace. No son to misinform. So many excuses. Nobody could forget all those times, even if Shirley thought she did. I wondered about Shirley's ulterior motives. She couldn't be so out of touch with propriety that she no longer expected to return a call, answer an invitation.

A flash went off in my brain. Could it have been, no, could it have been a racial thing? Could Shirley have felt that a party with so many white people would not be the place for a Black person? Hadn't Oprah said that her Black women friends were convinced that white people all secretly hated Blacks? Most of the time, I hadn't thought of Shirley in racial terms. Could race have been the reason? No, not between us. I couldn't believe it.

Growing up in a middle-class Jewish and Catholic neighborhood in Brooklyn, I didn't have many personal experiences with Black people. We had a cleaning woman, Carrie, who came to our apartment every Thursday, even when my father lost his business. I often watched her ironing, and she smelled of lemony furniture polish and laundry starch. She told me stories about her family down South. She asked me about school and my friends. I adored her.

In high school, I had lunch with a beautiful Black girl named Milly. She was president of the senior class and went on to an Ivy League university. She was the only Black student in school.

Then another flash went off. I remembered saying something to Shirley about a friend looking as if she had just undergone chemotherapy. Could Shirley have been insulted or hurt by that remark? Maybe Shirley thought I had forgotten about her own past cancer.

"No way," Denise told me. "Shirley knows what a sensitive person you are. She is not so thin-skinned."

The flashes of so-called insight never stopped. As the days passed, I tortured myself with every conceivable possibility: that Shirley was depressed, that she was embarrassed, that she had been sick, that she hated me, that our partnership and especially our friendship meant nothing to her all those years. And then I'd remember all the times Shirley told me how talented I was, how she bragged about me, how she depended on me in our business for the instant creative solution. How we laughed for hours, and how we regaled each other with the same old stories over and over again. Had everything been a sham?

I composed letters in my head, conducted pretend phone conversations with Shirley. In each, when I tried to imagine Shirley's responses, they were always the same: "You know I'd never miss your party.... You know how much I love you"—all the right words. Yet, no matter what I invented, nothing made any sense.

★ ★ ★

On another rainy afternoon, six months later, I looked through an old photo album. There was Shirley on her wedding day, wearing a beautiful sheer blue dress, her son, Elgin, about twelve years old, standing behind her, his huge Afro as proud as his mom's full-blown smile. As the minister spoke and Charlie repeated his words, Shirley's right fingertips stretched behind her, reaching for the hand of her friend, me, who stood as close as I could.

As I shut the album, a thought occurred to me, more insistent and overwhelming than my previous flashes. With tears spilling down on the green faux leather photo album, I understood immediately: I'd never know what happened with Shirley. I'd never know why my friend, who professed love and loyalty, couldn't show it.

# CHAPTER 38: YOU NEVER KNOW WHEN YOU CAN USE IT

### October 2005

As soon as my brother turned sixty-five, he bought a two-bedroom condominium in a Florida retirement community. Shortly before his move, I went to his ranch house in suburban new Jersey, where he lived after his divorce, and helped him organize his possessions, many of which he hoarded from various locations over the years, into a semblance of order. His taste was eclectic; he loved antiques, especially old toys and model airplanes, and he loved kitchen gadgets advertised on late-night television. Over the years, he spent many Saturdays and Sundays at flea markets and tag sales. When he picked me up at the train station, I got into his car. The back was jammed with ragged stuffed animals, bicycle parts, and stacks of old books and record albums.

When we reached his house, we transferred the items from his car. I held up a strange plastic box with an attached narrow transparent tube.

"What in the world is this?" I had asked.

"Waterpik," he said.

"You mean you will use someone else's?"

"Well, you never know when you could use it."

A month later, I took advantage of my brother's invitation to visit him in his new place in Florida. I thought it could be the time to confront Ben with my lifelong resentments. The question was, "Did I have the courage?"

I was prepared for Ben's arguments about throwing out his junk. After I stepped into his condo, I was shocked at how sparse and pristine everything looked. The beige tile floors that lined the entranceway and spanned the living room, were immaculate and shining; the black leather sectional was devoid of throw pillows; the galley kitchen featured uncluttered quartz countertops.

"Ben! What happened to you?" I cried.

"I decided to turn over a new leaf. I had hired a service to help me get rid of my stuff before I moved. After several anxious days, I felt a sense of utter relief when I watched the movers fill up only half of their truck. I am determined to play tennis on weekends and not attend one garage sale."

"Good for you." I stared at my brother's still-lanky physique and his salt-and-pepper beard. Was there hope that this man who clung to his anger and grievances had really changed?

On Sunday morning before I was going to the airport, I sat with Ben on the kitchen stools drinking a final cup of coffee.

"Can I ask you something?" I asked.

"Oops, that sounds ominous."

"Well, it's something that has bothered me for a long time."

"Okay, I'm game."

I felt overwhelming pressure around my eyes. I cried so rarely that I couldn't tell if this was the opening of the floodgates, finally. More than anything, I didn't want to lose it in front of my brother. I inhaled and took a sip of my coffee, now lukewarm. "I don't know how to begin."

"Then let me change the subject."

"Oh?"

"How are your freckles doing? Do they still point to your twat?"

Oh, no, I couldn't believe he was asking me about this before I finished my coffee. A wallop of heat overcame me, and I felt all my clothes fall off my body as if I were still the little girl in the country.

Perhaps my brother had sensed that I wanted to go back to our childhood, but I couldn't believe he would revert to this. Something snapped in me.

"You know Ben, you and your gang tortured me with your bullying. I want you to know that I really suffered from this, haunting me my whole life." Finally, I said it. I waited for something unnatural, like a hurricane blast or an earthquake's spasms. Nothing, I still stood in my brother's sterile kitchen.

Ben rose and I expected he would give me a hug. Instead, he moved to the sink facing the counter where I sat. He turned on the faucet and bent down, sipping the water directly from the spout.

"Believe it or not, at my age, I'm just happy I remember anything."

"That's all you have to say?"

"What do you want from me?"

"Nothing," I said. I walked to the hallway where my suitcase awaited. "I'm ready to go when you are."

★ ★ ★

A week later, Ben hanged himself when he was expecting a visit from Paula. She found him sprawled on the living room rug, his neck still tied to the ceiling fan, which had fallen on his head.

Ben had said that he was happy to remember anything, even if it was painful to someone else. Did he contemplate that his final act would be seared into the consciousness of all who ever loved him?

The pain was unforgettable.

# CHAPTER 39: JUMP-START

December 2006

One afternoon, mired in deep clinical depression, I turned on the television as I usually did when I couldn't do anything else. Oprah's show came on; she was interviewing Mia Farrow and her son. They just returned from Darfur and described the dire situation, showing footage of the suffering refugees. Though I had seen pictures of starving children many times, though I was researching my family's Holocaust experiences, delving into inconceivable human torture, and though I had felt useless for longer than my depression, and still trying to make sense of Ben's suicide, these Darfur images hit me like a hard and swift smack in the face. One little African girl's huge eyes bored into the camera, telegraphing her longing directly toward me.

Still mesmerized, I stumbled into my study overlooking the Hudson River, activated my computer, clicked onto the internet, and Googled two words: *Africa, volunteers*. Almost instantly, more than a million entries appeared. Daunting, overwhelming, yes. But for the first time in ages, I couldn't wait to click away. As a writer who now basically worked in isolation, and as a woman who had been battling psychological demons, this search felt like my last call to action—my jump-start to living.

After weeks of research, I narrowed the field to a humanitarian organization that offered a communal approach with supervised meal preparations and dormitory-style housing in a rural Tanzanian village. On the phone, Sharon, the program director, explained that the commitment was three weeks, a long time to be away from home. I approached Sergio with my plans.

"How would you feel if I went?"

"Without me?"

During our long marriage, we had traveled often together, especially to visit Sergio's family in Italy, and to take our daughters to France. This time, I needed to go alone. Sergio was a self-sufficient man who liked the routines of domestic life, including cooking and even ironing. When we once had a large hole in the upholstery of our old wingback chair, Sergio took out the sewing basket I inherited from my paternal grandmother and, with the finest of surgical stitches, mended the chair so that nobody was the wiser.

"Yes," I answered. "I'd go alone, but there would be other people in our dormitory."

"I guess I have no objection," he said in an unconvincing voice. He knew me better than I expected and kept his misgivings to himself.

I still had doubts: Did I have the skills and knowledge that could become appreciable service? Did I possess the sensitivities to bridge language, cultural, and age barriers?

Mostly, I worried about living in a shared living arrangement. I never went to an out-of- town college; I never went to a sleep-away camp; I never indulged in hippie communalism. My childhood sleepovers included one or two girlfriends, and sleeping was the last thing on our minds. There was my experience with Denise as Village roommates, and then our trip to Europe. That could hardly count as communal living.

Yes, I'd live and work with others, but I'd be on my own. I wouldn't have my daughters.

I wouldn't have my husband. I wouldn't have Denise. I wouldn't have my dog. I wouldn't know one living soul. Then again, no one would know me. I could be a new person. I could be anyone I wanted.

The potential seemed enormous. Maybe I could help women start a business. Maybe I could impart writing skills to children. Maybe I could promote a health-related group. Maybe I could adopt a child.

Certainly, I'd be surrounded by photographic and authorial material. I could delay my proposed Holocaust novel and write one set in Tanzania. I'd bring my Nikon and create a gallery photo exhibit. I could combine the two and create a photo book with essays.

Soon after I made the commitment, I learned that the seventy-year-old volunteer, the oldest one, dropped out. At sixty, I'd be alone at the top. Since estimates of life expectancy for Tanzanian women ranged from 45 to 49, close to the sub-Saharan area's average, I could be the oldest woman in Africa!

★ ★ ★

On the long plane ride from Amsterdam to Tanzania, I dreaded any bump or announcement of impending turbulence. I couldn't maintain this level of anxiety and swallowed a tranquilizer. As I drifted off, I thought of the reasons for my depression, which had revived my old phobias after I had been attacked and freaked out smoking pot. This go-round seemed littered with tragedies; the most recent and severe was my brother's suicide and the knowledge that his daughter would discover his body. These triggered memories of Aviva and even Marilyn. Underlying these was my constant search for creative fulfillment, and my fear of synthesizing my Holocaust research into a cogent novel that honored my family.

After a deep sleep, I arrived in Tanzania where a van took me in the dark night to our headquarters. I barely said hello before I tumbled into the lower level of an empty bunk bed and awoke to a cacophony of roosters.

This was the first day at my placement, the Children's Centre, primarily a preschool, also providing morning elementary-grade and remedial after-school programs, in Majengo Village near the town of Moshi. Amina, the founder and director, greeted me and we shook hands. An attractive woman in slacks, Amina was in her fifties with a bronze complexion and reddish-brown hair in tight cornrows lined with gray. I followed her on a tour, including an outdoor area, a middle room, a small library, and a back semi-open space for the youngest children, mostly four-year-olds. We returned to the outdoor classroom, where an older group of six-year-olds sat on small wood chairs facing rows of low benches serving as desks. She introduced me to a young, slim man, Ibada, the teacher, who shook my hand vigorously.

The large blackboard contained two columns of sentences in perfect script, ending with blanks. Ibada had instructed the children to copy the sentences and fill in the correct word at the end. I sat on the highest bench in the back and watched the children writing in their blue school booklets. Most used pencils, some of which were mere stubs.

There was also a smaller mobile blackboard on the other side of the classroom. There, Ibada wrote simple arithmetic equations: additions and subtractions. I was relieved that they were easy enough for me. Ibada informed the children to bring their work to me when they finished. He handed me a red pen.

A girl slowly walked to the teacher, and he nodded toward me. She thrust her booklet in my lap. I read her sentences. She got everything right, and I wanted to praise her. Near each answer, I made large, flowing check marks. On the top of the page, next to the date, I wrote, "Very good work" and drew a star. The girl grinned and squeezed by my side.

Very soon, there was a crowd before me, each child shoving, yelling, "Teacher, teacher, me." Happily, I read aloud each child's work, and when I found a mistake, I circled it and asked the child to return for a check mark and a star. After only an hour with the kids, I lost my voice.

Most of the children finished and encircled me. A few girls played with my hair, pulling it back in a fake ponytail. Others squirmed in my lap, vying for a good position. One girl placed her booklet in front of me; I had already given her "100 percent correct." So, I asked her name and, on a new page in her booklet, wrote "Lisa." Then I drew a ball and asked her to write "ball," which she did.

Before long, hands were jamming booklets in my face, each child demanding a drawing.

"Teacher, draw me a kangaroo," one asked. Another, "Draw me a cat."

On the next girl's booklet, I wrote, "Regina Goes to School," and fashioned objects she'd encounter, such as her clothes, house, books, and trees in the street. One boy's story, "Johnson Walks Home," included figures and names of his family members. The requests came faster than I could draw a circle. Only yesterday, I had worried that I wouldn't get a child's attention. Now, I couldn't get the children in order. Ibada brought out a tray of mugs filled with porridge, and the children sat down to eat. Afterward, it was time for them to go home, each one petting my ear, my nose, jumping, and shouting, "Bye, bye teacher Anita. See you tomorrow." I was in heaven.

* * *

That afternoon, Amina and Ibada took turns with the twelve to sixteen-year-olds in the main classroom. During the December holiday break, this age group brushed up on their

English and math skills for secondary school, which was conducted solely in English. Many of the students, Amina pointed out, were products of cheating teachers, so they had to take exams again.

Ibada tackled algebra, and Amina taught English. She asked me to tutor a boy named Jeremiah. His mother requested that someone help prepare him for his exams.

Jeremiah and I shook hands. Although he was sixteen, he looked no older than twelve. He asked me to call him Jerry. In a corner of the large classroom, he showed me his workbook.

Amina had given Jerry a pamphlet with exercises, employing the customary sentence copying and oral repetition, a more advanced version of the usual lesson. He copied them and checked his answers from a list of possibilities. I recognized the British English, and Jerry corrected me when I said "period." He called it a "full stop," which made a lot more sense to me. Many of the sentences were not grammatically correct, and I cringed silently.

When Jerry completed a sentence and answer, he showed it to me. He had beautiful, even handwriting. As was required, he first repeated the sentence and his answer aloud to practice his pronunciation. Then we went over each set together. Usually, it was easy, and I checked them and corrected him if necessary. Sometimes, I wrote a few explanatory words on the top of his booklet so he could study this when at home.

I was confounded by the selection of multiple-choice answers. In these cases, I could see from the way the question was worded that there could be more than one possible answer.

Shockingly, sometimes the expected answer was downright wrong.

I asked Amina what to do. Should I tell Jerry the answer they expect so that he was prepared for his exam, or should I tell him the correct answer that wasn't on his list, hoping he would truly understand my explanation? Amina said, "Most certainly, give him the correct answer." Finally, I instructed him, "Jerry this is the answer they want, and this is the better answer."

* * *

On our second day, my lessons with Jerry were boring; most of the time I watched him copy sentences. I wasn't sure whether I was accomplishing little more than giving him the answers or confusing him with two answers. I tried to enliven the sessions with mini lessons on plurals, verbs, nouns, and synonyms. I drew a crude map of the United States and pointed to New York. I added skyscrapers and placed the Statue of Liberty in the middle of the water.

My work with Jerry continued during my three weeks in Tanzania. Little by little, he veered from the rote exercises to being interactive. He asked me questions and added more creative answers, sometimes writing separate paragraphs based on my writing prompts. On our last day, when I exchanged addresses with him, I was astonished that not only did he have a post office box but two mobile phone numbers. I assumed these were for his parents or some other relative.

He asked, "What is your mobile number?"

I answered, "I work at home and don't use my mobile very often."

He looked at me as if I was weird. In a country where most children didn't have a complete family or the money to go to school, much less a nourishing meal, many of the older children had access to cell phones and email accounts.

* * *

Jerry wasn't the only one who changed. My three weeks ended, and I said my tearful goodbyes. On the way to the airport, the driver got stuck in traffic. When I thought I'd miss my plane home, a familiar onrush of anxiety overtook me like a reflex. It had felt good to put all that extra adrenalin to bed for three weeks, but scary to know that it could rear its ugly head at a moment's notice.

After we changed planes in Amsterdam, and I sat on the plane to Newark, I allowed my mind to float. In one sense, it seemed like I had left for Africa years ago and that a lifetime had passed. I hadn't left all my worries during those three weeks. But the anxieties were less about my abilities and shortcomings and more about responding to new situations—normal worries.

Daily, I went to the local internet cafe and typed emails to Sergio and my daughters. I wrote postcards to Denise because she would cherish the safari artwork and eventually cut it up and paste it on one of her beautiful collages that she made in her art class. I had wanted to send a letter to Cindy and include a beaded bracelet from our visit to the Maasai village, but I had no idea where she was.

I wished Marilyn were alive so I could share my experiences. She would have been rigid at the International Criminal Tribunal for Rwanda we had witnessed in Arusha, investigating the staggering 800,000 deaths of ethnic Tutsis and their Hutu sympathizers that occurred in just a hundred days in 1994. I would have told her about the wrenching visit to the Network Against Female Genital Mutilation (FGM) in the nearby town of Moshi where a member of the group showed us models of a normal woman's genitalia with three inserts depicting the anatomical results from different types of FGM, as well as a box of crude instruments used without anesthesia. Later, we saw a video showing a young girl of about five who was held down, tied by sashes, as someone cut into her vagina. Although my eyes had been closed, I heard the screaming, with the translation in a voiceover: "Mama, please help me."

Mostly, I wanted to communicate with Shirley and tell her about my new friend Amina, a Black woman, a single mother, and businesswoman. Two warm and compassionate women with commonalities, from different corners of the world.

The faces of the people I met drifted in and out of my consciousness as I looked out the window at darkness. The images of my last day at the school repeated. I saw the younger children swarming around me, nearly pinning me to the bushes. I heard their laughter and spontaneous singing; I felt the tug of their tiny hands on my skirt. I heard them calling me "teacher." Some part of me realized that these had been the best days of my life.

I came to jump-start my life. It was too soon to see if this worked, but I didn't want to return to my prior mental state. I had an inkling that I was on the correct path. Even on this plane, I hadn't resorted to my previous phobic reactions to every dip and turn. For the first time in over thirty years, I sat in the window seat, looking outside, admiring the clouds.

I was fearless.

★　★　★

After being home for almost two months, I didn't recognize my past *mzungu* (Swahili for white person) self. Who was that person who went to Africa? Did I live in a communal compound, sticking to a fairly normal eating and sleeping schedule, keeping up physically with women half my age? Did I teach children subjects I had long forgotten? Was that me?

Little by little, my pre-African life returned. I stayed up late again, eating leftovers and waking to a sour stomach. I was obsessed with things people said to me or what I said to them.

When friends and relatives asked me about my trip to Africa, I was hesitant to discuss the details.

I didn't want to reduce my experiences into pat generalities, into common travel stories centered on food and attractions. Mostly, I told people it was a life-altering experience, but I couldn't answer "how." I knew that for three glorious weeks in my life, I was another healthier self.

★ ★ ★

In the meantime, I revisited my Holocaust work. If Africa taught me anything, it was to stop concentrating within and turn more to the world beyond my reach. Suffering seemed to be a linear thing, stretching its tentacles, reverberating in unconscious transgenerational ways. I felt this especially when I found an old carton in a storeroom of my mother's apartment building. Only now did I have the mental fortitude to open it. Inside, I discovered my grandmother's and mother's naturalization papers; old letters from my mother's brother, who died in World War II; sepia-toned photographs of various villagers, the backs stamped with a photographer's name from Warsaw; several postcards with Yiddish writings; a tiny silver menorah and matching candlesticks. There was a treasure there; I had my family's history in my hands.

I had already amassed a great deal of materials: letters from Polish and Belarusian authorities, as well as the State Department; old tape cassettes of interviews my cousin conducted with my grandmother and her siblings; query responses from Holocaust and genealogical museums and organizations.

Amina wrote me a letter, thanking me for my service. She said Jerry often peppered her with questions about my life and background. I answered her, "Please tell Jerry I am getting ready to write about my heritage and hoped he would also appreciate his own."

# CHAPTER 40:
# MATTER OF DEGREES

### 2010-2014

It must have been the positive memories of teaching in Tanzania, as well as efforts to combat the constant rejections of my profession, that propelled me to investigate MFA programs, finally settling on the City College of New York for two reasons: It was a short subway ride from my apartment, and they accepted the most diverse students, of whom I considered myself as a woman approaching sixty-five.

With forty-three years between academic programs, I hoped the acceptance committee would forgive my lack of recommendations from former teachers in favor of professional colleagues. I was confident in submitting writing samples. But when I read that one of City College's requirements to the MFA program in Creative Writing was to pass a second language proficiency exam, I felt doomed to another failure. The only language for which I approached any proficiency was French, and the last time I studied that language was as a freshman in college over forty-five years ago.

What was I to do? My daughter Beth did what any good daughter did: she found a French tutor online. Marie (not with the last name of Curie) appeared at my apartment armed with books on French grammar, and everyday idiomatic conversations. After leafing through her stacks of materials at my kitchen table, my heart sank. My brain felt entirely too old to conjugate verbs. It would take me years to grasp enough French to even complain in a foreign language other than using the Yiddish *oy vey.*

"Marie, Marie, I really appreciate all your preparedness. But the test is going to be an essay, and I need to form a coherent written response. My speech will be inconsequential."

After a few months, Marie helped me formulate some decent paragraphs on literary topics, and I was more prepared for the upcoming exam. However, my fear was now bordering on terror. There was no way I would pass, and I would surely miss my dream of finally having my writing appreciated by knowledgeable scholars.

On the day of the exam, my alarm went off, and I awoke with a startle, stuck to my sheets in a layer of sweat. I staggered to the bathroom and popped the thermometer under my tongue. Sure enough, it registered at 102 degrees, and my throat felt like sandpaper every time I swallowed.

"I can't go," I said to Sergio.

"You should stay in bed," he said, bringing me a glass of water and an extra-strength Tylenol.

"Maybe this is a kinder way for me to avoid a failing grade."

"I'm so sorry," he said, and went out the door on his way to work.

I stretched on my bed, thinking of the last time I had been in France a few years ago. Sergio and I had rented a house in Provence. One day, we drove to a nearby village and Sergio visited the outdoor market to buy food for a picnic. I had been tired and crossed the street to wait for him and sat on a bench. An elderly man in a peaked beret and a denim short-sleeved shirt sat by my side.

"*Bonjour,*" he said.

"Ah, *bonjour*," I answered, adding, "*Ça va?*"

"*Très bien, et vous?*"

"*Bien,*" I replied. We seemed to have gotten past the introductory greeting.

After he asked me where I was from and where I was staying, we began a rudimentary conversation about the pros and cons of city life versus country life. Not once did he utter a word in English.

By the time Sergio appeared, carrying a basket with cheese wrapped in paper and two long baguettes protruding like crossed swords, I stood and shook hands with my French *ami*. I felt marvelous, or *merveilleuse*.

"I'm going to take the test," I yelled outside the front door as Sergio was waiting for the elevator.

"Are you sure you're up for it?" he asked.

"No, I'm not sure, but I can at least try."

★ ★ ★

An hour later, I squeezed into a narrow, hard-wooden folding chair in a large classroom with about twenty-five other students, all of them there for a second language and in most cases, it was their first. I received a test booklet with my essay question about Molière and his significance in French literature. It was a general question, and with the help of an allowed pocket dictionary, I first composed it in my head in English and then translated, resorting to words that were similar in English, such as splendid and important, just adding an *e* at the end. I fudged it the best I could, sucking on Lifesavers, unaware of the symbolism. When I finished two pages, I looked up at the clock and saw I still had a few minutes. It was then that I realized that my head was throbbing, and that I was shivering even though the room was overheated.

Wobbly, I stood and delivered my paper, certain that this would be my one and only visit to the City College of New York.

A few weeks later, I received an email from City College with my grade. Although I had recovered from my inexplicable "flu," I shook uncontrollably as I opened the file. Shock of shock, I didn't fail. This had surely been a mistake. In my world of professional rejection, I wasn't used to acceptance. But there it was, those magic words: "You have passed."

★ ★ ★

For my first semester as a graduate student, I enrolled in two courses: Global English Literature and a fiction workshop. It had been such a long time since I wrote a book report, and I dug in for my first assignment, *The Reluctant Fundamentalist* by Mohsin Hamid. Naturally, I began at the beginning:

Like every writer, I struggle with first sentences. Sometimes they come quickly; sometimes all I have is a first sentence; and occasionally, I strike the first sentence in favor of a temporary replacement. So it is with particular admiration that I note that Hamid's first sentence introduces the narrator/protagonist, Changez, who offers to be of assistance. Not only is he making himself essential to the story, he is setting up the style of the novel throughout: his listener is addressed as "sir," someone requiring deference because of his apparent difference.

From this starting point, my writing flowed seamlessly. My years as a writer of so many varied assignments, mostly geared to rigid requirements, gave me an unexpected ease of expression. Perhaps words had not betrayed me after all.

My report focused on the ending:

Hamid says in the interview at the end that the core skill of a novelist is empathy. The world is suffering from a failure of compassion toward people who seem different. Yet Changez does not seem to possess empathy. I think he is too mired in anger and self-justification to fully imagine the reality of what others feel.

He too is trapped by his own tragic perspective.

My fiction workshop didn't go as smoothly. The class comprised twenty-five students of various ages and nationalities, sitting around a long conference-room table. Our assignments involved submitting short stories to "workshop" in class. For my first effort, I submitted a story fashioned from the material I had been collecting on my extended family murdered in the Holocaust, their fates unknown, though some research pointed to their death in a village massacre. This story focused on the ghettoization of my main characters.

On the day of my critique, the instructor asked for a volunteer to begin the discussion.

One woman, a teacher from Brooklyn in her fifties, said, "This was very moving. You handled the research seamlessly." She handed me her copy and there were no editorial changes, but many positive comments. Another student, a young Pakistani man, said that the story helped him understand the Holocaust better. He wrote a few questions on the back of the story. Then John, a man in his twenties, good-looking, wearing a vintage green sweater with a shawl-neck collar, shot up his arm. "I would like to comment," he said. "I spent the summer working for a literary agency and my job was to read unsolicited manuscripts."

Ah-ha, I thought. Finally, I may have contact with a reputable agency, someone who will help promote the publication of my work. This was one reason I had decided to go to graduate school, to have people in the business help me.

John stood holding my paper, fanning the pages as he spoke: "I have to say that I don't relate to these kinds of stories. I would never read this on my own. I find them boring."

A hum of groans emanated from the other students, but the teacher didn't interfere. Seemingly emboldened, John continued: "After two months of reading all kinds of manuscripts, this is the kind I would put in the slush pile."

The class ended shortly afterward, and I walked down the hall toward the elevator. I felt tears gathering and my breath was coming out in snorts. By the elevator bank, two of my classmates joined me, one repeatedly plugging the down button. The other, the older woman from Brooklyn, tapped me on my shoulder. "Please don't take the words of that arrogant son of a bitch seriously."

"It's hard not to," I croaked.

"He doesn't know what he is talking about. Remember his stupid story about the bar scene, talk about a slush pile."

I thanked the woman, and we all rode the elevator down to the first floor in silence. I ran ahead and walked twenty blocks home with tears running toward my mouth as I swallowed the salty drops as if they were my last liquid. I kept an interior dialogue, repeating the refrain, "Is this what I went to graduate school for?"

★ ★ ★

Not everything in graduate school was an exercise in rejection. Unlike my experience in college, as a graduate student I received As and A plusses in every course. I received literary prizes in both fiction and creative nonfiction. The school did not open doors for me in the literary publishing world, but it helped my self-esteem. To my astonishment, I was a good student, and unlike my rebellion in college, I was attracted to the teaching courses.

On a warm day in May, graduate students joined the mob of undergrads in a ceremony, complete with caps and gowns and the strains of "Pomp and Circumstance." When my name was called, I walked down a long aisle to the stage. Even though there was crowd noise coming from hundreds of audience members, there were only two words I heard above the noise: "Mommy, Mommy." Without seeing their faces, I knew my two daughters were standing among the crowd waving frantically at the oldest graduate in the arena.

At the end of the ceremony, Sergio handed me a bouquet containing a mix of carnations and roses. There were too many people to compete for a taxi, so we took the subway downtown, and I sat in the middle of my family, my flowers resting on my lap, atop my black cap. For the celebration, we had the choice of many fine restaurants. I selected our local diner, and we all ordered our favorites.

I was eager to begin my official teaching assignment. Like all news graduates, I was assigned a required freshman com-position course that combined a research topic with a writing component. After two semesters of this course, the English Department awarded me my choice: to teach Introduction to Creative Writing. Without explicit parameters, I covered all forms of writing, from poetry to long prose.

I began by distributing printouts of how to critique prop-erly, keeping in mind all negators from my old writing teacher Broderick Sudberry to John in my workshop. I made sure that the students remained polite and encouraging, never using dis-paraging words such as "boring."

On the last day of this creative writing course, I brought a rolling suitcase filled with a blanket, paper plates, plastic utensils, and cans of soda. I had asked the students to bring food from their cultures. We spread out on a campus grassy hill and unfurled our goodies. There were stuffed grape leaves, tabouli salad, falafel, dumplings, sushi, naan bread, and a tray of assorted Dunkin' doughnuts. It was an eclectic feast. A few students read excerpts from their favorite pieces; one wrote a poem for the occasion. A young woman from China, who had been adopted in America after her parents abandoned her because they exceeded China's one-child policy, announced, "I have changed my major."

"Oh?" I said.

"Yes, I am going to major in English and concentrate on creative writing."

"Oh, no," I said. When I saw the girls' furrowed eyebrows, I realized I was inappropriate. "Sorry," I added.

"I thought you'd be happy," she replied."

"Well, I am flattered, very flattered. And you are a brilliant writer. I guess I am protective. Writing can be a lonely and frustrating career. But I would never discourage creative talent."

The girl relaxed her eyebrows to their natural state.

"But," I said, turning to the others, "this is a lesson for all of you. Make sure you have a backup plan."

# CHAPTER 41:
# A LETTER AND A WIG

## Fall 2016

All summer long I was bloated. I had trouble buttoning my jeans and was convinced that I had been eating too many desserts, especially since Sergio started baking cookies and cakes to bring to the hospital where he now had a cubicle office and attached waiting room in a long corridor of similarly appointed doctor cubicles designed for efficiency and not the luxurious quarters the doctors enjoyed before they were sucked into the vortex of the hospital. After buying larger sized pants and bulky shirts, I finally listened to Sergio and made an appointment with my gastroenterologist, expecting that my ileitis was the culprit.

Doctor Manny Lowell was a tall, handsome man in his sixties, with salt-and-pepper hair in a mild pompadour, as if he had modified his adolescent personal style. He tapped my abdomen several times and instead of the normal playful demeanor, his lips pursed and his nostrils expanded.

"What?" I said. "Do you think I have a bowel obstruction?"

"Let's not jump to any conclusions," he said. "But I want you to have a CAT scan with contrast to make sure that there is nothing to worry about."

With those words, I was worried. Sergio must have talked to Dr. Lowell on the phone and by the time I got home to my Upper West Side apartment, my husband called and arranged a CAT scan for the following day. Now I was very worried.

Sergio and Dr. Lowell worked at lightning speed, and after my CAT scan, they were both waiting for me as Dr. Lowell said the words: ovarian cancer.

"Cancer?" I asked, as if I hadn't heard him. "But cancer is not in my family. Besides, didn't Gilda Radner die from this?"

He didn't answer and shrugged. Sergio put his arm around me and shook in sobs. This was a man who never showed such emotion in front of a colleague. It must be pretty bad. I sat in absolute shock, unable to move, unable to shout, unable to cry. The first thing I thought was we had to tell our daughters. Oh my God, what if this is inherited and they get it, too? I've heard of such cases where the daughters have to get prophylactic hysterectomies. Now, I began to cry in earnest, if not for myself, but for my beautiful girls whose lives were now in jeopardy.

We saw the oncologist, Dr. Sternberg, two days later, accompanied by Giorgia and Beth. He said that the team at the Division of Gynecologic Oncology Health had agreed on the course of action: chemotherapy, surgery, and again chemotherapy. I would lose my hair, my long, silky hair that Sergio loved to pull out strand by strand to pretend he was using as dental floss. The PA informed me I didn't have to lose all my hair. Many breast cancer patients on chemo successfully used a cold cap procedure, which temporarily constricted blood flow to hair follicles, thereby lessening the chemical penetration. Some of these patients could keep at least half of their hair. What did I have to lose?

Magdalena, from the cold cap company, met me outside the chemo floor on my first day. Sergio and my daughters watched, aghast, as she loaded a strapped jockey-like cap with dry ice from a cooler, tightly tucked in packs, and applied a head cover. I sat back as the freezing air pummeled throughout my body and left me in a state that could only be described as post-frigid. I couldn't stop shaking and she covered me with a thin white hospital blanket. Thankfully, Beth came prepared with a satchel of warmth. She unfurled a burgundy woolen serape and wrapped it around me like an Eskimo on an Arctic journey. Magdalena secured my chin strap with a large gauze pad and Giorgia deposited a paper cup of steaming tea in my shaking hands. I clutched the cup for life.

Maybe twenty minutes later, Magdalena undid my contraption to refill the ice, and the oncology nurses started my chemo IVs. On that first day, I was nauseated, my legs shook in prolonged seizures, and I had to pee constantly, unhooking my IVs and dragging the pole to the bathroom outside my curtained booth. By far the worst torture was the cold caps, which continued the entire time of chemo and for two hours afterward. By midday, I was able to relax a bit and closed my eyes. A few minutes later, I heard Sergio talking to Magdalena. I opened my eyes and asked, "Is it time for the cold torture?" He said no, but he brought a plastic bag with our mail that he planned to open and noticed an envelope hand-addressed to me. Did I want it?

What the hell, I thought. Since the advent of emails, I got little physical mail, and I missed that excitement of opening a letter, like I used to receive from Denise.

On the outside of the envelope, there were various postal stamps and notices. Apparently, this letter had gone to our old address on Roosevelt Island and had been forwarded to the Upper West Side. The envelope was smudged and wrinkled; it looked like it had been through many time zones and weather conditions.

I saw the return address. It was from Cindy, my old dear friend. It read:

*Dearest Nita, Pita:*

*Here I am in San Fran. I had a dream about you and woke up and said to myself, "I have to write to Anita now!" The dream was weird. I moved into a new apartment on the top floor of an old brownstone in New York. There were two apartments on each floor. An Indian Sikh lived in the other apartment. He met me at the door with a hypodermic needle. He had been shooting coke. You lived on the ground floor. Jack and I visited you in the middle of the night. You answered the door with a pencil and notepad. You had been interviewing my old boyfriend, and you were stuck on a question. Don't ask me what this all means. I have no idea. At least it provided the spark for me to write to you.*

Well, this was a shot of light that I needed. When I saw Magdalena approach with the lethal ice cap, I lay Cindy's letter on my lap, excited to continue even if I turned into a temporary ice princess. Soon, I continued:

*How are you? How is Sergio? How are Shirley and Denise? I know it's been ages but I can't stop thinking of those days. I'm sorry I didn't stick around after Marilyn's funeral. And thanks so much for the wedding invitation. Are you still married? There is no excuse to miss your wedding to Sergio, dear man, except to plead poverty. I still can't believe that Marilyn is dead. What a waste of a beautiful and talented soul. I just couldn't take it in New York any longer. Nothing was happening for me. I couldn't get a full-time job, as you know, and ever since my father died, my family is falling apart, and they expect me to fix everything. And Jack wanted to get to California badly. As for me, things are going well. Can you believe that Jack and I lasted such a long time? My brother Dennis and Jack's sister and her son have been living here too. We were doing a lot of speed, and acid. I had a vision of our ignorance. Now I have been working as a bookkeeper and taking care of Jack's nephew (it's a long story) and then my sister Becky, who is beginning high school. This place is bursting with people and their problems.*

*And you, bubbeleh? Any kiddies? Did you write the Great American Novel yet?*

*I'd love you to visit. I like San Francisco. My only goal is to be happy. I love Jack like crazy. He's really a genius. He has all kinds of ideas. Right now, he's working on a watering system for plants. I'll let you know if he gets a patent. Please write soon. You are one of my dearest friends.*

*Love, Cynthia (Cindy) Morgan*

Why did Cindy include her full name (and her nickname in parentheses)? As if I could ever forget her.

Magdalena came by my side when I was close to the end of the letter, and I put my hand up to push her away. I wanted to take it all in. I missed Cindy like crazy. If she knew I was sick, she would be on the first plane here. I didn't want to alarm her, but I spent the rest of chemo composing an answer to Cindy in my head.

After two rounds of chemo with the cold caps, my hairbrush was twisted with thick strands that I plucked out and clumped together in my toilet like amebic beings. It was time for me to go wig shopping, and I took my backup team: my daughters and my best friend. Rather than visiting the salons that featured wigs from real hair, I opted for the less expensive synthetic emporium that my oncology nurse recommended as "just as nice, but a lot cheaper." In a tiny two-room office space on the third floor of a retail building with a coffee shop on the ground floor, we reached "Hair Delight" and were met at the door by Inez, who had thinning dyed blond hair with gray-brown roots. If anyone needed a wig, she did.

The wig room contained bookshelves filled with Styrofoam heads adorned with wigs of every style and color. I tried on a short gray one and Inez pulled its netting down and then the hair and brushed it in place. I looked at myself and saw my daughters and Denise watching me in the mirror, all with a very serious expression. Suddenly, Beth started giggling and we all burst out laughing. I was an ugly old woman.

I tried on several more and realized I would never be a blonde or a redhead. I finally settled on a shoulder-length bru-nette that parted on the side, similar to my natural hairstyle except it was a lot fluffier, even-toned, and perfectly trimmed than real hair. When I got home, I tried it on for Sergio. My team was still there, and they did their best to keep from laugh-ing. Sergio was a good sport. "It's lovely," he said. It felt like a tight, bulky helmet and I couldn't wait to take it off. I vowed to order colorful headscarves, and when my team left, I crawled into bed.

Before I wrote to Cindy, I spent hours flipping through dusty, crusty cellophane-protected photo albums, searching for her. I found an old photo of a party on Christopher Street. Sitting on pillows against the stained-beige wall are Denise, her neck-length, light-brown hair pinned up with stray wisps, sexy in a brown-flowered, low-cut dress, holding hands with her Arthur. To Arthur's right side, somewhat apart, is a radiant Cindy, her endless legs raised, her ring-bedecked fingers splayed on her knees as if she's playing the piano, and her broad smile crinkling her face.

Finally, I emailed her:

Dearest Cindy. I was thrilled, just thrilled to get your letter. A real live letter, how special! I am so happy to read all your news. I am attaching an old photo of us that I found. It brought back so many memories. I will still write a real letter back to you with all the news. For now, I just wanted to say hello and how happy I am to hear from you. You know you are always welcome to come to New York and stay with us. The sooner the better.

# CHAPTER 42: TOUCHING BASE

Fall 2017

After the last chemo was finished and I was ostensibly bald, my family joined me in Dr. Sternberg's office to review my prospects. He explained that there was an experimental drug used for breast cancer patients that he prescribed for some of his ovarian cancer patients. He didn't know yet if I was a candidate as I had to have some genetic tests, but he explained that this could be something to consider in the future. It had side effects like nausea, but patients usually did fairly well when the doses were titrated. Despite all my research on the Holocaust, I did not Google ovarian cancer and shied away from asking difficult questions. In my case, avoidance had been the key to my sanity.

I had absolute confidence in Dr. Sternberg and his top-notch staff. Sitting opposite him, I asked solemnly, "Before I agree to any protocols, can you tell me what my prognosis is? How long do I have?"

Sergio was in a chair beside me. My daughters stood against the wall of Dr. Sternberg's tiny office, flanked by two of his assistants.

"Well, Anita," he said, lowering his eyes, "normally, two years from diagnosis."

There were simultaneous gasps from my daughters. Beth ran into my arms and started weeping. With bent knuckles, Giorgia grasped the table's edge.

I focused on Sergio, who seemed to metamorphize in slow motion. His face blanched, his nostrils flared like a horse, his eyes reddened and watered, and he whimpered and croaked into his palms. Though Sergio teared up and sniffled at sad occasions, including discussing his own patients, I had never seen him uncontrollably shake and wail even at his mother's funeral.

Turning to the doctor, I whispered, "But that doesn't leave me much time."

Dr. Sternberg said little after that. He shrugged and lifted his eyebrows. His cellphone rang.

He excused himself and walked into the hall, still speaking on the phone.

"I guess I should start preparing my funeral," I said, as if I were reading a script. I thought of all my houseplants, including an array of orchids, lining a shelf against the window of my living room. Should I start giving them away? Perhaps Sergio would forget to water them; he rarely went into that room.

June, a nurse practitioner standing against the wall, came up to me. She had been the one in charge of organizing my chemo. "Oh Anita," she said. "I'm so sorry about what Dr. Sternberg said."

"I can't be angry at him. He has been amazing. No doubt, he saved my life, what's left of it."

"There is much more to the prognosis." She spoke in a confidential whisper.

From living with an oncologist all these years, I learned that medical personnel rarely criticized their colleagues.

"Dr. Sternberg was just giving you raw statistics. This may have been a standard prognosis before treatment. But you had extensive surgery and treatments, plus two separate courses of chemo. And there are several pharmaceutical interventions nowadays."

"That's true," Sergio said, finally piping up. "We will be hopeful." Undoubtedly, he had known my future was in jeopardy, but as a husband he ignored the facts.

All I could think about was an article I read about Gilda Radner and her husband, comic actor Gene Wilder. He said that after she died, he discovered a note she wrote responding to the question of what would make her feel unafraid. Her answer: "If someone could for sure tell me that everything would be okay."

I recuperated at home and finally finished sending our queries to agents and publishers for the novel about my Eastern European relatives. Somehow, all the suffering of the Jews at this time in history helped me put my own troubles into perspective. I could cry about people I didn't know, but I was stoic about myself. As I appeared socially without a headscarf, revealing a perfectly shaped skull of fuzz, I realized I had never fully responded to Cindy. I went into my office, turned on my computer, opened a new file on Word, and typed a letter:

*Dearest Cindy,*

*I was hoping it was you and checked your profile photo on Facebook. Though it was shrouded in purple gauze, the image of my remembered you emerged, as you were then. How could I ever forget our meeting in the basement of the General Post Office, giggling over the tedium of sorting zip codes in the airless caverns. You asked me about my life. I'll give you a quick summary.*

*We lived on Roosevelt Island for about twenty years, where we raised our two daughters. It was a magical place, a bedroom community of the United Nations, filled with people from all over the world and serviced by an aerial tramway that descends on Manhattan's East Side in a wondrous three-minute ride over the East River. We moved to the Upper (Upper) West Side about eighteen years ago. I'm still married to Sergio. I guess, by now I know it will last! Our daughters are grown. Giorgia is a filmmaker living in Brooklyn, and Beth is a Boston attorney. She has a live-in boyfriend, and they are trying for a child, so I may be a grandma.*

*I am putting the finishing touches on my second novel after years of disappointment and rejections. I was competing with younger and more connected writers. So, at the ripe old age of sixty-five, I went to graduate school for an MFA. I became an adjunct and taught creative writing to college students, most of whom were immigrants and had incredible life stories. Believe it or not, after all my bellyaching about women from our college ages being forced into teaching, I love it.*

*I am still very close to Denise; I hope you remember her. She is retired now but works part time with Alzheimer's patients. She married Arthur. Remember him? He died at age sixty. She has since remarried to a former stockbroker, but he's a mensch.*

*Oh, I forgot to mention our fearless shrink, Gregory. I continued to see him for another few years after you went to California. He helped me considerably, especially with issues relating to my brother. Gregory moved to California, and we corresponded for a while. I'm not sure how Kosher that was, but when you are in an intimate relationship like therapy, it's impossible to cut it off completely. Anyhow, he often asked about you in his letters.*

*That was my life in a nutshell. The times we had together were stimulating and formative, maybe the best years of my life in that they now stand out in relief like a marble frieze.*

*I look forward to hearing from and about you.*

*Love, Anita (aka Ani)*

As I reread my letter, I wondered: Did I sound like I was bragging about my accomplishments? Why did I insert my frustrations about my creative writing career, falling back on old habits as if I were the same insecure person she knew when we were in our twenties? I swallowed my hesitancy and pressed "send." I neglected to tell her about my cancer.

Cindy emailed me a letter within the hour:

*It's great to hear from you! Thanks for the photo ... that's how I remember Denise! I think this was Christmas time of 1973. I look happy!*

*So happy about your publication news. Proud of you.*

*I'm pretty busy this week as I've got to get my plants in the ground (my garden), but you can see some photos on my Facebook page. I think there might be some of my kids there.*

*A little recap of my life: The letter I had sent you was actually written several years ago; it was sitting in my desk and I finally mailed it to you without even rereading it. So I need to update you. I attended a photography program and got an Associate of Science degree. Never did anything with it because six months later we were living in the wilds of rural*

*California. I had three children at home. Jack and I moved south of S.F. and divorced after fifteen years.*

*When my kids were grown, I quit my job, packed up my belongings, and traveled to Europe and India, returning to S.F. where I worked in various low-level jobs until two years ago when I retired and moved to my own house in Oregon with its hot summers and rainy winters. My children live within a fifty-mile radius. It's a lot cheaper here than in CA and we have space to live and breathe.*

*Oy, vey! Please write back! Let me know details of Denise's life. Do you hear from Shirley?*

*Love, Cindy*

# CHAPTER 43: REGRETS

Cindy and I made a date to speak on the phone. I was nervous and excited. Nervous that we would have nothing to say to each other, excited to hear her voice again. I picked up the phone on the first ring.

"It's been over forty-three years since we've corresponded," Cindy said. Her voice was gruff, scratchy, the voice of an older person who once smoked and drugged.

"Are you planning to retire soon when your new book is published?" she asked.

"Writers don't retire. They just leave a lot of blanks in their résumé."

"I see you have the same sense of humor."

"Hey, when it comes down to it, a sense of humor should be a basic sense. Without it, the other senses may malfunction, but laughing keeps you going."

"Yes, that's true."

"I saw your children, or should I say your grown offspring, on FB."

"Yes, the tall one with a beard is Cory. He's a sound engineer. The one with the baby is Valerie. She is a computer programmer and works at home. She has two kids. The handsome one with blond hair, Logan, I call the milkman's son 'cause he doesn't look like anyone else. He's a PA and works in a hospital and is divorced with a son."

"How wonderful," I said. "You must be so proud of them."

"It's been very hard. Basically, I was a single parent. My husband, you remember Jack, left us when they were young and teens, and he's been mostly absent. He was more interested in drinking and drugs. I worked sometimes two or three jobs, and we moved a lot. But don't get me wrong, my children are everything to me. I loved every minute of raising them."

"It sounds like you've had a hard life."

"I have. I'm at peace now, with my own house. My children are all working and settled."

"Do you still play the guitar?"

"Yes, and the piano. My son Cory also makes musical instruments. He's working on a harpsichord now. If he can't sell it, he will donate it."

"Wonderful."

"I made sure that my kids could play a musical instrument. There was always someone playing in my house. Music is important."

"I am envious of that. I had such little musical training. It is a big regret of mine."

"I remember you once took guitar lessons."

"Oh, yes. My brother gave me his old guitar when he got a keyboard, with the stipulation that I was on my own. I studied with a Brooklyn music teacher and learned to read notes. I could play three songs. But the teacher never stressed listening. As a creative person, I don't take to memorizing. Now I see after all these years, that for me, I need to be immersed in something before I understand it."

"Didn't you also have that weird mouthpiece?"

"Yes, a melodica. I can't believe you remember that! My brother bought it for my sixteenth birthday before the guitar fiasco. One night I was stoned on pot, and I picked it up and played "Hatikvah" by heart. I was amazed that I could do that without looking at a single note. We don't know the full extent of what we know."

"That sounds profound," she said.

"Well … that is one thing I know."

She laughed.

"Do you ever come to the East Coast?" I asked.

"I come to visit my great aunt and my best friend in Queens. Do you remember Catherine?"

"Oh, yes."

I heard the phone click, and Cindy excused herself to take the call. "It was long distance," she said, as if our coast-to-coast call was around the corner. I usually got annoyed when people interrupted a phone call to answer another, but this time, I needed a break to organize my emotions. I got up, stretched, and looked out the window. The trees in Riverside Park were swaying, the orange autumn leaves scattered in the wind, and the sky was darkening. A storm was approaching, and I stood on my desk to close the window. I remembered the sweet smell of the budding linden blossoms, the first sign of spring, and I looked forward to walking among the blooming magnolia, cherry blossom, and crab-apple trees lining the interior corridors of the park. If Cindy visited New York, I hoped it would be in spring. I would take her on my park route, and we would sit on the bench and watch the parade of Upper Westsiders and Columbia University students. She had always been a great people watcher.

"I'm back," Cindy announced. "So sorry, I had to take that. You have to grab the insurance claim adjusters when you can get them."

"No problem," I lied. "Cindy, one more question. I have been asking older people this."

"Sure, shoot."

"Did you have the life you wanted?"

"You really get to the heart of things."

"Maybe it's our age. I'm obsessed with the concept of regrets and making amends while we can, I mean personal amends. My parents were such bad role models, and I never wanted to feel as unfulfilled or unrealized as they were."

"So, are you asking me if I have regrets?"

"Well, yes, if you don't mind."

"I can't really answer that. I try not to think that way."

"That's cause you're not Jewish."

"Believe me, being raised as a strict Catholic is worse. Seriously, I don't have much materially. But I don't regret anything. Honestly, I did so many wrong things, like being an enabler to my ex for many years. I wasn't confident, and I was raised to be the nice one who takes care of the family."

"Like many in our generation of women."

"I've had a lot of heartache. My older brother died of a drug overdose when he was thirty; my younger brother died of cancer. Now, my younger sister lives in Seattle; my older sister works in Vegas. Each has kids. They all come to me on the holidays. It's important for me to have family around."

"A lot has happened."

"And for you?"

"Well, not that different. Most of my extended family is scattered. My brother lived in Boston, retired to Florida, and committed suicide thirteen years ago; my sister-in-law, Aviva, died of breast cancer years ago."

"Oh, no. So sad to hear about Ben in particular. That must have been devastating."

"It was. Probably I will never get over it."

"How about Sergio's family?"

"Sergio's family, what's left of it, is either in Italy or his sister's son lives in New York and has two sons who treat us as grandparents. My daughters and their families all come to me for Thanksgiving, the one holiday when I cook."

"I could be depressed, but I'm not." Cindy said this without a prompt, as if I asked about her mental health.

"Why?" I asked, intrigued. I had battled depression most of my life, and it always interested me how some people managed to bypass it.

"I don't know, maybe because I was too busy."

We both laughed.

Now it was my turn to ask Cindy to hold on a second. My doorman buzzed and announced that he was sending a package for me in the elevator. I disappeared for a minute, waited for the elevator, and scooped up a gray spongy envelope. Probably a book, I thought. By now, my dog Ruby was barking and pacing from her living-room doggy bed to the front door.

Stimulated by the impending storm and the buzzing intercom, she needed to go out.

"Hi Cindy. It was a package. But let me call you in five minutes. I need to walk the dog before it downpours."

★ ★ ★

When I called Cindy back, I answered her questions about Denise and Shirley. After a pause, she said in a soft voice, "I was just thinking about your question."

"Which one? I asked so many."

"The big one about regrets. In a way, I feel like I wasted my life." Cindy's voice quavered.

Who was I to delve so deeply after all this time? "I'm sorry, Cindy. I didn't mean to open a Pandora's box."

"No, no, you got me to obsess over something other than garden weeds."

"Then I'm happy."

Cindy continued, "As for my life, I didn't go after anything for myself in a serious way. My father was a newspaperman. He could edit at lightning speed and form a headline before the story was finished. He expected me to have a career as a reporter or something in the field."

"And why didn't you pursue this? You are, were a great writer. Your blurbs at Theoretical were outstanding."

"That wasn't much of a stretch. I just don't think I had the discipline."

"My God, Cindy, you always did the *Times* crossword puzzle in ink."

"No, Ani, you were the real writer, the one with sheer guts and imagination. I just fiddled around. I let circumstances define me."

"You, like so many women of our time."

"Did I want to be more successful? Of course."

I took a sip from my water bottle, stood, and massaged the cramp in my calves from sitting too long. I put Cindy on "speaker" and paced my small square space. Thunder rumbled louder. I turned up the volume on my phone.

"Ani, you got me asking myself, 'Did I want to have a career and not a stupid nine-to-five job? Did I want to have a supportive spouse? Did I want to be thirty pounds lighter? Yes and yes and yes. It's too late now for me."

"It's never too late."

"I don't know about that."

"You may remember in our old consciousness-raising group that we often discussed our mothers," I said.

"Oh, yeah."

"I had mentioned that when I was a teenager, my mother tried to go to college but was discouraged because she had to take algebra and other academic subjects."

"I kinda remember. How old was she then?"

"Forty."

"Oh, my God."

"And Cindy, no one contradicted her. We accepted that she was too old. But I wouldn't let that happen to me. When I went to graduate school at age sixty-five, for my MFA, I was older than all the professors."

"Wow, Ani, that is so inspiring. Did it change you a lot?"

"Yes and no. Most of the instructors assumed I knew a lot since I had writing experience. For the assigned theses, my mentors spent little time on my work. Instead, they used me as a sounding board for their department's infighting. They didn't take me as seriously as the younger students. For my novel, my advisor told me to self-publish. I guess it was a form of ageism."

"So, are you sorry you did this?"

"No, of course it would have been better for me if I went to grad school when I was younger, at a more active school. Perhaps I could have benefitted from certain opportunities, like writing residencies and publishing referrals."

"Was it difficult to study as a senior citizen?"

"Also, yes and no. When it came to remembering anything, I was mush. But I did learn that unlike my undergraduate time, I was an excellent student. As a matter of fact, one of my fellow grad students, in her fifties, was flabbergasted about my grades. Once during a short-story class, when we got our stories back, she said, 'Why did you get an A+? Did you do anything differently?' I realized that someone was jealous of me. It was like a bomb fell on my head."

"That's so cute."

"Cute? I don't know if cute was the word, but it was mind-boggling. But fuck jealousy. I became upset if I only got an A. I spent years rejecting my old college counselor's recommendation that I teach, the only 'real job' for women."

"It's good if we have the time and energy to 'rewrite'—sorry for the pun—our misguided self-images. But for me, I managed to raise three wonderful humans and have a nice little house and a garden. Now, this is enough for me."

"Thanks so much, Cindy. You answered my question."

"I'm gonna call you when I come to New York," Cindy said.

At that moment, it would have been the time to tell Cindy about my cancer, especially given the "loose" date of our future meeting. I hesitated for a few seconds and just couldn't address the elephant in my room. "Please do," I said.

"Love you," she said.

I was taken aback. These were always difficult words for me to say, even to those closest to me. But I couldn't let the empty space hang in the air.

"Ditto," I said, and hung up the phone.

# CHAPTER 44:
# NO GOOD REASON

### January 2018

Still outliving Dr. Sternberg's dire prediction, I was soon happily diverted by an offer of publication from a small independent publisher for my new historical novel, now entitled *Blood Sprang from the Earth*, named after a line from a poem written about one of the Holocaust's largest massacres. The publisher had an unexpected opening slot in the spring, and I was busy with the editor and designer, and pre-publication reviews. I was, of course, thrilled, and was contemplating whether to plan another book party.

I was obsessed with all the writings I hadn't published: unfinished novels, poems, academic papers, and especially a collection of humorous personal essays that I had been accumulating for many years. If I could get these essays published in my limited lifetime, then at least I'd leave my best work for my daughters as their mother's legacy.

I knew this type of collection was practically impossible to get published unless you were Nora Ephron, but I persisted. An agent search was my first serious step. I took a break from sending out query letters and checked my email. Scrolling down the list of six messages, I saw the name. It didn't register at first.

Shirley Wilson. Could it be from Shirley, my Shirl, after fifteen years? Wilson was Shirley's married name.

I clicked on her name, dreading a hoax. There was a paragraph. In some kind of stupor, I scanned the first line. "Dear Anita," I read. "I am so very excited to come across your web page." I continued to read: "So much has happened since I last saw you. Please call me." The note included a phone number with a strange area code, which I Googled and discovered it was Mississippi. I returned to the email: "I want to preorder your new book but prefer an autographed copy." After sending regards to my family, Shirley included her full name with her maiden name in parentheses.

"Oh my God," I said aloud. "It's really her." I expected to feel shocked, almost speechless. Instead, I had a gnawing sense of something beyond curiosity, perhaps the old wondering, the promise of a mystery unraveling.

I immediately called the number. It rang a few times, and an automatic message came on.

I emitted tiny coughs. I was recovering from a respiratory infection and sounded phlegmy. "Shirley, I hope this is your number. This is Anita. I am so excited to hear from you. Call me." I left my home phone number even though it hadn't changed in the years of our separation.

Hours passed, and I paced my living room. Memories of Shirley came to me in waves: sleeping over at the Brooklyn brownstone as her eight-year-old son, Elgin, climbed on the top bunk bed; flagging each other from our chairs at Theoretical; Shirley standing on the deck of a summer weekend rental lake house in Connecticut, flinging her fishing pole like an experienced Southern country girl; Shirley and me, as we lounged on the couch of my apartment, creating a name for our new publishing business.

I had to speak to someone about Shirley, but I didn't want to tie up my landline. I picked up my cellphone and tapped Denise's number on my "Favorites" list.

"You'd never believe who called," I blurted, before Denise said hello.

"Well, hi to you, too. I don't know, who?"

"Remember Shirley Baumann, I mean Shirley Baumann Wilson?"

"Shirley, of course. She didn't come to your book party. Don't tell me she finally called."

"I got an email from her, and she included her number. I called and left a message. I'm expecting her to return my call. If my phone rings, I'll hang up with you."

"Wow, that's a blast from the past."

"I know. I can't imagine what her life has been like. She must be about seventy-nine now. I just can't picture us as a bunch of old ladies. How did this happen?"

"I prefer this to the alternative," Denise said.

★ ★ ★

By ten that night, the phone didn't ring. I couldn't stand the silence. I waited way too long. I went to my computer and replied to Shirley's email, reiterating my phone number.

Minutes later, the phone rang. The caller ID had that same Mississippi area code.

"Shirl?" I crooned, my voice a mixture of familiarity and surprise.

"Anita, it's you?"

"Yes, it's me."

"You sound the same."

"I have a cold." I coughed as if to convince her.

"You sound great, anyhow. How have you been?"

"Oh, a lifetime has gone by. I guess I'm okay and you? You're living in Mississippi?"

"Yes, after working at Princeton and another college, I retired again. I moved back home, not far from my sister."

We spent the next ten minutes taking turns, filling each other with information.

After a second lull, Shirley said in a lower voice, "You know I lost Elgin."

"Elgin? Oh, no?"

"Yes, it's three years now. He had a heart attack. Tumbled at work. Only fifty-seven."

"Oh, Shirley, that is so terrible. I am so very sorry."

Shirley related the story of Elgin's death and the family's reaction. And then, she mentioned, almost as an aside, that one of Elgin's sons also died. "Car accident. He was eighteen." She had four other grandchildren and a great-grandchild.

There were almost no words. Finally, I said, "What horrible news." As always, during times of tragedy, I resorted to clichés.

Somehow, Shirley redirected the conversation to her retirement, her new apartment near a university, her lack of a regular job for the first time in her adult life. "And your new book?" she said. "It sounds so impressive. I want to buy it, but I want an autographed copy."

"Well, when you come to New Jersey to visit your grandchildren, we can meet in Manhattan for lunch, like old times. And I will sign the book in person."

"I would love that. You know I have thought about you so much over the years. I haven't stopped caring about you. I tell everyone about you."

"Me, too, Shirley. Me, too."

We hung up with this unknown future date between us. I went to the bathroom and glanced at my reflection in the mirror.

Not bad, I thought, for an old lady of seventy-two. And Shirley, her voice was still sophisticated and velvety, the voice of a woman who wore her tragedies like a much-mended lining of a mink coat.

Sergio went to bed. I needed to retain Shirley's voice in my memory. Too late to call anyone, I longed to communicate about Shirley. I typed an email to Denise.

"I spoke to Shirley," I wrote.

Ever the night owl, Denise answered immediately, "So did you ask her?"

"What?" I wrote.

"Did you ask her what had happened? Why she didn't come to your party?"

"I couldn't," I answered. Then I wrote a summary of what had happened to Shirley. "After all she went through," I wrote, "after all the years passed, it seems so meaningless. She lost so much. She had breast cancer. I had cancer."

"Did you mention yours?"

"No, I didn't have the heart, especially after she recited all her tragedies." I had thought of telling Shirley during our conversation. On some level, I longed for her motherly compassion, for that symbolic giant hug. I couldn't trust her with that kind of information, not when there were still some unspoken issues between us. And I suppose I didn't want to crack my defenses, so fortified by now. If there was one person who could do it, it was Shirley.

"She would want to know."

"What does it matter now?"

"Of course it matters," Denise wrote. Denise also had her share of sorrow, having lost Arthur, at the age of sixty from a ruptured aorta. She had remarried recently but her new husband, who at eighty, was showing signs of dementia.

Yes, it was true, I thought as I readied for bed: I would never really know what happened with Shirley fifteen years ago. This spring, we were supposed to meet for lunch. And there was always the possibility, over our coffee, that the subject could come up. If it didn't, the mystery would remain between us.

# CHAPTER 45:
# NOTES FROM BETTY

July 20, 2018

*Ms. Rappaport*

*In your husband's office. I could not get the cover of your book out of my mind—I had to read it. It is a wonderful book—It took me a long time to finish—so hard to go on. So hard not to go on. When it is my turn I am going to have the book club I belong read it—Three cheers for you.*

*P.S. Please sign my book.*

July 30, 2018

*Dear Anita*

*I am so sorry this is so late. I have been in and out of NYC. That your apt. was in 165 Christopher St. Kismet.*
*The Book Club. We are 7 ladies—close in age to each other. We meet monthly at my apt. We bring a snack or a dinner. We eat and talk about the book. I would be so happy if you would join us when we read your book.*

*Please come—I would love for you to be with us when we meet to talk about  the book—I will let you know when we will meet.*

September 6, 2018

*Dear Anita*

*The book club has come together. The book Dance of the Jakaranda is  what we are reading. We will meet Oct. 4, 6 p.m., my apt. The next book my pick. Blood Sprang. You must come. You know the way here. Please come. Betty.*

# CHAPTER 46: BOOK CLUB

October 4, 2018

Iemerged from the Christopher Street subway station with time to spare. The book club meeting was scheduled for 6:00, and it was only 5:30. I didn't want to arrive early and disrupt Betty's schedule. So, I headed to Christopher Park, whose benches and redbrick walkway were inhabited by scattered people, interspersed with George Segal's white-lacquered, dual-couple sculptures, called *Gay Liberation*. There was an empty space next to the seated lesbian twosome. The female figure with the long hair sits with one hand hanging loosely on her thigh, resting against her knee, and the other touching the thigh of her partner. The partner's fingers reassuringly pat her friend's wrist while her other elbow brushes against her friend's shoulder. In this way, these women are deliberately casual, oxymoron withstanding, and their faces turn toward each other, confirming their essential intimacy. And so it was for the real-life males standing in front of me, one arm on the other's shoulder, his friend relaxed with hands in pockets, both absorbed in a private conversation. All of us—animate and otherwise—posed opposite the Stonewall Inn, sure that this birthplace of revolution had our backs, and we could relax in our own space.

Across from me sat a family of four. In their forties, the parents were consulting a guidebook and their cellphones. The daughter, about twelve, leafed through a Harry Potter book—I recognized the artwork on the cover but not the title—and her brother, about sixteen, was engaged in a scissor sprawl of his long legs, sipping from a plastic water bottle. Tourists, no doubt. I sat back on the bench to improve my posture since the mother took numerous photos of my white-painted friends, especially when her daughter sat on the other side of the women and smoothed the nearby figure's thighs. I had seen a photo online of these statues, their necks festooned with rainbow-ribboned garlands, a sign at their feet announcing, "Just Married." I didn't necessarily believe that marriage guaranteed anything; their union, though forever stationary, made me feel peaceful. They could, so they should.

Finally, it was time to make my way, and I crossed Seventh Avenue and noticed that jutting out on the triangular wedge between West 4th and 10th Streets, the Riviera Café's windows were boarded up with wood panels, though empty tables were visible in the outdoor seating area. I quickly Googled the restaurant and read that it was closing after forty-eight years. Remembering the countless hamburgers and coffees I had consumed there, and the confessional talks with Cindy, Denise, Marilyn, and sometimes Shirley when she came to visit, I had a stab of pain that went directly through my stomach as surely as if I were kicked by leather boots decorated with brass tacks.

Crossing the street, I continued on Christopher, observing a billboard atop Village Cigars that said, "Make Google Do it," and I realized I had already followed that order. Had I seen that sign when I first got out of the subway and internalized the message? I felt happy, though, when I spotted the sign for McNulty's Rare Teas & Choice Coffees. Underneath the sign was the reminder, "since 1895." A male and female couple pushed the wide handle of a three-wheeled stroller past me, and I realized their heterosexuality seemed out of context. I needn't have worried because the next store featured skimpy male briefs and female lingerie with exposed breasts, and I knew I was closer to home. And so it was for the Lucille Lortel Theatre, whose marquee jutted out behind the purple banner of the Musée Lingerie. Built in 1926, known in my day as the Theatre de Lys, it was a great place for Off-Broadway, and I remembered seeing Bernadette Peters there in the musical *Dames at Sea* in 1969. I was also heartened to see the iron-and-glass marquee announcing "Hudson Tunnels" of the PATH train station to Hoboken, in business since 1908. Even older was the Roman Catholic Church of St. Veronica, established in 1887 and built between 1890-1903. I stopped to look up the date as the imposing crimson Victorian Gothic Revival building hit me with a thud. How was it that this lovely edifice with three arched doors and a stained-glass rose window could have eluded my memory? Did I pass this building every day and never go inside? I remembered the redbrick Federal Building with the Post Office across the street from my old building, now a ten-story apartment complex, but St. Veronica remained submerged in my unconscious.

Alas, I reached 165, which I had seen several times over the years, but not for the last ten. The white-brick building was stained darker and more weathered, punctuated by the black outlines of reinforced windows and rust-colored fire escapes. On closer inspection, the bottom brickwork around the street-level apartments was brown and framed by a short metal gate containing bushes and other unhealthy-looking greenery. To the left of the entranceway, behind a circular-trimmed hedge, were the iron vertical window bars of my former apartment. I recalled passersby sitting on the ledges, discussing everything from truck-space availability to anal size, but now there didn't seem to be space for seating. It was time to walk through the doors and leave my reverie for the scene of Betty's reality.

The lobby was plain with black leather furniture. An off-white desk displayed a clipboard announcing an exterminator sign-up list. A man behind the desk wearing an official insignia type vest sat in a swivel chair. He directed me to the elevators, a section of the building I had never seen since I had lived on the ground floor.

★ ★ ★

The door to Betty's apartment opened before I rang the bell, and a petite woman, barely tall enough against my shoulder, embraced me before I entered the apartment. At first, I wasn't sure if this was Betty as her very short white hair and large oval-faced, black-framed eyeglasses, and black turtleneck sweater gave her an androgynous look until she spoke in a soft, feminine, breathless tone as she welcomed me inside her one-bedroom apartment, the mirror-twin of the one I had so many years ago.

I sat on a tan velveteen couch with framed black-and-white drawings above. A woman with neck-length white hair and bangs, wearing a green spiral designed sweater, sat next to me and, without introduction, deposited the book on my lap and asked me to sign it. Kitty-corner to me were two women sitting on dining-room chairs, each holding up my book as I snapped a photo with my cellphone. Three women in mismatched occasional chairs faced me. Betty appeared on my other side and produced her book as well, whispering, "I loved your book so much." Her gray tabby perched on the couch's arm and watched us as I signed my dedication. All seven women positioned their chairs, with three sitting and four standing behind, for the group portrait, four holding my book as the other three having read it on Kindle. With the official business over, we reconfigured in a semicircle in the living room area, and Betty again sat by my side, her slight frame pinched against mine.

"Can you sign my book?" she asked, her large whitish teeth in an innocent smile.

I was about to say I signed it already, but I didn't want to insult her, so I took the book and turned to the signature page and smoothed it over, then handed it back to her. She put her arm around me and squeezed. I looked around the room at the seven women, all in their eighties, white-haired except for one who had short brown hair, sprinkled with gray. She was the one who sat erect in her chair despite her apparent rounded back and announced, "I have read many, many Holocaust books and yours, dear Anita, was the very best. It affected me the most. I cried and cried at the end. It really touched me."

Unlike my first book release, I had decided against a launch party. I felt too exhausted to arrange such an event, although Denise and my daughters offered to help. Instead, I had an opening at an uptown bookstore, attended by about forty friends and relatives. Although these were certainly "friendly" readers or potential readers, I dreaded the reaction since the theme was so horrific. I expected something like my former classmate John, who said he would never read such a subject. When anyone discussed my characters, I held back profound disbelief that my fictional people could have a life outside the page. If someone enjoyed the book and found the characters relatable, I suspected the sincerity.

These women's apparent approval relaxed me, though no one else felt emboldened to make such an endorsement as the brown-haired one, especially since Grace, the most outspoken, said that they had been meeting for almost fifty years and have read every book imaginable.

"Do you have a favorite?" I asked, suppressing a hidden wish that they selected mine.

"Oh, yes. We just discussed this," Grace said. She wore a deep-purple sweater offsetting her blue eyes and rouge-accented apple cheeks. Her sparse white hair was swept up in a bun. She had an aristocratic stance and spoke with a hint of a Scottish brogue. She let it be known that she still worked for a nonprofit and it was difficult to find time to read, but she always met the group's deadline. Undoubtedly, she was a woman of whom people said, "She must have been gorgeous when she was young," as if beauty had an expiration date.

I was immediately intrigued. Was it *War and Peace*? Maybe *Gone with the Wind*? Maybe something more esoteric like *Ulysses* by James Joyce, or more contemporary like *Beloved* by Toni Morrison, or more related to their time like *The Group* by Mary McCarthy? These were women of the West Village. Maybe the selection was more feminist. But no, it was a contemporary book, *A Gentleman in Moscow*, which, by another coincidence, my husband had been reading on his Kindle.

"Why did you choose this book?" I asked.

The woman who loved my book said, "It had all the elements we like: good characters, good plot, historical context. Have you read it?"

"No, but I certainly will. With your recommendation, it means a lot."

I wanted to hear opinions about my book, so I asked, "Was there anything about my book or any characters that you identified with?"

"Oh, I liked Aunt Fanny the best," a woman with a blue sweater said, and then disappeared into the hallway leading to the utility kitchen. I could see her arm picking up a wall phone and slamming it down, repeating the action until she connected with someone. I couldn't make out the conversation but recognized the tone of frustration.

No one else commented on my book except for Betty, who hugged me again and said so softly I wasn't sure of all the words, but repeated something like, "I loved, loved your book so much." Perhaps she asked me to sign it again. I couldn't be sure, so I gave her an extra squeeze. She rose and crossed into the hallway, where the two women seemed to be busy with the telephone. I noticed that whenever Betty moved, the women followed her movements with their eyes and if Betty disappeared, one of them rose and moved in Betty's direction. I looked at my phone and noticed that it was close to seven. I saw no sign of dinner, though the long oak table near the windowed wall was set with paper plates and plastic utensils.

Within minutes, the women relaxed into a more informal conversation and the one with dark hair, now identified as Edna, mentioned her hatred of Trump. Each woman voiced her distaste of him preceded by, "Can you believe?" Clearly these octogenarians, two who mentioned they were in Europe during World War II, both Christians, Edna in Prague and Grace from Edinburgh, had seen much in their multinational years, but nobody liked Trump.

"I am curious," I said, "how has the West Village changed during your time?"

"Oh, it's too expensive to live here," Edna said, admitting that with her teacher's pension, she now lives in a small apartment on the Upper West Side.

Another woman, Josephine, said that she has lived in the same apartment for fifty years with her husband, and they have a convoluted rent arrangement with the city, maintaining an organic food delivery business in the basement of their building.

She was the "boss," she said jokingly, as her husband preferred playing chess in Washington Square Park and schmoozing with his pals.

"We still look out for each other," she said, eying Betty as she returned to the wall phone.

"Yes, I can see that," I said. "Women are always the thread of our societal fabric."

"Unfortunately, we sometimes get into knots," said the former silent woman in the green spiral sweater, now introduced as Janie.

"So true," I said.

The question that had been haunting me since I had heard of Betty, and of which I relentlessly queried my long-time friends, popped up. I figured I had a unique assembly of opinionated Villagers.

"Tell me," I asked. "At this time in your life, can you look back and evaluate whether you had the life you wanted, or you expected?"

"Hmm," Grace said, untying a yellow striped silk shoulder scarf and laying it behind her chair. "An intriguing question. I came here with my family as immigrants when I was a teenager. We were happy to find a place to live, and my father worked at the docks, each day wondering if he could get a job."

"And then what happened?" I asked.

"As I got older and more financially secure, I allowed myself to dream big—to be a famous singer or musician. But then I had two children and divorced. I had to earn a living. I abandoned my fantasies. My priorities changed. It wasn't until my children were grown that I considered what I wanted, and even then, it was more like what I could get."

"Yes," Janie said. "We were children of the Depression. We were interested in security first. We didn't question whether we liked what we were doing."

Edna stood and sat again. "That question is very interesting. Like Grace, I was an immigrant, and my family constantly told us to be grateful to be in America. When I retired, I started to explore some of my interests."

"Like what?" I asked, hoping I didn't appear too nosy.

"I took a film course and learned how to throw a pot. I would have bought a wheel but didn't have room in my apartment."

"Did you enjoy these?"

"Believe it or not, I have a more complete life now and am happier than I've ever been."

"That's so great," I said, feeling that I had much more to look forward to in my life.

"For me," Josephine said, "even with my long marriage and business, I've had a lot of heartache. I had serious cancer and was given a very poor prognosis when I was a young mother. Then, I doubted if I would have a life at all."

"Oh, I'm so sorry. But obviously, you survived." This confession buoyed me.

"Yes, but we also lost our son in Vietnam."

"Oh my God."

"I don't want to sound so sad. There were many wonderful things:, travels, friends. It wasn't the life I envisioned, but it was the one I've had."

As if forming a coda to the conversation, the doorbell sounded, and Janie and Grace joined Betty at the door. It was a gray-bearded man holding two pizza cartons. Janie kissed him on the cheek. "That's Janie's husband, Frank," Josephine said. "He had to pick up the pizza.

Betty had some trouble ordering with her credit card on the phone."

"Oh, nice," I said, quieting my stomach's growling with an air swallow.

"Sometimes, it takes a man," she said.

Before long, Frank left, and we sat at the dining table eating cold pizza. I didn't hear all the ins and outs of ordering the pies, but I realized that it took two hours for them to come. Still, I was hungry and had two slices and a spoonful of salad.

Shortly afterward, I told them I had to get home.

"Me, too," Janie said.

At the door, Betty brought her book and asked me to sign it again. I took out a pen and pretended to sign.

"Oh, please come back to our next meeting," she said.

"I'm sure she has a busy life," Grace said.

"No, I'd love to," I said, even though Josephine squinted at me, probably suspecting I was just being kind to Betty.

Betty picked up a postcard from the nearby hall table. "Your husband's office sent this with his new address. I'm going to see him tomorrow."

"But it will be Friday, and he doesn't have office hours."

Betty raised her gray eyebrows. "When should I go?"

"The appointment says next Wednesday," I said, glancing at the postcard.

"Oh, next Wednesday," she said. "But you'll come back soon."

"Yes," I said.

On the way home, down Christopher Street, I called my husband. "Please call Betty and make sure she knows where and when to go for her next appointment, Wednesday at eleven."

"Will do," he said.

Across from the station, he called me back to reassure me that he had called Betty.

"What did she say?" I asked.

"That she loved you very much and really wants you to come back."

As I sat on the subway, I thought about the book club women, who gave me a unique glimpse into the lives my friends and I would have in the next decade. Two of the women still worked in satisfying careers, the others loved living in New York and reading books, and one had Alzheimer's. Christopher Street still looked beautiful.

# CHAPTER 47: FINAL NOTE FROM BETTY

December 2018

I received a greeting card with the cover quotation, "Let your Light Shine. Matthew 5:16," superimposed on a gold sun. Inside it said:

*Anita*

*I love your book. Thank you for Blood Sprang. I loved meeting you.*
*Please come back and visit.*
*You can come with a book you like.*
*The book club women would be happy to read with you*

*Much love, Betty*

After fifty years of meeting, Betty's book club's favorite book pick intrigued me and I ordered *A Gentleman in Moscow* from Amazon, though my husband offered me his Kindle version. I had vowed (to myself) never to read an e-book. First, as a longtime writer (and reader), I needed to feel the crisp yet supple texture of the paper page, run my fingers down the smooth surface, inhale the musty smell of embedded ink and binding glue, feel the rough-cut deckle edges of a hardcover, and straighten out the slipped dust jacket by knocking the bottom of the book as if it were a deck of cards. And, as an author who counted my number of rejections to be on the list of the *Guinness Book of World Records,* I felt an inexplicable loyalty to the paper world of printed books. Besides, I based my home decoration ideas on floor-to-ceiling white wooden bookcases. Over the years, I reorganized the books in different configurations: from oldest to newest, those with book jackets, and most recently, like my old shrink, Gregory, placing hardcovers on the lowest, easiest accessible shelf. How could a Kindle viewer remember the red cover with the yellow all-caps title to *Catcher in the Rye,* or the light green cover of *Ulysses?*

When *A Gentleman in Moscow* came in the cardboard mailer with the black Amazon curved arrow, I ripped open the package and began, eager to write a note to Betty announcing my agreement with the book club's all-time favorite book. On a two-week winter retreat at a lodge in upstate New York, while Sergio recuperated from rotator cuff surgery, I settled down with Count Alex. I immediately admired the concept of exploring what life was like when forced to live in one constricted place, this time the Old-World luxurious Metropole Hotel. Did author Amor Towles conjecture that, unlike life in a prison or even in a Siberian Gulag camp, this hotel's isolated setting put different strictures on the protagonist's independence, allowing for limited but necessary elevated creature comforts? As I read each chapter, I admired the prose. Also stuck in one place, taking care of an invalid, I felt an almost symbiotic attachment to the Count's claustrophobic environs. I entertained fantasies of retreating to the porch with *People* magazine, losing myself in the world of pop stars I no longer recognized.

Then I thought of Betty's group. These book club women obviously must have read hundreds of books over their years of meeting. They admired this book above all others. I kept reading. I recalled the story of when my mother was about eight, an immigrant living in Brooklyn. She had caught diphtheria and was quarantined with her mother for two weeks in a rented room near her family's tenement. Over the years, she would show me the large dent in her thigh where the doctor thrust several injections. She'd retell the exaggerated details of how she died and was revived, but most longingly, she remembered her mother lovingly spooning chicken soup and wiping her perspiring forehead. It was the only time in her traumatic, pogrom-scarred childhood that she had her adored mother to herself in prescribed isolation, and she didn't mind almost dying to attain this state of nirvana.

* * *

Throughout *A Gentleman in Moscow*, I was aware that there was a writer in this story. He was directing us through his repetitious experiment. I was surprised that the women of the book club would be attracted to such complex contrivance; though perhaps it was the Old-World ambience that seduced them.

Toward the end of the book, the ponderous pace picked up as the Count devises a meticulous strategy for his daughter, Sonia, to leave Moscow and for him to escape the hotel. The book suddenly feels like a portentous mystery, awash in melodrama. But, alas, the ending is ambiguous; the woman waiting for him is unidentified except for a gray streak and the description of being willowy.

For the next few days, however, I couldn't wait to begin a new novel, this time a contemporary story of a single mother relocating to London. As I read about her moving to a house that needed renovation, getting her hair dyed for the first time,

I longed for life in the Metropole. I missed the hotel. I missed being an observer of a cohesive and well-run enterprise, where everyone had work that he/she enjoyed and was good at, where everyone knew his/her place, and where growth and change were as imperceptible as the first sign of a neurological tremor. Was this what the women in Betty's group had so admired, this sense of belonging, this bygone life—a place frozen in time within the boundaries of proletariat change, a bastion of refinement in a world that no longer prized taste? Were we all, figuratively and literally, willowy waiting women, "hair tinged with gray"?

# CHAPTER 48:
# UNTOUCHED BY TIME

## April 18, 2019

It was a crisp, sunny morning, the type of day I associated with 9/11, cloudless and bright, though chillier, filled with the promise of a walk and a talk. I called them "bottle days" to be clearly encased, blocking impending fog. Denise was scheduled for a cleaning at her dentist and already called me twice to say she may be late. She was the only one I knew who was as pathologically punctual as I was. My reputation was such that my mother once called Sergio because I had been five minutes late to meet her outside of Macy's.

I was expecting to snap photos before I met Denise, so I wouldn't bore her with my incessant need to record our past. I began with the first place I saw after exiting the subway on Seventh Avenue, Village Cigars, sporting the same white lettering on vertical placards advertising CIGAR & CIGARETTE as if these lethal habits were singular and had never been banned in restaurants and other venues. I stood in front of the park, across the street, and aimed my Nikon to get a wide-angle shot and then zoomed into the sign. Then I crossed Seventh Avenue for a close-up of the windows. It was time for me to enter this anachronistic establishment and see for myself. Surely, the inside would display trays of gluten-free cookies, vegan peanut-butter squares, organic cigarettes, or even vaping products, befitting the cornerstone of health-conscious former hippies. Instead, there were drawers of individually cellophane-wrapped cigars in opened wooden boxes, and trays of smoking paraphernalia, as well as men lined up to buy lottery tickets.

A faint aroma of stale smoke reminded me of my father's chewed stogie cigars that protruded from his brown-juice-stained lips, as he occasionally spit the sputum out the car window driving from our apartment in Brooklyn to the Catskill Mountains where he played pinochle with other cigar-expectorating men who wore handkerchiefs over their bald spots to prevent a crown of sunburn. I had to leave the store before this phantom smoke clouded my senses and headed east across Seventh Avenue to examine Christopher Street at its beginning on Sixth Avenue. Since Denise and I lived near the western end and normally took the subway on Seventh Avenue, we didn't explore this section on our daily rounds. Even when we met friends to shop on Eighth Street or to gather in Washington Square Park, we often crisscrossed West 4th Street, which short-cut through the maze of West Village streets.

At the Stonewall Inn, attracted by the rows of tiny rainbow flags waving from the faux balconies under the three first-floor windows and the large rectangular rainbow banner covering the middle window, I stopped to examine the announcements lining the storefront window alongside the "A" rating. Here there were posters displaying a busty, Brigitte Bardot-wigged Diva, announcing a drag review; a lesbian dance club featuring a scantily clad woman whose boobs spilled out of her bra; and a female impersonator in a gold headdress and filigreed bathing suit. I didn't have the proper vocabulary to describe these over-the-top lingerie-type getups, but I felt a wave of disappointment that friends of the hallowed Stonewall Inn hadn't progressed to less stereotypical female role models.

Recently, Denise and I had been watching Caitlyn Jenner on television as she stood awkwardly in a black stringed bikini, her chemically and surgically altered face and boobs erect in a Botox-frozen stance, and I observed, "Why does she have to pose as a much younger sex symbol? Why can't she be who she is now, a female senior citizen who is comfortable in her hard-fought-for body?"

"Maybe this is what she always wanted to be ... and couldn't."

Did Denise come up with the more compassionate answer because of her social work experience or because she was someone who didn't allow her personal anger to interfere with her judgment? Probably, I thought. Her response made me think of when my daughter Giorgia announced when she was about eleven, "Mommy, I decided that I want to be a nurse."

"What?" I had cried. "Why can't you be a doctor?" I didn't wait for her answer and continued, "A doctor is much more involved in deciding the patient's care. She is more in control."

Giorgia had mumbled that she still wanted to be a nurse.

I thought about the book I loved the most at her age, *Cherry Ames, Student Nurse*, and could still picture the cover of Cherry's beautiful face and full ruby lips, her nurse's cap jauntily perched atop her long brown hair, her expression the right mix of deep concern and congeniality, while another dark-haired woman leaned against a fluffed-up pillow in a hospital bed framed against a light-filled window and a huge bouquet of orange and yellow flowers. Nothing sickly or dangerous in this photo. In my memory bank, Cherry didn't remain a student. Her books followed her adventures as a senior nurse, army nurse, cruise nurse, dude ranch nurse, chief nurse, boarding school nurse, flight nurse, island nurse, rest home nurse, companion nurse, and even department store nurse undoubtedly combining her female need to shop. Nobody questioned why Cherry changed her jobs so often. With such an adventurous life, who wouldn't want to be a nurse?

But Giorgia didn't read such books. Then I realized maybe my daughter just wanted to be a nurse, and that she had no preconceived notions. Nurses were the first responders, the ones with the most direct contact. Nowadays, there are many male nurses. Who was I to judge?

Within a week of Giorgia's announcement, I had a talk with her, female to female. "If you really want to be a nurse, there is nothing wrong with that," I said, with stifled superiority.

"No, Mom. I've changed my mind. I think I want to be an actress."

Oh my God, I thought, with visions of Marilyn Monroe and other blonde beauties laying on the director's couch. "Are you sure?" I asked.

"Yes," she said.

That time, I kept my big mouth shut.

★ ★ ★

A plaque on the outside brickwork displayed a short history of The Stonewall Inn and that it was declared a New York State Historic Site in 2016. A standing chalkboard easel announced Stonewall's Happy Hour until 7:30 and times for its "sensational" cabaret and '90s karaoke. I pushed open the steel bar on the door and entered the wood-paneled bar area. White netted gauze draped the ceiling, and three small skulls hung on the wall near the bar. As I aimed my camera for a photo, a man appeared and yelled, "We're closed!" I mumbled that I was so sorry and backed out. Was I sorry that I had intruded, or that I didn't ask whether I could go further inside to explore and record, knowing that I couldn't explain why this place was so significant to me even though I had never stepped inside?

I continued onward and past the pet store with a large purple neon sign, "Puppies" atop a window poster announcing, "We have Frenchie." I didn't stop to examine the puppies nestled in a hill of newspaper strips as I felt sad when I saw dogs in store windows, certain of the lasting cruelty of such confinement. As I walked further east, I looked for the street sign of Gay Street.

I crossed to the other side of Christopher and walked down a lovely side street and looked up, Gay and Waverly Place. Wow. It appeared that Gay Street was on my right side, heading east, not on the left of my memory. Happy that such an old and beautiful street remained, I was nevertheless sad that something I was so certain of was, in fact, on the opposite side of my memory. I have had this feeling many times over the years, so often that my husband playfully remarked on a regular basis, "Are you menstruating?" referring to an old study that investigated the hormone levels of women and compared their senses of direction to their cycles. I couldn't remember now whether your period made you more or less off-center, but given my postmenopausal status, I knew whatever I had was permanent.

Gay Street seemed untouched by time, a quiet and pedestrian-empty enclave of brick townhouses and black wrought-iron gates and staircase railings. I backtracked and under silver scaffolding I saw the sign I was looking for, Christopher Street and Gay Street. I lifted my camera for the shot.

# CHAPTER 49:
# MEMORY'S TRICKS

I spotted Denise across Sixth Avenue and called her name to no avail. Finally, I waved frantically as I crossed closer to her, standing on the corner of 8th Street, our appointed meeting place.

"I was waiting there," I said, pointing to the small seating area bisecting the avenue. "I thought I'd be early, so I began my investigation, hoping to spare you some of my nostalgia."

"I told the dentist's hygienist to simply do her cleaning, even though the dentist planned to also replace a filling," Denise said. "Next time, I told her, not wanting to be late."

"I wouldn't have minded," I said, knowing that Denise's anxiety about being late was equal to mine.

As we reversed course and walked west on Christopher Street, now beginning at the beginning, I recalled my observations, and Denise was glad to stop at the Stonewall window to note the signs.

"We were so stupid in those days," she said. "We didn't know about homosexuals and certainly didn't know we were moving into the heart of the activity."

"I don't think we knew about it, even when all types of men swarmed the streets, cruising for action. I only realized it when Jabari and I slipped into a gay bar, and I was the only woman. If he hadn't explained it to me, I still would have thought the men had been watching football on TV and that was why they all congregated there."

In front of Village Cigars doorway, Denise said, "I wonder if that triangle is still there."

"What triangle?"

Sure enough, on the ground, there was a double-lined triangle with a mosaic tiled message: "Property of the Hess Estate which has never been dedicated for public purposes."

"I never noticed this before," I said, bending to get a close-up.

"I don't remember the exact history. It had something to do with a dispute between the city and a landlord and the question of eminent domain. The city wanted the area for the construction of the subway."

"The history of this street never fails to astound me," I said.

"When you look for something, it's great when you find it."

"I wish I could agree about Gay Street."

"Why does that bother you so much?"

"Sometimes, if I am exiting a subway stop or even leaving a restaurant bathroom, I am so sure of which direction I have to go and so many times, I am wrong. You would think that with the probability of error being so high, I should go against my gut instincts."

"I think you may be saying something more profound. As for me, I am satisfied when I get to the refrigerator and remember why I opened the door."

I laughed, but something in my chest tightened. This visit to my past, our past, was so much more than a stroll down memory lane.

At No. 81, we passed another landmark. The plaque read, "St. John's Evangelical Lutheran Church ... in modified Federal style, was built in 1821." It became the house of worship for the church in 1858. With three arched doors, three arched windows, and an imposing domed cupola, this building was another example of a place I passed twice a day for three years, of which my brain located no imprint. Denise had no memory of the church either but recalled something about an organ and musical events. It was difficult to tell if our information was gleaned through experience, hearsay, or our dedication to reading the daily *New York Times*—Denise still in the newsprint and me scanning online.

I asked Denise if she wanted to go inside so we could correct our shrinking hippocampi, and she said no, but I opened the door to take a photo. The image I captured showed an outlined crown of my brown, silver-streaked hair, my fist raised to depress the button, superimposed on a white-painted narrow interior with three stained-glass windows at the altar. Now there would be no question that I was here; the question to any inquisitive heirs would be: Is this ghost image really Anita?

I supposed this was the danger in revisiting old haunts, deciphering the puzzle of memory's tricks: figuring out what you saw and when, comparing your idea of an event with what you gleaned from photos and retold *Rashomon* stories, and deciding what to believe. I had enough therapy to realize that the only reality is what you think of that event at the time of discussion. What you didn't know for certain would never be certain without branding the numerical evidence on your forearm like an Auschwitz ID number.

A few years ago, I dragged Denise to my old Brooklyn tenement apartment, where I had lived as a young child. The current occupant allowed us to photograph inside the tiny four-room flat. I was surprised that it wasn't smaller than I had remembered as attested by similar accounts of those returning to their childhood homes. It was plenty small, though. The renters had jammed so much furniture into my old bedroom that I had been aghast that it all fit in the space where my brother's bed jutted against mine, separated by a tall black-board for privacy.

And when I coerced Denise—poor Denise—to the house I lived in years later near Madison High School, I was struck by its layout (confirmed by snooping in the window), exactly repli-cated by my memory. What impressed me the most was that it looked so dingy. The front porch was removed and paved over with mismatched bricks, the colorful garden replaced by unruly hedges and brown grass. I knew it had been more beautiful in my youth because I had sat on the front porch and tended to the flowers. And somewhere, I saved white scalloped photos and garish Polaroid shots of the house, if only I could find them.

Denise and I hurried past the Hartwick Seminary plaque, a pair of handcuffs and what appeared to be stirrups in one win-dow, a store displaying adult toys with names like Daddy-O and Surrenda, McNulty's, and the plaque near the Theatre dedicated on October 26,1998, claiming to be "New York's only per-manent monument to great Playwrights whose work has been performed at the Lucille Lortel Theatre and other Off Broadway Theatres."

We both stared at the boarded-up storefront across the street that used to be Li-Lac Chocolates. "I used to drool looking at those windows," Denise said. "And a few years after we moved here, I spent Saturday brunch eating an everything omelette and potato pancakes at David's Pot Belly. Do you remember that place?"

"Oh, it was heavenly," I said, recalling my indecision look-ing at the various omelette choices. Our minds were on eating, and I was intent on having lunch on Christopher Street.

Inside the doorway of the PATH, facing the staircase, was an arresting mural of an androgynous couple, one depicting the back and the other face forward, each going or coming. Appropriately called *Ascent-Descent* by artist Biff Elrod, the mural was one of others painted on site in 1986, and the center of a trio, framed in a curvilinear top that further directed the viewers' eyes.

We next passed an intriguing cafe called the Sweet Life. A papier mâché tuxedoed mannequin with dilating eyes and Dracula features stood in front, as if to dare us to enter. All we had to do was cross the street, and we saw our old apartment building at 165, peered into our bush-shrouded windows, and glanced across at the former Federal Building. As we walked to the end of Christopher, we again recalled how we had gradually discovered the gay nightlife on this stretch where we never ventured.

"I remember men in suits arriving by limo and meeting young studs and heading for the piers," Denise said. "They were fucking in bathhouses, trucks, bars."

"I once saw photos of naked men sunbathing on rotted piers. It was like a scene from *Lysistrata.*"

"I think you have the wrong analogy. Wasn't that a play about women denying sex to stop a war?"

"Well, probably Aristophanes wrote something appropriate."

"There's no denying this all happened literally under our noses," Denise said, probably feeling guilty for correcting me. She then Googled her phone and announced, "June 28, 1970 was named Christopher Street Liberation Day, and the beginning of the Gay Pride marches."

"We take the marches for granted now."

I had one last stop before lunch and that was to walk down the final diverting street, Weehawken, whose signpost revealed the street as New York Preservation Commission's Historical District. The plaque said that the street contained "14 buildings dating from 1830 to 1938," capturing a colorful history filled with unique maritime and residential buildings, only a few of which looked inhabitable now.

We stood opposite the piers as a sweatshirt-hooded man jogged across West Street to Hudson River Park. By eye, I followed the jogger's path across the stone promenade and knew that walking uptown was something I would reserve for another day. I grabbed a picture of his back. It was time for lunch.

# CHAPTER 50:
# ODDITY OF PERCEPTION

We returned to the Sweet Life and sat at a window table facing the redbrick of the former Federal Building. I opened the menu and happily noticed it said all-day breakfast and lunch. We both ordered a cappuccino. I couldn't have been happier.

The young server brought our coffees, and after I observed the tin ceiling, I asked her if she knew the history of the cafe.

"Oh, I think it used to be a pizza place, maybe twenty-five years ago."

I laughed. "That's too recent for us. We lived here over forty years ago."

The woman's eye bore into mine as if she didn't know if I was kidding or not.

"We were only babies at the time," I said, trying to diffuse potential tension. While she was there, I felt that we needed another record of Denise and me. "Can you take our photo?" I asked, handing her my camera.

She held it in her palm as if she had never seen a camera before. "What do I do?"

I showed her how to hold it and press the button. I moved my chair to Denise's and put my arm around her. We both smiled. I didn't check it, sure that we both would find fault. We returned to our menus.

I ordered banana pancakes, and Denise, who, unlike me, could have afforded the extra bulk, ordered a spinach and feta omelette.

"That reminds me, do you still associate Paula with spinach?"

"It's broccoli. Yes, she will always be broccoli."

"Is that like that famous line from *Casablanca,* 'We will always have Paris?'"

"Funny. The daughter of one of my patients, Claudia, wrote a book about synesthesia. Do you know what that is?"

"Something to do with words?"

"Yes, but literally it means joined sensation. It's when one of the five senses is stimulated, but more than one responds. For example, when you hear a word, you also see it."

"Did this woman Claudia have it, too?"

"Yes, when she was sixteen, she was talking with her father about how she learned the alphabet and mentioned that the letters were colored when she saw them. Her father was astonished. She had never known that this was unusual and thought everyone was like this. She saw each letter as a different color. They appeared automatically and never changed."

"Like your food associations."

"Exactly. And it's not just about colors and words, but it could be about tastes and shapes. Some famous musicians say they can feel the texture of certain chords."

"Fascinating."

"Claudia began to formulate this question, 'Do you see what I see?'"

"That reminds me of our old consciousness-raising questions, how you see yourself as opposed to how others see you?"

"Yes," Denise said, her cheeks taking on a rosy quality. "Some neurological studies say that we all have these cross-sensual capabilities, but it's on a spectrum, from mild to strong.

There may be unusual cross-activation in color processing, and synesthesia is more likely to occur in creative types. It's an oddity of perception."

"I know as a writer, it's always been difficult for me to describe colors, or any senses for that matter. I mean, how many times can you say the person has brown hair? And then if you use words like chestnut or burnt sienna, it sounds so phony. I always try to use analogous imagery to describe it like, her hair was the color of a paper bag, maybe not the best example."

The server brought our order, and I poured on the maple syrup, plunging my fork and carving out a tiny pancake triangle.

"You are a creative type, and you are probably more sensitive to cross-activation."

Denise rubbed her eyes with her palms. "But what about me? I'm not that artistic."

"First of all, I think you are. You make collages. You love to cut up images and glue them together, to see the possibilities in shapes. You are just modest about attributing this to any special ability."

"Maybe, but get this: when I told Claudia about my food associations, she said it may be a form of synesthesia. I could also be a synesthete. I love that word."

I held up a tube of lipstick and twisted it until the red tip was prominent. "I wonder what letter this is to that woman, Claudia, I mean. Has all this discussion influenced your idea of what you have?"

"Not really, but it makes me feel more normal."

"So, look at me now. Do you have a food association?"

"Sorry, Ani. That hasn't changed. Nothing comes to mind."

After finishing our food, I asked the server for another cappuccino. I stirred in two packets of raw sugar. I seemed to need more and more sweets, tempting me to squirt maple sugar into my coffee mug. I pitched into the table and asked Denise, "Well, I've been asking this question lately. I may as well ask you, too."

"Not more about the food business."

"No, this is something a little more serious."

"What?" she said, staring back at me, responding to my tone.

"When I came to Christopher Street to that book club of the elderly women I told you about, I realized it was the perfect opportunity to ask an older group of women this question that has been haunting me."

"Which was?"

"Did you have the life you wanted?"

"Wow, what did they say?"

"I got some amazing and surprising answers. A few appeared to be having the best life in retirement when they could finally focus on themselves. At the time of their youth, most didn't have the luxury of fulfilling their desires or of even knowing them."

"That question is surely a gut kicker. I don't think in those terms."

"Cindy said something similar. Although after she tried to answer my question with a summary of her family and where she lived, she added later, almost as an afterthought, 'Maybe I wasted my life.' As soon as she said this, I felt terrible that she had been happy believing she did well in life, and then I upset her. Maybe I should have kept my big mouth shut."

"Don't worry, I can handle your questions."

"You could always put me in my place."

"Wherever that is. Anyhow, to be serious, I never had specific goals. I always wanted to work with people. My aim was to do good work, though I wasn't sure what that would be."

"Then you did accomplish your goal. After all, you worked for Social Security, patiently answering endless questions and dealing with the bureaucracy. When you were fifty, you got your MSW and worked with caretakers of the sick and elderly. It was difficult to go back to school at that age and stage in life. You were a role model for me."

"I remember the day of orientation at social work school. The welcome woman said to us, 'Stand if you are older than the President of the United States.' It was Bill Clinton at the time. Another woman and I were the only ones standing."

"All the more wonderful."

"Yes, but I feel like I fell into it. It wasn't a well-planned decision."

"You chose it, whether you wrote it down or not. After all, you're still going to the Home for the Aged to visit your clients with Alzheimer's like you do for that woman, Nina."

"I don't do it for them, though."

"Then who do you do it for?"

"For their families. Like for Nina, it means a lot to her daughter to know that someone who cares is going to see her mother, someone other than her."

"Would you say that inadvertently, helping others also helps yourself?"

"Yes, I would. Ultimately, is there any selfless thing on Earth?"

"I don't think so," I said. "But some selfish things are worse than others."

"You sound so sad," Denise said. "I guess I didn't fully answer your question."

"You said a lot."

Someone opened the front door, and the breeze blew my napkin to the floor. As I picked it up, I noticed that Denise's feet were pigeon-toed, her shoe tips touching, something she did when she was tense.

"Why are you so obsessed with this question?" she asked. "Is it your fear of returning cancer?"

"That's probably a big part of it."

"Can I assume that you didn't have the life you wanted?"

"Yes, and no. Maybe I can't answer my own question. I'm not talking about marriages or children or friendships. I can't imagine my life without them. I'm focusing on the paths we took to get where we are today. It's more about professional goals, not just a job or even a career, more of a clarity of creative vision and opportunity. I don't know how to explain it."

"You're doing a good job. Do you think you wouldn't have become a writer?"

"Oh, that I don't question. But the path to it was so long and torturous. Growing up, I never had anyone who praised me or encouraged me to pursue any talents. The most I got was my mother saying I wasn't plain like my childhood friend or that I wasn't good at math like my brother, but more like her, good in English. Even that came with a caveat, because I don't think she appreciated her own mastery of English until she was old."

"That's too bad. I always felt that she was proud of you, in her own way, of course."

"Maybe, but her appreciation was always loaded. She was jealous in a way that I did more than she did with my writing and was also critical that I chose that as a profession."

"Like all our mothers, she wanted you to have security."

"I suppose. But I must say that both my parents were terrible role models. I always saw them as frustrated people, as failures in their own minds, even if not fully realized by themselves. Even in their relationship, they seemed to stay together out of a sense of giving up."

"It's sad."

"And my brother didn't help matters."

"Wait, Anita. I must use the restroom, or my bladder will burst."

When she returned, I mentioned a sudden flash of our CR group and how we took regular what we called "biological breaks."

"I also remember one of our popular topics," Denise said.

"Not about our mothers again?"

"No, but whether it was better to have diarrhea or constipation?"

"Leave it to you to remember the essentials."

"Yeah, I voted for constipation. Seriously, though, what were we talking about before my 'biological break?'"

"I need one, too. But we were discussing my brother," I said. "His actions definitely affected me deeply."

"Yes, he was often a sadistic, sick person."

"I never told you about my visit to Ben before he died."

"I figured you would when you are ready."

"I don't know if I'm ready. Anyhow, I told him he and his gang tortured and bullied me."

"Oh my God, what did he say?"

"Believe it or not, he laughed. He said, 'At my age, I'm just happy I remember anything.'"

"That is so sick."

"Yes, a week later he hung himself before Paula was coming. He knew she would find his body. I will never forgive my brother for that."

"It is entirely unforgivable."

"But I may have been a party to it."

'How?"

"I had been visiting Ben for the weekend when we had that conversation about my childhood. Is it possible this contributed to his suicide?"

"His reaction to your confession was typically Ben. As far as he was concerned, he had no regrets. And even if he later changed his mind, there's no way that this would have driven him to suicide."

"Can we ever be sure?"

"You must know, suicide is very complicated. He was depressed, narcissistic, and his old familiar ways of dealing with people no longer worked for him. He had so many repressed angers. If anything, you tried to help him when he wouldn't have done the same for you."

"I suppose so. It's like a very bad plot from a very bad novel, if it weren't so tragic."

"Sometimes you just can't make up for someone's past traumas."

"All I ever wanted," I said, "was not to be like my parents, not to be like my brother. I didn't want to die with regrets."

"And you, Anita, have fought this, admirably, I might say. Didn't you write a wonderful childhood novel and a book about the Holocaust that has helped many? And follow that up with your witty book of essays?"

"Which nobody wants to publish."

"Didn't you go to Africa when you were so depressed you couldn't go to the store? Didn't you battle diseases your whole life, including very serious cancer? Didn't you care for your mother during her long illness? Didn't you go to graduate school when you were sixty-five? Haven't you been teaching college students and adults and getting rave reviews? I'd say you *are* a woman of courage. Whew, I rest my case."

"Thank you, sweetie. Certainly, going to Africa was a turning point for me and propelled me toward graduate school. But even that took me so long. If I only had a mentor, a teacher, someone who encouraged me to become a literary writer, helped me get into a good graduate school with contacts to the publishing world, who nurtured my career, it wouldn't have taken me so long to get my work published, even in low-level places."

"I say, shut up your inner voice, and stop asking women this question."

"I want to. We women of a certain age were so influenced by societal norms that paralyzed our life choices."

"Well, we know this is true. Maybe the real question you should ask is 'Did we have the life we should have had?'"

The conversation stopped. Denise's eyelids drooped, and my voice was hoarse. Denise grabbed the bill and covered it with her credit card. "My treat. For your birthday."

I didn't argue. We had been celebrating our birthdays together for over fifty years.

I didn't press Denise any more about the choices she made in her life. She had been a widow and remarried. Her second husband was showing signs of Alzheimer's. Like me, she had serious cancer. You don't get to be our age without scars, and I certainly had a body full of them.

Psychological scars, internal scars, were impossible to see. If only there was an MRI that recorded our eroded self-images and repressed hurts. If so, would we have believed such proof?

"Denise, right now I feel content."

"Why now?"

"Because I am here with you, where we lived at a time in our lives when we were free yet encumbered, excited yet repressed, learning yet uninformed. And don't forget the old standby, diarrhea and constipation."

"We were oxymorons," she said.

"Hopefully not morons."

"Maybe I should add, dumb and smart."

Denise slipped on her sunglasses and placed her wallet in her backpack. I ran my fingers through my shoulder-length hair, the same basic style I had since I was a teenager.

"Ready to head for the subway?" Denise asked.

"Let's stop one more time in front of our old apartment and sit for a while."

"Sure, I'm in no rush."

★ ★ ★

Although the wrought-iron bars took up much of the ledge in front of our old street-view window, we squeezed our butts against the peeling, black-painted metal. The sun was bright, and I slipped on my progressive eyeglasses, whose lenses darkened.

Recently, on one of our regular walks through Riverside Park, I asked Denise why she needed to take a backpack. She showed me what was inside: her cellphone, charger, keys, credit cards, IDs, purse with money, a paperback, gloves, thermos, a sweater, and two shopping bags. Digging deeper, she unearthed a tin with ibuprofen, aspirin, and Rolaids, tissue packs, lozenges, and sucking candy. Woven through the zipper hung keychain toys, animals with sounds and jingles that annoyed me when we walked.

"Why do you need those?" I had asked, recalling our days of spontaneity in Europe.

"If we meet a child, I like to have something to entertain them."

I had been smug, with a tiny silk bag I had bought in Cambodia. It was barely wide enough to hold my cellphone, keys, and a few tissues. Occasionally, though, I would run out of tissues and ask Denise for a replacement. A few times, she noticed I patted my lips and complained of parchedness. She delved into her backpack and handed me a ChapStick. Maybe that was the real reason I took little with me on my walks with Denise. It wasn't about being free. If I needed something, I could always ask Denise.

"Wow, it's hot today," Denise said. She unzipped her backpack and, like a magician, produced a Day-Glo pink baseball hat and pulled it down over her soft, curly gray hair. "You want a cap, too? I have another."

"Of course you do."

Within minutes, Denise secured one on my head. It was dark blue with a white "B" for Brooklyn.

"Well, here we are, two old broads from Flatbush," Denise said.

"We would never have used the word 'broads' back in the day of our CR group."

"That's the beauty of old age," she said. "We can do what we want, sitting here on our old ledge, watching the world go by, on Christopher Street."

I took Denise's hand and rested it on my knee, laying mine on top. Yes, I thought, there was no better place to be.

# EPILOGUE

On the first Monday evening in May, Sergio walked through the front door of our apartment, put down his briefcase on the hall bench, and yelled in the hallway to the kitchen.

"Guess who I saw today?" he said.

"The Queen of England?"

"Close, but no cigar," he said, stepping into the kitchen where I was washing the dishes by the sink. He kissed me on my cheek.

"Royalty ... maybe a royal pain in the behind?"

"Hardly. It was Betty. She came with her daughter."

"Oh, Betty," I said, wondering why I hadn't gotten a note from her in months. I had repeatedly asked my husband if she had come for a medical visit, and he reported he hadn't heard from her. "How is she?" I asked.

"Not good. She has deteriorated. She's very thin."

"Oh, no. She was already a toothpick when I saw her last fall. Did she or her daughter tell you why you hadn't heard from her?"

"She now lives in a residential facility and can no longer take care of herself."

"She left Christopher Street?"

"Yes."

"Did she recognize you?"

*"Who knows? She seemed to and even remembered you. She said that she loved meeting you and hopes you will come to the next meeting."*

*The tears came before I realized it, and I wiped the back of my right hand across my nose. With the sink water still running and my left hand clutching the saucepan I had been scrubbing; I turned off the water and grabbed the dish towel hanging from the cabinet knob. I placed the towel within the well of the pan, catching the wavering reflection of my hairline. I traced my finger along the circular rim, patting down the cotton material to contain the residual moisture.*

-THE END-

photo credit: Penny Laitin

# ABOUT THE AUTHOR

ANDREA SIMON is the author of three award-winning, published books: the groundbreaking memoir/history, *Bashert: A Granddaughter's Holocaust Quest*; historical fiction, *Esfir Is Alive*; and a novel-in-stories, *Floating in the Neversink*. Andrea holds an MFA in Creative Writing from the City College of New York, where she has taught writing. Students from her online course "Writing About Your Mom without Guilt," created a published anthology, *Here's the Story ... Nine Women Write Their Lives*, of which Andrea is the editor and a contributor. Andrea is a great believer in the power of female friendship and support. A native New Yorker, she has a grown daughter and lives in Manhattan with her husband.

# ACKNOWLEDGMENTS

For this book, which spans many of my lived decades, there are bound to be parallels between Anita and me, even though many of the events and characters are fictional. As such, I am utterly grateful to all those friends and relatives who have taken part in my life's journey and served as inspiration and support for my literary endeavors. Alas, there are too many people to list and, as memory does, some have merged into the very personal and distinct fabric of Anita's story. So, thank you to all those who patiently endured my questions and gave me fodder for creative reimagining.

For her astute and encouraging guidance, I am indebted to Sara Kocek of Yellow Bird Editors. Huge thanks (as always) to my long-standing writing group, inspired by the workshops of Madeleine L'Engle: Patricia Barry, Stephanie Cowell, Jane Mylum Gardner, Katherine Kirkpatrick, Pamela Leggett, and Sanna Stanley. I am also beyond grateful to my newer writing group (some members are in both groups) called The Lady Bunch, so named after the iconic TV series *The Brady Bunch*, for our Zoom online format: Amy Baruch, Stephanie Cowell, Linda Aronovsky Cox, Karen Finch, Jane Mylum Gardner, Rhonda Hunt-Del Bene, Katherine Kirkpatrick, and Kathleen M. Rodgers. Not only did these women encourage the development of *Did You Have the Life …* but many read (and re-read) the manuscript, pored over cover designs, gave me wonderful blurbs, and helped me secure important reviewers. Thanks to early reviewers Mary Caputi, Stephanie Cowell, Katherine Kirkpatrick, Helen Schary Motro, Ruth Pennebaker, Kathleen M. Rodgers, and Mark Wisniewski.

Of course, I couldn't have produced this book without the loving support of family and friends, many of whom have experienced events that mirror this book: longtime cherished friends: Helene Ebenstein ( a great proofreader), Cora Harrison, and Penny Laitin (who patiently took great headshots); cousin and onetime Villager, Amy Lew; lifelong sister/friends Joan Katz and Carol Schweid; and with great love, my daughter Alexis Neophytides and my husband, who also happens to be an astute typo catcher, Andreas Neophytides.

To the courageous and innovative women of Sibylline Press, who dared to create a unique publishing model, my enduring thanks for their expertise and compassion: Vicki DeArmon, publisher; Julia Park Tracey, executive editor and founding partner; Suzy Vitello, managing editor; Maxfield Fulton, copy editor; Aaron Laughlin, layout and production; Alicia Feltman, cover design; and Sang Kim, publishing systems manager.

# STUDY GUIDE QUESTIONS

1. Why did the author begin her book with the quotation by Carl Gustav Jung about the strong psychological influence of the unlived life of the parent?

2. Anita's husband, Sergio, delivers a note from his patient whose address is the same building that Anita lived in as a young woman. Has a similar coincidence happened in your life that caused you to reflect on the past?

3. The gang attack in Brooklyn has a profound effect on Anita. Why does she repress her reaction to this traumatic event?

4. There are many instances of sexism in this book, including the remark by Anita's female unit supervisor who accused her of wearing her dress too short, thereby provoking sexual violence. Does this surprise you?

5. Racist attitudes also play a part in this story, including the relationships between Blacks and Jews and interracial couples. Do you think attitudes have changed since the 1960s and 1970s?

6. Anita's work at Theoretical Press introduces her to Shirley and Marilyn. How do female relationships play a significant role in this book?

7. In the consciousness-raising group, a recurring theme is "How We Perceive Ourselves and How Others See Us." Can you relate to this topic?

8. How do the revolutionary events of the time (school strikes, feminism, Stonewall, Attica) form the backdrop to this novel?

9. Anita never finds out why Shirley didn't come to her book party. Have you ever suppressed your confrontation to a friend's disappointing behavior that has bothered you for a long time?

10. Do you think Anita has answered her own life question? Do her friends' responses surprise you? Have you ever asked yourself and/or your contemporaries the question: Did you have the life you wanted?

**Sibylline Press** is proud to publish the brilliant work of women authors over 50. We are a woman-owned publishing company and, like our authors, represent women of a certain age.